Tales From

The Golden Tree

Book 1

The Lost Kingdom

By M.V.R.

"The cure to boredom is curiosity. There is no cure for curiosity."

– Dorothy Parker

© 2021, Marina Vidal de Ritter
TWENTYSIX
Eine Marke der Books on Demand GmbH
Herstellung und Verlag:
BoD – Books on Demand, Norderstedt
ISBN: 9783740783938

Preface

In the country that we today call Germany, there runs a middle-sized mountain range or highland called the Taunus, which stretches between the Rhine and the Main rivers and is gifted with bountiful valleys, richly green forests and several geothermal springs. No one really knows why this name was given to the range, or even where it comes from. Some speculate it was given by the Romans, who occupied the region in the past. Still others are convinced the name is much more ancient, derived from a word of attributed Celtic origin for hill fort.

I consider myself lucky to enjoy life in this beautiful corner of the world. And it is this landscape that has inspired me the most. For me, the name of these German highlands comes from an altogether forgotten time, a time without memory, where no witness remained to recount the deeds and stories, the language and culture of the people that lived here. All we know has been deduced or told by the Roman conquerors, much later.

As if under a spell, it is my wish to take my readers to a magical time when in these very mountains a kingdom emerged that would change the minds and landscapes of Europe forever. A kingdom that would leave no traces or clues to its downfall, as if it had been silently swallowed by the mists of time, waiting for the right moment to tell its story. The story of a mighty civilization that over thousands of years united the continent of Europe, a civilization that brought hope and glory, but carried the seed to its own downfall, as well. This saga will be told in the trilogy 'Tales from the Realm of the Golden Tree' and will begin with the story of the Lost Kingdom.

It would not be fair to take credit for my work, however, without thanking the rich imagination of mankind for the countless fairy tales and legends, the incredible hordes of mythological beings and the bounty of well-written fantasy stories, as well as the inspiring sense of humour of the people in my home town, Cordoba, where my taste for figurative language was first developed.

Moreover, I would like to thank my mother for giving me the best education one can get, my father and grandmother for their patience and creativity in story-telling, and my young family for giving me the space and time to write, and for encouraging me with my work. It would not have been possible for me to write this book without them. In addition, I would like to thank my colleague Vera Mark for giving me good tips and helping me with the revision of the text, and the artists Meme Friquet, for giving me a hand with the beautiful maps, and Solnyshko, for illustrating the book cover.

Further, I am convinced that trees and rocks, being ancient witnesses of time, possess a remarkable treasure of memories of the past. This is why I love the forest and the tales it tells. This is why I often silently walk its winding roads, always listening how the wind in the trees whispers stories in ancient tongues long lost. I have been lucky enough to understand their language. For this, I'm very grateful, and therefore, I would like to dedicate this book to Mother Nature for her generous bounty and forbearance; for all the trees and plants and their ancient memories, and begging for humble forgiveness for the extent of human impact on this planet. Sometimes I do wonder...

Contents

PROLOGUE   15

CHAPTER ONE: 17
The Host Country

CHAPTER TWO: 34
Arachtan Skyarach

CHAPTER THREE: 46
The Forest Of Dreams

CHAPTER FOUR: 64
Reaghil Bheallemer Na

Caydùllien Ore

CHAPTER FIVE: 70
Swallowed By The Earth

CHAPTER SIX: 77
The Children Of The Rheann

CHAPTER SEVEN: 87
In The Dragon's Lair

CHAPTER EIGHT: 107
A Journey Through The Rheann

CHAPTER NINE: 124
Annea's Story By Lughan

CHAPTER TEN: 127
Daing Mhuir

CHAPTER ELEVEN: 140
A New Life

CHAPTER TWELVE: 165
The Green Terrace Of The Dragon

CHAPTER THIRTEEN: 190
The Hidden Passage

CHAPTER FOURTEEN: 203
A New Home

CHAPTER FIFTEEN: 232
Drkenstar

CHAPTER SIXTEEN: 244
Treacherous Valley

CHAPTER SEVENTEEN: 261
Asttrian King Of The Skyarach

CHAPTER EIGHTEEN: 279
The Anairarachti Princess

CHAPTER NINETEEN: 311
The Vwylrynn Kæyn

CHAPTER TWENTY: 322
The Golden Cage

CHAPTER TWENTY-ONE: 343
The Magic Stones

CHAPTER TWENTY-TWO: 352
The Warrior Queen And Her Dragon King

CHAPTER TWENTY- THREE: 367
Troubled Seas

CHAPTER TWENTY- FOUR: 375
Of Noble Hearts

CHAPTER TWENTY- FIVE: 385
The Underground

CHAPTER TWENTY- SIX: 392
The Plan

CHAPTER TWENTY-SEVEN: 401
Lady Of The Thriar

CHAPTER TWENTY- EIGHT: 408
A Family Reunion

CHAPTER TWENTY-NINE: 419
Polarys

CHAPTER THIRTY: 437
Dryemoshach

CHAPTER THIRTY-ONE: 461
Drkarach's Secrets

CHAPTER THIRTY-TWO: 470
To No Fair End

EPILOGUE 479

GLOSSARY OF ARACH LANGUAGE 482

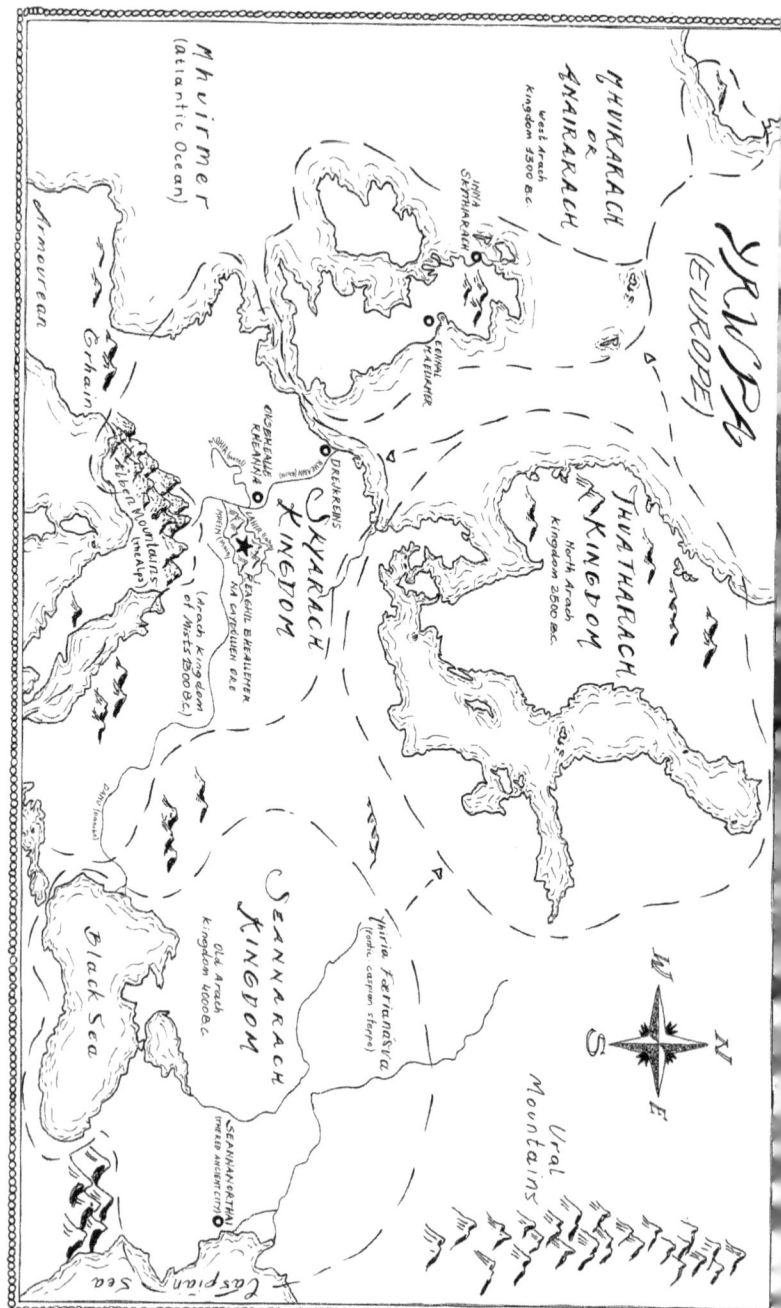

The extraordinarily gigantic shadow carved the blue out of the

ocean...

A blinding white light and a blast,
and then,
utter silence...

Prologue

1st day of Nwyr, Year of the Dragon 298 (around 1000 BC our count),
Reaghil Bheallemer na Caydúllien Ore[1]

    Fire, fire everywhere. Inside and outside, there was no escaping it. His people, burning all around him.

He had to save them! It was family fighting family!

Urarathan had seen it all before, why was it all coming back now? In his mind's eye, this picture was as clear as the icicles now licking at his bare hands.

Suddenly, he turned his gaze down to the snow-covered forest ground, he thought he had heard some dripping sound.

The king went down on his knees.

Now, he could see it: a pool of deep, red fluid had formed around him.

Was he dying?

---

[1] Great Royal City of the Golden Apple Tree also known as The Golden City, area corresponding roughly to today's Heidetrank Oppidum, Oberursel, Germany.

This could not be...

'I have to ride back and summon my council,' the king thought. 'I have to bestow the sword and free the dragon before it's too late. My brother Thuarnach and the Thriar in full have to bear witness to my last wish... if Arachtan doesn't reach Reaghil Bheallemer on time, not just the Skyarach Kingdom, but all of the Arach kingdoms will be in great peril... My Love, what have I done?'

At that very moment, miles away, on Inna Skythiarach, Queen Scaìthara woke up with a start.

"He is in pain," she said almost in a trance, "I can smell the blood, he has been severely wounded and has no one to turn to. I see the arrow of treason piercing through his heart."

After all these endless years when time had stood still for both, Great King Urarathan of the Skyarach would be parting this world... alone.

Chapter One: The Host Country

The party

April 20th, 2022
Premises of the UNC (National University of Cordoba), Faculty of Philosophy and Humanities, Cordoba, Argentina

"Annea, where are you?! Everyone is waiting for you! Annea!" She heard her best friend Lola calling outside in the corridor.

She had been hiding in the library all day, a perfect place to do so, and had made sure to turn off her mobile, too. She was hoping, as it turned out in vain, that everyone would forget about this silly idea of a farewell party.

This had been all Lola's fault, of course. She had insisted that Annea couldn't leave for two whole years without a proper party with friends and colleagues. Only, Annea did not like big parties…

And now here she was, stuck in the library, when she should have been collecting her passport, arranging some last-minute errands, and packing. Yes, packing, she was so bad at it, and she still had all those warm clothes to fit in her suitcases!

As most of the time these days, her thoughts took her readily back to the issue at hand: her imminent journey to Germany...

For the first time in her life, Annea would be taking a flight, facing, once and for all, her innate fear of flying.

'There is no going back, I have to see it through, I am going to find him even if I have to fly to the moon,' she thought.

Annea knew little about Germany. As a matter of fact, her interest could be reduced to one specific event in her life that had bound her destiny to it: Germany was the last place her father had been sighted before he had mysteriously disappeared, sixteen years ago.

"There you are!" called Lola out loud, "you won't escape me, no matter where you hide, little Pandora!"

"Shush, Lola! Please, don't use that name here," whispered Annea uneasily.

But once Lola let loose her contagious laughter, Annea couldn't be mad at her any longer. In fact, in a funny way, she was thankful that her light-spirited friend was rescuing her, once again, from her troubled thoughts and self-imposed confinement.

"Sorry, Lola. I know, I promised to come, but I can't, I simply can't," she admitted, while nervously collecting her books and throwing them into her leather backpack.

"I really need to get going. You know my mother, and I still need to finish packing. Plus, that professor I'm staying with hasn't been answering my messages!"

"Annea, darling," said Lola patiently, "I know you don't like big parties, and I know you really hate the idea of flying, and, hey, let that poor professor breathe for a day! He'll be there as he promised, trust me."

Lola steadied her friend's hands, looking pleadingly into her troubled silvery eyes. "Please, Annea, they just want to say goodbye properly. Who knows when we'll all meet again? I promise, you needn't stay long, okay?"

Annea felt terrible, even more now, seeing that tiny flicker of sorrow in her beloved friend's round face: Lola would miss her, and she would miss Lola, too.

By the time they had started their courses to become history teachers, Lola and Annea had been best friends since kindergarten. The rest of their fellow students all came from every corner of Argentina, with no friends or family in the city. It had been Lola's open-mindedness that had helped many of them. She loved to make new friends, meet new people, and be in the spotlight, while Annea preferred mostly the backstage of social events. That's how they were, and their friendship would endure through time and space.

Annea knew Lola was right, their classmates were nice people, and she wasn't being fair.

"Ok, I'll come with you. But only for an hour, otherwise the passport office will close and I won't be flying anywhere tomorrow. Deal?"

"Deal! And don't worry too much about your family tonight," continued Lola, "they will ignore you, brag about themselves, and eat as if it were their last supper, as they always do. And, maybe after that, they'll go on to praise each other on their high IQs."

Annea had a chuckle at this.

"So, you see," Lola went on undisturbed, "nothing out of the normal, really. You, my darling, should rather focus on packing all those thick jackets you bought," and with that, she finished collecting the rest of Annea's scattered stationery and led their way out of the library.

'What have I signed up for?' thought Annea.

Although it was late April, the day was extremely stuffy. On top of that, the college classroom, where the farewell party was already up and running, was completely packed. So, as soon as she opened the door, Annea's instincts warned her to turn on her heels and run.

Seeing as she had no other option - she had Lola at her back – Annea reluctantly entered the crowded room.

"Annea, finally! So good to see you." Roberto the Relentless, as they had nick-named him, came up to her, simpering.

"We thought you might be already depleting the stocks of warm underwear at the mall," he added, trying to sound funny.

Annea and Lola exchanged looks for a millisecond, with their usual synchronised sighs and raised eyebrows.

"Hi, Rob. Good to see you, too," answered Annea, "tell me, when was the last time that you hunted for new underwear? 1999 perhaps?"

She hadn't meant to be mean to him, she knew she possessed a sharp tongue when provoked, but she was starting to feel overwhelmed. Why couldn't he just let her be?

"Sorry, Rob, I didn't mean to–"

"It's okay, I'd better get you something to drink."

"Ouch!" said Lola when he was gone, "Annea, you'll have to moderate your temper, or you'll have him crying in the corner all afternoon."

Everybody knew Roberto was desperately in love with Annea – like most of their male peers. Shy as she was, she still seemed to exert an irrational appeal on both men and women alike, which made her feel even more uncomfortable in big gatherings. In truth, Annea seemed to be completely resilient to any romantic encounter, having put off all advances right from the beginning. She had no interest in dating anyone, not at the moment, at least.

As they moved on through the crowd, many friends as well as teachers came over to wish Annea good luck in her Masters years in Germany. And slowly, without noticing it, she started warming up to the happy spirit around her…

'Yes,' she thought, 'I will miss them, too…'

She had chosen a Master's Degree in Anthropology of Neolithic and Bronze Age European Culture at the University of Mainz. She was 23 years old, and this was going be the first time in her life that she left the country all on her own. She was absolutely thrilled, and absolutely terrified, at the same time.

In fact, no one had ever imagined her doing something like that. Annea suffered from a condition known as aerophobia, the fear of flying, and there had been no power on earth that could move her to board a plane, until now. And as Annea also tended to be quite introspect, most people mistook this for lack of confidence.

She had had no easy childhood. Dr Julio Menard, Annea's father, had disappeared without a trace when Annea was only seven years old and had left her immersed in a family that despised her. But with the passing of the years, she had grown strong, and her determination to find out what had happened to her father had almost turned to obsession, giving her the strength to face her deepest fears and go her own way.

Lara Menard, the woman she had learnt to call mother, while openly favouring her younger daughter Bella, seemed to find pleasure in punishing Annea randomly. She would always undermine her accomplishments and complain about her to any one that would care to listen. Her sister Bella, on her part, so used to her queenly place in the household, utterly despised Annea, and never forgave her for the loving relationship she had with their now dead grandmother Emma, who had been determined to help Annea achieve what she herself could not: find her missing son. In fact, it had been Granny Emma to support Annea all along, and Annea missed her terribly… It should have been her to see her off tomorrow, not them.

To make things worse, Annea possessed, unlike Bella, a rare jewel: a distinguished, old-fashioned charm. Something about her fascinated, almost enchanted people, who, as if under a spell, wouldn't be able to stop staring at her to the point of embarrassment.

Perhaps it was her nostalgic silvery gaze with its deep pools of liquid metal. Or perhaps, her absurd paleness in such a sunny country, or the torrent of golden, red locks framing her lovely oval face. It was difficult to tell, there was so much more beyond her purely physical beauty: she possessed an inner light, an iridescent soul.

"Annea, are you okay?" called professor Martinez del Castillo, "you look even paler than usual."

"Oh, sure, sure, professor, it's just... You, you were saying?" answered Annea, trying to focus back on her teacher's monologue.

"I was telling you that Professor Beckmann has sent his greetings and asked me to let you know that everything is set for your arrival. He apologises for not getting in touch, he has been having problems with his internet and just got them fixed today. Either he himself, or his wife will be there to pick you up from Frankfurt Airport, so you don't have to arrange a taxi. They are very nice people, you know. I stayed with him a couple of years back. Did you know they actually live outside the city of Frankfurt? But surely, he must have told you this already?" continued the scholar.

Annea had been so busy arranging everything related to her trip that she hadn't given it further thought.

"No, professor, actually I haven't talked much about the place with Professor Beckmann. He did mention, however, that Oberursel is a picturesque little town. Please do tell me all you know about the place, it will surely help me figure it out faster," she answered.

Professor del Castillo, like most of his kind, enjoyed entertaining his audience with knowledgeable accounts of the many places he had visited, and today was no exception.

"Right. So, the town of Oberursel am Taunus is about half an hour drive from Frankfurt. It will take some time to get to Mainz from there with the train, but since you're often driving with Dr Beckmann, it should be okay. While the whole area is very beautiful and green, Oberursel's old town is especially charming and has an exquisite old market area. Most of the residential neighbourhoods are surrounded by old forests or fields, where people go hiking or biking. I'm sure you will have fun living there. And don't mind the weather too much, Annea. Yes, it can be quite cold and damp, and the summer is not as warm as it is here, but... you know," the professor said, with a compassionate smile.

It was, of course, quite plain to Annea what he was thinking. Literally everybody who had approached her lately pitied her for Germany's hostile weather. But she was absolutely determined to go, and the weather and such things were of no true concern to her. This was the chance she'd been waiting for all her life, and she wasn't going to waste it. She was going to find her lost father come what may.

"Thank you, professor," she replied politely, "I'd better get going now, or I'll be late. Have a good couple of years! And I promise I'll start a blog to post any news – even weather news – related to my stay."

And with a wink, Annea grabbed Lola's arm and surfed through the cheery crowd as fast as she could towards the exit door, the last good-byes still hanging in the air.

'I wonder,' she thought, 'will the weather in Germany truly get as crazy as most people predicted?'

Farewell

April 21st, 2022,
Ing. Aero. A. L.V. Taravella International Airport,
Cordoba, Argentina

"Lola, I told you, stop acting like a paparazzi and taking pictures of all my movements, would you? Besides, I couldn't sleep last night, I look like a ghost."

The moment they had entered the airport, Lola had started taking pictures of Annea, and it was becoming irritating even for those watching the scene.

Lola started laughing wholeheartedly at this.

"Annea, you're so pale, you always look like a ghost, but a friendly one, at that. Oh, and did you remember to write down what time Ludwig has his meals? You know I have no idea how to look after a cat. I'm still wondering what made me promise you I would take him in... With my expert care, I will manage to kill that poor beast before you even touch German soil! Why did you accept, anyway?" she asked in a dramatic note, making her friend smile.

"Just unwind, won't you? You offered because you know I love that old cat with all my heart, and no one at home would have taken care of him. Besides, Ludwig loves you, too. He is used to having you around, and when I'm gone, the two of you will keep each other company. And yes, of course, my dear Lola: I have included all sorts of notes on how to feed him, sleeping time, outdoor time, and the vet's number. But I'm not vanishing into thin air, am I? If anything is the matter, just get call."

For Annea and Lola, who had practically grown up together, it was going to be tough not to see each other daily. At least, Lola possessed a cheerful, energetic nature, and a warm and caring family, too. That was partly why Annea thought it a good idea to have her look after her cat; that, and the fact that her own mother and sister would have definitely killed the cat as soon as she had stepped out of the front door.

"Have you got all your stuff? And the pills?" inquired Lola.

"Yep, all inside," she answered, pointing to her leather backpack, "it seems I won't jump screaming out of the plane after all. The doctor assured me the pills are strong enough to put an elephant to sleep, so don't worry, I won't even notice I'm flying," said Annea trying to sound reassuring.

"Darling, I know you better than that: they will need ten people to knock you out. I'm so regretting that I'm not coming with you…"

Lola had always felt protective towards her friend. Maybe because Annea had lost her father so early, and her mother had certainly not been the caring type, or just maybe because she saw Annea as some kind of ephemeral being, too delicate for this world. She was not quite sure why, still somehow, Lola had always known her friend needed a shield to protect her from a world that would threaten people like Annea simply for being different. And Lola had willingly become that shield.

"Girls, hurry now. It's about time Annea gets going to the gates," Lara Menard's voice thundered across the empty departure hall.

With her usual severe look, the woman managed to make everyone anxious.

"Annea, you know what uncle Bernardo told you, yesterday. You need about an hour to get through all the security checks they have now, and he knows better than anyone because he still flies for his conferences all around the world. You don't want to miss your plane, do you? If your sister Bella were here, she would never be losing her last minutes discussing 'cat' matters. Besides, think a little about me, too, airport parking costs a fortune!"

At that point, Annea and Lola could only stare back in disbelief. Neither of them could articulate a reasonable response, so they opted to silently, but openly ignore her pleas.

"Your mother has lost it, Annea. I never thought she could be that selfish! One day, I will tell her in her face what I think of her," whispered Lola through gritted teeth.

Annea tapped her friend gently on the tip of her tiny, round nose.

"No, my dearest Lola, you're not. That won't make her change a bit. Besides, she has never cared about others, that's how she is. I bet that is why granny never truly liked her… and she got worse after father's disappearance. You know, sometimes, I don't even blame him for leaving us."

"OMG, stop it! We don't know for sure what happened to him, remember? Your mother has injected her venom long enough, but you know he would never have left you or your sister behind. Have you stopped believing in him, Annea?"

"No, how could I?" replied Annea, "it's just, from time to time it is hard to understand how he could have vanished like that… you know, there are nights, in which I can still hear his voice like a whisper before I fall asleep, like when he was telling us bedtime stories. Lola, it is so sad to admit this, but I can't remember his face clearly, not any more. Lara took all his pictures away, and now there is nobody behind that voice: he is literally gone."

"I'm sorry to hear that, darling." Lola caressed her friend's cheek.

"Most disturbing of all," Annea went on, "after all these years, I'm more and more convinced that my mother's bitterness is related to both my father's disappearance and my staying behind, as if she was blaming me for it. I believe she'd rather have me disappear sixteen years ago… And then, of course, all those eccentric parties, the alcohol… Well, it hasn't helped much either."

"Annea, the life she's chosen is not your fault," Lola replied with a determined voice, "your father's disappearance is not your fault. Look, you've come so far, you've worked so hard for this trip, why look back now? Don't think too much about her or Bella, they don't deserve it. Now, well, just go for it, Little Pandora!"

Annea had to laugh at this. 'Little Pandora' had been her father's nickname for her as a child.

"My dearest Lola, you always know how to cheer people up!"

"Promise you will keep in touch daily, Annea."

Annea hugged her best friend, whose eyes were by now all red and swollen, and whose face was completely covered with tears, the two staying for a couple of minutes in this never-ending embrace, until Mrs. Menard interrupted again.

"Annea, have I already told you? Bella says good luck and apologises for not making it to the airport; she had an important lesson on subatomic matter and she couldn't possibly miss it. Poor Bella, she works so hard..."

Annea started wondering why Lara Menard had come to the airport at all. Possibly just to make sure she would board that damned plane. So, to put her out of her misery, Annea moved on to say good-bye to the woman.

Just then, an unexpected tear peered out of the corner of one of her mother's eyes, and as many times before, Annea wished the distance between them had never existed. But she had learnt to accept her place in that woman's heart, a heart that blamed her for all that had gone wrong in their lives. Lara Menard would always see Annea as the daily reminder of the existence of the man that had left her behind like an old pair of shoes.

'This is it,' Annea thought, 'the point of no return...'

Turning to Lara Menard, she said, "Good bye, Mum. Please, take care of yourself and Bella. And above all, remember to be happy. I'll call as soon as I can." And with that, she headed straight towards the entrance doors to the passenger area. She hesitated for a second, and then with renewed hopes she stepped through the threshold to her unknown journey.

Chapter Two: Arachtan Skyarach

The Summons

16th day of Nwyr, 299 YD[2] (1000 BC our count),
Drejkreins[3]

He hadn't been able to sleep that night. It was the twelfth month of the Dragon Year, the month of Nwyr, the dark god of winter. It was bitter cold, but bastard prince Arachtan's mind was still on fire.

He had left the fortress of Daing Mhuir, on Inna Skythiarach, ten days ago, and he had talked to no one, except for his two half-brothers, Thuaìden and Skeorden, who he had brought along as requested by the druid.

Arachtan had to reach Reaghil Bheallemer, the capital of the Skyarach Kingdom, within a fortnight, at the latest. The errand was urgent, delicate and dangerous. And although the three had departed swiftly, they all knew very little about the reasons behind the druid's summons.

---

[2] Ynar Drkent or Year of the Dragon
[3] Modern-day Utrecht

The importance of this missive, however, had been clear to Arachtan from the beginning. Not that Thuarnach was prone to write in full and in detail, but this message had been written using the secret druidic alphabet, which not many could read. His druid uncle was urging him to come without delay and to stay undercover, he was convinced that Asttrian, Arachtan's cousin and new king of the Skyarach, would do anything to stop him from reaching the Golden City alive.

Fortunately, the three princes were all well-trained for any journey, and knew their ways through the rough territory they had to follow. They were strong sailors, better horsemen, and they had been prepared to range mountain and forest alike. Of course, this had been part of their upbringing at the fortress of Daing Mhuir. Their mother, Queen Scaìthara of the Anairarachti, being a skilful warrior and ranger herself, had seen to it. In particular with Arachtan, who was her first-born, bastard son, Scaìthara had been uncompromising, and had determined that everybody would treat him as they would her other three children.

For this, Arachtan was thankful. He had always been loved and respected by the Anairarachti, his mother's people. They had been mostly kind and generous with him. For them, however, he would always be the fruit of his mother's young love for a Skyarach knight who had died in battle when his kin had split from the

North Arach. Legend had it, he had easily captivated the heart of young Scaìthara, making her forget about her great disappointment in love.

As it was, no one ever questioned her choices. Scaìthara was a Dragon Queen of the oldest Royal Arach. She was a born warrior, just and wise, yes, but also very powerful. She had led her people victoriously, time and again, out of terrible odds. Her people loved her, but most of all, they respected her.

But Arachtan's heart was, above all, loyal to the Skyarach of the Golden City. His mother's cousins, King Urarathan and Druid Thuarnach had always been close to the boy Arachtan. Even as a child, he had spent many a training year in Reaghil Bheallemer, without returning home to his mother. So, now, the druid's summons had prompted him to leave without much questioning.

They had departed that same night, while the rest of the castle had been busy celebrating Meadh a'Oigche, the winter celebration marking the return of light. And they had been able to keep good pace for two full days, until they had reached the trading port of Eonnal Skethemarbheal na Maelirmer.

There, they had been much delayed by bad weather. The seas had been terribly upset, and most sailors had been forced to return to their homes, refusing to offer passage. They had tried to persuade them offering large amounts of gold, but to no avail. People in town were very superstitious, and wisely abstained from daring the powerful forces of nature. But due to this, it had unexpectedly taken Arachtan and his brothers ten full days to reach the continental port of Drejkreins.

To avoid curious eyes, they had decided to camp in the forest just outside the port city. Still, they couldn't linger long, or they would risk being seen. Many people here knew Arachtan well and, this time, it was certainly not to their advantage. They still needed to follow the course of the Rheann for several days on horseback without being discovered to reach Reaghil Bheallemer on time. Their cousin Asttrian, suspicious as he was of his own relatives and old allies, wouldn't have taken it lightly if he had found them on their way to pay him an unannounced visit.

They had to avoid going close to the waterways as much as possible. The Rheann, being the biggest river in the kingdom, was the main trading route and was busy at all times of the year, even during the winter. Currently, it was even more dangerous for them, for it was being jealously supervised by the feared Drkarach Kechtás, the Dragon Knights of the Skyarachti.

Despite his weariness after the journey, Arachtan couldn't seem to find sleep. He thought time and again about the strange summons from druid Thuarnach, and somehow a strong feeling of uneasiness took over him, he was simply restless.

It was strange for a man like himself. He had always known how to wait, when to move, what to say, when to say it... Even as a young child, he had shown he was capable to choose his actions wisely. Arachtan was known to be patient. It was the one trait even his most envious foes knew to acknowledge.

Tonight, however, it was different...

Dangerous Secrets

16th day of Nwyr, shortly after midnight, 299 YD,
Drejkreins

In the cover of night, while Thuaìden was keeping watch and Skeorden was resting, unconcerned, Arachtan decided to pay a visit to their loyal friend Tschiaran, who possessed a vast network of spies around all port areas. Arachtan wanted to hear what news he might have about the fragile situation in the Skyarach Kingdom, where now his cousin Asttrian was king.

In previous letters, his uncle Thuarnach had cautiously implied a delicate matter pouring over the edge between King Asttrian and their cousins Ealator and Skymnia of the western city of Reaghil Ovsbhealle Rheanna.

It wasn't a secret, of course, that the new king was much less than a tolerable leader. From a very early age, Asttrian had shown weaknesses of character that had made his teachers despair. The Skyarachti had trusted their old king to survive them all, and resolve any disputes about the succession to his throne before dying, but this was not to be.

Urarathan, the old king, had died unexpectedly and under most peculiar circumstances, about a year ago. He had left behind a son,

Asttrian, and a daughter, Shya, none of whom possessed the nature of a true Royal Arach to lead the kingdom into the future. On the contrary, both were arrogant and selfish, showing no respect or empathy for either subject or enemy, friend or foe. Urarathan's twins were cruel and thirsted for power, taking advantage of their position to let the people they disliked or mistrusted suffer at their pleasure. But most dangerous of all, both siblings were ambitious beyond measure. And so, most members of the court and neighbouring kingdoms were very concerned about the current rulers of the Skyarach Kingdom.

Tschiaran had been expecting him.

He knew Arachtan wouldn't risk daylight. He had been waiting since the moon started its nightly race through the sky, at their usual meeting place, the Lion's Den, a shabby old cottage close to the harbour, used mostly by gamblers and smugglers to meet undisturbed.

Arachtan came later than usual, though, and seemingly troubled.

"Hyo, my friend!" greeted him Tschiaran, "not in a good mood, I see! But what is this? You don't bring any merry company? Where have you left your girlfriend, or should I call her your guest wife now? Does the Druid know? The Queen? They won't like it a bit, Ara, no, they certainly won't..." He hesitated for a second and then went on, "As always, Tschiaran is not telling, but they will find out soon enough."

Arachtan gave him a scolding glance.

"Oh, don't look at me like that, you know me, Ara, Tschiaran always knows things."

Arachtan smiled amused, shaking his head at the same time.

"You will never change, Tschiar, nothing escapes your ears! But I'm not here to talk about me tonight, we'll discuss Ryssa another time. I need to hear everything you know about the conflict between my Rheann cousins and Asttrian. You know messages are being delayed, or they simply vanish before reaching Daing Mhuir. We haven't been getting any critical information from the Skyarachti, for months now."

"My dearest friend, where do I start?" answered Tschiaran, looking grave now, "The death of an Arach King has always been ominous. Who is his dragon going to follow? Will it fade? Which Arach has the right to succeed him to the throne? All these questions... many are worried... your uncle Urarathan was most beloved and honoured by his people, and no one really expected him to die so soon, least of all under such dubious circumstances. These are indeed dangerous times for the Dragon People, my friend, we are being throttled by snakes."

Arachtan was becoming impatient at his friend's ambiguity. He didn't want to be solving riddles at this point. He knew his history, and he did not want to talk politics for the sake of it, right now. The druid's letter had been ambiguous enough.

"Now, Tschiar, I know all this, everyone is mourning his death, I am too. But surely Thuarnach has already–"

His own words suddenly echoed in his head like a thunderbolt. Of course, this must be it! That is why Thuarnach was summoning him: he must have found something wrong about the Old King's death, something that he would only tell him in person!

Tschiaran interrupted his thoughts. "Not everyone is mourning!"

"What do you mean?" asked Arachtan.

"Just that, my friend: not everybody is mourning the king's death. There are rumours, you know, involving his offspring."

Tschiaran paused and scanned the room around them as if fearing someone might catch a word of what they were saying.

"It is told that no sooner was Urarathan dead, Asttrian crowned himself king without the support of the Thriar.[4] After that, he

---

[4] Council of the Wise, made up of a male druid and two royal women.

proclaimed a thorough reform of the Royal Contract of the Dreà Arachti,[5] changing the rights and obligations of the King and the royal family, all the while with princess Shya's support. They say their mother, Host Queen Umbriel, is not holding court anymore, her mind, weak as if a shadow has fallen over her. Princess Shya and her brother Asttrian, on the other hand, are feasting lavishly in his honour. It is also said that they have banned your cousins Ealator and Skymnia from Reaghil Bheallemer, ordering them to stay within the boundaries of their castle at Reaghil Ovsbhealle Rheanna. They aren't allowed to travel north to the Thuatharachti, nor west to the Anairarachti, and they aren't allowed to use the waterways of the Rheann, either."

"I knew Asttrian was capable of many things, but this? What has befallen my cousin to act like this?"

To his own surprise, Arachtan's dismay was turning into anger.

"Has he forgotten what happened during the last Arach War when the Skyarachti split from the Thuatharachti in the North? It was his own father, back then crown prince, who started the war through his decision of marrying a Host Maiden[6] against the Royal Arach Contract. King Urukaracht had no choice but to fight his

---

[5] Ancient treaty signed with blood by the founders of the Red Ancient City of Seannanorthai, the Dreà Arachti, first ancestors of the Peoples of the Dragon.
[6] "Host Maiden" were young women from honourable "host families," i.e. educated or rich merchant families as were native to the territories the Arach incorporated into their Kingdoms. These natives were usually assimilated in the executive management of the realm, but always remained subjects.

own son, then, and that war is still fresh in our bones! Is my cousin out of his mind?"

"Ey, it's true, it was King Urarathan who split the Skyarachti from the North Kingdom in that bloody conflict," replied Tschiaran, "but he was wise enough to make peace, soon after. He never meant to take Drkarach with him, the dragon followed him. He always respected his father and mother. He despaired when hearing of his father's sudden death, and took great care to leave all matters settled with his mother and all his siblings, those that had stayed and those that had followed him. We all know this."

Tschiaran went silent for a moment, and then went on, "but after that day, king Urarathan followed the Royal Contract of the Dreà Arachti almost to obsession... No, Ara, it would be unfair to compare the father with the son. Urarathan's biggest mistake was certainly to take lady Umbriel as his wife, but he could never have guessed–"

"True, but he was not just any Arach, he was the crown prince, he had the responsibility to choose wisely, and he failed. Now, we are still paying!" interrupted him Arachtan with bitterness, "but, after all, I'm no one to question the great king of the Skyarachti, I sure had my own decisions to make..."

Arachtan went silent for a moment, and then added with concern, "I'm supposed to travel straight to Reaghil Bheallemer, that's what Thuarnach would have me do, but I can't leave my cousins alone, imprisoned in their own fortress, Tschiar. I will have to delay my arrival, and see if all you've just told me is true. You send word to Thuarnach for me, will you? I know he won't like it much, still he'll have to understand. Please, remind him he can trust me, I know what I'm doing."

"Ara, never forget your cousin Asttrian is half-Arach, too. He might not be as clever as you lot, but he is cunning and ruthless, and he is the one with the last dragon."

" We'll see… Drkarach chooses whom she follows, Tschiar."

"Maybe, or maybe not. Why is the dragon still at Reaghil Bheallemer, then? Why hasn't she disappeared or flown away like the rest of them? What is she waiting for? Such an ancient and wise beast that came from the very bowels of old Seannanorthai, why hasn't she left yet?" countered Tschiaran.

Arachtan left that night without being able to answer these last questions, which stayed in his head, hunting him long after the meeting with his loyal friend.

Chapter Three: **Forest Of Dreams**

The Taunus

April 22nd, 2022
A5 highway, close to Frankfurt, Germany

She had a terrible headache; the back of her eyes was throbbing inside her skull like drums to an African beat.

What were those pills made of?

Her panic to fly could have ruined everything, and she simply couldn't risk it. So, without asking too much, she had swallowed the pills right after boarding the plane.

One thing was for sure, the doctor knew exactly what he was doing: she had slept through – or rather stayed unconscious – for the whole flight. It had then taken some three people to shake her awake, and rather ungently, too.

Actually, she still felt pretty much stunned, as if her head was filled with lead bricks, so she closed her eyes tightly, and prayed the pain would go away. But sitting in the car with Professor

Beckmann, who was cheerfully offering her some accounts of their journey home, the headache was becoming worse by the second.

He was definitively a kind man, she could tell, and a smart one, too. Tall, lean and well-dressed, he appeared younger than she knew he was, and although they had just met, he was the type of person that makes others feel comfortable around them. She very much hoped that the same applied to his wife and children, since she would be staying with them for two whole years.

Very slowly, she dared open her eyes.

The scenery instantly captivated her: a colourful sunset reflected on what looked like thousands of tiny mosaics cutting out the profile of the Frankfurter Skyline, while on the other side of the highway, the view of the great orange disc gradually sinking behind the mountains felt strangely familiar...

How odd, she had never been here before.

Now, the mountains seemed to be getting ominously closer; she could almost touch them. Absentmindedly, she reached out to touch the cold glass of the car window. Those very mountains were the last place her father had been to, before mysteriously disappearing. She tried to remember their name, but her mind was still clouded. She wanted to ask the professor, but her throbbing head stopped her.

She sighed.

There was nothing she could do about the pain, so she closed her eyes again. But just as she let herself go, a soft whisper calling "Thaunaan" settled in her mind.

Night Bird

June 30th (dawn), 2022,
Oberursel, Germany

Annea was floating, hovering some distance over the ground in her room.

How...? This could not be real.

But it was.

She had full control of herself, and as she hovered always higher and higher, she decided to fly out of the window.

But, wait, this couldn't be true! She was afraid of flying!

She flew out all the same.

Her heart was pounding madly, it was exhilarating! She flew this way and that, found a little lake and overflew it a couple of times, then, she discovered little, winding paths in the forest that had been hidden by the incredibly tall trees. It was simply magical, and she could not get enough of it.

All of a sudden, however, she felt a longing presence up above her. Someone or something was waiting for her.

She had to fly further up.

Then, she saw it: a massive winged shadow swallowed all the moonlight around her.

Still, she felt the urge of going further up, she had to reach it...

Just then, to her utter amazement, the shadow turned into white flames and the green forest below was erased by a storm of ashes.

She heard a man's voice shouting out her name: "ANNEA, ANNEA, ANNEA!"

She woke up shivering. In spite of the cool damp of the night coming in through the window, she was soaking wet. She had been dreaming again.

Since her arrival two months ago, Annea had been having the same kind of dream over and over again. Still, she couldn't make up her mind whether it was a nightmare or not. Paradoxically, her fear of flying had no place in her dream. Instead, she truly enjoyed the feeling of being weightless, boundless energy, free up in the air. However, it always ended the same way: licking, white flames turned the green of the forest into a desert of grey ashes...

She stood up and walked to the window to close it.

It was a mild, starry night. One of the first ones this year, and she rejoiced in its fresh breath.

Every night, before going to sleep, she would follow the same ritual. She would open her window for some time and try to make out the sounds of the forest. It seems that tonight, she had fallen asleep while doing so.

She thought of how much she was enjoying her stay in Germany, but how the search for her father, in contrast, was proving nothing but fruitless.

The professor's family, made up of his lovely wife Masha and their two energetic boys, Henry and Peter, had proven to fill a void in Annea's life, giving her exactly what she was needing: a warm family home.

The boys, in particular, had truly made her part of the family, and she was really fond of them, too. In this short time, they had become like two little brothers to her.

Masha Beckmann, on her part, was a very kind but very silent person. She loved gardening and painting, and could seclude herself for hours in the little attic room, where her empty canvases waited patiently for a spark of colour to ignite them. She was always in a good mood and had taken it to her heart to help Annea with anything she needed. And while you couldn't precisely say that they were intimate, they got on very well with each other. Annea helped with the chores at home, and with various family errands, whenever she could, too.

By now, she had been introduced to most family friends and relatives, and whenever there was time, the family would take her sightseeing, too. So yes, she was having a great stay at the Beckmann's.

On the other hand, and much to her disappointment, she had learnt absolutely nothing about her father's disappearance.

More than two months already, and nothing! She had searched several places and talked to many scholars and experts around the area: some from the University of Mainz, where she attended her classes, some from local museums, and even tourist guides that specialised in tours of this particular mountain chain. And still, nothing! As if the earth had opened up her great brown jaws and devoured her father entirely...

Professor Beckmann's house was very close to the forest of North Oberursel, so in her free time, Annea would regularly comb the slopes of the Altkönig, the Heidetrank Oppidum and the Bleibeskopf, three of the well-known Taunus mountain tops of archaeological importance. Only one of these, the Heidetrank, was easily accessible to her, though. But since she was herself an archaeologist to be, and already possessed a profound knowledge of history, Annea was eager to survey all the sites on her own.

She was absolutely puzzled by the archaeological richness of the area. The evidence pointed towards rather ancient settlements. Precisely, her father's favourite.

Experts talked about very extensive Bronze and Iron Age Celtic settlements in the area that had been all connected to each other, something like 3000 years ago. She was more than sure her father would have been obsessed with exploring those grounds…

Unfortunately, all college professors that had known Dr Julio Menard, Annea's renowned father, and his work, assured her that they hadn't seen or heard from the scholar for years, now.

But she wouldn't despair, she was here now, and she was not going to give up so easily. She was in the right place, she knew it. There must be something she was missing, some piece of the puzzle that could lead her to him. She just had to be patient.

When Annea had been seven years old, Dr Menard had retired from scholarly life, although he had been too young for that, of course, being only 45 years old. But no one had questioned his decision. He had a beautiful family, and being a prominent archaeologist, he had spent most of his life digging in foreign countries, far away from home. Annea had always loved her father dearly. He had been a good-natured, truly patient and loving father to her and her sister, and she could still remember how glad she had been when he had told them about his plans of staying home to spend more time with them. Ironically, things had not turned out quite that way for them, since merely a year after retirement, during what was supposed to be a short trip to Germany, he had disappeared from the face of the earth without a trace.

The Forest Walk

The next morning, Annea was again suffering from a very bad headache.

That mysteriously recurring dream she had, and all those thoughts in her head that wouldn't leave her, were not contributing to her spirits either.

She stretched herself slowly and trudged across her room to open the window, which offered an ecstatic view of the Taunus hills.

Then, she saw it...

Despite it being mid-June, the beginning of the summer, an unexpected delicate whiteness had silently but conspicuously covered the world:

Snow, snow in June!

As every Saturday, she would stay to have breakfast with the Beckmann's, and since Masha was an early bird, she always had breakfast ready before most of the family were up. Both Henry and Peter were very much like their mother, and today was no exception. Annea could hear them already playing soccer downstairs in the living room and couldn't but smile: Masha was telling them off, but could not prevent another of her decorative vases from crashing down raucously to the floor. They seemed to be particularly energetic today…

'Not good for a headache,' she thought.

As soon as they heard Annea walking down the stairs, both boys sprinted towards the feet of the staircase to be the first ones to greet her.

"Sleepy head, sleepy head," called Henry, the older of the two brothers, "you will miss it, come, have a look outside. It's snowing! We've got to get out, Annea. Please, please, you have to come with us to the woods, today. What do you say? We could build a base in the snow. Please, please, come with us?"

Peter, who was two years younger and much wiser, waited until she turned the elbow of the stairways and could finally make eye contact with him. Then, stretching his arm towards her, he offered her a tiny, truly melancholic daisy he had picked from the garden ten minutes ago, and with a big bright smile, he gave it to her intently, forming the word "PLEASE" with his lips.

He was absolutely adorable, and she knew she was in for it.

And so, for the rest of their breakfast, they all enjoyed an energetic brainstorming on the shape, the materials and the location of the would-be base.

Right after, the boys got ready to go out so fast that Annea's ungovernable hair was still all over the place, and she barely had time to pick some warm clothes from the storage room - where, a month ago, all the family had put away their winter garments. Fortunately, she did find her beloved lamb boots, which she put on hastily to follow the boys out.

This kind of weather in June was absolutely mental. Still, Annea pondered, the coolness outside might help her get rid of that headache, plus, she always had a great time playing with the boys. So, inspired by the children's burst of determination, she went out in high spirits to join them.

As soon as they were out, Annea noticed something strange in the colours of the sky. It wasn't a dull grey, as it mostly is when it snows. The sun had managed to pierce the clouds and the background gained a strange hue of orange while further off, towards the mountains, an astonishingly bright rainbow floated as if painted against the white canvas of the snow. It was surreal!

'Where is my phone,' she thought, 'I have to take a picture and send it to Lola, she has to see this.'

She looked for it everywhere, but of course, she had forgotten it.

"Henry, darling," she called, "do you happen to have your phone with you?"

The boy searched all his pockets, and nothing...

A few seconds later, little Pete admitted, with sheepish eyes, that he had taken Henry's phone, and hidden it in his own jacket, where he was pulling it out from this very moment.

"Here, Annea," he said, "take a nice picture for Mummy, please."

"You, again!" protested Henry, "it's always you! Give me my phone back, now!"

"Ok, you two," –this was not helping against the headache, and Annea knew it was time to intervene– "just quit it here, will you? I won't go a step forward unless you start behaving as the good brothers you are. Pete, dearest," she addressed the little one, "I know you would love to have your own phone. This one, however, is not yours. So, you have to promise not to steal from Henry anymore. Now, I will take the picture, and I will be giving the phone back to his rightful owner after that," and turning to Henry now, she added, "if it's ok with you Henry, of course."

The boy nodded his consent reluctantly.

"Do we have an agreement, then?" she asked, looking sternly at both boys.

They both nodded, and Pete handed over the device in question.

By then, the clouds had already turned hues of a reddish pink, and it looked even more breath-taking.

'This isn't true. This is what people call a miracle, a godly painting.' she thought.

So, to have proof of this wonder, she decided to take a selfie, too.

'Just perfect,' she mused, 'now, Lola can't argue I would download the picture from the internet.'

As the boys were growing tired of Annea's photographic experiments, they started narking her, so they finally started hiking up, singing and whistling through the snowy landscape.

For half an hour, they plodded their way up the hill with increasing difficulty. The boys in their hurry hadn't brought proper snow boots, and the forest ways were by now deep with snow. Altogether, Annea was starting to doubt this expedition had been a good idea, after all. This kind of weather was quite exceptional, and who knew what awaited them further up the mountain...

"We know the place, Annea, promise," Henry tried to motivate her, as if he had read her mind, "let's just rest for a while, it won't take much longer. It's perfect, wait until you see!"

"I must be mad to follow you out here, guys," Annea answered, "we could have chosen some place nearby, you know. There are so many places with enough trees closer to your house, why on earth do we need to go up this far? This place you chose better be really special!" she told them with a smile, "but yes, we can rest here, and we'll still go a little further, just a little. Now, here, look what I brought for you," and saying that, she pulled out three deliciously red apples from her pockets.

During their short break, Pete wanted to take a peek at the pictures Annea had previously taken with Henry's phone. So, the three came closer together, while Henry searched for the photos.

Like thunderstruck, the three stared onto the screen of the cell phone in disbelief: instead of the beautiful light-soaked landscape they were expecting, the pictures were bathed in just one colour: the colour of blood. You could make out shapes, like the trees, but most surprisingly, the last picture, Annea's selfie, she just wasn't on it. As if she had been made of some transparent matter, Annea was not showing on the selfie. In her place, a bright shape of light pierced the blood-stained background. Now, that looked truly surreal!

The boys were the first ones to come around, for they desperately wanted to reach the building site for the base before Annea would call the whole expedition off.

They started laughing uncontrollably, while Annea still took some time to shake those images out of her head.

She told herself this incident would surely have a most trivial explanation. She was certainly no expert on using cameras. And trying not to give it another thought, she collected their things and ushered Pete and Henry to get going.

This was a big mistake; she would later realise with some bitterness. There had been so many signs warning her against the journey she was about to undertake. So many strange things happening. The dreams, the snow, the pictures… She should have paid attention, she should have been more cautious. But back then, she simply had not seen it coming. And, how could she? She had never given any credit to superstition in her life, she did not believe in fairy tales or supernatural beings, she was a rational historian through and through. And so, the merry company started off again, towards the place at the feet of a steep slope, which the boys had selected for a perfect forest base.

Chapter Four: Reaghil Bheallemer Na Caydúllien Ore

1st Day of the Dragon Month of Aarglas,[7] 300 YD,
Reaghil Bheallemer na Caydúllien Ore

Thuarnach had been busy all day, trying to talk young King Asttrian out of beheading the fortress's latest smith, Ranor the Black, for an iron sword he had delivered to the king, which was lacking the royal hilt, the dragon head made of gold. The smith had sincerely replied that he had had no access to gold for months now. The kingdom's gold was being jealously hoarded by the king himself in the gold chambers of the castle, for, among other things, he was fearing a revolt and wanted to buy sell-swords to strengthen his power over the realm.

This was no exceptional day, though. Things had been going on like this for a year, since old King Urarathan's sudden death, but the royal druid of Reaghil Bheallemer knew better than to rush things.

Thuarnach had been Asttrian's childhood teacher and was, in a peculiar way, still close to his nephew. The druid would continue advising his nephew, trying, sometimes in vain, to control his

---

[7] January (aprox.)

temper. In this way, he was buying time for Arachtan to reach the capital. Thuarnach knew the kingdom's last hope was in Arachtan's hands now, that was why he had urged him to come, but he had not told Arachtan the whole story, not yet.

Today, however, the druid felt strangely uneasy. A month had passed since he had sent word to Arachtan that his presence was urgently needed. In normal circumstances, it would have taken him just about a fortnight to arrive, the Dragon roads connected the most distant places across the Arach kingdoms very efficiently.

True, it was the dark season of Nwyr,[8] rivers were partly turned to drifting masses of ice and roads were laden with heavy snow, not the perfect weather for a journey from Inna Skythiarach to Reaghil Bheallemer. This Ynar Drkent, in particular, was proving to bring extreme temperatures and wild wind storms. Thuarnach knew it was no coincidence, of course. But he also knew Ara's temperament well, he was not one to be defeated by weather conditions. He was an experienced ranger, and he would have been able to find his way through any blizzard. No, it was not like him to take this long...

As it was, however, he still had no news from his nephew, and to worsen the situation, Thuarnach could not send any more birds.

---

[8] Winter

The jays weren't flying without king Asttrian's or princess Shya's consent. In such fear of a rebellion they were, that they were strictly censoring communication with the other two remaining Arach Kingdoms, the Anairarach in the West, and Thuatharach in the North. Had the druid sent another jay to Queen Scaìthara at Daing Mhuir, he would have raised suspicions...

No, this time he would have to keep waiting and pray to the Dragon and the forces of Nature. He would have to steer the situation alone as long as it took Arachtan to arrive. But how long still?

They had to talk, Thuarnach thought. It was past time Ara knew some well-hidden secrets that would change his life forever, and there was also that old prophecy. But what if Ara never made it to the Golden City in time? What if he was caught?

No, this was an option he would not consider for now.

Well past midday, Thuarnach swiftly stole himself away from Drkent Har, and went to visit his friend Lughan, who lived an hour's walk from the fortress.

He had to hurry, or Lughan would have all his family sitting at dinner with him, and he needed to have a word with his friend in private…

Lughan, who he had personally trained for about ten years to help him with his work as medicinal master of the Golden City, had also become his most loyal friend.

As Lughan had been found wondering astray and belonged neither to the host families, nor to the Nachtural Brean or native farmers of the realm, he was taken in as a guest person by old King Urarathan himself, on the condition that he was to contribute peacefully like any other to the health and wealth of the kingdom.

A middle-aged man, very smart and educated, Lughan had come to Reaghil Bheallemer around 16 years ago. He was not physically strong, making a poor worker for the mine or the fields, so it had been easy for Thuarnach, who had been given charge of organising and administrating social structures in the Kingdom, to soon discover in him a most skilful apprentice.

Lughan had learnt fast and was keen to learn, he had an interest in politics and a good hand with mixing potions. Thuarnach used to sit with him long hours debating what could be best for the kingdom in these difficult times. And as the years passed, they also started sharing many well-kept secrets. Lughan told

Thuarnach all about the world he had left behind, while Thuarnach instructed him on the Arach ways. Theirs was a true friendship.

Truthfully, the Skyarachti were known for their justice and generosity towards strangers. In other places, someone like Lughan would have been taken as a slave, sold or exploited. Not in the realms of the Dragon People, though. Lughan had eventually been given almost all the rights of a true citizen, if not the title, for proving through the years to be a faithful and responsible person. He was allowed to leave or stay at will, as long as he respected all Arach laws as delivered by the Royal Contract of the Dreà Arachti.

Lughan, for his part, preferred to stay away from the castle as much as possible, and Thuarnach agreed that he could keep on living in the guest quarters, at the edges of the Golden City, even if he worked for him as an apothecary. Out of sight, out of mind, in this way, King Asttrian, who was known to mistrust foreigners, would take no notice of his loyal helper.

Thuarnach made his way through the crowded market place, where still some merchants were closing their stalls and packing up for the evening. He took a sharp turn left into a little alley with a dead end. It was dark and it was snowing heavily, which made it extremely difficult to pierce through the thick white curtain. He stopped and waited to make sure he was not being followed.

The alley was completely deserted, so he opened the secret door that led to the tunnel underneath the market square.

Finally! Now, he was invisible in his own underworldly kingdom.

The underground tunnels of this great city had been his most ambitious project, and he was proud to know each and every secret passage in Reaghil Bheallemer. This particular one followed the stream known to everyone as the Sryath, and then bent west towards a deep ravine, where the settlements of most guest peoples were.

When he arrived, Lughan was preparing a medicinal potion out of the soft, bluish green needles of the pinus cembra, or stone pine. The Skyarachti attributed healing properties to its resin, and it was preciously valued in the ancient kingdom.

"Hyo, Thuarnach!" greeted him Lughan, "take a look at this, it is so pure, it can cure an elephant! The quality delivered by the Quaranien is unbeatable. Do you think we'll be getting more in, this winter?"

"Hyo, my friend," answered the Druid, "I'm afraid not, the King has ordered to close all trading points with our Southern neighbours as long as winter lasts. We'll have to make do with what we have. Asttrian is becoming increasingly weary of his foundering alliances, he mistrusts everyone… have you heard word from Daing Mhuir yet?" he asked with concern in his voice.

"No. It's over a month now that the last bird was sent. It never came back, Thuarnach… it could be caution, or it could have been intercepted. Arachtan, though, should have long arrived. Do you think something's happened to him along the way?"

The druid grew thoughtful, deep furrows of concern in his brow.

"Lughan, we will deal with what we have, but yes, we are indeed running out of time. The Drkarach doesn't wait for us to act, the Dragon gives and the Dragon takes… if Asttrian continues ruling this way, the Drkarach will awaken, and then, I'm afraid the degree of destruction escapes our imagination, my friend. I need Arachtan here, it is imperative that he knows the truth. As for Asttrian, he will never change, and nor will his efforts to destroy everything that his father held dear. He has his mother's ambition, not just her dark sight, and his mind is set on clinging to the power of the Arach, which he was not born to wield…" he hesitated for a moment and then continued, "the Dragon will not tolerate it, she chooses whom she follows. I know the time has come, Lughan. The prophecy, I feel the portals shifting again, we cannot wait for Ara much longer. The maiden will be here soon,

Lughan, you know who I'm talking about... We have to find her first, we have to find her before Asttrian's or Shya's men do!"

Chapter Five: Swallowed By The Earth

June 30th 2022,
Oberursel, Germany

Annea and the boys had reached the feet of the hill both tired and cold, and although they were quite enjoying themselves, it was not as easy to build a base in the snow, as they had previously thought.

Twigs and branches were hidden by a white coat, and so were stones and leaves… The base turned out to be more of a challenge, in the end, than the way up had been.

So, as they couldn't find much building material around them, they decided to split and explore the area. The boys went together to the left of the slope, while Annea took to the right.

After a short distance, however, the hill took a turn, and Annea was completely on her own. She could not see the boys, and they could not her.

She walked a little further up and, to her surprise, she discovered a barred entrance to something that looked very much like an abandoned mine. Behind it, a big rocky hill bulging to her right, which seemed taken from a blood-curdling fairy tale, raised strong and solemnly. On top of the rocks, Annea could make out a dense grove of looming twisted oak trees.

'They must be ancient,' she thought.

Like enormous shadows of an old forgotten forest, they were watching over the stones as if a treasure had been hidden there.

'I've never seen something quite like this before, the whole landscape is so...' she had to admit it, '...magical...'

She was so taken by the landscape, that Annea felt the urge to explore a little more of her surroundings. She decided to follow the rocky hill yet another turn to the right, so as to see what could lay beyond...

What she saw then, was nothing she had been expecting. There, at her feet, opened up a massive hole in the ground, the size of a crater left by a mine explosion.

'Second World War,' she remembered.

She had forgotten Germany wore the visible and invisible scars of one of the bloodiest wars in history, 'a battered land with half open wounds,' she reminded herself.

Taking a closer look, she saw to her surprise that there was even more snow swirling at the bottom of the crater. She felt a sudden urge to reach it, to touch its surface.

'Only once,' she told herself, 'I want to feel the rough ground beneath.'

She knew she was acting strange, but somehow the whole atmosphere invited her, seduced her to explore. As if it had a voice of its own, that icy emptiness of the crater hole was calling for her.

Annea descended slowly, careful not to slip all the way down. The snow on the surface of the crater had turned into ice, which made her descent quite difficult. She should have put on crampons, she mused sarcastically, even a snail would go faster than her, right now.

Suddenly, a flock of jays took off from a nearby tree and brushed her head with their wings. She instantly lost footing and slid all the way through, reaching the bottom turned more or less into a ball of snow, twigs and leaves, all nicely bundled up together.

'Splendid, Little Pandora!' she scolded herself, 'now enjoy the crater ground as long as you want! Who knows when Henry and Pete will find you in here?'

She sat there for a while, evaluating her options. There was no use in screaming, the snow would muffle the sounds so effectively, that no one would hear her calls. Trying to climb was hopeless, too. Should she just wait?

She couldn't...

Annea was extremely beautiful and smart, she was brave and independent, she was certainly headstrong and some even said 'wise' at times... But patience was certainly not among of her virtues.

Restless, she started surveying the bottom of the crater, which was slightly bigger than a medium-sized car, pacing from one corner to the other like a wild animal trapped in a cage.

She had to think how to attract the boys attention.

Then, all of a sudden, she stumbled over something hard that was sticking out of the ground. She kneeled to take a closer look, and the ice beneath her cracked loudly. There was something down there, she couldn't see what it was, for it had been covered by earth, leaves, and snow.

Seeing that the ice was splintering, she rapidly looked for a stone to hammer the ice open. She then carefully dug out the earth beneath with her bare hands, it was bitterly cold.

'God, I should have brought those spare gloves Marsha offered me! My fingers will be falling off any minute!' she reflected.

A couple of minutes later, she found what she was looking for. It resembled a doorknob. Made of golden metal, it was perfectly shaped into a smooth ball with swirling engraved patterns.

Curious to understand what she had just found, she went on to clear as much as she could from the surrounding area.

'It looks like gold,' she thought, 'but so massive...'

She kept digging bare-handed until she was able to make out the shape: it resembled something like a big, round door!

She kept staring at it in disbelief, when suddenly she realised that it seemed to be slightly open, and there was more ice coming out from beneath it.

'I wonder, maybe I can manage to open it just a little further,' she mused, 'I'd like to catch a glimpse of what lies behind it...'

Taking a closer look, she discovered mysterious, engraved patterns all over its frames, and in the middle, somewhat worn out by time, there was some sort of more detailed design. She thought it actually had the appearance of a dragon head of some sort.

In all the years studying history at university and reading through her father's extensive, private collection, she had seen many different types of symbols and written archaic alphabets, but never, never something quite like this.

The surface of the door was incredibly shiny, as if it had been polished yesterday. The engravings and the drawing, on the other hand, were fading away.

'This is just amazing! Father would love it… How I wish he would be here with me…"Go for it, little Pandora!" that is exactly what he would say!'

This was certainly a major archaeological find. Should she truly try to open the door by herself? She would certainly risk breaking things. And then also, what if there was something dangerous behind it, like a forgotten Nazi bomb? What if she fell down a shaft of some sort? There was the old mine quite close to the place, so this was certainly a possibility to consider…

But being all alone and with nothing better to do, temptation got its way over reason.

What damage would it cause to have a quick look? For what she knew, the door might be even locked or barred from the inside.

She pulled hard on the door knob. It was slippery, and she couldn't get a good grasp of it. She tried pulling at the edges of the door, but it wouldn't move a bit.

Overwhelmed by physical exertion, she went back to the centre of the door, where the outline of the dragon head was, and sat down to rest for a while. She would try again later, there sure was a way to get it open. In that precise moment, however, the earth started vibrating, and then shaking madly.

An earthquake, she thought, perfect, just what I needed!

As she tried to pull herself up, her surroundings became blurry, and the next second, everything around her was turning at the speed of light. She couldn't see, it was utter darkness, she could only feel on her skin what seemed to be snowflakes hitting her hard, racing past her in a storm of swirls.

She could not keep up, any longer! She was herself a snow flake now, she was levitating, floating, being carried away and finally, swallowed...

She was no more.

Chapter Six: The Children Of The Rheann

1st Day of Aarglas, 300 YD (1000 BC our count),
Reaghil Ovsbhealle Rheanna, the Royal Western City of the Rhine, today's Koblenz

"It is snow,

It is now,

it is the turn of the tide,

And when the shadows shall lift,

realms shall reunite,

peace the Dragon shall bring.

Behold their beauty,

Behold their white flame,

For you shall never

see them again.

And you,

vapid, spiritless men,

fill your hearts with awe,

and tell your friends:

A new beginning with the rising sun,

All turned to ashes,

All,

but one."

"Bravo!" clapped Skymnia spontaneously, "Thuarnach would be proud of you, big brother!"

She signalled the service maiden to bring in the Rheannvid, the rich red wine that was cultivated on both sides of the Rheann valley, and which was considered the most exquisite red in all of the Arach Kingdoms.

She sipped with pleasure at her now full glass, and then added, "You have finally managed to recite that ancient prophecy in full and with no mistakes! Here is a toast to you, Eala!"

The hint of a smile appeared on Ealator's face for the fraction of a second, to then disappear even faster, "I never truly understood it, you know…" he sighed and joined Skymnia with the wine.

"No one ever did, I think," replied Skymnia thoughtful, "Thuarnach was the best teacher one could dream of, but we were so young… we wanted to have fun, enjoy each other's company, not learn silly prophecies by heart."

She ambled in deep reflection across the exuberantly ornated hall.

"I miss our Anairarachti cousins, Eala…" she went on, "I'm concerned about Ara, Asttrian always hated him the most, and he hates quite a few people. He and Shya are sending Kechtás to every corner of the realm, it seems that now, more than ever, Ara needs to stay away."

"I know, but there is no way to warn him, sister," answered Ealator drily, "and this is all my fault! I should have never reacted like that in front of the Death's Assembly. I just... I couldn't let those two destroy our kingdom's laws, the laws their own father vehemently defended! Damn them both! What they did was a blunt betrayal to our people! But mother–"

"You did what you had to, Eala. You can't blame yourself for it, they would have taken her and banned us one way or the other," interrupted him Skymnia, "as long as we stayed in the Golden City, we were a threat to their ambitions. We know too much, we ask too much, and we are both royal Arach. And while defying our cousin Asttrian in front of the Death's Assembly at Drkent Har certainly didn't help –I'm still relieved Host Queen Umbriel interceded– they had been plotting to get us out long before that. I'm glad we're back home, though. Reaghil Bheallemer will never be the same without the Old King, not even Thuarnach will be able to stop them for long."

"You might be right... Still, that doesn't explain the disappearance of the king's Chlìar Drkent.[9] Where is that bloody sword? Where is

---

[9] The royal sword or Chlìar Drkent was the most powerful symbol of Arach power. Crowns were seen as merely decorative, in contrast. Something only to wear at court assamblies. Costumarily, the Dreà Arachti, the true Arach people, passed on their ancient steel swords forged by dragon fire from father to son.

Drkenstar?[10] Somehow, I perceive wise uncle Thuarnach's touch behind this."

Lost in his thoughts, Ealator refilled his cup for the fourth time consecutively with the deep, red liquid, and then continued, "Well, I suppose it is better Drkenstar is gone than in Asttrian's hands. However, I don't understand the old king's intentions behind his last wish, I still can't believe he meant our bastard cousin Ara to have his sword!"

They had all been summoned to the royal chambers when the King had been brought back from his daily ride. He had been badly wounded, a deadly arrow had pierced him from behind. It was treason, no doubt, but who and how had they managed to get so close to the king unnoticed? His Kechtási guard had been redoubled after the uprisings at the borders, Ealator had seen to that himself. Indeed, the circumstances of his passing had been quite peculiar.

Urarathan had been still alive, if breathing heavily when they had laid him on the bed. All the family had gathered close to him: Skymnia, their mother Lady Skenya of the Rheann, Queen Umbriel, her two children, the druid Thuarnach and Ealator himself. The King had wanted them all to be present, the Thriar and his family in full, and he had addressed them all together.

---

[10] Name of Urarathan's sword.

Now, no one could deny his spoken words and his healthy state of mind before his last breath.

"He said we should trust Ara to lead the way although our cousin had stayed away from the kingdom since the revolts started. He ordered we shall give him the Chlìar Drkent, Drkenstar, to protect the people."

He looked speculatively towards his sister, a long silence filled the hall.

"He had never talked to us so openly about Ara," Ealator said finally.

Although everyone knew how much the old king appreciated Ara, for some it still came as a shock that he would choose him over his own son, or even over other more noble young Arach who had served him loyally.

"The honourable bastard son of our powerful aunt, Queen Scaìthara of the Anairarachti and the brave Skyarach warrior! The very same who always wanted to become a druid, and is now married to a slave girl! Is that the rightful bearer of Drkenstar? Tell me, little sister…"

Looking at her with contempt, he shook his head and went on, "I say, he is not! It is but a sad joke the old king played on us all. And deep inside, you know it, Skymnia, he is not a man to be trusted!"

"My poor dear brother," replied Skymnia looking into her brother's face with watery eyes, "our king loved all his family, but he also knew what we're all made of. He was a wise man, and he knew exactly what he was doing."

She turned away, and moved towards the big glass doors that opened to the royal terraces overlooking the Rheann and its rich valleys, now all dressed in white.

"For our dear king we were all his children, he always treated us as equals, it was his way, Eala. But with Ara, well it was always different. He is different from the rest of us, you have to admit that…"

She opened the massive doors to let the cool air in.

"I won't believe the court gossip about the slave girl, brother, not until I hear it from his own lips."

Ealator knew he was being unfair with Arachtan, but he was driven by jealousy. The king had thought Ara would be the best choice for their kingdom although he, Ealator, had been the one at the king's side, and had been leading the king's attacks bravely in his name throughout the revolts, without but a hint of acknowledgement from the king. He was of more noble blood than his bastard cousin, he deserved that sword! He had earned it!

A sudden gale of damp, icy wind swept across the room, upsetting the long, heavy curtains that framed their view over the valley.

Skymnia turned to face her brother again, her cheeks now a deep red.

"Ara has always been kind and protective to us. He is the smartest, strongest and most noble person I know, and independently from his birth rights as a royal Dreà Arach, he has proved himself may times. Consequently, it comes as no surprise to me that the King chose him to rule over the Skyarachti people. That's what he meant by bestowing the royal sword onto him. And surely enough, he was counting the Thriar would support him, too. He never dreamt his own son would annul the council he held so dear, or imprison mother for openly protesting against that annulment..."

She hesitated for a moment, and then added, "I wonder how she is faring..."

As if he had seen a ghost, Ealator's face turned pale all of a sudden.

"In his last letter, about a week ago, Thuarnach assured me, he was doing all he could to help her. We can only hope it is enough, sister. I fear the worse, however. You know Asttrian and that devil of a sister he has. And now, he is thirsty for revenge against our whole family… It would be very much like him to send us a painful warning, he loves this kind of games."

And he added through gritted teeth, "if only Arachtan had been there when uncle died… If he is so noble as you say, why didn't he come as soon as word was sent about the King's sudden death? Thuarnach sent word to Daing Mhuir, I know it. Maybe he enjoys his new life with the slave girl so much that he has no time for our royal troubles."

"Brother, these were only Asttrian's vile lies to hurt his dying father even more. Besides, we don't know for certain that the jays made it to Daing Mhuir in time. The situation was already tense before the King's death. And then all happened so fast."

Skymnia was trying hard to soothe her brother's restless mind and broken ambitions.

"Maybe, but I wouldn't be so sure about the slave girl. You've heard the stories, and I know Arachtan well enough to know that he does as he pleases. Why did he not return two years ago to go back with us to Reaghil Bheallemer? He gave no explanations, he just said his errands were taking longer! And when things were starting to get dangerous, did he ever write to you that he would come to help?" continued Ealator, "I bet not even the king approved of his favourite's doings then. Skymnia, you have to face it, he went away when the kingdom most needed him."

Skymnia looked her brother in the eyes pleadingly, "Eala, we must hold together and trust Ara, he must have had a good reason for leaving and not coming back. Why judge our cousin now? Let him tell his own story. We're not to believe envious court gossip, mother always told us, and it is most wise not to do so. Ara is the best man, I know it. And I won't believe a word until it comes out of his own mouth!" ended Skymnia defiantly.

Ealator gazed at her filled with disdain and answered briskly, "that's because you are in love with him, you've always been, sweet sister. Blinded you are, like all of them!"

To put an end to this conversation, he walked out of the royal court hall into the terrace overlooking the Rheann river with its frozen shores.

Despite the crispy snowflakes that were now eagerly covering the landscape, there he stayed for a long while, staring down at the loaden vessels bringing their precious cargo to the Golden City, as always, as if nothing had changed.

The only disruption to this so homely scenery was the omnipresence of the Dragon Knights, the most feared Drkarach Kechtás of the royal guard, in their dark blue cloaks and their golden armour, with their always vigilant eyes fixed on them all.

'No,' he thought, 'the Rheann is not ours any more, we are but prisoners in our own fortress!'

Chapter Seven: In The Dragon's Lair

The Royal Knights

1st day of Aarglas, 300 YD (1000 BC our count),
Reaghil Bheallemer

She was cold, ice cold. Her head, throbbing. For how long had she been sleeping? One hour, two?

She peered up to the sky and noticed the sun had already given way to a lovely starry night.

'Four, at the very least,' she deduced.

The ground was hard, her back was aching, and her whole body felt stiff. She stretched herself, while scanning the ground beneath her.

She stopped short in disbelief.

"But… it doesn't make sense, where's the door?"

She kept looking for it, now digging somewhat anxiously beneath the snow-covered ground, her frostbitten fingers aching painfully.

Nothing.

"It's gone! There is absolutely nothing here!"

She had to sit down for a moment to gather herself.

"It must have been a dream, quite a vivid dream... That's the only reasonable explanation. It seems this country is not suiting me, after all. Mental note: first thing once I get home, shrink's appointment."

Her head throbbing, she got up with difficulty and started her slippery ascent. The steep crater was thickly covered by ankle deep snow, so every now and then, she would lose footage and slide back downwards a few steps. By the time she had finally managed to clamber all the way up to the top, Annea was completely exhausted. To her surprise, an absolute darkness surrounded her now, making it almost impossible to make out any path.

"Well, Dad, it seems your Little Pandora has done it again! A short off-the-beaten-track adventure with an open-air, overnight stay. Just wonderful..."

She searched the darkness for any sounds, but she could hear none.

"Where could the boys be?"

After a moment, she started off all the same. She tried to follow roughly the same direction, she thought she had come from earlier. Only she could not figure out the shape of the rocky cliffs now. Somehow the hill itself felt much higher than it had done before.

"Hmm, not a single leaf is moving… I had never noticed how still the forest could be…"

The only sound that now filled her ears was her tedious ploughing through the snow.

Where could the boys have gone? Maybe they had already called the police and they were searching for her at the wrong place… Maybe she should try calling out for them.

"Henry, Pete…"

She kept calling out for some time, but no sign of the boys.

Suddenly, she heard somebody or something approaching in haste.

"Over here!" she cried.

"Thay! Rem oan Thay er! Qven er Thay?" thundered a male voice, piercing the empty darkness, "Thay er go Pennian na Myrd an tanbredien Drkent Teyn Asttrian na Skyarach. Neyen vyen da Krayn na Dkrarach!"[11]

Now, she could see him: a tall man dressed in a golden armour yelling at her some thirty feet away, blocking the way, sword in hand and looking very angry.

Annea held her breath, what was this stranger up to? She couldn't understand a single of those angry words.

'What should I do? Maybe I should introduce myself first. He obviously speaks some kind of German dialect I have never heard before, and he definitely does not look happy to see me… but he might know where Pete and Henry are…God, look at that armour! He looks hilarious with that heavy thing on and half buried with snow.'

In truth, he looked quite menacing, a torch in one hand and a sword in the other. Annea, however, could not distinguish this well, in the dark.

---

[11] "You! Stay where you are! Who are you?"…" You are under punishment of death as decreed by the Royal Dragon King/Chief Asttrian of the Skyarach. No one enters the caves of the Dragon."

"Hallo, mein Name ist Annea. Ich wohne in Oberursel mit Dr. Beckmanns Familie. Ich suche zwei Kinder. Haben Sie sie vielleicht gesehen?" she introduced herself in German, asking the man whether he had seen the boys.

He stopped short, but then he started mumbling something to himself. He looked extremely uncomfortable, even more annoyed than before, and without wasting any more time, he covered the distance between himself and Annea in the blink of an eye, grabbed her very ungently by the elbow, while shouting at her in that strange language, whatever it was.

At that moment, however, a second man in golden armour appeared.

'What is this?' she thought, 'is it some kind of film set? I have to get out of here and find the boys before it gets more bizarre!'

She struggled to free herself from the stranger's iron grip.

"Let me go! You brute, you're hurting me!"

The men exchanged worried looks and started arguing, the first man dragging her along like a sack of rice, while approaching the other.

She was honestly at a loss. She did not know what to make out of this situation. Most of all, however, she was worried sick about the two boys, now. She had felt so secure in the forest during the day, she had never considered something like this could happen...

Then, all of a sudden, everything went blank.

Asttrian's Royal Knights, the feared Drkarach Kechtás, had knocked her down without further ado, and were now carrying her off swiftly up to the fortress of Drkent Har, the Dragon's Hall, the heart of Reaghil Bheallemer and the centre of power of the Skyarach Kingdom.

The Dragon's Hall

2nd day of Aarglas, 300 YD,
Drkent Har, Reaghil Bheallemer na Caydúllien Ore

Steel in her eyes and closely escorted by two weary guards, Princess Shya strode briskly along the Snake's Tunnel, a narrow corridor connecting the royal chambers with the court hall. She was in a very bad mood this morning, and this long, windowless, grey snake of a corridor was nagging at her spirits even further.

She wanted to get it over with, she had other plans for the day... What was her brother thinking, sending those Kechtás to escort her straight to court?!

'Fool of a brother! I'm running out of time, I have to send that jay to the Kechtás positioned at the Lahir river if I am to be the one catching our stealthy cousin...' she thought.

Shya knew the druid had sent a jay about a month ago, asking their bastard cousin to come, and she had kept this information for herself. If they were to defeat the lot of them, they had to be just as cunning as they were, and her brother Asttrian was far too emotional about Arachtan. And so, she had let the jay carry off Thuarnach's message, while knitting her own plan.

Arachtan, however, had not been seen, so far. What is more, he seemed to have evaporated in thin air. All port cities from Eonnal Maelirmer to Drejkreins had been searched. Her spy on Inna Skythiarach[12] had lost trace of Arachtan about a month ago. He and his two brothers were missing, but no one had seen them leaving. Shya was keeping a tight watch all over the Rheann and Reaghil Ovsbhealle Rheanna. She had explicitly given order to seize him as soon as he was sighted. And still, nothing.

'You were always a tricky one, dear cousin Ara,' she reminded herself resentfully, 'I would have given you everything, a kingdom, a dragon, my soul if you had wished for it, but no one was ever good enough for you… now I promise you this: your loyalty to the Skyarachti will be your doom.'

When she reached the enormous wooden doors that led to the Dragon Hall, she stood there for a moment, then took a deep breath, and pushed them open.

She didn't like what she saw…

They were all standing in a circle talking to each other in a whisper: Asttrian, two Drkarach Kechtás, and the hated Thriar in

---

[12] The Island of the Winged, as the isle of Skye was called.

full, apparently even Lady Skenya had been allowed to leave her chambers to attend court.

Something was very wrong!

Moving forward, she noticed a red bundle at their feet. Someone was lying motionless on the stony floor of the Dragon Hall. For the fraction of a second, her heart leapt, she thought it was Arachtan.

Coming closer, Shya recognised a female shape, and felt instantly relieved. But it did not last long. Once she was close enough, she could see, to her shock, that the most beautiful woman she had ever seen was now lying literally in front of her feet and was dressed in a very strange fashion. Most outrageous of all, she was wearing the royal colour red!

"But..." she managed to produce, "she looks like the legendary Altásva[13] of the old legends, the fierce Horse Ladies or Witch Queens who founded the ancient Arach Kingdom of Seannarach. What was it they said of them?" she continued absentmindedly, "ahh, now I remember: 'Their hair, golden streams of a stormy sunset over the ignited plain; their bodies, sculptured out of the palest of stones; their red lips, the ripe fruit of the Caydúllien

---

[13] Altásva was the name of the Horse Ladies or Witch Queens of the ancient Seannarachti, founders of the Arach Family. There were many old legends telling the stories of these extraordinarily beautiful women.

Ore...'[14] What is this creature doing here?" she ended, without looking up, while the rest of them chose to ignore her and continued their argument.

Shya's both exotic and extravagant beauty had never been challenged before within these walls. Of all the Royal Skyarach women, she had always been described as the most enchanting beauty of the kingdom. Her mother, Queen Umbriel, had also possessed great beauty, which time and life-long sadness had now erased. It had been mainly due to King Urarathan's lack of affection that bitterness had overcome the queen, some even believed, it had been the king's love for another that had eventually weakened her mind. Whatever the true reason behind it, Queen Umbriel had turned into a bitter old woman within a year of the Old King's death.

Her daughter Shya had inherited her charms, and was not only handsome, but also most extravagant. She loved to live a luxurious life, and would have her jewels and dresses brought from every corner of the world, even beyond the Skyarachti Kingdom, and some say, even beyond the ancient Arachti Realm.

For Shya, then, finding out that this stranger's beauty could indeed surpass hers, both annoyed and infuriated her even more than this unexpected gathering at the court hall...

---

[14] Golden Tree, it was the name given to the ancient apple trees that had been brought by the Arach from the Seannarachti kingdom itself, and that always marked special places, like central squares.

Ice daggers were drilling through her head now.

"What is this?! Explain yourselves!" she addressed the two Drkarach Kechtás first, interrupting their discussion. "What is this person doing in our hall?"

Now she turned to her brother, who overtly avoided her gaze and sighed deeply.

Thuarnach was the only one who answered. "Good morning niece, woken up on the wrong side of the bed? Thankfully, nothing really serious is affecting "our hall" today. These two most vigilant Dragon Knights found this poor lady astray, close to the Tyarsach Drkent.[15] I'm sure no harm was intended. Look at her, she doesn't seem like a threat to me. She is just a foreigner who doesn't speak our language, or so the guards told us. That is why, I've brought my dear friend Lughan here, who is a master in foreign tongues."

Thuarnach smiled kindly to his niece, and was about to turn to King Asttrian, when Shya cut him rudely. "Then what are we all waiting for?"

Turning to the servants that were standing at both sides of the throne, she signalled them to approach and ordered them to pour

---

[15] The Portal of the Dragon, entrance to a dragon's lair.

the content of their jars onto the unconscious girl that was still placidly lying on the floor.

The King wasn't giving the order, though, so the poor servants hesitated a second too long.

Shya, seemingly vexed, grabbed one of the jars from the closest servant and readily poured its contents onto the motionless girl, as if she could erase the scene at her feet with one stroke.

Icy water trickled its way down through her…

Annea opened her eyes confused and shivering. "What on earth!" she cried instinctively.

Wherever she was, this was certainly not a warm welcome.

She was forced to kneel and look to the ground. Her vision still blurred by the dripping water, she couldn't see clearly where she was. There were quite a few people in the room. She could discern their shapes like the shadows of looming trees in a forest of stone.

Was it daytime? Where was she? Was she having nightmares again? Where were Pete and Henry? She was trying to think hard, what was the last thing she could remember…

All of a sudden, someone pulled her up. She could barely stand, and she could not see clearly yet, but she knew to keep calm.

The next moment, a woman's voice was yelling at her angrily in a strange language… Was it the same language those two men had used before? Annea shook her head a little to dissipate the fog in her mind. She could hear several voices arguing now.

'But, wait a minute,' she thought, 'that language… that can't be German! But then, what is all this? Are my nightmares taking over my mind? It all feels so real, I truly need a doctor!'

Trapped in her tribulations she missed out on most of what was going on around her, until suddenly, she caught a familiar male voice over the rest. There was a pleading urgency in it.

'Wait a moment, I know that voice… but… it can't be…' she was assembling her memories like long scattered and splintered mosaic pieces of an intricate puzzle work.

Very slowly, she cleared the remaining moisture from her face with her hands. Now she would see better, but would she dare open her eyes?

She did. She opened her eyes and, mouth wide agape, she took in her surroundings in complete shock.

She was standing in the centre of a very spacious room. It resembled something like a royal court or meeting hall.

'If this is not a dream, then this place must be part of some very costly film set,' she rapidly deduced.

Surrounding the centre of the room, two lines of interspersed, delicately ornated golden tree-shaped pillars rose to support an extraordinary dome dominated by golden branches of blooming apple trees. Light seemed to be entering from every corner of the room. She noticed very high stained-glass walls with elaborate designs on each side, which beautifully lightened and warmed this interior, built mostly out of white stone. There were incredibly luxurious fabrics and materials on display, and the people... Their costumes and jewellery were mind blowing, everything looked so real–

Then, she saw him...

Lughan had been forced to witness the scene from the threshold to the hall, not intervening in the discussion until now, while holding his breath with effort, from the moment he had seen her.

She had been so young the last time... His head was exploding... Would she ever understand? Would she be able to forgive him?

He had attempted to enter, but the guards on both sides of the doorways had readily stopped him, and Thuarnach had given him a warning glance.

'I have to get her out of here, Thuarnach doesn't understand what it is like. Annea doesn't belong in this place!' he argued silently to himself through gritted teeth, both hands balled into fists behind his back.

"You, foreigner, what was your name again?"

King Asttrian addressed Lughan for the first time.

"Lughan, muin Reaghil Drkent Teyn, at your service," answered Lughan politely looking at the floor.

"Come closer now," said the king, waving him to move forward.

"Let him talk! He has been invited by my good uncle Thuarnach, we don't want him standing outside our hall. Come on, what kind of manners will he think we care for at Drkent Har?" he told his guards, while staring fixedly at Lughan.

"Come, come, tell us what you came to say, I'm sure it is most interesting..."

King Asttrian was getting bored by the arguments at court, even more so since his sister had joined them. Never a true statesman, he wanted to end the matter now. What a waste of words and time, when he had actually already made up his mind...

At Drkent Har, all matters ended the way it pleased him, nowadays, and he intended to make sure this time Shya couldn't lay hands on this girl. This one was going to be his toy, and his alone.

Lughan stepped into Asttrian's court, knowing well the precarious situation he was in. Nevertheless, he strode decidedly towards the little crowd at the centre of the court, always keeping his eyes to the ground.

He knew Annea, like all the others, had her eyes fixed on him, but he did not dare look at her.

"Your Highness," he started cautiously, "I would be most pleased to assist you on this matter. Please, allow me to serve you well," he said while kneeling before the king.

Asttrian enjoyed being honoured.

"Go on, try to speak to this lost maiden, so we might find out what she intended to do at the Tyarsach Drkent, I'm most curious."

And smirking to his sister, he walked to his throne and made himself comfortable. This was going to be most interesting...

Lughan slowly looked up. For the first time now, he locked eyes with Annea.

There it was, a minuscule tear slowly describing a path down Annea's cheek... But her eyes, they were smiling at him.

She had grown so much since the last time, and she possessed a devastating beauty. Those eyes, how often had they begged him to stay... It hurt him to remember, and now, she was in such great danger!

He turned to her now, and pleadingly said, "please, trust me. We cannot talk much right now, we need to get you out of here," and still holding her gaze he added, "now, tell me your name, your age and where you come from. Do it as if you were introducing yourself to a stranger. They won't understand what we're saying, but they'll gather we can communicate."

"Dad?"

Now a river of tears cascaded down her cheeks and was making it difficult to speak.

"Is it you?"

He had to remain detached or else they would realise something was wrong, "your name, please," he said fixing her intently.

She did as she was asked, without blinking or looking away, "Annea Menard, 22 years old, student of Anthropology at the University of Mainz, resident in Oberursel, Germany. What is this all about, Dad? For years now, Granny and I have been looking everywhere for you..." Now her eyes turned the colour of steel, and she wasn't smiling any more.

"I can explain," he whispered, and then turned to the king and their audience, using the difficult Arach language as best as he could.

"The girl's name is Annea, she has seen 22 cycles of the sun, my lord, and she comes from a land far away, beyond the Mhuirmer.[16] She speaks my language." He had to stick to the truth as much as he could, or else they would realise he was lying.

"Ask her which land is that, and what did she intend to do at the Krayn na Drkarach," commanded Asttrian anxiously.

---

[16] Great Ocean

Lughan locked eyes with Annea, "Annea, listen to me, you are not where you think you are, these people are extremely dangerous. Please, follow my lead." Lughan made sure she was paying attention to every word he said, "do you understand me, Little Pandora?"

She nodded somewhat in trance, 'how long since he had last called her that?'

"I will have to invent a story about you, just as I did for me," continued Lughan, "we have some friends here, they will help us get you out of this place, trust me, please. Now, I need you to talk to me as if I were interrogating you, and you were answering me. Is it a deal, Little Pandora?"

He had given her that name long ago, as a small child crawling her way through the world, inspecting anything she would come across. Possessed by an endless curiosity, always wanting to know it all, Annea had put herself at risk many times before, and he had been at her side helping her out of trouble, just like today. Dr Menard had even read the Greek myth to her about Pandora several times, in a hopeless attempt to temper her curiosity. Yes, her father knew her well, and even though the situation was most awkward right now, she felt indescribably relieved to have found him, after all.

"Okay, Dad. I guess we do have to get us out of this crazy place asap, but I do have so many questions… I truly don't know where to start, I mean, it's been so long…"

"We'll have time for that later, don't you worry."

Annea was feeling dizzy and quite confused about the situation. She was overwhelmed with happiness for having finally found Dr Menard, but, on the other hand, as hard as she tried, she could not make out what these people and this place were. Why was her father all of a sudden standing in front of her? Why was he dressed in that same queer fashion as the others? And, above all, what had kept him from reaching out all this long? It just did not make sense at all!

Chapter Eight: A Journey Through The Rheann

2nd day of Aarglas, 300 YD,
Rheann valley, close to Reaghil Ovsbhealle Rheanna[17]

Contemplating the vastness of the now frozen Rheann valley, Arachtan stood tall and threatening, his brow furrowed.

'We have lost so much time... we cannot afford to lose more, we'll have to risk it!' he thought.

The icy winter temperatures, frozen grounds, and strong blizzards had forced them to lose precious time, but moving like night shadows, all three Anairachti princes had successfully managed to travel through the densely populated Rheann territory without being sighted, so far.

They had carefully trailed the river valley without touching its streaming waters. Sometimes on horseback, sometimes on rudimentary Sgythi,[18] sometimes on foot, the company had

---

[17] Royal Western City of the Rhine, today's Koblenz, known also as The Green Terrace Dragon.
[18] Sgythi was the name for skis, and represented a traditional means for mobility in the winter. Mostly their ancestors, the Thuatharachti or North Arach, had perfected the technique of moving over ice and snow. There were many different types, depending on the terrain that had to be passed. They all had in common, however, that they could be easily carved out of any wood and formed to their

strenuously covered over three hundred kilometres since Drejkreins.

They had managed to hunt small game and had eaten mushrooms, nuts and the fruit they could find, which was not much right now. In fact, in most forest areas, the only edible fruit left were the little chequers now bletted enough to be edible. Fortunately, they still had some of the provisions they'd brought with them, so they had managed well without exposing themselves.

It had been far from easy, of course, and it had taken them almost a fortnight from Drejkreins to reach Reaghil Ovsbhealle Rheanna. In all check points, small coastal villages and greater cities, there had been positioned a large number of Drkarach Kechtás from the Royal Guard.

These were no common knights. They were most skilled, well-trained soldiers who had been handpicked by the old king himself. Some of them were even descendants from the warriors that had once come with Urarathan from the North, their most important trait being their undisputable loyalty towards the royal family.

Never into politics, most of the Drkarach Kechtás would support the son of their king without hesitating, and no matter the odds.

---

purpose, whether it was sliding down a steep open slope or a dense forest. Most children learned how to make their own Sgythis from a very early age.

Their loyalty was better not put to the test, and Ara was not going to be the first one to do so.

He and his half-brothers were only three men, but they knew the area well enough to go unnoticed. They had chosen to ride smaller, less crowded roads, consciously avoiding all Dragon Roads, even if it took them longer. More often than not, they had camped in the woods, under the cover of ancient forests, where only wild animals would bear witness of their doings. And, of course, they had consistently kept away from the waterways, which were being tightly controlled by the royal knights.

Ara had certainly anticipated that Asttrian would send some Kechtás to secure the area, but this? This was beyond his wildest dreams.

The now white plain, where the Mohir river mouthed into the Rheann, was literally infested by patrolling knights from one end to the other. It seemed excessive even for his cousin to retrieve so many Kechtás from the capital and boundaries, and position them all here... Somehow, Ara couldn't get rid of the strange feeling that the royal knights had been sent to do a special job: hunt him down.

On the positive side, this meant that Reaghil Bheallemer and Drkent Har had been left quite unprotected, so once there, it would be easy to get to the king. It was not like his cousin, though, to risk such a bold move, unless he was certain that their enemies would be coming this way...

So Asttrian was convinced that Ara would never be able to pass the Rheann, now... What other traps had he set for him? Were his Rheann cousins Ealator and Skymnia part of the plan to stop him?

Arachtan knew that now that King Urarathan was dead, the clock was ticking fast for his older cousin Asttrian, and he would stop at nothing until he saw Arachtan destroyed. No matter the reason behind Thuarnach's summon, their enmity went far back to their childhood years, when they spent long hours together, being both instructed by the royal druid himself, at Drkent Har. Asttrian had envied Arachtan's strength and wits, but above all, his close relationship to his own father. King Urarathan had always been distant and cold to his own offspring, but not so to Queen Scaìthara's bastard son...

Arachtan had not been at the Rheann for quite a while, but Reaghil Ovsbhealle just never disappointed him. With its breath-taking views both over the Rheann and the Mohir valleys, it continued to be the most charming and cheerful city in the whole Skyarach Kingdom, if not of all kingdoms of the time. The Green Terrace of the Dragon, as it was known for its usually bountiful green valleys and hills rich in vineyards and fruit trees, showed little signs of the increasing unrest rooted in the hearts of its people. Just the paleness and stillness of the snow reminded Ara that he should not expect a warm welcome here this time.

On the left bank, the urban settlement usually stretched like a masterly woven tapestry of bright greens interspersed with the myriad of reds, oranges and ochres of its buildings. Today, Ara contemplated a more monochrome landscape in shades of white and grey, but his heart, nevertheless, instinctively jumped at the sight if the city's most dominant feature, a true masterpiece of architectural engineering: the port.

The largest city on the banks of the Rheann possessed a magnificent port with a large docking area bursting with life even in the winter. Serving both the Rheann and its smaller tributary, the Mohir, right under the vigilant gaze of the exquisite Green Terrace of the Dragon, on the opposite side of the great river, the port was the true beating heart of Reaghil Ovsbhealle Rheanna. It was surrounded by dozens of shops and several market squares, which were ingeniously connected through busy, winding lanes. The city itself, however, had only one main Dragon road leading from the bustling city centre straight to the port for especially bulky cargo that could not be carried through the narrow alleyways.

Surveying the landscape further, he held his breath.

'There it is,' he thought…

The royal fortress of the Rheann with its beautiful terraces and balconies, perched over the river and the surrounding vineyards, now all in a ghostly disguise, took him straight back to all those unconcerned childhood summers spent here with his cousins.

Arachtan loved every stone of this castle, every grass on those hills, and of course, the Rheann wine.

'Once we cross the river, we are in! No one knows those maze-like corridors better than we do,' he mused.

And in fact, the fortress's hidden passage ways had been long out of use, and the children had been allowed to play and explore them at their pleasure. Their prime advocate for these adventures had been Thuarnach himself, arguing that no one really knew if it wouldn't become handy one day to know "alternative" ways around the castle.
And he had been proven right, after all. Now, thanks to those unforgettable expeditions, the secret entrances, hidden doors, and dark corners of that beautiful building were tattooed by fire in his and his brothers' minds.

'We can't wait here any longer, we have to make for the crossing tonight or tomorrow, more knights are being sent every day.'

Arachtan had been observing the river valley and the city from the top of a nearby hill, for some days now. He had a fairly good idea of how the Kechtás were strategically positioned and knew every change of guards. In the cover of night, he had also visited several of the city inns, which were open till very late. If one wanted fresh news, these were the right places to look for it. And indeed, he had been lucky. He had overheard local people complaining about the Kechtási knights' merciless behaviour and brutal methods, which had taken Ara by surprise. This was not the way he recalled his uncle's royal knights to be… As it was, people here seemed to be running out of patience and understanding for the new king's policies and men.

Since the surrounding plain was usually flooded, Ara had early on been speculating that the somewhat chaotic meander of the rivers close to their confluence would be their gateway to reach the fortress on the other side. It had seemed like a good plan, then. They would have been able to mingle among the illegal, but tolerated fisher boats that entered the Rheann through the Mohir without registering or paying any fees. These vessels were smaller but sturdier than the licensed ones. They would have surely helped them carry the horses to the other shore for some Anairarachti gold.

Unfortunately for them, this winter had been a particularly frosty one, with both valleys and mountains, all white coated. So, at the moment, no fishers were coming out of the Mohir, and no transportation was readily available for them.

The crossing was tightly watched over by the guards posted on both banks of the Rheann, whereas the port area was buzzing with Kechtási knights.

No, this time the overseers held a tight grip on whatever goods or people went over the river. They would have to find another solution, a creative one if they didn't want to get caught in Asttrian's web.

Arachtan was chewing on one particular idea, 'the way they are strangling traffic, no wonder trade is suffering, and many tradesmen here are already getting more and more impatient at Asttrian's erratic disposal… I'm sure we can use this to our advantage. I shall arrange things tonight.'

The strategic position of the city, at the junction of the Mohir and the Rheann, had been
the main factor why Reaghil Ovsbhealle Rheanna had successfully flourished in the first place, and why it was still a very wealthy and powerful city in the kingdom.

Trade was key to the city's development and prosperity, and trade was evidently suffering from the new regulations the king had put into place to keep the Rheann under his foot. As a consequence, on the streets, in the city markets and inns, everywhere, words of unrest were silently but rapidly spreading.

The Rheannar, as the citizens of the great Rheann city were called, were not fond of this new tyrant king, who had always shown little interest for them, and who had now sent in his Drkarach Kechtás to massacre the true ruler over this city: trade.

It came as no surprise, that people were increasingly upset. And this, of course, was something Ara and his brothers could certainly harness to their advantage.

'But where are Skymnia and Ealator? We have to find them before something terrible happens,' Ara thought, 'and where is their mother?'

Being a member of the Thriar, Asttrian would need to keep Lady Skenya close by, at least for some time… But before they continued their journey to the capital, they would have to make sure their cousins were not being kept prisoners within the Green Terrace of the Dragon.

'Cousin Asttrian,' he sighed tiredly, 'I know your weak heart, but how could you betray the memory of your father like this? I should have never left, I should have stopped you long ago…'

Arachtan hurried back down the rocky, icy slope that took him straight to their camp site. He still needed to tell Thuaìden and Skeorden what news he had brought from the city, so they could decide together on the last details.

"Hyo, Ara, you came just in time to cook us breakfast," Skeorden teased him, "are you bringing those chequer berries again, or have you found a juicy rabbit for your younger siblings?"

Showing his empty hands, he answered, "No, Skeor, no rabbit today, berries and roasted beechnuts will do. They're redoubling the Kechtás every day."

"How many do they still have?"

"Ey, well, Asttrian seems to be recruiting new men."

"You were in the city, last night, any other news?" intervened Thuaìden, "you know I have my girl, there, Liena. She is always willing to see me. I could visit her and ask–"

"No, brother, that is exactly what they'll be expecting. Liena is being watched, and the inn is being watched, too. This time, we'll look for help somewhere else," gave back Arachtan somewhat irritated.

He couldn't hide he was upset by this proposal, he knew Thuaìden was clever and brave, but sometimes he could be a danger even to himself. What was he thinking? This was no training journey with Thuarnach, it was the real thing! There was so much at risk, and Thuaìden was only thinking about his mistress!

"I see…"

On his part, Thuaìden didn't like to be treated as a child, either. This had turned out to be a nightmare of a journey, and his only desire was to finally see it end.

"Thuaìden, brother, we are all weary, but we cannot act carelessly, we cannot afford any mistakes. Truly, Thuaì, this time, I have a very bad feeling about all of it…" Ara started kindling a small fire together with Skeorden and added, "but yes, I have news, and I think they are useful."

He went on to explain then to his brothers what he had seen and heard, and what he thought might be their only way out.

"I reckon fresh diary and fish are brought over from the green markets in the city to the castle almost daily, as well as precious southern Rheannvid from the south valley. Every day, Ealator's

Green Lady[19] sails across the Rheann escorted by the Drkarach Kechtás. We just need to convince the traders to let us take their places. Most of these Kechtás are new, they haven't seen us at Drkent Har, so they cannot recognise us straight away. And once we're crossing, we can easily overwhelm them. It is the right plan, they won't be expecting us in their midst."

"What about our horses? We'll be needing them again at some point, and our provisions, too. It is still a long way to reach the Golden City, brother," added Thuaìden with scepticism.

"If what I've heard is correct," started Ara, "we won't be having any trouble to convince the traders and fishers to take our side, Thuaì. They're suffering, their families are suffering, they hate our cousin's tyrannic rule, and I'm certain they will agree to help us with the transportation of both horses and provisions. I will go tonight to see Rhyan, my contact in the guild, and try to settle everything to set off tomorrow. If they agree, we would first need to hand everything over at dawn, some 10 miles north of the Mohir's Neyst.[20] Meeting point would be the Nwyr Krayns,[21] where they all, smugglers and official crown suppliers alike, meet

---

[19] Ealator's royal sailing boat, which was being used to bring supplies to the castle.
[20] Mohirs Neyst is the name given to a particular twist of the river Mohir. Legend had it that this river was actually the enchanted serpent Mohir that, being exhausted after setting up its beautiful nest, went to sleep forever. And so this area became known as the nest of Mohir. Today, the river is known as the Mosel.
[21] The Nwyr Krayns were hidden caves that locals used for smuggling on the coasts of the Mohir river. Mostly known only to local traders, no official control posts were set in the area, and their location was kept a secret for generations. The entrance to the caves was expertly covered by dense bushes and trees.

regularly to discuss their businesses. What do you think, brothers, shall we?"

Thuaìden was not yet fully convinced.

"Ara, what if this all was a trap to get you out of Daing Mhuir in the first place, and then take revenge on you. Now that King Urarathan is gone, who is going to stop Asttrian, and Shya?"

It was true, Asttrian was not alone at Drkent Har, and Ara knew never to underestimate his ambitious cousin Shya. If he wasn't sure, exactly which role she had played in all this chaos, he was certain about two things.

Above all, Shya wanted revenge for him turning her down not one, but several times. The last couple of times, it had been so obvious, that her father, the King, had sent her away for a season in the North with her grandmother, when Ara had come for training at Drkent Har.

She was like that, everyone knew. Whenever she wanted something, she would go to all extremes to get it. And if she couldn't, she would get out of control with rage, and destroyed whatever was at her reach. That was irrevocably her nature. But most important, she possessed the wits her bother lacked. She could be very irrational and emotional, but a clever and ruthless enemy. If there was a master mind behind this plot against him, it was undoubtedly hers.

"I know, Thuaì, this has been in my mind, too…" said Arachtan, "I agree, if that coded letter Thuarnach sent, reached me under the circumstances, it was meant by all to do so, in which case Ealator and Skymnia do make for a good bait. Asttrian and Shya foster no love for them, our Rheann cousins are but an obstacle on their way to seize absolute power, so they have sent them back to their home, back to Reaghil Ovsbhealle Rheanna. It could have played to our advantage if the Kechtás weren't here, the fortress has many entrances and tunnels. But again, this would also explain why we have encountered such a tight control over all ports: someone is expecting us and assuming we know our younger cousins are here…"

Skeorden had been silent and listening all the while, but now he had too many questions in his mind.

"Ara," he said, "I don't understand, why would they have them brought here if they suspected security would be much easier to breach? What do you propose we do once we reach the fortress?"

"I think our Rheann cousins were intended as a bait, but they never expected us to get this close to the fortress. Now, we will need you most, Skeor," Ara continued, "some of the knights here are so young, they don't even have the honour of being acquainted with you, my younger brother. So, you will be the one to knock on the door for us. The sooner we act the better."

"Knock on the door?"

"Ey, Skeor, we'll knock on their front door!" said Ara, "Asttrian and Shya both are aware we know the castle like the palm of our hand. But so do they, don't they?"

"True. They have spent as many summers here as we have…"

"Exactly. They will see to defend every single entrance to a hidden passage, there will be no escaping there. But, you see, their arrogance is blurring their actions."

"What do you mean?" put in Thuaìden.

"They won't have enough men to guard the enormous main portal to the Green Terrace because they simply won't anticipate us entering and leaving through the main entrance, as their guests. We will be carrying with us the trading documents with the royal seal of our helpers, and you, Skeor, will be leading the party. They won't think of checking the Drkariaen[22] on the shoulders of some trades men."

---

[22] Drkariaen were minuscle golden dragons painted onto the skin that identified the royal Arach. To make these markings visible, a dragon flame needed to be used to illuminate the patch of skin bearing them.

"I'm in, Ara," said Skeorden intently.

"And me,' Thuaìden moved closer to his brothers and laid a hand on both their shoulders, "until the end."

"Until the end," Arachtan and Skeorden echoed at the same time.

After whatever awaited them in the castle of Reaghil Rheanna, Arachtan and his brothers would need to continue their journey steadily northeast. This was a painful and even longer route than the one the Rheann offered, but it was the only way for them to avoid the great river's dangerous sentinels.

This time, they would have to stay on the right bank of the river, for close to the Ovstbheallean fortress, another river, the Lahir, entered the Rheann. The Lahir was a small disused navigable waterway that would take them to a journey north of Reaghil Bheallemer. For the company, this meant that they were going to need their horses again to make the descent, valley after valley after valley, from the very heart of the Thaunaan Mountains.[23]

This area was characterized by quite a few unimportant villages scattered alongside the river, with a merely decent trading connection to the capital. On the other hand, the druids had built

---

[23] Thaunaan was the name given to the mountain chain that is today the Taunus.

a spiritual trail that mirrored the constellations above, right through the Thaunaan range, placing several meaningful temples across the landscape. The First of these temples was an important druid training centre at the junction of the Lahir and the Vwyl rivers, which Ara knew well. He was sure he could find out more about the situation at Reaghil Bheallemer, once they reached the temple. The druids were his best hope, now. Besides, no one would be expecting them to come this way. It was, after all, a journey full of dangers, and it was certainly going to take much longer.

Chapter Nine: Annea's Story By Lughan

The lands beyond the Mhuirmer, or Great Ocean, were thankfully so far away from any Arach Kingdom, old and new, that almost no records existed with any detailed description about their people, culture or geography.

Over the millennia, the Dreà Arachti had expanded their civilization to bring wisdom and knowledge, the Wbent Teyn Drkent, as they called it, to the world. It had been this felt duty that had been at the heart of their culture, and had motivated their expansion policies, not the thirst to dominate the peoples they encountered.

They had founded their great cities, integrating amiably all native peoples and becoming their educated ruling class. They had named their realm the Arach Confederation of Knowledge,[24] and while they had secured a tightly knitted communication network over time, they had only sent but a few explorers to the distant corners of the Earth – most of them never returning.

And so, it was, that there were few accounts of what lay beyond the Great Ocean, and Lughan knew how to play this to his advantage.

---

[24] Arachti Wbent Teyn Kydrachs

He told the King and the Thriar that Annea originally came from the lands beyond the Mhuirmer, and that, during a terrible storm, her ship had been hit by lighting and had foundered, mentioning she had barely survived because she could swim, while the crew had drowned. Grabbing a floating log, she had been brought ashore by the currents off the coast of the territories of Grhain.[25]

Not surprisingly, they wanted to know more. They inquired why she had been sailing towards Yrwpa[26] in the first place, and how Annea had managed to reach their city and pass unnoticed by all. This part of the story, then, became much trickier, so Lughan turned to the very same plot Thuarnach had used for him several years before.

She had asked people for help, fishermen, road merchants, even nobles travelling the Dragon Road. No one could understand her tongue, of course, but they all guessed she was lost and needed help. And so, one thing after the other, she ended in Reaghil Bheallemer na Caydúllien Ore, the Golden City of the Skyarachti. She had never intended to go anywhere near the dragon, she simply was not aware of its existence, and did not know the rules or laws of the kingdom, either. She had wandered off the city market to rest from the hustle, and had unintentionally stridden towards the fortress grounds. That is when the guards had found

---

[25] Coastal area of today's France
[26] Ancient name for Europe in the Arach language

her. As to why she was sailing with a merchant boat, Lughan invented a supposed arranged marriage in a distant land.

And so, slowly and consistently, a plausible story was masterly woven by the hands of the man, who, many years before, had given Annea the family life they had both now left far behind. And just as it had happened with Lughan, the story luckily convinced the Thriar and the King. Only Shya, as expected, remained suspicious. But again, such was her nature.

It was well past midday, when the Court finally reached a decision on Annea's future. She was to remain in Reaghil Bheallemer as a guest to Thuarnach for the teaching of their language and customs. King Asttrian made sure, however, that she was given the status of special guest visitor to the court during this time, so as to see her more often. Once the training time was completed, she would transfer to the fortress to serve as handmaiden to Queen Umbriel, at Drkent Har.

And although, in many ways, this could have sounded like a favourable outcome, only one person was sincerely content with it: King Asttrian. Everyone else at his court had good reasons to doubt the benefits of such accommodation. But for now, it was all Lughan could do for his Little Pandora.

<u>Chapter Ten:</u> **Daing Mhuir**

2nd day of Aarglas, 300 YD,
fortress of Daing Mhuir on Inna Skythiarach

"Answer me, girl! Lord Rœhen tells me you have been exchanging jays with Drkent Har, is this true? What business do you have with my cousin's son at Reaghil Bheallemer?" asked Queen Scaìthara exasperated.

This slave girl was head strong, she had to give her that. After several nights in the dungeons of the fortress, she was still looking defiant and proud.

"I told his Druid Highness, Lord Rœhen, that I have been made responsible for some precious goods that reach this castle. And so, it happened, I was expecting a silk delivery for the palace seamstresses that should have arrived about a month ago. Such a delay is very uncommon. I was worried those precious fabrics could go lost. This is why I sent the jays, muine Drkarach Qvynne," [27] Ryssa's calm but pleading voice bounced against the intricate, ornated walls of the Anairarachti court hall.

---

[27] My Dragon Queen, title taken by Scaìthara of Daing Mhuir in her kingdom. When visiting the Skyarach Kingdom she was not allowed to use it, for this term was used to address the Skyarach Queen, Urarathan's wife Umbriel. Scaìthara would be then addresse as "Drkent Qvynne na Daing Mhuir", in more general terms.

Her good fortune was saving her once again...

Ryssa had perfected her persuasive arts since very young. When she was eight, her mother, father and three siblings had caught a severe lung infection, which left Rhyssa alone and unprotected.

For a short time, she had managed to live from what she could find on the streets of Cællen, the biggest port on south Armourean.[28] But very soon, she had been taken by slavers, and carried away in endless journeys. She had received no formal education, and wasn't a very pretty girl, but Rhyssa had learnt how to survive under most adverse circumstances.

In her case, the law was very clear, and she knew it: if there was no proof that she had misused the birds for herself or sent messages of treason against the realm, she could not be held prisoner. And, fortunately for her, the seamstresses had supported her story.

"Very well, Ryssa, you are allowed to return to your houses and to your services. However, next time you consider there is a need to use our royal jays, you will take advise from Lord Rœhen."

Scaìthara was not eager to pass this sentence, she did not like the slave girl, notwithstanding the rumours about her son...

---

[28] Name used for the southern most territories of today's Spain and France.

"Ey, muine Drkarach Qvynne, you are most just and fair," curtsied the girl, honey-tongued.

The Queen nodded and signalled her to leave, but before the girl could leave the court room, Scaìthara descended from her throne and bridged the space between them in the blink of an eye, as if she had grown wings. She was tall and looming over the slave girl, now.

"Ryssa," she whispered threateningly close to her face, "listen to me, and listen carefully: you are oath-bound now, these birds are extremely valuable to us, and none should be sent without mine or the druid's consent, do I make myself clear?"

The girl looked intimidated. She had never stood so close to the queen before. Of an otherworldly and powerful beauty, Scaìthara, the warrior queen, certainly was a presence to fear.

"Ey, I understand, muine Drkarach Qvynne. It won't happen again," and with a cautious bow, she turned and left the court without looking back once.

Scaìthara followed her with her gaze until she was but a tiny speck at the end of the main royal corridor.

If rumours had it right, and she hoped not, Ryssa had managed to awaken Ara's interest in women...

As queen of the Anairarachti, Scaìthara had learnt to pay no heed to court gossip, she wanted to hear it all from her son's lips. But where was Ara? And where were his younger brothers, Thuaìden und Skeorden?

She had been surprised by their sudden disappearance, and was increasingly irritated by the lack of information. She was trying to be patient and controlled her temper, but she was, after all, a true Arach warrior. She did not know how long she would remain diplomatic with Umbriel's mischievous twins. Besides, Urarathan's death had changed things radically...

She knew Ara was behind this, though. He had left her his Anairarachti warrior ring on her pillow, almost a month ago. The message, although unspoken, was as clear as water to her: he was heading East into the Skyarachti Kingdom.

Whenever her first born son visited her cousins, she made him leave behind his warrior ring. It was like a secret ceremony between them.

As her son, Ara was entitled to one of the three Anairarachti warrior rings. These had been passed from generation to generation within her family, and the queen was the only person responsible for choosing her champions from among her children.

As a Skyarach druid apprentice, however, he was also expected to renounce his title as Anairarachti warrior and, of course, the ring.

But because he had been so young when he had made up his mind to become a druid, his mother and his uncle, the king of the Skyarach, had decided to tolerate both his origins and educational paths, as long as they wouldn't interfere with each other.

Following this arrangement, Ara possessed his own Skyarachti druid[29] ring with his name seal, too. This he was expected to wear always at Drkent Har, although, interestingly enough, King Urarathan himself had not been very keen on the future the Skyarachti ring forbode.

He had always hoped Ara would enter the order of the Drkarach Kechtás, when reaching the appropriate age. And so, Queen Scaìthara, in the end, had always been able to convince her cousin to let Ara write his own destiny, and keep his two rings for longer than it had been prudent.

---

[29] The rings worn by the druids were known as the Drkent Dryd Nuar, and were standard through out all Arach kingdoms, where druids could travel and educate, exchange information and represent their respective kings freely.

"Is this all about the shift in power at the royal capital? What has my brainless nephew Asttrian done for you to leave like this, Ara?" she spoke to the empty blue ceiling above her.

She had heard about the dissolution of the Thriar, it had been officially communicated through royal sealed mail. She had awaited more news from Thuarnach right after, as he always did in such delicate circumstances, but none of his jays had reached her fortress on the isle, no more messages from her druid cousin.

Since Urarathan's death, her druid cousin had been very cautious to avoid any mention of the political situation in Reaghil Bheallemer, and due to his silence, she had been forced to find other ways. She had attempted to make contact with her cousin Skenya, but neither at the capital, nor in Reaghil Ovsbhealle Rheanna had she received any answers. The only intelligence she still received was from Tschiaran through Drejkreins, and it was always very vague.

As a seasoned warrior queen, Scaìthara understood very well what this all meant: a breach of power. It had happened many times before in similar circumstances, and it had always ended with the loss of a dragon and the death of many innocent people.

At least, she knew the wise and ancient Drkarach would never accept Asttrian as king. But the days of the Dragon were numbered, and it would only come out again to intervene if a true

Arach stood up to reclaim power. So, although she wanted to keep good faith with her late cousin's children, she was not willing to sacrifice her own in the process.

Asttrian and Shya, even united, were certainly not as clever as her sons. Yet, let loose with so much power and without any instrument to control them, her niece and nephew represented a genuine threat to the stability of all Arach kingdoms put together.

Had Ara consulted with her, however, she would have done all she could to stop him from going. The situation, as it was, was extremely delicate and dangerous, especially for him. Both her husband Drearyan[30] and herself had considered that the best strategy was to wait, while silently mobilizing their fleet, troops and agents, but without letting any of their children in on the secret. Maybe this had been a mistake, after all…

On the other side of the fortress, meanwhile, Ryssa was in the kitchens organising some wine and delicacies for those friends who had supported her during confinement.

One of her most loyal supporters, as always, had been the cook. A middle-aged, round-shaped women with a warm breast for the

---

[30] The wise king consort, as Scaìthara's husband was known.

poor and helpless, Næore,[31] had practically adopted Ryssa as her own daughter, and unknowingly had helped her to win Ara's favour.

The slave girl, on her part, knew how to play her, and always obtained what she wanted from her.

Today, she had expected to get some special treats that would normally be reserved for the royal family, but the cook was proving stubborn. The castle was nearly empty, and the queen had given specific orders that no extra meal be prepared for her. So, the celebration was not going as Ryssa had planned.

"Næore, please, take out some of that delicious cold meat from the pantry, no one will notice. It's just this once," pleaded Ryssa.

Like most of the times when she started begging like that, the poor cook started getting all anxious and sweaty, and had to take a seat.

"My dear, I'm so very happy for you. You have proven your innocence," she said short-breathed, "I knew the good queen would never do you wrong. You have to admit you were a little reckless this time, sending those jays out like that…" she added rolling her eyes at the girl, "but all is well that ends well, isn't it, my dear?"

---

[31] Nick name given to the cook, meaning "the golden nanny".

She then stood up and hobbled all the way to the pantry, while drying her sweat off her forehead with a smelly kitchen towel.

"Here," said Næore, bringing out something from inside the pantry that was supposed to get Ryssa's spirits up again. "I've prepared a special meat pie for you, I heard the seamstresses and that stable boy Gœllen, the one that stares at you too much, are joining us? Well, I'm afraid there will be no wine today, I do have some fresh raspberry juice,[32] though."

"But Næore, this is not fair," complained Ryssa.

"You don't want any more trouble, do you?" reminded her the cook, "I say, no… Maybe we can have a second celebration when Ara returns from wherever he's gone this time…"

And approaching the girl she added compassionately, "when he hears what has happened to you, dear, he'll sure see to it. Now, go, go, girl, bring the others!"

The mention of her missing "husband" annoyed Ryssa even more. After all, she had to be treated as his wife, that was the law of the Anairarachti kingdom. But Ara, of course, had not made it official, yet, he had said he was waiting for the right moment…

---

[32] The "rasperry juice" was in truth no juice, at all; it was an alcoholic drink, instead. It went through a special process of fermentation and a little red wine and spices were added to it so as to make it taste better.

This whole waiting was most unnerving for her, however. Now, she would have to swallow that ordinary pie down with juice, as an ordinary guest maiden, which she definitely wasn't... Or, at least, so she thought.

True, her husband had never shown any signs of loving her, but his kindness had sealed his fate, and now, he was bound to her by law, and no one was going to change that. And although she found him the most handsome and attractive man of all, she had no deep love for him, either.

In reality, she had no deep love for anyone else but herself, she was a born survivor. She knew to trust no one and was skilled on how to use people to her benefit, and she surely knew to cut ties before getting too close.

Following this scheme, in many a lonely night, Ryssa would pay a visit to Gœllen the stable boy, who being five years her younger and thankfully mute, never complained.

Ryssa had tasted power, and she wanted more.

Ara's disappearance without any trace represented an unwanted flaw in her plans, and she was determined to fix it, after all, she was risking her own life.

'Where is he? Curse it! It's almost a month...' she thought.

Ara had left Daing Mhuir sometime around the midwinter celebration of Mædhr a' Oighe,[33] when the castle passes from darkness to light in a majestic and exuberant feast. The druids say it is the time of the year when the white fire of the dragon, the Wbent Teyn Drkent, brings back life to the world.

This year, the druid feast came and went, but darkness still hovered in every corner of that fortress. All three princes were missing, and the queen was restless and dangerous.

To counter this, her husband, Drearyan, had engaged the court in an early hunting game, which had started a couple of days ago, and was meant to last for a week. The royal Anairarach, as well as most host nobles, were to travel together through the island and camp overnight. The queen, as expected, participated reluctantly and only some days, riding back and forth with her splendid black mare, Mæres. Most of the times, though, she stayed in the castle with her strong-headed 17-year-old daughter Anuelle, the only child she had left.

---

[33] The first of the four yearly nature festivals celebrating the cycle of life in the mystic Arach tradition.

An ever-inquisitive mind, young Anuelle was very attached to her older brothers, especially to Ara, and was steadfastly determined to find them. On her own and on the sly, she had started a sound investigation of her brothers' whereabouts, and, while she, very much like her mother, instinctively disliked Ryssa, she had come to realise that some lines of inquiry about Ara had ended with the slave girl's name. So, she had decided to follow the slave girl around Daing Mhuir.

It had been thanks to her vigilant eye, then, that Anuelle had discovered how Ryssa was sending out jays to the continent; and it had been Anuelle, too, who had informed Lord Rœhen about this. She had made him promised by the Fire of the White Dragon, that he would never mention her name to her mother, to which the druid, knowing the queen's mind, had promptly agreed.

Anuelle knew her mother well. Queen Scaìthara saw her daughter as a child, and was not going to tolerate her meddling with her older brothers' affairs.

Although herself a warrior queen, she saw none of her strength in her daughter, and had interrupted her warrior training at an early age.

Surely enough, the girl could swing a sword and ride a horse to battle, as it would be expected of any Arach princess. Scaìthara had been forced to admit, however, that her virtues lay somewhere else, and had ordered the Skyalla[34] of Daing Mhuir to introduce Anuelle to the healing arts. At the age of 17, Etayn Anuelle was an excellent healer, always welcome on hunting expeditions, where she really enjoyed helping the wounded.

This time, though, it was different because it was her dear brothers who needed her. She was not intent to sit back and listen to her mother. No, Anuelle was not going to let go! She was determined to find them, and no one was going to stop her.

---

[34] "Skyalla" were the priestesses/ teachers of princesses at the castles. While women were allowed to take up formal druid training, the first years of it were always introduced by the royal skyallas.

Chapter Eleven: A New Life

The Maze

2nd day of Aarglas, 300 YD,
Reaghil Bheallemer na Caydúllien Ore

Life was taking an unrealistic turn for Anneal, her heart, at this very instant, pounding loudly with happiness and excitement: she had finally found her father! But she could not entirely understand what kind of game was being played around them, nor could she make out her father's role in it...

Lughan and Thuarnach made sure to take her out of Drkent Har swiftly. They insisted, they needed no Kechtási escort, arguing Lughan knew the newcomer's language and it was apparent that she presented no threat.

So, having no guards to see them off, the two old friends guided Annea, who was still very much in a state of shock, through what seemed to her as a never-ending maze of staircases and corridors.

The first of the corridors had no windows, but it was warmly illuminated by torch light. Several statues of what looked like real-life, graceful white horses stood on both sides of the doorways leading out of the hall. Along the way, strange golden objects adorned the wall niches. A thin, golden line parted the corridor floor in the middle. One side was made out of the same white quartz stone used for the hall, while the other was made of colourful mosaics displaying beautiful spiral shapes.

They took many turns before reaching a broad, majestic staircase that was filled with daylight from a roof opening. Annea couldn't tell if its ceiling was made of glass, or if it was completely open to the sky, but she could smell the scent of fresh air, and felt a placid breeze soothing her burning cheeks.

They, then, followed the stairs to an enormous, empty, bright hall with beautifully decorated walls and floors.

"Arsant Har, the Hall of the Arts," said Lughan, watching Annea gape in surprise, "it's beautiful, isn't it? Its entire front is made of glass, so the sun bathes every corner of the room with light."

She stopped for a second to take in the place.

"I have never seen something like this place before, this room is just magical. I could stay here all day…" she said.

"No time for that, I'm afraid," said Lughan, urging her to move on.

They soon turned left and took another quite winding corridor that would end in a smaller and less prominent staircase that led them to the kitchens of the castle.

Every now and again, Annea could take a glimpse of the surrounding landscape through narrow, windowlike openings on the outside walls. Some of these were sealed with pale yellowish glass, and some were left completely open.

'Everything looks so strange... the forest outside seems to have redoubled overnight,' she thought, 'I don't get it, this place seems huge, how could I miss it, when I was searching for twigs? And where are Pete and Henry gone? God, I have the feeling, I won't like the answer...'

They wouldn't leave Drkent Har through the main entrance, though. It was far too busy, too many eyes. Thuarnach knew they had to keep a low profile, and hide Annea, as well as they could.

So, once they had reached the royal kitchens, and before anyone could ask, they took another, this time sombre staircase that led them to the bowels of the castle, below the dungeons. This was one of the hidden passage ways Thuarnach had customized for himself, so that he could come in and out of the fortress undisturbed.

When the three were well under the castle walls, the two men stopped, and Lughan turned to his daughter.

"Annea, I know your head must be spinning by now, and you must be full of questions. And I promise, we will have the time to talk, I will tell you everything, all you want to know. But for now, my Little Pandora, please, I need you to trust me."

Annea didn't quite know what to think of this whole thing, but she was so happy to have found her dad, she just wanted to get out of here with him, as soon as possible.

"You know I do, I've never stopped believing in you, Dad," she said, looking deep into his eyes, "but you have managed to exceed all possible expectations I've ever had about our reunion!" and after a few seconds she added, "actually, now that you mention it, there is something else I'm truly concerned about. I was with my German family's children in the forest when I lost consciousness. I looked for them everywhere before those mad men caught me. They're nowhere to be found, Dad!"

"I see... I'm sorry it had to be this way," he said, "I'm afraid you won't find them here, either. We will talk about it, I promise. Now, we have to get you out of this place–"

"And you? Don't we also have to get you out of here?" she interrupted him.

"Annea, you have to understand," he answered, pleadingly, "we've been very lucky today to be able to leave the castle without further damage, believe me! The people you met up at Drkent Har are extremely dangerous and unpredictable, child."

"Dad, please, stop worrying about me as if I was still a girl, I'm fine. I'm not your Little Pandora anymore," she tried to sound convincing, "I'm so glad to have found you, I cannot put it into words... Granny and I never stopped believing in you, you know, even when mother assured us that you would never come back..."

She felt a knot in her throat, but she went on all the same, "Dad, I know something terrible must have happened for you to stay away from us all this time. I know you have a good reason why you couldn't return, and I know I can help now, I'm a grown up. We can talk it all over when we get home."

"Annea, listen to me!" he replied anxiously, already fearing her reaction once she finally understood what was going on, "we won't be going home anytime soon, it isn't possible!"

She looked at him with concern.

"What do you mean?"

"As I said, there is no time to explain right now, please, whatever you see, whatever you hear when we come out of this tunnel, just follow me. We'll get you to a safe place, and we will talk further there. Promise me you will stick to me… You have to promise," he urged her.

This whole situation was getting weirder by the second. She didn't want to quarrel with her father, it was certainly the last thing they needed. But what on earth was he talking about? Oberursel was a safe place, the forest was always full of hikers, surely there was enough help waiting for them out of this unbelievable film set… or had they been brought to another place altogether? She could not remember being in any means of transport… actually, she could not remember much of that day, at all. There was the huge, golden door in the ground that would not open, the snow and frost covering it all, and then nothing…

Her head was now throbbing again with the exertion. There would be time for an explanation, she said to herself. Besides, not everyone on set could be so uncivilized and rude as those would-be knights and that neurotic would-be princess… Sure, they had truly played their part well, she had to give them that.

"Ok, fine, I won't look right or left. I will just follow you," she finally answered.

Ten minutes later and countless steps in the darkness, they emerged from the dimly lit tunnel into the blinding light of a perfect snowy day.

At first, they couldn't see much, the light was so bright. A few seconds passed, and their eyes finally started distinguishing shapes.

Annea couldn't but hold her breath entirely not to scream.

She started mumbling something incoherent as they pulled to get her going, but her feet were firmly anchored, as if ten tons of lead had been bound to them. She was thunderstruck, and they couldn't convince her to take another step forward.

"How?" she managed to mumble.

"Annea, darling, you promised to follow me. Come on now, help me here," Lughan begged her patiently. He could very well imagine what was going on in her head.

"It makes no sense, there is no way they could have built a site of these dimensions overnight! Where are we, Dad?! You could tell me at least that."

"Reaghil Bheallemer na Caydúllien Ore, the Great Royal City of the Golden Apple Tree," replied Lughan, "now, darling, let's move on, please."

From a very young age, she had been this very rational and logical little person, who had never appreciated fairy tales of any kind, dismissing them as 'childish memories of immature civilizations.' She had always questioned their content and moral, and she used to be quite stubborn in her own beliefs, having no love for religion or superstition, and wanting to find out the scientific truth behind every phenomenon. Yes, that was his Little Pandora! He could bet that she was going to fight this new world with all her heart...

Seconds, minutes, hours, she could not tell how long she had been standing there paralyzed.

It had stopped snowing, now, and the sky was clearing, but everything was covered in white. She didn't know if it was the brightness of the icy layer, the sheer size of the mighty buildings, or the noisy buzzle of the crowd: she was absolutely overwhelmed. She knew she wouldn't be able to take another step if she looked back, so, at some point, she nodded her consent to her father, and as they started down a busy road, she focused her attention on the strange hooded figure guiding them.

He was tall, but somehow delicate. Annea could tell he was not young. His long white hair, his grey beard and his gaze, it was like looking into the eyes of an ancient stone. She instinctively felt she could trust those eyes, they looked determined, and at the same time, filled with infinite kindness.

Despite this, there was something unfitting to his character, something quite special but difficult to tell at first sight. After a moment of reflection, it struck her that he moved so swiftly and gracefully that, when hooded, it was impossible to tell he was actually an old man.

'What had father called him?' she tried recalling, 'it was something like Turnak... what a funny name, though, it must be very old and very German!'

Immersed in her own thoughts, she hadn't realised that they were now entering something like a tunnel system under the streets. The passages were again very dark, and only the intersections exhibited torches that merely helped distinguish the underground crossings.

Druid Thuarnach could navigate them blind. But if by chance someone discovered his tunnels, the person would not be able to find the way out again. It was a master piece he was proud of, a tangled maze for the skilled wizard he was.

He tugged inside his long, hooded coat, and a second later he was pulling out some kind of stone that produced an incredibly bright iridescent light. With that, he led Lughan and Annea through his subterranean labyrinth to their final destination: the Tyarsach Drkent or Portal of the Dragon.

The White Dragon

2nd day of Aarglas, 300 YD,
Reaghil Bheallemer na Caydúllien Ore

Thuarnach understood his dilemma, he had to show the girl the full scale of her situation, otherwise, she was going to refuse to believe Lughan's explanations. They had no time to lose, so he was going to risk a very bold move, and a dangerous one, for it. She was not ready, not yet, certainly too young and unexperienced in the Ways of the Dragon. She could be rejected… In other circumstances, he would have himself been against it, but now, Thuarnach was determined to let Annea swim in icy waters or face defeat. They simply could not wait.

At the end of the corridor there was a dim light, and Annea could see what looked like a door. She could see that it was made of some kind of metal, bronze perhaps… It was glimmering like unpolished gold, maybe it even was gold, after all.

When they got closer, she could see spiral carvings all over the surface. Hadn't she already seen them before?

In the middle of the door, a prominent bulge with a perfect circumference around it and a central cavity started glowing as they approached. Thuarnach turned to Lughan with a nod, and placed the stone he had been carrying in the door's central hole.

Lughan seemed very nervous when he turned to speak to her, "Annea, my darling daughter, I wish I could have been there for you all these years…you must know that…"

He looked from Annea to Thuarnach, and then continued, "now, before we enter, you have to understand that this will be something like a trial, and I have all my faith in you. If you succeed, we'll come out of this together and we will have time to go through the questions you have stored in that beautiful, stubborn head of yours."

"Dad, what do you mean?" she asked impatiently, " is this joke of some sort?"

"No, it is not, but it is necessary. It is the only way for you to understand who I am and who you are, now."

And without saying further, the doors to the Tyarsach Drkent were opened.

There was an inviting stillness to the place. It was so bright, nothing like what one could expect so deep under the earth. The air was fresh and sweet, Annea thought she could even smell the old magnolia trees that stood once in her granny's garden...

A strange place it was.

The men made way for her to step inside, and she entered into an enormous chamber made out entirely of thousands of crystals.

'So that's why it is so bright in here,' she mused, while carefully touching the walls of the cavern.

She looked up to the ceiling and to her surprise, very high up, the place ended in a distant vault with an opening to the sky, 'and that's where the fresh air comes from... it's amazing–'

A bloodcurdling roar thundered against the cavernous walls, suddenly interrupting her thoughts. She turned and found the men still standing close to the door behind her, right there where she had left them.

'Great! So now I'm supposed to lead the way!'

She walked further into the cave, and the roaring became even louder. She didn't know how much longer she could restrain the urge to run back to the door and hide behind her father.

Something was telling her, however, that that was exactly what she should not do. Her heart was about to burst out of her chest with fear, but she kept going slowly further into the cave.

She felt a breeze starting up, now.

After a few moments, it got stronger and wilder. Now, up in the air, she could literally see wind gusts swirling madly. She wasn't going to go any further, the wind was gushing so violently, she even saw objects, maybe rocks, being lifted and smashed against the adjacent walls.

'We have to get out of here!' she thought with increasing terror.

But before she could think any further, a pair of very big, extremely green, and extremely frightening eyes were staring right at her with a mischievous expression.

The wind stopped. The roaring ceased.

"I know what you're thinking, I know your heart," said a strangely deep, female voice in her head.

'Perfect! Now, I'm the one going mad,' thought Annea, 'not only do I see things appearing out of thin air, but I'm hearing voices, too!'

"You see nothing, you are blind! You are not ready yet... Why are you here? Dragons are no pets," the voice continued.

"It wasn't my choice," answered Annea confused.

She closed her eyes, and made up her mind, 'what am I doing? This is all madness, I must leave!'

When she turned to leave, a fierce gust of wind gushed through her, making her stumble and fall to the cold stony floor. A gigantic white beast covered by shiny scales appeared in front of her.

"Madness it is to deny me, Daughter of Daughters! I have found you, and I will tell you when it is time to leave."

This whole day was becoming a real nightmare!

Annea tried to stay calm, "I never meant to be disrespectful. It's just, I don't understand what you're talking about. I just came to this country to find my father, and now, everyone seems to be intent on driving me crazy. I'm even talking to a fully-grown dragon, right now!"

She tried to focus at a distant point in the darkness, behind the dragon, where the two shadows were still standing in silence.

"Them! Yes, I know they're here. There are few you can trust in this corrupted kingdom," replied the beast in her head.

"With all due respect, which kingdom is that again?" Annea inquired carefully.

"One answer only," conceded the ancient voice, "Daughter of Daughters, Priestess of the Althayan, defender of the peoples of this world, you are now in the mighty Skyarach Kingdom," and after sometime the dragon added, "now remember, you shall not come to me again until you accept who you are." And having said that, the white Drkarach disappeared as it had come, making the air rebel against the cavernous walls and floors, and leaving Annea crouched on the ground still in shock.

'And I always thought I was brave…' she said to herself.

Lughan

2nd day of Aarglas, 300 YD,
Reaghil Bheallemer na Caydúllien Ore

After leaving the cave, Thuarnach, Lughan und Annea took a long walk around the surrounding forest, and the druid wisely left father and daughter to talk undisturbed.

They found a quiet grove, surrounded by coppiced trees, and made themselves comfortable, using the tree stumps as seats.

Annea was starting to notice the cold. The icy air was making her shiver uncontrollably. She hadn't had time to look for a warmer winter coat back at the Beckmann's before she left with the boys, and Marsha's thin leather jacket was no match for the weather.

'I wish I had dressed for the weather, my teeth will fall off if we don't get inside soon!' she thought, looking at her clothes, 'at least I did manage to put on my red cashmere jumper and my lamb boots...'

Realising how she was feeling, Lughan promptly covered her shoulders with the hooded cloak he had been wearing. A fine example of Skyarachti tailoring expertise, winter coats were made of a precious thick wool and had furs attached to them, depending on their hierarchy and their income. Lughan, as a guest citizen providing services to the Royal House, was allowed to use the colour black and a red fox's fur.

Now that she could think again, Annea fixed her dad intently.

"That's it, I'm done, Dad! What is all this?! I mean, I was talking to a monster in my head a few minutes ago, which is actually impossible?! Why are we here? What do you want from me? I've come all this way to find you! You owe me an answer… is it, is it possible we're both dead?!"

"I'm sorry child, I know this must be very disturbing," he sighed, compassion in his eyes, "but no, we are not dead, and you're not where you think you are, Little Pandora."

He observed her beautiful features for some time, she had become the most beautiful woman.

"To be more precise," he went on, "we are in the same place you were yesterday… only in a parallel world, 3000 years before our time. We have the year 1000 BC, and you, my darling, just like me before you, have travelled back through the veils of time."

Annea was thankful, she was sitting and had her father beside her. For the one thing, she did not know what to do of this statement. Had he gone mad? Time-travelling? That was out of the question! But she could not deny she had seen many strange things, most of all that beast in the caverns under the fortress...

She hesitated for a moment, but then summoning her courage, she inquired further.

"What was that thing in there? It talked to me..."

"Did she? Well, that ancient beast you met inside the cavern is the Royal Drkarach, the mighty White Dragon of the Skyarach."

"A dragon?! Dad, those are creatures of myth and legend! They don't actually exist!"

She looked around her desperately for some hint that would contradict what her father was telling her.

Lughan took her hands in his, before speaking again.

"Yes, Annea, here they do, as well as many other things."

"But–" she began.

"It is only natural that you don't want to believe me, Annea," he went on, "but it is of utmost importance that you do... We are living in dangerous times, there is a war coming. The Drkarach is a wise and ancient she-dragon of the old world, she is the last one of her kind, and she is the protector of our Kingdom."

"She spoke to me, Dad, she could hear my thoughts!"

"That is quite peculiar. I need to ask Thuarnach, I'm no expert in dragon-lore, but as far as I know, dragons can't speak, my love."

He looked at her with pity in his eyes.

"Do you intend to tell me, you didn't hear what that thing said?" Annea asked.

"Not a single word."

"But you could see it, right?"

"No, Annea, for Thuarnach and myself, it was just the crazy swirls of a violent gust of wind."

"It said things, I swear it called me names! It said it knew all my thoughts!"

"Well, I have been told that a dragon can communicate with the power of its mind, maybe it is that what you are referring to. We will ask Thuarnach about it, Annea. Now, you can relax, you have passed the test, the White Dragon won't hurt you or any of us…"

He observed her delicate face and saw mistrust in her eyes.

After some time, he went on, "yes, it was a risk to take you there, but we needed you to see her. You would have never believed me otherwise... and I know it sounds unreal to you still, but you have to befriend the idea that you are living in another era, we don't have much time, love."

She looked away for a while, her eyes burning, her face still impenetrable. Streams of tears were now tracing patterns of sadness on her beautiful, reddened face. She wanted to be strong, she was always strong...

"I've missed you terribly Dad... nothing was ever the same again in that house, after you left... Granny died two years ago, but you know, until her last breath, she never gave up on you. She told me all she knew, she helped me prepare, she wanted me to come looking for you..."

"She knew me well, Annea, and so do you," put in Lughan, "believe me, I miss her, too. But there was nothing I could do–"

She went on, not listening to him now, "and then, she left us with no warning. I used to imagine how terrible it must have been for a woman to lose her only child, I used to wonder how could she still have any faith left – I had so many doubts myself. I saw her crying, many times, without her noticing me, of course… But all through the years, Dad, it was her who was my pillar of hope. I swore to myself I was going to find you and bring you back, for me, for mother, for Bella, and above all for Granny Emma… and now, you stand in front of me, and you're telling me it's all been for nothing?!"

Lughan moved closer to her, and put an arm around her shoulders, while kissing her forehead.

"No, it's not, Annea! You kept your promise, and here you are! That is what matters, now!"

She turned her gaze to him again.

"What good is it? You said it yourself, we are both stuck here now, and she will never know!"

"We are not, we are meant to be here, darling. With time, you will understand… You see, these people need our help more than anyone, and my mother knew it, she understood the price, Annea, and she never doubted that it had to be paid. She did what she had to, she did it although she suffered, and she also did it for you."

"What help could I be for anyone? This is all madness! I don't even understand what they're saying! I don't know their ways! How am I supposed to act? This is like being stuck in an hourglass!"

"Annea, now listen to me: I, very much like you, keep my promises, and it was my duty to come, I gave my word that when the time was right, I would be here. My mother, your Granny, she knew it was necessary. I am so, so sorry, there was just no other way–"

"But, how could you survive? Who are these people, anyways?"

She had so many questions, her head was going to burst!

Lughan sighed and slightly nodded to himself in self-reflection. Then, a content smile set on his face.

"My daughter, a scholar through and through! Didn't I tell you not to step into your father's shoes?"

She had to smile, too, "well, I was never too stubborn."

"That's true," he replied with a broad smile.

"So, are you going to let me into your little secret?" she insisted.

"It has been hard, sometimes harder than others… I first met Thuarnach, he can speak something that relates to both old German and Greek, and with that, he slowly taught me his language, a dead language, for that. Archaeologists tap only in the darkness here. There was no way to study it before coming, Annea. This place has as good as completely disappeared from all history records, and no one knows why."

"So, is this Thuarnach your friend?"

"He is a very old friend, Love," smiled Lughan, "I met him on my second trip to Germany. You can say, we've shared a good reason to keep in touch with one another. Some twenty-four years ago, he urgently needed my help, and since then, we have been working secretly together. When I finally arrived here, he taught me all I needed to survive. He is an excellent teacher, you know. Thuarnach is Drkent Har's royal druid, Annea."

"Impressive!" she said with a tinge of sarcasm in her voice, "and now, he is going to teach me so that I can help him, like you did? How selfless of him!"

"No, he will teach you, Annea, because that is his duty, and he will protect you because that is his duty, just like mine," and standing up somewhat too hasty, he added, "so, for now, it is all you need to know."

"So, now you decide for me what I need to know? I have done without that for sixteen years, I think I can manage!"

"I didn't mean it like that," Lughan was tired and did not want to get into more detail, "we can keep on talking more of this later."

He hesitated and then went on, "but there is one more thing I need to tell you before we get going. Since the new king has taken over power, they have curfew hours in the city, and my home is on the other side, across the stream."

"What is it, then?" she pressed on.

"I married again, Annea, and I have two children."

Chapter Twelve: The Green Terrace Of The Dragon

The Way In

3rd Day of Aarglas, 300 YD,
Reaghil Ovsbhealle Rheanna

    The crossing had gone as planned. Early that day, the three brothers had cleared their camp and handed over the horses to the traders, and smugglers, who had been waiting for them at the Nwyr Krayn caves. They had been lucky to find men that were not locals, and henceforth not easily identifiable. So, once all details had been set, the three princes had taken on the identity of the Mohir traders responsible for providing new southern wine to the fortress of Reaghil Ovsbhealle Rheanna. After checking the documents, they had made their way back to the main port, bringing the Rheannvid with them. They had waited at the reserved docking area for what felt like a lifetime, but just when they were starting to lose hope, the beautiful green vessel, Ealator's Green Lady, had finally made its appearance.

The Kechtás were very well-trained and watchful, but as Ara had predicted, they had never imagined them amid their own people.

So, while the port commander and the Kechtás were discussing traffic matters, Ara had prompted the servants to start loading the wine onto the boat, and in that brief moment of chaos, no one had noticed them getting onto the boat and hiding themselves like shadows, in the dark corners behind the casks of Rheannvid.

Midway on their crossing, the three had taken the Kechtás unawares, knocking them out for the rest of the journey, or rather for the rest of the day. Nobody on the boat seemed to notice, and by the time the Kechtás would be discovered soundly sleeping among the casks of wine, the three brothers would already be out of reach.

They took the Kechtási uniforms, which felt so uncomfortable that a thought crossed Ara's mind, whether the soldiers needed more discipline to wear those uniforms or to follow Asttrian's mad orders. And so disguised, the they were able to reach the other shore without being further disturbed.

From time to time, however, all three wondered what was going to happen with their horses and their provisions, since if they wanted to be successful in their endeavour, they were going to need those horses. And despite the fact that the traders were all on their side, these people were also in urgent need of feeding their own families. Knowing this, Ara had promised them a generous reward, once they reached the last port on the Lahir river, where they would meet in three days' time. In case they were delayed, however, they had agreed that their helpers moved on, with their possessions, further into the Vwylr[35] Valley, to the first and smallest of the Kæyn an Drkent Dryd.[36] For this eventuality, Ara had made sure to give them his druid ring as a token of good faith, and to make sure they would be admitted inside the sacred site. It wasn't the best solution, but it would have to work. The druids would recognise the ring without a doubt, and would understand the circumstances of the arrangement, without asking uncomfortable questions. Besides, Ara could do without his hard-won druid ring on him, which could expose him any time.

Once they had reached the other shore and left Ealator's proud ship behind, the three escorted the servants with the first load of goods, through the royal gate and all the way up into the fortress on the top of the rocky hill. It was snowing slightly, again, and the stairs were already frozen. One misstep could lead to a fatal end, and so the selected little crowd made its upwards procession slowly and carefully.

Once at the top, they accessed the fortress through the royal service gates that led straight into the kitchen storages, and the wine cellars. So far, everything was going according to plan.

---

[35] Today's Weil river.
[36] Name given to the temples of the dragon druids.

As they passed the second entrance, they noticed the absence of guards by the west tower. This was the one chance they had been hoping for.

They swiftly turned left instead of right, and ended up right where they had wanted: the side entrance to the west tower that connected the royal chambers with the court room.

Ara stopped his younger brothers, "Skeor, as we have talked before, I need you to lead the way, Thuaì and I will follow ten steps behind, forming the dual Kechtási wall,"[37] and he added in a reassuring voice, "you'll see, they won't recognise you."

"I don't like all this, it has been too easy, Ara," put in Thuaìden, "are you sure you don't want to try the hidden tunnels under the tower? They always worked well when we were children."

"That's just because, then, no one but Thuarnach knew about them, brother!" replied Skeorden, "I figure out Asttrian has made sure to change that. Ara is right, we cannot risk going that way."

"But if they do recognise us, you know the Kechtás won't hesitate," countered Thuaìden through gritted teeth.

---

[37] Patrolling formation, in which the drkarach kechtás were expected to march.

"Ey, it is the one risk we are taking," answered Arachtan, "once we have reached the third level, though, it would only be one Drkarach Kechtá against three of us. We'll have to act swiftly, but we can make it."

After checking the entrance was still clear, he added, "are we ready?"

His brothers nodded their consent, and the three started their perilous ascent.

On the first level, as expected, they met three control points, right there where the corridors intersected with other main entrances. At this level, the castle of Reaghil Ovsbhealle connected most rooms and halls with its four towers, making it more accessible for the servants, who needed to cover the long distances regularly. Ara and his brothers could have taken one of the corridors at this level to move forward to the royal chambers, but they knew it was too risky for they would meet far too many Kechtás.

On the second level, also as expected, they met no one. Luckily, the West Tower presented no corridors to other parts of the castle at this level, merely a small watch room, which was usually empty, and mostly used as service storage room. And so, they were able to reach the third floor without having once had to identify themselves.

But they knew that the most rigorous test was coming next, and sweat was running under their armour and making the itchy uniform feel even more uncomfortable.

Skeorden entered the spacious room first. Thuaìden and Ara followed, as it was customary, building the dual Kechtási wall behind the leading knight.

The Kechtá at the control point was so concentrated working on some papers, he didn't even bother to look up from whatever he was doing.

"Drkarach ney, Bran!"[38] he said, "your business?"

"Drkarach ney, Bran!" answered Skeorden somewhat too readily, "I was sent with news from the town for Lord Ealator and Lady Skymnia about the southern red wine shipment for the capital." He tried to sound as calm as possible, but within his helmet, cold sweat pearls were slowly crowning his forehead.

Ara had come up with the idea of the red wine shipment, and luckily for them, there were so many valuable goods traded at the port of Reaghil Ovsbhealle, that this had been a perfect excuse to get through to their Rheann cousins, without raising suspicions.

---

[38] Official salutation among Drkarach Kechtás, the word "Bran" meaning "brother".

"What news are those, brother?" the Kechtá wanted to know, while now frantically searching his improvised desk for something he had evidently misplaced.

"There have been some problems with the quality, I'm afraid. The traders have written it all down. Here, " and he produced what looked like sealed documents from out of his coat and extended them to the Kechtá, who being still busy with his search, would not dispense a second to look up from his desk.

With a mere wave of his hand, the Kechtá signalled them to move on towards the royal chambers.

It was their lucky day, or so they thought, for a short instant. If their cousins were not at the court room, but in the royal chambers, the chances of finding Skymnia and Ealator alone were definitely higher.

They passed in front of the Kechtá strictly keeping the Kechtási formation, but when they were just about to reach the door to the corridor, the Kechtá looked up and called them to a stop.

"I almost forgot! Your name and number, brother?"

They moved swiftly. They had to.

They turned around keeping their formation, and while Skeor started mumbling something incomprehensible, the three simultaneously jumped onto the confused knight, who never stood a chance. They overwhelmed him before he could make a sound.

After that episode, they had to be fast, so they left him unconscious inside one of the trunks together with all his papers, and then, not wasting any more time, they made their way straight into the corridor that led to their cousins' chambers. They shut the doors behind them and kept the keys.

Once they had reached the main building, they went for Skymnia's chambers first. They found her sitting close to her balcony, looking outside her window, so lost in her thoughts, that she didn't hear them entering the room.

"Hyo, cousin!" called Ara casually.

She turned around wide-eyed and open-mouthed with astonishment. She just could not answer coherently.

"Ara? What…? Where…?" she managed to produce.

He moved closer to her and embraced her tightly. He was very fond of her young cousin, and was worried sick something bad could have happened to her. He knew Asttrian wouldn't hesitate to inflict pain on the people he cared for.

'Thank the Dragon, she is alright!' he thought.

After some time, she delicately pushed him away and confronted him, "they have imprisoned our mother, Ara! We are nothing more than baits to lure you here, you are all that stands between them and their father's throne. Asttrian and Shya are after you, you have to leave, now! There is nothing you can do for us here! They would do anything to get to you, Ara! Look what they've done to us, to our beautiful castle! It's but a prison, now…"

"Ealator?" asked Ara concerned.

"He is alive, and he is here, but be warned, Ara, he is not half the man he used to be. Bitterness has clouded his mind," she replied, sadness in her voice.

"I understand…" he put a hand on her shoulder trying to comfort her.

She moved away.

"No, Ara, you can't! How could you? You weren't there! You don't know!" she glowered at him, tears running down her cheeks, now.

"Then tell me, Skymnia, please, I'm here now, I'm listening."

Ara assumed his cousin was blaming him for not listening to her before, when she had tried to tell everyone what was going on in the capital. She might have even sent letters that had never reached him... But what was most important right now, was that he was here to take them with him. He could not change the past, and some day, he would have the chance to explain, but only if they managed to get out of Reaghil Ovsbhealle Rheanna.

She turned around to face the distant Rheann valleys, which were now covered in snow.

"You have the right to know. I don't think my brother will talk about it, Ara, but..."

"What?"

"The old king, he wanted you, and no one else, to have Drkentstar. He made the Thriar in full issue a royal promise that they would find you and hand over his sword to you..."

She turned to face him now.

"You know what this means, don't you? After the king died, Asttrian set out to destroy everyone that witnessed the king's last wish. We have a death sentence hanging over our heads... The day they find you, well, they have no use for us left!" her voice began to break as she pronounced the last words.

After a moment she continued, "you shouldn't be here, this is not home to us anymore... and you, Ara, you are the enemy."

Without saying one more word, Ara left Skymnia's chambers. He left Thuaìden to guard her, and Skeor to guard the corridors, and then continued into Ealator's chambers.

'This cannot be,' he thought, 'why would the king name me his heir? He knew I was to become a druid. There must be another explanation for this, and Thuarnach must know... Skymnia must be mistaken!'

He found Ealator thoughtful, bent over a piece of paper with the Royal Drkarach Seal of Reaghil Bheallemer.

He stood there for a while, observing his cousin, without saying anything, until Ealator looked up from his reading, his red eyes now fixed onto Ara's with a strange glint to them.

"Arachtan Skyarach, my virtuous Anairarachti cousin, coming all this long and dangerous way from Daing Mhuir to rescue us," he laughed sarcastically.

He was drunk. Skymnia was right, Ara couldn't recognise this man.

"Ealator," called Ara.

"Ahh, my loyal cousin!" greeted him Ealator, with open sarcasm in his voice, "tell me, for what were all those training years good if you fall for the simplest of traps?"

"My kin are first, Ealator, always, traps or no traps!" cut him Ara.

"Ahh, so typical!" replied Ealator with bile, "now, do you feel any better now, dear cousin? If so, I'm glad to have cheered you up. Unfortunately, as much as I would like to continue this conversation, the moment the Kechtás come in from that door, we are all dead men anyways: you and me, and my little sister, and anyone that has followed you in here. There is no way out for heroes this time, Arachtan, we are in the viper's nest…"

Stranded

6th Day of Aarglas, 300 YD,
Reaghil Ovsbhealle Rheanna

"What shall I do?" countered Ara to his brother Thuaìden, "I cannot leave them here at Asttrian's and Shya's mercy! We have to get them out and bring them to a Kæyn, the temple is the only place they can be safe, now."

"But we have lost precious time, and the route ahead isn't going to be any easier! You said it yourself, we cannot afford to wait, we have to reach Reaghil Bheallemer before Asttrian gathers an even bigger army and finds the sword!" gave back Thuaìden in frustration.

"I'm aware of that, brother... we'll need to change our plans, and go from here straight to the Kæyns."

"What about our provisions and horses? Do you think we'll ever see them again?"

"I trust these people, Thuaì. They are on our side."

Arachtan turned to the open window of his cousin's dressing chambers, where they had been hiding, for four very tedious days.

It was true, time was pressing, they had to leave, tomorrow at the latest.

After their swift arrival at the Rheann fortress, the three Anairarachti princes had been forced to linger much longer than they could afford. But as much as they used to love their stay at Reaghil Ovsbhealle, things were quite different this time. Both their Rheann cousins were as good as broken, and they were in grave danger, too. Ealator and Skymnia had not welcomed them, yet they hadn't given them away, so far. With their mother Lady Skenya held hostage hundreds of miles away, however, who could have blamed them if they had? Indeed, it was but a matter of time, and they would be forced to make a choice. Every second they all spent here, their whole mission threatened to fail. Ealator and Skymnia had to understand that coming with them was the only chance they had to survive. Ara was convinced he could get Skymnia see reason, but he doubted her brother would consent to accompany them, or let his sister go…

"See, there?" Arachtan pointed to a distant figure, looming distrustfully at the feet of the steep hill the castle was built on, "the Kechtás are positioned to cover all possible entrances. Our last hope is the druid tunnel, we'll move in the night. But Skymnia and Ealator are coming, with or without their consent."

He was referring to the one tunnel, in this castle, that Thuarnach had shown only Ara as part of his druid training. The Reaghil

Dryd Sljk, as this system of druid tunnels was named, ran completely underneath all other passages without crossing them. In the Rheann fortress, the tunnel had been especially designed for the Drkent Dryds' use, and had the advantage of connecting the Rheann with the Lahir river beneath the hills. However, finding it again was going to pose a major challenge, for the entrance was well hidden, almost invisible to the bare eye.

"You think you'll be able to find it? The entrance to the Reaghil Dryd Sljk?" asked Skeor.

Arachtan nodded, and then added, "the Kechtás don't suspect us behind the assault, we have good chances of reaching the gardens unscathed under the cover of night. The entrance to the tunnels has to be there."

Luckily for all, Arachtan and his brothers had been so careful not showing themselves, that by the time all the Kechtás had shared their accounts, nobody had ever suspected them being inside the castle. Rather, the Kechtási knights thought they were dealing with a band of smugglers, and were therefore preparing their official written complaints addressed to the port master. So, them using the traders documentation had paid off in the end...

The whole truth be told, however, the situation had unexpectedly blown up in his face. Arachtan had never expected to be rejected like this by his cousins. He was dismayed. The Arach cousins were not just relations, they were dear friends, who had shared a lifetime. They had played together as children, travelled together, lived together, trained together... They had undergone many training seasons at Reaghil Bheallemer, and shared many summers, mostly at the Rheann, but also at Daing Mhuir. They should have known him better! How could they ever doubt him like that? How could they have thought he had abandoned them, or the kingdom in the hour of need?

It was true, a little longer than two years ago, he had left Reaghil Bheallemer in haste, after his six months' retreat at the Elthanin Polarys Kæyn, where the main druid temple was. That had been the last time he had seen his Rheann cousins. Arachtan had been 28 years old then, and only two years away from his Drkent Dryd na Wbent Teyn.[39] It was also true that he had promised to meet them at Reaghil Ovsbhealle Rheanna after Thuaìden's warrior initiation, dah Kaicht Kryn Fæstal,[40] which had taken place at Daing Mhuir under Queen Scaìthara's meticulous supervision. Ealator himself had invited him to spend some time with them at the Rheann fortress at his return to the kingdom. He had said he wanted to discuss delicate matters under his own roof, and had

---

[39] The Druid Dragon of Knowledge trial.
[40] The order of the Anair Kaicht was created by Queen Scaìthara herself and was reserved for the royal warriors of the Anairarachti only. This order foresaw an initiation ceremony at age 23.

asked Arachtan to travel back to the capital with him after… but this was not to be.

As Skymnia's jays started arriving, urging him to return hastily to the capital, so did Thuarnach's, pleading him to stay at Daing Mhuir and to interrupt all exchange of information with the Skyarach Kingdom. After long nights, discussing the matter with his mother and his step father, Drearyan, who had still had active spies in Urarathan's kingdom, they had all agreed that Thuarnach's advise was to be followed. But this had meant that, even as the messages from his Rheann cousins had continued to arrive, he had been forced to silence. By then, it had started to be obvious that the developments at the capital were taking a dark turn, which ended tragically with the old king's death. Soon after that, the jays had stopped bringing any news to Daing Mhuir…

Arachtan would have handled differently, of course, had he been free to do so. But shortly after his return to Daing Mhuir, he had made that unforgivable mistake with the slave girl Ryssa, which had done away with many plans, including his lifelong ambitions of becoming a Drkent Dryd. Faced with no viable alternative, he had chosen to marry her in secret, there would be time to explain it to his family after. Arachtan had been aware that he would never love Ryssa, and that he would now never be accepted by the Drkent Dryd Kydrachs, but in this way, no Arach law could harm her or the child.[41]

Arachtan Skyarach, however, was no person to hide behind fortresses or walls. He was someone who faced any challenge, no matter how hard, no matter how impossible. He did not know fear, and staying away from the Skyarach Kingdom had been the hardest trial to his will he had ever had to endure. He could not forgive himself for not having been there to protect his beloved uncle Urarathan, his heritage and his Rheann relatives. Things might have ended quite differently had he not listened to his mother and Thuarnach…

So, here he was now, after the longest two years of his life, fighting to free his cousins and yet stranded again.

'We cannot wait for them to see reason, and even if the journey is dangerous, I have to take them with me. There is no other way… if they stay, they die,' he reminded himself.

---

[41] By the Arach Law, if a True Royal Arach had an offsping with some person from the common folk there were two options accepted: a) they would marry for a lifetime, with no option to trial time; b) the subject and the child must die.

The Way out

7th Day of Aarglas, 300 YD,
Reaghil Ovsbhealle Rheanna

They were waiting in the dark, four black shapes, and their burdensome load, shivering in the cold dampness of a wintery night...

It had been snowing all day, and it was bitter cold and windy. The Rheann had been punished by a mighty blizzard, and the castle life had concentrated mostly around its hearths. Even the Kechtási knights had gathered in the tower keep, which they had taken as their living quarters.

It was the opportunity Arachtan had been waiting for, and he wasn't going to waste it.

Early that morning, feigning a headache, Skymnia had asked her chamber maiden to bring her some water to boil, a glass filled with the strongest beer that could be found in their cellars, and some medicinal herbs that were kept in the apothecary's closet, down at the buttery. Specifically, she had asked for large quantities of valerian root and dried chamomile flowers, that grew in the area and were used as sedatives.

Skymnia herself had no use for all this, of course. Arachtan, on the other hand, had learnt how to prepare all sorts of medicinal potions as part of his druid training.

Once they had gathered the ingredients they needed, he had wasted no time, and had prepared a strong herbal brew that could have knocked a giant troll out. He proceeded to add hops, the only one they could find was the one in the beer, and then some other more exotic extracts he had in his druid pouch, like magnolia bark and a few drops of lavender oil from the Southern Seas.

When the potion was finally ready, it was Skymnia's turn. She stole into Ealator's room and poured it unnoticed in his wine jar.

At first, she had been very anxious about the idea of escaping this way, the Drkarach Kechtás were lethal weapons in the hand of her tyrant cousin. On the other hand, she trusted Ara, and she knew in her heart that it was the only escape they could risk. Besides, it had been somehow fun to watch her brother drink until the very last drop of that awful liquid had disappeared down his throat. He had had so much alcohol in his bloodstream already, he hadn't even noticed the difference in taste!

That part had been easy, but now, they were all here, hiding in the darkness, with Eala's motionless body lying limply in an even darker corner beside them. If the Kechtás found them, they would all be dead come morning, she knew as much. Those knights had specific instructions not to let anyone leave the fortress alive, Skymnia had been there when Asttrian had given the orders, and she had accepted to help her cousins, nevertheless. She could see that it was their best chance, and she knew their mother would have approved of her decision, especially now that Eala had given up on them all.

Now, however, engulfed by the frosty claws of the night, Skymnia was starting to doubt, yet again...

Just then, Thuaìden gave the signal across the great courtyard. They had to get going.

Skeorden was covering their rear, with his arrows ready to shoot, and Ara was carrying Eala's bulky hull over his shoulders. Her brother was not particularly large, but one could see Ara was struggling to keep pace with the weight.

They weren't a second too early. Just as they had found cover behind the stables, two Kechtási patrolling parties appeared from opposite sides of the courtyard, surveying each entrance to the royal towers. They had been lucky this time, but they needed to hurry out of the fortress, or they would likely come across more knights.

They took to a badly lit gallery that connected the stables with the potter's workshop, and this to the glassblower and glazier's. They stopped to rest for a few minutes, taking care not to break anything. There were hundreds of empty wine bottles waiting to be filled with the precious fluid of the Rheann, so they had to be very careful, any sound could give them away, since this area of the courtyard had always been intensively guarded for its costly materials and products.

Arachtan had patiently observed the Kechtás' movements all these days, and he knew there was a change of guards happening right now, in front of the entrance to the royal gardens at the back of the fortress. They had to wait a little longer, and they would be able to ambush the new guards without anyone noticing until early morning, when the next change was scheduled. True, the new guards would be more vigilant, not as tired, but if they succeeded in overwhelming them, it would give them precious time to escape through the hidden Reaghil Dryd Sljk, without anyone looking for them that way. They would need to be very careful, though. If any of the guards managed to blow his horn and call for reinforcements, they were lost. They all knew this was the most challenging part of their plan...

When the time came, Ara told Skymnia to wait with Ealator inside the glazier's, while he, Thuaì and Skeor sneaked themselves out of the shop and carefully crept closer to the new Kechtás watching over the garden gates. In the cover of darkness, they managed to get as close as one could get without being noticed, now was the time to strike!

Without hesitating, Skeor loaded his bow and shot.

His arrow was silent and precise, taking down the first Kechtá by complete surprise. The two others reacted almost immediately, and grabbed to their horns.

Luckily, Thuaì, who was not as good with an arrow, had brought his daggers with him, and he certainly knew how to use them. He threw the daggers aiming at the Kechtás' hands, preventing them from taking hold of the horns. Simultaneously, Ara charged out of the darkness with his long sword in one hand and his dagger in the other. Thuaì followed him, while Skeor went back for the two Rheann siblings.

The fight didn't last long with one Kechtá already down, and the other two with wounded hands. Although they knew how to dance to a sword, the Kechtás were no match to the Anairarachti brothers. Ara and Thuaì had the advantage of having learnt both Skyarachti and Anairarachti combat techniques, and together they were lethal. Their queen mother had trained them personally, and she was famously unbeatable.

Skymnia and Skeorden, with Ealator over his shoulders, came just in time to watch how Ara dealt the final blow to the last standing

Kechtási knight. They could tell it had been a hard battle, as both Ara and Thuaì were sweating despite the freezing temperatures.

Together, they then pulled the motionless bodies of the knights to the side, and rushed into the royal gardens, so far unnoticed.

The Arach people had always protected forests and worshipped nature and its forces. As a testimony to this, they always included a garden or two within their castle walls. These were true feats of landscape architecture, and were always extremely beautiful, with a mixture of regional and exotic plants, and several water streams and fountains. They also usually offered several delightful secluded corners, where to rest the mind. This time, however, there was certainly no time for that...

The Rheann gardens presented an exuberant vegetation even now, and provided good cover. They had been built like a maze to provide a peaceful and secluded refuge for the lady of the castle, and also to act as an open-air temple to nature herself. Unfortunately, this, paired with the frozen and slippery ground, was not helping them. On the contrary, it was making their progress especially difficult.

Arachtan, knowingly, turned to the one person that knew these gardens like the palm of her own hand: Skymnia. He trusted her with the impossible task of finding the centre piece within, the Caydúllien Ore, the Golden Apple Tree.[42] She had spent most of her childhood with her mother in these gardens, and knew every plant and stone inside them. If she could not find the tree, then no one could. On his part, Arachtan had been shown how to use the Reaghil Dryd Sljk, how to navigate within, but because these corridors were a well-kept secret, each druid had to prove himself in a quest to find them and opening the druid gates. From Thuarnach's words, however, he had gathered which was the place, where the entrance should be hidden: the Caydúllien Ore of the Rheann garden.

---

[42] Each Royal city of the Skyarach had its own Caydúllien Ore, its own golden apple tree. The capital city, accordingly, exhibited the most ancient and biggest of them all. This species of apple tree came from the East, from the native lands of the Dreà Arach, and was the symbol of their people.

Chapter Thirteen: The Hidden Passage

7th Day of Aarglas, close to midnight, 300 YD,
Reaghil Ovsbhealle Rheanna

    The Caydúllien Ore of the Rheann fortress, which had surely proven to be quite hard to find, was not as monumental as its counterpart in the capital. It was, however, a beautiful and generous tree, with some golden apples hanging from its branches, even in the winter.

When the Anairarachti brothers and their two cousins finally found it, they were all out of breath and exhausted, Ealator still unconscious and being more or less dragged along through the dense vegetation. They had wasted precious time searching, but still it was their best chance.

Skymnia collapsed onto the nearest bank, and Thuaì, with Skeor's help, laid Ealator's limp body next to her, countless drops of sweat running down their foreheads despite the chill. Ara, who knew they could not afford to waste more time, went on to search the place for the hidden entrance to the tunnels.

The tree stood solemnly, the icy wind deftly bending its lightly laden branches in all directions.

The last time they had been talking about the Reaghil Dryd Sljks, Thuarnach had spoken in riddles. He had told Arachtan to look without, to find within, and to look within, to find without. Ara knew his uncle, he had a passion for riddles and, of course, he was not about to let him into the secret just like that.

"What did your wise words mean, uncle?" asked Ara aloud, "what is it I'm missing?"

He sat down and contemplated the ancient Caydúllien Ore, trying to make sense of his uncle's words.

There was something strange to this tree… Arachtan was not yet able to see what it was, but he was sure it had to do with its appearance, its shape.

Engulfed by the stillness of the frozen gardens, he sat there deep in thought for a while, until an unexpected burst of hysterical laughter brought him back.

It was Skymnia. She stood up and came closer to him.

"Sorry," she apologised, "but it is indeed ironic that we shall end our days here, at the feet of the very tree my father and mother promised each other eternal love…" she continued, "it was the end of summer, they say, and the Caydúllien Ore was bent by the weight of its golden apples. The Dryd who married them had them pick the highest apple on the highest branch of the tree, to symbolize the extent to which they were ready to fight for each other. He told them, marriage is the fight you should never win or lose."

She sighed, and then continued in a sad voice, "look at it, now, this tree is the very reflection of ourselves, all bent and torn by the gale…"

Ara hadn't heard about this family story before, but after hearing it, he saw the tree under a different light, now: the symbol of her aunt's and uncle's union.

It was true, it was not as full with apples, as he remembered it. Still there was something most peculiar, the biggest and freshest apple was the one hanging from the very top of the highest branch… Right there, where his uncle and aunt had harvested their wedding apple, long ago… Could it be possible?

"Of course!" said Ara all of a sudden, "the Dryd replaced the apple back then, and made sure that no one would collect that apple ever again, by giving it a sacred role in the marriage ritual of your parents," he went on, "over there, it is the highest fruit. I'm sure it hides the entrance to the tunnels."

"And how do you suggest we will reach that high, brother?" asked Thuaì already knowing he would not like the answer.

"Well, as you can see that apple is extremely high up, and we have no ladders here, so the answer is quite plain to me…" Ara looked at Thuaìden, with a grin.

"Oh no, no, not this time! I might be good at it, but I hate heights!" answered Thuaìden, shaking his head with determination.

"Come on, Thuaì, you are by far the best of us all," put in Skeor, "and besides, I'm too short, and Ara is too heavy for the poor old tree."

"We will pull you up to the first branch to avoid the slippery trunk. You are the only one who can do it, Thuaì," persuaded him Ara.

At that point, Ealator shivered uneasy in his sleep, and Skymnia looked at his cousin Thuaì pleadingly.

Thuaì shook his head slightly, "this is incredible! You are doing it again! Just as when we were young, you three against me, and Ealator reading from his book of old codes of chivalry!"

They all couldn't refrain from laughing at that… Although Ealator was not precisely reading this time.

Ara stood up and together with Skeor they propelled their brother as hard as they could all the way up, to the lowest branch of the apple tree. Thuaì was barely able to get hold of the lowest branch, which was extremely thick and slippery. He managed to pulled himself up, in the end, and so slowly, and very carefully, he started his ascent.

It took him quite a while to reach the densely branched upper crown of the tree.

"You're almost there, Thuaì!" whispered Skymnia to him from the ground, "go a little left, now, the branches are thicker there, they will hold you better!"

A little while longer, and Thuaì reached the final part of his climb. He had to concentrate not to look down at the others, or he would feel dizzy, and it was easy to fall off from the frozen branches.

"Right in front of you now, Thuaì, you can do it! Just clear those dried leaves to your right, and stretch your arm, you should be able to reach the apple from there," guided him Arachtan from below.

Stretching himself to the limit, he delicately tapped the apple with the tip of his fingers, making it move to and fro. After sometime and with extreme difficulty, he was finally able to get hold of it, and then, without further hesitation, he gave it a strong pull.

The apple was his.

After what only felt like a few seconds, the earth underneath the tree started rumbling and shaking. It almost felt like an earthquake and everyone, except Thuaì, who was now wrapping himself around the closest branch, jumped away from the tree as fast as they could.

With a whoosh, the giant tree roots moved to the side, revealing an enormous black opening underneath the tree, which looked very much like the open jaws of a monster, ready to swallow anyone who dared enter…

They had found it: the entrance to the Reaghil Dryd Sljk!

As soon as they were all together again, they rushed into the unfathomable gateway to the tunnel. Inside, they found a staircase leading to the very bowls of the earth.

It was pitch-black, so without losing time, Arachtan fashioned a torch using a green wood stick, a piece of cloth and some tree sap to soak it with. He then used his igniting stones and led the group down into the deep, with nothing but his improvised torch.

The stairs turned to be extremely steep and long, and to make things worse, after a few minutes descent, the opening above sealed itself closed again, leaving them in utter darkness. It felt like being swallowed by some kind of underground creature, and they all instinctively came closer together.

Still carrying Ealator's body over his shoulder, Skeor was at the rear of the group, which made his descent especially strenuous. With this dead weight and almost blind, he unluckily missed a step, and lost balanced, falling over into the black abyss to their right.

Skymnia bolted just in time to feel, rather than see them falling, and desperately grabbed after them, while Thuaì, who had been walking right in front of her, jolted back to help her get hold of Skeor.

This time, it had been really close, they had been lucky. However, with the strain and darkness surrounding them, it was a matter of time, and it could take anyone right down to the endless bottom of the pit.

They were not going to risk it again, so Thuaì offered to change position, and took up the rear with its heavy burden. After this event, they all felt even more uneasy in the menacing, cavernous darkness.

Some minutes later, they reached what felt like the bottom of the stairs, and it became easier to move forward despite the absence of light. The strain was now starting to weigh down on them, but they continued walking. They had a long way still, and the Kechtás had by now certainly raised the alarm.

At some point, however, Skymnia tripped over her own feet and plummeted to the ground. She was exhausted, and seemed to be unable to pull herself up again.

In truth, everyone was feeling the exertion of their adventurous escape. They would have to rest for a while, even if it was risky, there was no way they could continue like this. So, one after the other, they made themselves as comfortable as they could with their backs to the cold, wet walls.

Ealator, on his part, was starting to move uneasy in his sleep, which was a sign that he would soon be awake.

'No good news,' Arachtan thought, 'I'd better go and see we find that bloody chamber before it is too late. It has to be somewhere close…'

Addressing everyone, he said, "any moment now, the wounded guards are going to be found by their peers, if they hadn't been already. You can be sure they will come after us like hungry dogs, and will stop at nothing, until they see us in chains. We have to get going… but I see how worn out you are, and this place is as safe and as warm as we will get, so you stay here for a while, I will search for the path and come to get you. I promise, I won't take long."

He left them the one torch they had, and without another word, he disappeared in the underworldly darkness.

Skeor who had brought some Kyllanan[43] from Daing Mhuir, which was especially tasty and invigorating, offered it to his cousin Skymnia.

"Here, drink something. This will help you keep going like a horse, cousin," he smiled at her in the dimly lit tunnel.

"What is it?" she asked while he was handing her over the worn, leather flask.

"It's what we take during training season, when we go ranging for long. It's Kyllanan and no, it is not as good as your Rheannvid, of

---

[43] Kyllanan was a powerful elderbeery tonic used for energising both body and mind.

course, but it makes you as strong as a boar," he answered with a contagious laughter.

She took it with obvious scepticism and a pinched nose. She knew the juice very well, Kyllanan was a widespread medicinal beverage taken for many ailments. She had never liked it, too strong and sweet for her delicate Rheann palate, plus it reminded her of disease and illness. The Rheann druids used to prepare different syrups of the kylla beery and flowers to keep everyone healthy through the winter, too.

He was amused by her disgusted expression, "come on, you don't trust me anymore, little cousin? Try it, I promise, it is not bad."

She summoned all her courage, and tasted it. To her surprise, this one was much better than the one she used to have as a child, so she kept on drinking wilfully.

Skeor observed her all the while, and although she looked quite composed, he could read her better than anyone: she was extremely anxious, even desperate. But then, who could blame her?

These last couple of years since the old king's death had been a nightmare for his Rheann cousin. She had suffered much, and all alone. Her mother imprisoned, her brother turned into a maniac, Asttrian had not hesitated to take her and Ealator hostage and used them for his plans. She had been abandoned by her brother, who had taken to drinking and swearing, and the Anairarachti princes, who were her only closest family left, had kept away from the Kingdom for very long, too long in Skeor's opinion. Of course, he knew Ara had good reasons for this, but it was now surely difficult for her to trust anyone.

"Thank you," she said, a little embarrassed that she had emptied half the bottle.

He held her eyes for a while in the blackness of their surroundings.

"He knows what he is doing, you know," he put in with conviction, "there is no need to doubt him."

Skymnia looked away, and shrugged.

He frowned, "sure you must have heard stories about him, he has many enemies, cousin, we all know that…" His voice now loaded with conviction, he added, "my brother is the best man I've ever known."

Skymnia didn't answer, but it didn't escape her that Skeor had not bothered to deny the stories as being false. She felt a chill run through her spine, and shuddered.

At that precise moment, Ara reappeared with a broad smile on his handsome face.

"I've found it, I've found the wheeled chamber! Follow me."

After some hundred metres, the tunnel took a turn to the left, and right in front of them, there was a lighted chamber. Like a beacon in the dark, its luminescence flickered defiantly, showing an open space with strange objects in it. Yet to the right of the chamber, there was another opening that led into darkness again.

"Tyarsa Ræth an Fael, the wheeled chamber! Our way out!" explained Ara satisfied, pointing at the strange vehicle-like objects aligned one after the other in front of the black opening, "this isn't just a normal tunnel under the mountains. The druids have designed it to be used in times of extreme danger and urgency. They have created here a way to travel faster under the earth."

"What...?" Skeor stood still at the entrance of the chamber, completely dumbstruck.

Thuaì was as speechless, but after a while he moved closer and scrutinized the artifacts first hand, "are you telling me that we have to ride these to get out of here? Have you ever considered that none of us has seen, let alone used such an object before? Truly, brother, I have no clue how we are going to get these things going!"

Ara laughed wholeheartedly. Thuaì was such a pessimist, as always.

"You don't have to do anything. You just sit inside, and the wheeled Cathrie[44] will lose itself from the lock and dart down the tunnels for quite a while. And don't worry, it will eventually slow down and stop by its own accord. Once it does, we'll know we have reached the underground caves of Daing na Lahirynn.[45] Now come, we have no time to lose!" said Arachtan to his widely perplexed audience.

---

[44] Word for seat in the Arach tongues
[45] The Lahir Valley Fortress was located where today's city of Bad Ems is.

Chapter Fourteen: A New Home

The Guest Maiden

18rth Day of Aarglas, YD 300,
Reaghil Bheallemer

She had been trapped in her new existence for a few weeks now, and her everyday life was proving extremely challenging. Annea was not entirely able to come to terms with her novel reality, and was bitterly fighting it from within.

Every morning, for the seconds it took her to be fully awake and open her eyes, she still feverishly hoped this incredibly fascinating and, at the same time, nightmarish place, would have vanished overnight, and she would find herself and her father in the twenty-first century, eating some ice cream.

'Is this my own personal fairy tale, or is it a perfect nightmare? If the latter, this one is positively turning out to be as real as the sun and moon!' she said to herself.

One way or the other, Reaghil Bheallemer na Caydúllien Ore, the Great Royal City of the Golden Tree, was her home, now. This magnificent walled city, with its many neighbourhoods, shops and well-laid network of interconnected roads and alleys, was a true architectural feat.

Perched on a natural rocky hill, and divided by a generous stream of water, which people here called the Sryath, the city enclosed gold, iron ore and quartzite mines to the northeast, and a natural valley to the southwest, which the Skyarach used to secure rich crop farmlands in case of social turmoil outside the city walls. It had never happened before, but the city had been laid out to be unbreachable, and it was self-sufficient in all ways possible.

Several cisterns had been placed across the capital, where clean source water from the Sryath was collected and made available to the many neighbourhoods allocated to the different groups of citizens, which were strictly organised in a very hierarchical manner.

Annea, of course, had to learn her way around the city very quickly. As a foreigner, she had been admitted as a guest maiden, and lived with her father at the guest quarters, close to the Drkarach Kechtási training arena, towards the northwest of the city. She was allowed to move as she pleased within the city, but she could not go near the ore mines, trespass the farmlands, or enter the castle without an official invitation from the king. Guest citizens were also allowed to leave the city, but needed registration at either of the two main gates if they intended to return.

The Nachtural Brean, or native farmers, had their homing between the guest quarters and the Sryath, and primarily took care over the crops and could move freely on the valley and all civilian neighbourhoods, but not the mines or castle. They were free citizens, and were allowed to travel in and out of the capital at pleasure.

And while the Skylliad, who were the craftsmen and tradesmen, housed closer to Drkent Har and the main market centre around Reaghil's golden apple tree, it was the host nobles, or Harkan Næl,[46] who had the honour of living directly around the main square facing the beautiful Kynna Tyarsa or King's Gate, and who, of course, had the most privileges of all.

In all of the Arach kingdoms, there was a tradition of engaging the host nobles in the management of the realm. They were part of courtly life and would share almost the same privileges as the king and his family. This was because they were also considered and honoured as an educated ruling class. A Drkarach Qvynne or Kynn[47] would always keep a large number of Harkan Næl to help

---

[46] Harkan Næl was the name given to the local nobles that became host nobles after the Arach took over the territories these people once had ruled over.
[47] Drkarach Qvynne or Kynn, as well as Teyn (which was an ancient word), were the official title given to the queen and king of the Dreà Arachti respectively. The title was originally carried by a queen rather than a king, but this changed with the millenia and the word "Kynn" was used more frequently those days.

her or him cover all the areas of government in a knowledgeable and efficient way.

This decision was a wise one. These people had been the original nobles of the area and knew their culture and environment better than the newcomers. The Arach, in this case Urarathan, had sealed a pact dating three hundred years back with their old chieftain, guaranteeing the native nobles that they would live as the king himself, as long as they proved loyal, respected the Arach Law and worked towards the benefit of the kingdom. This deal had been honoured so far, and the Skyarach Kingdom and the capital had enjoyed the longest period of peace ever recorded in local history.

And it was due to that, that the Harkan Næl lived at the most impressive and beautiful area, except for the fortress itself, in Reaghil Bheallemer, and whereas each community had a functional central square, where people could gather freely at will, the host neighbourhood exhibited the richest and most spectacular market square in the whole kingdom, and that, right in front of the King's Gate.

An ample marketplace that had been laid in front of Drkent Har, where the king lived and held court, was the main trading centre, as well as gathering place for citizens of all kinds. At the heart of the square, a majestic, ancient apple tree stretched proudly, with richly ornated white stone banks surrounding it. The Caydúllien

Ore, as Annea learnt, was revered and protected by all. It was the most precious symbol of the city's pride, but what was most impressive was that the tree bore fruits even though it was midwinter.

When the busy hours were over, the citizens of Reaghil Bheallemer would gather at this central square and play games, sing songs, or sit there and leisurely spend time with others. Tribunes had been built with the same white stone all around the place, which made these gatherings an everyday scenery in front of the castle. From time to time, minstrels, bards and other wandering artists would also come and entertain the people under the vigilant eyes of the Drkarach Kechtás, the royal knights, always watching, and merciless if any trouble arose.

Annea had seen them in action several times by now, and she honestly preferred to get out of their way as much as possible. She had to admit that she had even developed some kind of paranoia, or so it seemed to her, for she had gained the impression that the Kechtás were somehow always following her. No matter where she went, she always seemed to meet them...

'Without a doubt,' Annea thought, 'the citizens of this city have no reason to feel unhappy. They truly live a pleasant, organised and comfortable life. I would have never imagined it possible in ancient times...'

And most people in the streets were cheerful and friendly to each other. Whenever someone needed assistance, there was someone else, or many, trying to give a hand. It was a society living in full abundance.

This, on the one hand, made her feel strangely at ease in this completely unknown and complex environment, and still, she could not help but feel utterly inappropriate for far too many reasons…

'Yes,' Annea thought, 'I have to find a way to close Pandora's box, or die trying! This just could not be it: finding Dad and then remaining stuck here forever? How could he expect me to accept that?'

She was not about to give up hope of bringing him back with her so easily. She couldn't wait to see Lara Menard's expression when she saw her husband again, and her sister Bella's, who had always doubted her.

'He will eventually come to understand that we have to escape somehow… but how?' she wondered, 'for now it is better to pretend I surrender, no matter how hard it is. If life is daring, so am I!'

Life here was certainly not being all too easy for her. Everything was different, everything was new. Starting with the clothing, all the way to the food, people's behaviour and that awfully complicated language, Annea was having a hard time trying to keep up with it all. Let alone the fact that she actually did not belong to this parallel world, or whatever it was.

As soon as she had arrived to her new home, Annea's father had begged her to change clothes, and keep her old ones well hidden. She had been quite comfortable with what she was wearing, notwithstanding the chill, but had seen the point, and had accepted her new wardrobe without too many complaints.

Having passed on the itchy, woollen socks, she had been at least allowed to keep her warm lamb boots, which, in any case, were not that different from the footwear most people here used. The clothing, however, was a completely different story. She had to wear three layers of clothing, which took hours to put on and were altogether rather heavy.

To be fair, she had to admit that these people did seem to know how to process wool. For the winter chill, she was given thinly-knitted, undyed, fine woollen underclothing, which actually turned out to be very warm and comfortable. She wore a thicker, natural, woollen blouse, and leather pants over the woollen underwear. And because she was expected to acquire the necessary skills to protect the kingdom, and therefore, had to train bow and arrow, as well as horse riding, she was given a masterly woven tartan tunic in the Gænnæriati[48] colours, which were grey, brown and green. The tunic was pinned together over both shoulders, using small, spiral-like, iron clasps called Triskele Fibulæ. Besides these and a bigger iron Triskele pinned in the middle of the tunic for festivities, she was not expected to wear any jewellery, and had only a leather belt to fix the tunic around her waist. On top of these garments, however, she was expected to wear her own Gænnæriati tartan cloak, with a hood made out of brown rabbit fur, which was extremely warm and kept the wind out when riding. To train, moreover, she wore leather gloves and a leather bracer or armguard to help her when shooting while riding. This was the perfect horse-maiden outfit.

But, yes, not just the garment was different and complex, what was expected from her was beyond her wildest dreams.

If she wanted to stay a citizen of the Skyarach Kingdom, she had to master horse archery as a basic skill. And although riding was no big problem, riding while simultaneously shooting with arrows was a different matter altogether.

She had always loved horses... A long time ago, as a little girl back in Argentina, her father had taken her to their family ranch to enjoy many a wild ride. Unfortunately, after Dr Menard's disappearance, Lara Menard had sold the ranch with horses and

---

[48] Gænnæriati means "of the guest people".

all, so Annea had not been able to go to her horse refuge ever again. From time to time, however, a friend had invited her to spend the weekend on the mountains, and there, she had been able to give free reign to her passion for horses. She had ridden for hours, until the sun was down and the mountain lion started roaming around the prairie. Yes, Annea's love for horses went a great deal back, and sure enough, this part of the training was not unpleasant.

The bow and arrow, on the contrary, were not really her favourite. She disliked shooting at things altogether, and this composite bow was too dangerous for her own sake. An impressive weapon made entirely out of bone, it could produce a very powerful and accurate shot over long distances, perfect for shooting while riding… If held properly, which she so far had not managed. But alone the thought of shooting at a living creature made her blood curdle. So, most of the time, she was fighting her inner self to please her father and that strange friend of his, Druid Thuarnach, in their everyday quest for instructing her in the use of bow and arrow.

When were they going to stop? Didn't they have better things to do?

Truth be told and in spite of her lack of skills, the bearded druid had been more than kind and patient with Annea. Meeting regularly for her training, it seemed that even someone as wise and learned as Thuarnach was finding it difficult to keep her on her mount. But while her father had early on escorted her to facilitate translation, with time she had made enough progress in the Skyarachti language to be left on her own. Lughan had now officially returned to his daily chores, and Thuarnach had fully taken over her instruction.

The Teacher

18th day of Aarglas, YD 300,
Royal Kechtási Training Arena, Reaghil Bheallemer

It was the fourth time today that she had fallen headfirst from the horse, and the third bow she had managed to break. She had been training mounted shooting from early in the morning, and she hadn't had anything to eat, yet. She was desperate for something decent to eat, something ordinary… A nice hamburger, a bag of chips, an ice cream, just anything familiar.

Her father would say it was all her fault, of course. She was not accepting the early breakfast she was offered at home, and therefore arrived everyday starved after morning training.

At least today, they would only be having language classes after lunch, she thought. But again, lunch was not much better than breakfast…

She knew she would have to give in at some point, not least because she was being extremely rude to her new 'family'. By now, the children were always staring expectantly when she was presented with a new dish, while Lughan's new wife was at a loss. The poor woman did not know what to cook for her any more, and she could not possibly continue living just on bread, milk and eggs for eternity.

But how could they expect her to eat all that disgusting stuff?! It looked and smelled awful, and on top of that, when they would try explain what the meal was made of, it would just make things even worse. Better she did not know what was inside! Roasted frog legs in lemon and wood garlic for breakfast? No, no way! She would stay firm or die...

Oh, well, so there she was, having to climb up that horse once again with nothing in her belly.

The snow was starting to melt, after all it was Wbentas and it was past time the extreme cold would loosen its tight grip a little. The landscape was slowly recovering some of its brown-green colours, and as a consequence, the Royal Arena was basically all mud.

When Annea finally got up on her feet for the fourth time, she was all covered in a thick layer of half-crusted mud that started to peel off while she staggered her way reluctantly back to the horse.

Witnessing this, Thuarnach saw her exceptional determination and understood, she was never going to quit. Even if she had to drag herself all bruised and broken back on top of that kind beast, she would do it, but this was not the purpose of her training for now, they just wanted her to blend in, that was all...

"Oan ra, Anneya? Ista neya sfie? Yai sona echt!"[49] called the druid from the other side of the arena.

"Sfie ista neyan, muin Eonar Drkent Dryd Thuarnach."[50] she answered politely and turned back to the task of mounting her horse.

"Sfie, Yahæn Ær! Thay har trvælien sfie av da Ásva hor! Ant Thay ra esmerian Schva,"[51] answered Thuarnach determined, and without another word, he called the horse to his side and walked it back to the stables.

Annea felt exhausted, but she was not looking forward to the food or her classes... She truly needed a break from it all.

Thuarnach came back a minute later, while she was packing with trembling fingers the spare arrows in her quiver. The bow itself was useless, again, she would need a new one for tomorrow... Right now, however, the druid had other things in mind for her.

---

[49] "Where do you go, Annea? Is it not enough? I say yes!"
[50] "It is never enough, most Ancient Dragon Druid Thuarnach."
[51] "Enough, young one! You have worked enough with that horse today! Now, you go eat something."

"You have trained hard this month, Yahæn Ær. You have made big progress, but your heart is not here, yet."

She looked up from the quiver surprised by his words.

"Neya, muin Eonar Drkent Dryd Thuarnach, my heart is not here," she answered sincerely, "how could it be? I don't belong to this place, I never will. My father does not belong to this place, either. This is all wrong!"

Clumsily, she dropped the quiver and all the arrows scattered once again on the ground.

The druid came closer and kneeled down. He patiently collected all the arrows without saying a word or looking at her, his long white beard slightly brushing the ground.

Annea was still standing there motionless like a statue, she did not know what to say. She was ashamed, but at the same time surprised at her own honesty.

Thuarnach got up with some difficulty and addressed her once more, "Anneya, Oreash.[52] Time can only heal, time is the Dragon's friend, and time is your friend, too."

---

[52] Patience

Coming closer, he put a warm hand over the girl's shoulder, and gave her back the quiver with all its arrows. He then turned, and they both started walking back in silence to the entrance of the arena.

"Here," he said all of a sudden, extending what looked like a chunky, dry cookie to her, "it will keep your belly and your brain content for some time," and after a while he continued, "we'll do something different today, I want to take you back to a special place, a place where we can talk undisturbed. You will have your meal there."

They walked for about an hour without saying anything to each other. They crossed many busy neighbourhoods, the city was vibrant at this hour. They went through several twisted alleyways, and then they took to the dark Reaghil Dryd Sljk – to finally lose the Kechtás that had been following them.

"What do they want?" inquired Annea a little exasperated.

"Oh, they? So, you have noticed them, ah? Good, good," Thuarnach answered obliviously.

"So?" she pressed on.

"Those are Shya's men, not the king's. Don't you worry about them…"

"But what do they want?"

"The king's sister wants to know everything, Yahæn Ær. Your father and myself, we are being followed most of the time… And now, so are you."

He met her eyes with a tired smile. Was it pity she saw in those compassionate, aged eyes? She wasn't sure, but after that brief interaction they continued in silence for the rest of their underground journey, until at some point, Thuarnach turned right, and opened a door that led them straight out in the open again.

She did not recognise it at once, her eyes needed some time to get used to the light again. Then, unexpectedly, it dawned on her where they were: the little grove of coppiced trees she had been to with her father and the druid, on the very first day of her arrival!

It surely looked different without the snow, or was it her? She hadn't noticed it before, but the place had a generous waterfall, forming a gracious little pool, like a natural bath tub below it. Some kind of stony shrine had been placed beside the rocky elevation the water sprang from. Behind the coppiced trees, a row of higher trees had formed a perfect circle, a clearing in the forest, where the rays of the sun could kiss the grass undisturbed, and a patch of celestial blue sparkled the stream crossing the grove.

It was such a wonderful and peaceful place, she thought...

Thuarnach had, in silence, been watching her taking the place in for the first time. He knew very well how the magic of the place worked on the troubled mind.

"Ahhh, so you like it, then? See, not everything is terrible or challenging here. This is my favourite place in the city, my refuge, Yahæn Ær, and I'm happy to share it with you. Whenever you need time on your own, you can escape to this place. Just make sure you're not being followed..."

After a short pause, he continued, "Annea, you have seen much of the Arach ways by now, and still there is so much more... 'Ours should be the kingdom of wisdom and love,' those were my brother's own words when he planted the sapling of the great Caydúllien Ore of Reaghil Bheallemer."

He hesitated a little, but then went on, "you must know, Yahæn Ær, my brother's son is not much like him, the Skyarach Kingdom is being ruled by a selfish and arrogant tyrant, now. Asttrian is someone who does not listen to any counsel, and while his twin sister is his closest ally, no better she is. In fact, Shya is more dangerous than her brother, for she not only carries an envious soul, but she is also clever and cunning. As sad as it is to say this, Yahæn Ær, my nephew and niece are trying to destroy their father's life work, they are threatening to destroy this kingdom and with it their own father's memory. They are filled with hatred and revenge towards the Arach. Now, King Asttrian has done away with the rule of the Dragon Law, and is not honouring his father's wishes regarding his succession."

"But why, muin Eonar Drkent Dryd Thuarnach? What can motivate the king to destroy his father's heritage?"

She was shocked to hear this, not in her wildest thoughts could she understand why would someone do that, especially considering the evident success of the old king's reign.

"Da Drkarach Qvynne onn Kynn, a Dragon Queen or King, rules for centuries, Anneya, even millennia. Asttrian is not a true Arach. His mother, Queen Umbriel, was a Host Maiden and after Dragon Law, will always remain one. Just like her and his own sister, he could only enjoy longevity as long as his father, my brother Urarathan, lived and the magic of the dragon worked. Now that his father is dead, they will all last a normal human lifespan… But Asttrian and Shya are not bothered by such things. They have no interest in preserving their father's legacy for future generations. They'd rather live a short life in power, than a long one following the Arach Law."

"Oh, but, so what you're saying is that the old king was almost immortal?"

"Not quite, as you see, but it isn't an easy task to wound and kill a Dreà Arach."

"What do you mean?"

"Only dah Drymæd, the Three Evils, can kill us. The first is the most potent potion ever made out of devil's cherry, hemlock and wolfsbane. The second is a metal weapon tempered exclusively with dragon fire. The third, the deepest of sorrow. These three are lethal for us."

"What happened to your brother, then? Was he poisoned?"

"Wounded, a deadly arrow pierced him."

"I'm sorry…"

"So am I, Yahæn Ær."

"So, now, what's next?"

"Well, Asttrian is not interested in consolidating or keeping peace in the realm, so that the people of this kingdom thrive for generations to come. The people are not important to him, they never were, and my brother knew it. My nephew is driven only by revenge and envy towards those that were chosen to lead the kingdom into the future."

Thuarnach stopped and sighed deeply, his eyes suddenly covered by a cloak of sadness.

"We want to spare our people the pain that a war will bring, we want to help keep the realm at peace, and above all, we want to restore the rightful heir to the Skyarachti throne, my nephew Arachtan of the Anairarachti. I have summoned him, and he should have long arrived, but Asttrian and Shya are expecting Ara to come, Yahæn Ær, and have sent his royal knights to all corners of the realm to stop him. I fear that if he doesn't come in time, we will be forced to evacuate the city, with as many as we can take."

"What exactly do you mean, Thuarnach?"

"There are refuges, several in the mountains, druid temples guided by the stars and protected by Drkarach's magic, not even Asttrian would dare break into those sanctuaries and he has no Reaghil Dryd at his side to enter the temples. I'm his only contact with the druid order."

The druid fixed her eyes and continued, "Anneya, this place is becoming more and more dangerous for you and Lughan, by the day. Asttrian and Shya profoundly dislike Gæn Ær, like you, and after your arrival, you are both now under their focus…"

He stood up and walked around the grove, touching carefully the budding branches of the trees.

"You will be called to court soon, Anneya. Asttrian wants you to stay at Drkent Har as a Royal Guest Maiden to the queen, and we will not be able to stop him for long. If it comes this far, we will need to handle even without my nephew Arachtan's help."

"But I don't want to go anywhere, I've just found my father! Please, Thuarnach, you have to help us! We have to get back home!" she pleaded sincerely.

The druid turned to her, "Yahæn Ær," answered Thuarnach patiently, "I would do anything to keep you safe, and to help you. But as much as I want, I cannot help you with that… and there is not much I can do about Asttrian without further raising his suspicions, either. It might be that you will have to hide for some time, away from your father, away from Drkent Har, and you need to be ready for it, Anneya. Lughan loves you more than his life, that man would do anything for you, so don't break his heart. Learn your skills, learn to survive here and now, Anneya. Do it for you, and do it for him!"

"Drey teyn meist, right?" said Annea.

"So it is, Yahæn Ær, always try your best!"

"But where would you be sending me? Even if I make it out of the city, without you, how would I be able to find my way?"

The druid smirked at her, "I have my resources, Yahæn Ær. You wouldn't be alone, you would be travelling with Lughan's wife and the children, and some other friends of mine. They are also your family, now."

Lughan's Family

The day Annea had first arrived, a round-faced, little girl with cherry cheeks and a broad smile had been longingly waiting for them at the doorway of a perfectly round house.

'A Celtic round house,' she had wondered… She had seen them before in her history books, and now, along their way, there had been many like it.

This particular home, however, had nicely painted patterns decorating the outside walls that had called her attention. Colourful, spiralling animal forms were represented in an ecstatic dance towards the door opening. There were no windows, and it had a large, thatched roof overhang.

The small girl, of about four years of age, seeing that she would not approach the building any further, had moved towards her timidly. She had realised, then, something she was not entirely prepared to accept: the girl actually wore an unmistakable smile, her father's!

'A younger daughter,' thought Annea with a sting.

The girl had been holding a fragile daisy between her tiny, dirty fingers, and had stopped in front of Annea to offer her the flower, with a cheeky, toothless smile.

For a moment, she had reminded her of Pete and Henry... Where would they be? People must have been looking for them, for her... She had been extremely worried about the boys, but in her present situation, there was absolutely nothing she could have done to find them...

As soon as they had reached the threshold, a boy had come running and calling out from inside the house, and a few seconds later, a slim, middle-aged woman ambling her way between the two children, had taken Annea's hands in hers, with tears in her eyes.

She had said something to Annea, something that she, obviously, had not understood, at the time. She had seemed sincerely pleased to see her, for she kept smiling at her wholeheartedly. She had a beautiful smile, which was accompanied by sweet, bright coffee eyes, while her hair, pinned together behind her head, left her kind, delicate face exposed.

'She is not an exuberant beauty, but so pleasant to behold,' Annea thought, 'nothing like mother, really...'

Caught in her own thoughts, she had not realised that she was being literally dragged into the house by the children, Lynthor and Lynne, who were now engaged in a lively, indistinctive chatter.

Once inside the building, she could see there was a hearth fire burning in the centre of the room, and all felt warm and cosy. The smoke was being channelled through a hole in the ceiling, right above the hearth. Beside it, a rough, wooden table had been set with several colourful, ceramic bowls containing some kind of hot liquid that was smoking timidly.

Annea was starving, and she felt relieved to be welcomed somewhere, at last. It had been such a long night followed by an even longer day...

And so, she ate and drank without asking that day, and she slept soundly, without even noticing that she was actually sleeping with her newly-found, younger siblings. So much so, that she slept through for two whole days. She heard voices in the background, and felt the touch of someone on her cheeks from time to time, but no one dared disturb her sleep.

On the third day, Thuarnach finally came back to Lughan's home to inquire about the newcomer. Annea had been having breakfast with the family, or rather watching them have their breakfast, for the first time. Lynthor and Lynne were enjoying some kind of porridge, while the adults were eating some kind of meat and a soup. There was milk and eggs, too, but she didn't feel like eating any of it, she was craving for a fresh pastry with marmalade and a coffee, but unfortunately, these seemed not to be on the menu, today... Slowly, it was dawning on her that this might be her daily breakfast for the rest of her life if she stayed here, and this might just be the beginning, who knew what other surprises were awaiting her... Oh, how she wanted that coffee!

Seeing that she wasn't touching anything, her father's new wife, looked at Thuarnach concerned and said something to him.

Thuarnach took something out of the leather pouch hanging from his belt, and gave it to the woman, who readily put some water to heat over the hearth.

'If they think I'm drinking that...' Annea said to herself.

But her father interrupted her thoughts, "child, you need to have something. If you don't eat, at least try what Rasmei is brewing for you. Thuarnach is the best herbalist I know, all I know, he taught me."

"Right, so he won't be poisoning me, just yet," she answered with a grin, "anyways, what herbs has he chosen for my pottage, may I ask?"

"Oh, no, my Little Pandora, it's just a herbal infusion this time. He knows how you must be feeling, but also knows that we want to keep you going for a couple of hours - you need to start your training today, I'm afraid. We cannot afford to lose more time, you see. So, he has brought dried melissa leaves, dried camomile flowers and some mentha pipertia, that is, peppermint leaves. Together, these three will take the anxiety away and help you concentrate. We'll brew enough, if you want more, later."

And with a smirk he added, "I will make sure to find some sausage and bread for you for lunch."

"Oh, dad, how very kind of you, but don't you worry, as soon as I feel better, I will eat whatever it is you are eating."

"Dried frog-legs with wood garlic sauce?" he laughed whole-heartedly and winked at her.

"Ok, maybe not," she admitted sincerely.

Her dad had not changed much after all, she thought. He had always been good-natured, and he definitely knew how to cheer her up. They could still talk and laugh for hours together. However, all dressed up like the rest of them, and so comfortable in their language, at times, he seemed a complete stranger, too.

He looked happy, though, and this made her happy, in turn. She could also see why. He had a beautiful family with Rasmei, who was always kind and patient to everyone. What's more, seeing him like this, she honestly could not imagine him back with her mother, Lara Menard. He truly seemed to fit in... At some point, however, they would need to talk about their return...

Annea did as she was told, and slowly sipped down the herbal infusion from the beautifully decorated ceramic cup she had been offered. And while Lughan and Thuarnach were engaged in some important conversation, she saw the opportunity to silently observe the children and their mother collecting and storing the leftovers for tomorrow's breakfast.

Rasmei was tall and slender, she moved gracefully around the house, and from time to time, she would look up to her and smile. She wore a long tunic, more of a long dress, in the exact same colours and pinned like her own with iron brooches in the form of the triskele. Now, that she thought about it, the little girl was wearing the same colours and the same brooches on her tunic, too. She wondered if there was a reason why they all wore the same stuff. She would ask her father later...

Lynthor had been sent out and came back a little while later with two buckets full of water. He was tall and slender, too. She could see he was still quite young, maybe 10? He was very energetic and liked teasing his little sister whenever possible, but both children laughed a lot together, and were kind and helped their mother without hesitating.

Her father's was a happy family, they all treated each other kindly and helped out in the house. Just like the Bergmanns, the children were joyful and smart, so very different from her own family. She felt extremely happy for him, however, happy that he had found a home, even though it was so far away from their own. She could understand now why he would not see the need to hurry his return, or even why he would rather prolong his stay indefinitely... It was all so very different from the family she had had! She remembered the fights, the screams, her parents had always been in disagreement about something, and as much as she tried, she could not remember the two being happy together. She was very young, back then, to remember any details, but she had felt the tension between them, her little sister crying in the corners, her granny taking them by the hand, bringing them out to the gardens to distract them. Later, her sister Bella always distant and rude, her mother, blaming her for all ill that had come to the family. No, in fact, the family her father had left behind was all, but a happy one.

Chapter Fifteen: Drkenstar

18th day of Aarglas, YD 300,
Dryd Slijk, beneath the procession road to Drkarach Ælbstæl Cathrie

The druid was breathing heavily. He was in a hurry, there was no time to lose, and he knew he was being followed by the Drkarach Kechtás.

In truth, every druid journeying through the kingdom without a royal permit was a potential traitor to the crown, or so had Asttrian decreed, and therefore, any travelling druid was being followed.

Dryd Rayka had just managed to lose the royal knights in the village, at the crossroads to the procession road. He had used the crowds at the market to disappear into the hidden Dryd Sljk that connected both the old Myzar Kæyn and the Drkarach Ælbstæl Cathrie. But it hadn't been easy, the Kechtás had keen eyes and were in exceptional form, Dryd Rayka, on the other hand, was not a young man anymore, and he needed breaks to rest, making him slow and easy to follow.

His old friend Thuarnach had given him specific orders. He had been entrusted something very precious, something that demanded utter secrecy and swift handling. It had taken him already too long, but it surely had been the safest way.

Thuarnach had been quite clear about Rayka's end destination, too.

Once he had reached Reaghil Bheallemer and taken the sword, there was no more time to lose, or their cause would be lost. Drkenstar had to be brought to the best guarded place in the whole kingdom, the Drkarach Ælbstæl Cathrie,[53] where not even the Kechtás would go searching.

Now, within the bowels of the earth, druid Rayka felt more confident that he would be able to reach his final destination, even though it was still a long way to walk and a steep ascent inside the tunnel, with little light, and even less air.

The Reaghil Dryd Sljk to the Ælbstæl temple ran underneath the most prominent procession road of the kingdom. Placed halfway between the Myzar Dryd Kæyn, where Urarathan and his people had founded their first settlement, and the booming capital of the Skyarach, the Ælbstæl procession road was also most of the time deserted. This had a good reason, of course. Only during druidic

---

[53] The Drkarach Ælbstæl Cathrie, the Seat of the White Dragon Star, was the most sacred and best secured of all Dryd Kæyns. It was situated where today's Feldberg is, between the Altkönig, where the Myzar Kæyn was, and the Hedietrank Oppidum, where Reaghil Bheallemer was situated. A dragon road and a procession road joined the temples with the city, and some little satellite villages flourished along this way.

festivals, did other druids were summoned or given access to the temple. In regular days, like this one, no one was allowed to enter the royal druid temple of Ælbstæl, that is, no one but the Ælbstæl Reaghil Dryds, one of which was Thuarnach.

His old friend had taken him once to visit the temple, shortly after its completion, he had been so proud... Rayka would never forget the impression it had caused on him: for a moment, he had thought to be back in Seannanorthai.[54]

Druid Rayka, on his part, had never aspired to enter the order of Ælbstæl. He praised himself for having remained a humble country druid, a druid of the people. One who helped and schooled his people whole-heartedly, Rayka preferred to consider himself a devoted mystic with a soft spot for engineering, astrology and the working of metal. And although he had loyally followed Thuarnach on his many journeys through most kingdoms of the Dreà Arachti, and had helped him build up temples and schools all over the Skyarach kingdom, the centres of power had no meaning for him, anymore.

Rayka himself not being a Thuatharachti, like Thuarnach or Urarathan, had always missed the ancient ways of the old Kingdom of Seannarach. After the foundation of the Skyarach Kingdom, and when his part had been completed, Rayka had silently settled in the village of Neybhrealle, a small town known

---

[54] Ancient Red City of the Arach.

for its good craftsmen - one of which he had proudly become - and had served as Drkent Dryd at the Polarys temple nearby, but had never accepted to become its master. He was most content leading a peaceful country life.

He had met Thuarnach long ago, in the western mountainous region of the Seannarach Kingdom, centuries after it had lost most of its glory. It had been a dark time, then, when dark lords toyed with dark magic. But ancient wisdom had been most jealously kept within the walls of the oldest of all Arach cities, and druid Rayka had been very lucky to have been taught by many wise masters, until the day he had been forced to escape the city with a most well-kept secret, a secret he would only share with his friend Thuarnach.

Yes, the two druids had known each other for far too many years to count them, now, and they had shared too many adventures. Rayka trusted Thuarnach with his life. However, their friendship was being put to the test, once again.

Rayka owed many favours to his friend, and although his mission was more than extremely dangerous, he had committed to the cause, as soon as he had heard of it. As the wise and seasoned man he was, he had understood the dangers of absolute power in the hands of a mischievous tyrant like king Asttrian, and he knew his friend would have never asked, if it hadn't been a matter of imminent importance.

There was one thing that was bothering him, however. He could not get rid of the strange feeling that his friend was hiding something, that he was not telling him the complete truth...

It all had started about a year ago, when a jay from the capital had brought a sealed druid letter with a coded message from Thuarnach. The king had died under unclear circumstances, no one was to be trusted, and he needed his skills and help. It was not like Thuarnach to ask him like this, he knew. This was something altogether different.

Druid Rayka had never liked power, and after a long life in the service of the common people, he had come to despise it altogether. Ever since he had left Seannanorthai, Rayka had sworn to himself to stay clear from any centre of power, be it the court or any capital city, and Thuarnach had respected this all along... Until now.

So, how could he say no?

Thuarnach had the right and the duty to sit at court and protect his and his brother's heritage. They had both worked ceaselessly to build up the Skyarach kingdom, assuring its political stability, social welfare and great prosperity. He, Rayka, did not need to understand Thuarnach. He knew that whatever his friend was up to, it was for the best of his people.

And so, late that Annoras,[55] druid Rayka had left the little town of Neybhrealle behind, with two newly forged treasures for his old friend Thuarnach.

The first of the two had been his own decision. As a proof of his loyalty and trust for all these years of friendship, he was bringing with him a true one-to-one copy of his astronomical metal disc, the Rœnneral.[56] The same he had brought from the ancient Seannarach kingdom to help his druid friend design his new cities and temples, the very disc he had used to save his most precious treasure...

He knew Thuarnach had always longed for one, but had never dared ask. Ahh, yes, old venerable Thuarnach! His friend had always respected Rayka's ways.

Rayka, on his part, had always secretly suspected that Thuarnach would have handled differently with his treasure if the disc had been in his possession, and so, he had never been truly inclined to share it with him. But things were different, now.

---

[55] Month of the fruits and the colour red, 6th month of the Arach calender
[56] Rœnneral was the name the Arach gave to what we know as the disc of Nebra.

As useful as it once had been, Rayka knew all too well how the wisdom and power contained in that metal disc could become extremely dangerous if seized by the wrong hands. But most of all, its linked magic posed the greatest of threats to all he had once held dear. He had to make sure no one would ever be able to find it again. From now onwards, it would rest safely hidden beneath the earth, under the great Polarys Kæyn, and it would remain his secret until his very last breath.

Thuarnach's copy, on the other hand, only contained the astronomical wisdom and magic portal powers unchained and without binding spells. Rayka would leave an encrypted message for his friend to know its exact hiding place, safely beneath the great Ælbstæl Cathrie, together with the sword...

To this purpose, however, Rayka would finally have to face the White Drkarach, and this was the greatest challenge of all, something he had been avoiding ever since the day he had first set foot in the kingdom. He owed the dragons, he had stolen from them, and his heart had been broken from it. He would never forgive himself, but he would do it again if it was necessary... For her, for Ærynel.

Under other circumstances, Dryd Rayka should have had nothing to fear about. He was a good man, he had a good heart and had helped many, in his long life. The White Dragon, as Drkarach was known, was ancient, wise, and just, but it was known that only those of pure soul, those who had nothing to regret, would come out alive from Ælbstæl Cathrie. Having denied the dragons what was rightfully theirs, it would now depend, whether Rayka was given the chance to explain himself to Drkarach, or not.

It might turn out to be his very last trial, he thought, but he and Thuarnach had come this far together, and he was not going to let his friend down now. No, he was finally letting Thuarnach into the secrets of the disc's magic, yet another secret the two druids would share together and take to their graves. Unless, of course, the right person could be found and entrusted with the knowledge, once they faded away.

The second of the two treasures he was bearing was currently the most problematic of the two: he had left the little town of Neybhrealle with a newly forged copy of Drkenstar, the old king's sword.

He had been the master smith to forge Urarathan's sword in the first place, and so it fell to him to produce a perfect enough copy that would live up to its original. This would prove a feat almost impossible to achieve, and it would require all his skills. Drkenstar had been one of his masterpieces, a splendid sword, intended as a very special gift from Thuarnach for his brother, the king.

Urarathan's sword was an outstanding example both of druidic art and metallurgic mastery, at the same time. Made entirely out of a single steel core, its double-edged blade was smooth as silk, and as sharp as a woman's tongue. On both flat sides of the blade, a magical druidic inscription in ancient Seannarach read: "This is the Dragon's gift, humanity's shield, Urarathan's Drkenstar."

Through this sword ran a very powerful spell forged with dragon fire. If its point was directed to the firmament, the sword was able to clear the skies surrounding its holder. It thus could break storms and winds as its owner pleased. If directed to the heart of a person, something astonishing would happen: that person was compelled to speak the truth and only the truth, and if his or her heart was treacherous, the person would instantly die. This made Drkenstar a very powerful and dangerous object to possess.

But on top of this, the king's sword was also regarded as the most precious jewel symbolizing the sceptre of Skyarach power. Its entire hilt was shaped in the form of a golden dragon, the guard representing its open wings, in its centre, a prominent transparent white gem that was called the heart stone, for it glowed and changed colour showing an opponent's true feelings. The pommel, in turn, was delicately sculpted and carved in the form of a dragon head, with curled spiralling ears and bright green gems for eyes, which gave the illusion of an intense, ever staring green glance. Nothing like it had been seen before in the new Arach kingdoms.

The challenge facing Rayka was that the original and its copy needed to be identical, like two drops of water, with one important difference: the second was never going to be given magical powers to wield upon the world. Physically impossible to distinguish from each other, only well-seasoned druids would be able to recognise one from the other with certainty.

Druid Rayka had made sure to use a stone that resembled the heart stone but manipulated it to produce three different colours, tricking its user into believing every one favoured him.

By replacing the sword, they would be able to permanently hide the true sword from the new usurper king, without raising more suspicions. And even if Asttrian ever discovered the sword was a fake, by then, it would be too late.

Yes, Thuarnach's plan was thought through, but the risks of being caught on the way were also very high.

While he would use the Reaghil Dryd Sljk whenever possible, Rayka would still be easily recognizable as a Polarys druid in the capital. He had to be very sneaky, and keep a low profile so as to exchange one sword for the other without ever meeting his friend Thuarnach. It was of utmost importance for the success of their mission, that they never met.

And so, they had set a specific place in the druid tunnel, where Rayka would find the king's sword and replace it by its replica. Then, the old druid would continue his journey out of the city, up towards the Myzar temple, and after the second village, he would go undercover again, so that no one would really know his whereabouts.

He had no idea what exactly Thuarnach intended to do with the new sword, and this was fine. In case he would be found and interrogated, he would not be able to tell them anything, for he knew nothing. Before leaving the capital, however, Rayka would make sure to let Thuarnach know about his intentions with the Rœnneral disc. A pity they were not going to meet this time, he would have sincerely enjoyed one of those long talks he used to have with his life-long friend... He was feeling worn out by time these days, as if he himself had also been buried under the temple with Ærynel's Rœnneral.

Well, it was duty calling, perhaps his last mission, he could feel it in his bones... There was little hope after meeting Drkarach, and even less of making a safe journey back to Neybhrealle. It had already taken him so very long, much longer than usual to reach Reaghil Bheallemer. He had had to stay alert and avoid all roads, coming all the way through old, forgotten mountain trails, under druid tunnels, and avoiding any big town on the way. Rayka was too exhausted, by now. He felt his strength leaving him...

'I'm an old man,' he thought, 'when have I grown this old? When have I grown this tired?'

With a sigh, Rayka finally came out of the last stretch of druid tunnel, and continued his ascent towards the unknown, now blended by the setting sun. The majestic Drkarach Ælbstæl Cathrie, all carved out of white stone like Drkent Har, already loomed on top of the highest peak, shining brightly like a star while a red sun kissed the snow-covered landscape with its last, timid rays.

"It was the day when I let you go… The day when I left you by the Caydùllien Ore, that was the day I became an old man," he answered to himself, and then, druid Rayka patiently hobbled up the last part of the empty road.

Chapter Sixteen: Treacherous Valley

18th Day of Aarglas, 300DYD,
somewhere in the Lahirynn,[57] close to the town of Aarfael

The charming Lahirynn, with its beautiful little villages, and it's narrow gorges and valley expanses, had proven to be more of a challenge than expected.

Arachtan and the others had reached Daing na Lahirynn, the Lahirynn fortress, through the Dryd Sljk, only to find out that the little trade and taxing town, as well as the fortress itself were fully in the hands of king Asttrian's Kechtás. To make matters worse, Ealator, waking up right after their crazy ride through the druid tunnels, had been in a very bad mood to discover himself kidnapped by his own sister. He had put up such a fight that Thuaì had to give him a black eye to make him stop complaining. And although Ealator did not like it in the least, he was made to understand that he had no other option now, but to come with them.

Luckily, they had found a little, snow-covered barge at the mouth of the tunnel, which ran right pass under the fortress, and ended

---

[57] The Lahir valley, the word "Ynn" meaning valley.

about a mile further upstream the Lahir. As things were, however, this had not been of great help to them.

They would have to go against the now heavy current to reach the first Kæyn, and to use the barge, they would need strong draft horses to tow them upstream, which they did not have right now, let alone the fact that they would be completely exposed if they were to use the waterway here. On top of that, their helpers, the smugglers, having waited for them the agreed time with their horses and provisions, had eventually been forced to move forward to the first Kæyn. So, while Arachtan aided a much reluctant Ealator to walk steadily, Skeor and Thuaì carried together the frozen, flat barge over their heads.

With their new load, the company left the Dryd Sljk on foot, and by the cover of night to avoid attracting attention, only the animals in the surrounding forests took note of the strange, little crowd. But carrying this extra weight made them a little slower by foot, so from time to time, they risked letting the barge in the water to carry their satchels, as well as Skymnia and Ealator, who were both weary and could not walk long distances, along the slippery and uneven riverbank.

After some time, they reached the village of Seannæhg,[58] named after a sacred well of the same name. They were thirsty and hungry, and luckily for them, this medium-sized village, which specialised in the cultivation of apple and sheep breeding, proved to be exactly what they were needing.

Apart from the fact that they were now far away from the Rheann and this area was of no interest to their cousin Asttrian, the people here were friendly and welcoming to strangers.

A farmer's family opened their home to them and offered them fresh, bubbly cider and some mutton soup, which was still warm. It was a most welcome gift, for they had not eaten properly for a long time, and the month of Wbentas was showing no mercy to them, either. The icy temperatures kept the trees and the birds tinkling with frost, while tiny icicles glinted over the landscape.

Sitting at the warm hearth together with the seven-headed family, the company asked their hosts if they could spend the night there to gather new energy to continue their journey upstream, the next day.

Ara further asked if they could buy a draft horse to tow them upstream, until they reached Aarfael, the rock of the Aar, where they would need to go into hiding again. Ara was expecting

---

[58] Today's city of Nassau

reinforced security around Aarfael and Har na Lahirynn,[59] and he did not want to risk using the boat after the confluence of the Aar and the Lahir rivers.

And so, they spent a restful night hidden in the village's mill, and they were given cooked eggs, sheep milk, three sheep skins and traditional bread balls, as prepared by the locals, as well as three full bottles of delicious cider to take along the way. The family also arranged for them to get a horse the next morning from the village's stock, and they took no payment for it...

"It's been an honour to serve you," the farmer's wife said.

"Sorry, it is us who are honoured to have made your acquaintance, muine Ærin," answered Arachtan, wondering what she actually meant, "but meaning no offence, you have given us more than enough. It is a most generous offer, but we can only accept under the condition that we will both pay you back for lending us the horse, and make sure to have it returned to you, as soon as we get to our destination."

"Do not fuss about that horse, muin Ærn, it's the least we can do to help you. Now, give those monsters the slip!" she answered, "and be very careful, they have eyes and ears everywhere, in the

---

[59] Today's cities of Diez and Limburg respectively.

Lahirynn, too. Muinærnd[60] saw two prowling downstream this very morning!"

Visibly surprised by the last remark, Arachtan hesitated for a moment.

"Thayng Thay, muine Ærin," he said finally, with a light bow.

Arachtan then urged the others to get going straight away. He would have wanted to ask more questions about the Kechtás stationed on the Lahir region, but there was no time left for that now.

They had been towed by a strong, muscular Aaraden[61] horse for about three hours, when, suddenly, they saw a boy upstream, standing as if petrified on a lonely rock, close to the southern shore. He was staring at them, red eyes and a panic face.

He continued fixing them, but did not move. After some time, however, he started calling out after them.

Thuaì, Skeor and Ara instantly knew that something was very wrong. What should they do? If they crossed, it could be a trap.

---

[60] Husband
[61] Local breed of draft horse, tireless and stout.

Besides, the current could easily take them... But leave the panicked boy there?

They decided to wait until their barge came closer to the rock the child was standing on. They, then, would see how to best make it over to the other side, or if to tow the child over to theirs with the help of the horse.

Just then, out of nowhere, three huge dragon horses sprang towards them from the other shore, crossing the river at the same point where the boy had been standing. The boy, in turn, pointed his finger towards them, and started screaming madly the word Nyamás, death, while falling into the heavy current of the Lahir to irreversibly disappear stream downwards.

It all went so quickly, no one really knew how it happened.

One thing they could all gather: three Kechtás had been hiding in the bushes with their horses, patiently awaiting their prey. They might have heard word or just been patrolling the area for weeks. Either way, Ara and his brothers had not expected them there and then, and it was this encounter that would mark a decisive turn in their journey.

Ara, Skeor, Thuaìden and Ealator had to somehow tow the barge with all their strength as close to the shore as they managed, arrows whistling past their heads, just in time to jump out of it and charge against their aggressors.

Standing up to their knees in the bitter, cold water, they could not move freely, but they understood to attack the horses first, while commanding Skymnia to untie their horse and flee with it as fast as she could.

The strenuous fight went on endlessly. The three Anairachti princes were well-trained warriors and in good shape, a good match for the almighty Kechtás. Ealator, on the other hand, was just barely being kept on his feet by all three in joint effort... It would have been much easier to fight without him.

After they were able to dismount the knights, each prince took up one to fight against. This time surely until death decided who to call first.

At some point, Thuaì dealt a decisive blow to the fastest and strongest Kechtá, who had actually been leading the raid. He pierced his right hand with his short knife and was able to push him into deeper water, where he lost foot, and was rapidly swallowed by the strong current. This one was not going to bother them for now.

Thuaì then joined Skeor, and together they killed the second Kechtá rapidly. While Skeor was an excellent swordsman, his older brother was a master in throwing knives. So, while the Kechtá was concentrated fighting Skeor, Thuaì expertly launched his short knife, which landed straight through the Kechtá's heart.

Ara was holding his attack. He kept his young Kechtá busy, while observing how his brothers were doing. He didn't want more people to die for Asttrian's madness. His druid soul bled every time he saw people dying and suffering. A part of him had always refused to become the full-blooded warrior he was expected to be. And now, despite the urgency of using his physical strength to stop this evil, he still respected and cherished the Kechtási Order...

But Thuaì, without thinking it twice, took his short deadly knife out of the dead knight's heart, and in one fluid movement, threw it towards the still standing Kechtá. The pain took the knight by surprise. The knife pierced the knight's thigh in the exact moment when Ara was charging with his sword, and he could not parry the blow anymore. Ara's sword cut off his right arm clean.

Ara got hold of the knight before he fell into the water and dragged him all the way to the shore, both covered in mud and blood, and shivering. The young Kechtá, with an excruciating effort, managed to produce something out of a pouch hanging inside his armour. He tugged at Ara's muscular arm and asked him to stop.

"En er muin Kechtásinuar,"[62] he said, "it was given to me by the old king himself... please, find my wife! Find Arnya and give it to her! Let her know I died fighting bravely..."

He breathed heavily, his sight was blurring, but after a few seconds, he managed to go on, "I am no one to question my king's commands, and I don't know what it is that you have done, but I can tell you are a fair warrior, a true one, may I ask your name before I die?"

Ara nodded slightly, "Arachtan Skyarach is my name."

The Kechtá opened his eyes in utter amazement, he obviously had not known who they were chasing after, he had been given a physical description only, no explanations. In truth, most of the Kechtási Order was being kept in the dark about the true intentions of the king. Only a few, selected knights truly understood what they were doing.

With a last effort, he pleaded again, "please, find her, find Arnya! My name is–" But then, he died.

Finding Skymnia turned out to be a hard task. The Lahirynn roads were narrow and winding, in bad shape and not properly traced,

---

[62] "It is my Kechtási ring."

the faithful product of a whimsical landscape. From time to time, the greyish, slate face of the mountains would end so steeply into the river bed, that it would cut off the road abruptly, at which point, another winding path, all the way up, would have to be followed to reach to the other side, where the next part of the road continued.

They had been walking for about three hours, with no signs of their cousin or the horse. They were exhausted from the fight and the ascent, and, now, the river took a sharp turn westward and a big, stony wall raised solemnly before their eyes.

Here, the only way to pass to the northeast Lahirynn route was through the river. There was no path or stairs, and the cliffs were so steep, there was no way anyone could climb all the way over to the other side.

"Where could she be hiding?" wondered her brother.

"She must have taken to the water, Ealator, she is fleeing but she's not mad," answered Skeor, "the current here is strong, but not deep."

"That would be madness!" put in Ealator, "my sister can't swim! Plus, there is no way you can guess what's on the other side…"

"True, but we told her to get as far as she could get, remember?" continued Thuaì, "I think Skeor is right, this is the only way to continue northeast."

Ara had been weighing their options, but he agreed with Skeor, too. They were going to get waist-deep in the icy water and tow the barge with their belongings behind them to the other side, or else their journey had ended here.

"Skymnia is a good rider, cousin," he said, "your sister is brave, she must have chosen to risk her way forward on the horse… we will go the same way."

After some discussion as to who would be covering the front and who the rear, they started off with the crossing.

They could be seen from far away, and from many directions, now. It was a tedious and slow march against the current, and they were all too aware of their being exposed, but no matter how hard they tried, they could not move any faster.

After what felt like hours, they were able to reach the edge of the wall. Soon they would be able to see what was on the other side.

Feeling the exhaustion in his bones, Ealator stumbled uncontrolled, and would have been carried away by the current, had Skeor not been close enough to get hold of him just on time.

Pushing their way further, they could now hear a moaning female voice, and a horse neighing nervously in the background.

"Do you hear that? It must be them," said Skeor.

As they finally were able to turn around the great wall and see what lay beyond, they were not happy with the view they were presented.

Right behind the wall, and rising halfway to the northeast shore, there was a small islet. From their position, they could only see a pile of undefined mass all scrambled together, resting on top of the small islet. But the sound was coming straight out of there, and the closer they came, the more it was clear that it was Skymnia...

The four men fought the current and the cold as their most hated enemies. Suddenly, they all lost foot, and could only continue swimming. They struggled greatly to reach the islet, which was surrounded by a rocky bed and dozens of whimsical swirling pools. This made it even more difficult to climb on top of it. They tied the barge to a large rock so the current wouldn't steal it, and moved on out as fast as their feet would carry them.

Ara couldn't help but wonder, how on earth had the horse managed to get up there...

"Sister, are you ok?!" cried Ealator.

She was not conscious, but she was moaning in pain. The horse had a broken leg and was lying over Skymnia's legs, her beautiful golden hair, scattered in the mud.

They would need to raise the horse and pull their cousin free. But as sad as it was to leave a loyal friend behind, the animal was not going to make it out of this. It would not be able to walk again, the bone had been cut through, and this would lead to its certain death…

Skeor was the first one to reach the two. He bent over Skymnia and touched her brow.

"She is very cold, brother, she is shivering," he said to Ara, "we shouldn't wait too long."

All rapidly moved closer, while Ara took his knife out of its scabbard and promptly slit the poor beast's throat. Then, he carefully placed both his hands on the horse's head.
"I thank you, my friend, for your loyal service and carrying her into safety. Rest now, Yhiria Færianásva[63] is calling you, there is nothing to be afraid of…"

---

[63] The wide green plain of horses, the place horses go when they die.

A few seconds later, he turned to the others, "Eala, you will carefully pull your sister from under the horse when I give you the signal. Thuaì, Skeor, we lift the horse up, come on."

And so, the four men worked together harmoniously for the first time in their journey. They managed to take Skymnia from under the horse, and slowly placed her in their barge, covering her with their woollen cloaks and furs, which were still dry. They moved the horse and buried it hastily, as they had done with the last Kechtá. There was no time to lose, however. By now, the rest of the Kechtási unit that was stationed at the Lahir had certainly heard about the incident close to Seannæhg. It was of utmost importance they avoided any further encounter around Aarfael and Har na Lahirynn. They could not afford exposure with Skymnia like this.

They pressed on through the whirling currents of the Lahir, dragging the barge with Skymnia behind them. The water was ice cold, and the ground was so muddy and uneven that they often lost footing, making the progress tedious and wearisome.

Just as they managed to reach the nearest shore, and find cover beneath a group of trees, a group of three Kechtás appeared around the far corner of the grey wall. What would they do now?

Luckily for them, the knights did not come over to this side of the shore. In truth, these Kechtás did not seem to be after someone in particular, they were simply patrolling the area. Most probably, they had not yet heard about their narrow escape.

Skymnia did not recover consciousness for two long days, so they had to delay their journey once more.

They were lucky to find cover in an ancient, abandoned Krayn,[64] where they kindled a fire that burned day and night to keep Skymnia warm and any marauder animal away.

Ara had then enough time to examine her exhaustively. He checked she had no wounds on her head, or anything life-threatening. Her legs, though, had been smashed to the ground by the impact and the horse's weight. Even if she waked up now, she would not be able to walk for quite a while.

Still, luckily for her, the ground had been soft, and she had suffered a couple of superficial scratches but no major open wounds. Her right leg, however, would take longer to recover. It had been twisted in an awkward angle, and Ara was certain that the thigh bone and maybe the knee cap had been broken and the muscles torn… Yes, it would take some time to heal, but he could help her to some extent.

---

[64] Cave

He had some powerful medicinal herbs, seeds and roots in his satchel that would help alleviate the pain considerably, and he would treat both legs with special ointments, and immobilize the broken one with the twigs they could find, and the bandages made of flax he always carried with him in his journeys.

But it would take some time. They would have to brew the tea out of the hemp roots, and then make a decoction of its seeds to mix with marmot and lavender oil. First, they would need to somehow make her drink the tea to ease the pain, and then gently rub the oil onto her legs, to disinfect and reduce inflammation. Skeor offered to assist Ara with Skymnia, who continued moaning in her sleep, and so the two spent most of the time working together.

Thuaì and Ealator, on their part, had to put up with each other's company while hunting and taking turns as sentries. The Krayn was well concealed among old trees and thick bushes, but that would not help if the royal knights came searching after them. At least, Ealator's attitude appeared to have changed, he seemed more determined to cooperate, now.

So far, they had stayed unnoticed, but time was pressing. Skymnia would need more medicine than Ara had with him, and a more thorough therapy if she was to walk again, anytime soon. She needed enough rest and druidic care, and this Ara could not provide here, in the middle of the forest, and being chased by the dangerous Drkarach Kechtás. Now, more than ever, they needed to reach the first Vwylrynn Kæyn swiftly.

But how? They had no horse, they had to keep hiding along the way, and they would have to carry Skymnia in the barge all along…

Chapter Seventeen: Asttrian King Of The Skyarach

5th day of Wbentas[65], 300YD,
Drkent Har, Reaghil Bheallemer

Asttrian was alone, waiting impatiently on the west balcony of Drkent Har, staring at the distant walls of his city.

"Where are they? They should be here already!" How dare they keep him waiting...

He had been waiting for this day to come for quite some time, now. He had suspected his uncle Thuarnach would try delaying the matter, so he had made sure to commit them to bring the guest maiden to court for royal scrutiny around a month after her arrival.

In reality, he just wanted to make sure nobody was going to spoil his new toy. Sure, the girl would need to master the Arach tongue before serving him, but, most importantly, she had to be acquainted with the Arach traditions concerning the art of love and especially how to please her king. And he was sure nothing of

---

[65] Second month of an Ynar Drkent.

the sort was going to happen under Thuarnach's or his guest friend's supervision.

Therefore, King Asttrian had swiftly made up his mind, he was going to have his guest maiden brought to court as soon as she could decently communicate, no matter what his council, his uncle or his sister thought...

Shya, of course, was going to give the girl a hard time, but as long as she did not inflict permanent damage to her, she could have her share of fun.

He heard the trumpets announcing the court summoning, and went back in. He would walk the Snake's Tunnel on his own, he needed some time to go through his arguments on the way to court. He would leave the druid no chance to counter his will this time...

The great carved doors made of pure gold that led to the White Hall[66] stood wide open, expectant to receive the young Skyarach king, the sound of the trumpets now announcing his entrance. Instantly, everybody turned and stood up to greet His Majesty,

---

[66] White Hall or Hall of the Dragon is the name of Drkent Har's main dragon courtroom.

and contrary to every expectation, he entered alone, without his sister or his mother.

The king strutted across the hall somewhat irritated. He scanned the crowd to see that his uncle was not there yet, his frustration slowly flaring up into fury …

He sat on the throne and nodded to his subjects, they all went back to their seats.

'Pack of weasels!' the king thought when looking at the crowd surrounding him, 'you're not coming to party in my honour, but you infest my hall to get a peek on my new toy! Well, I'll please you tonight… It'll definitely be fun, at least for me.'

The Hall of the Dragon was fuller than usual. In fact, it was so full that a large number of seats had been added, and the room felt overwhelmingly crowded.

Almost every noble family had come to see the new guest maiden the king was so interested in. Word had it that she was of an outstanding beauty, yet almost no one had ever met her. People also said, the king had invited her to become a royal guest maiden to Queen Umbriel, which was something very uncommon for a stranger, a newcomer who did not even speak their language well. Of course, malicious gossip had it, that the maiden was actually meant for the king himself and he wouldn't be much bothered if she was speechless altogether.

If this last piece of information was true, however, the noble host families and Arach families of the realm had another reason for concern.

Their erratic, new king, who was still unmarried, tended to make his decisions without consulting anyone. No sooner had his father died, he had done away with the Thriar, the king's small council, and the Dragon Law, only extending more power to his Drkarach Kechtás. There were rumours that he had even imprisoned his aunt Lady Skenya of the Rheann, and her two children. Several advisors from the noble families that had served under his father's rule, had been all promptly dismissed, too. For these positions, he had chosen men from the Drkarach Kechtás, who despite being great, disciplined soldiers, made terrible statesmen, as it was well known. Thus, most of the host nobles were by now seriously concerned about how Asttrian's rule endangered the wellbeing of the kingdom.

As a consequence, noble families were increasingly speculating with getting the king married to one of their daughters, and in this way regain some degree of influence in His Majesty's court. They were, of course, not counting with this foreign girl to cross their plans, and they were surely going to do everything in their power to get rid of her.

At that moment, Shya entered the hall so briskly that she did not give the trumpets enough time to announce her properly. She fixed her eyes on her brother, and walked straight to him, without looking right or left. Everyone could see that she was fuming…

'What was he thinking to summon a public scrutiny? Isn't enough shame that he wants to bring a new guest girl to our castle? Of course every host noble was going to come! Look at them, all dressed up in their cheap silks and their jewellery…'

When she got close enough to the king, she whispered through gritted teeth, "mother is not coming, Asttrian, she is not feeling well. Let's get on with this circus, now, we'll talk later, in private!"

The king put on a smug grin. He saw that man Lughan talking to the Kechtá at the entrance to the hall.

They were finally here…

The king turned one last time to his sister.

"Dearest sister," he said just before standing up, "thank you for attending this scrutiny, I was sure that even though mother doesn't seem to have any interest in it, you weren't going to miss one bit. And of course, rest assured, I'll pay her a visit tonight. And now, let the show begin!" he concluded, directing his gaze towards the doorway, where now Thuarnach, Lughan and Annea stood.

Shya frowned.

"A strange company those three!" she said to herself.

The crowd slowly followed the king's gaze and went suddenly silent.

Grey furred hood still pulled up, Thuarnach was the first one to enter the hall, his walking stick hitting the stone floor with determination. As he moved forwards, his bison grey cloak fluttered so, that the tiny crystalized snowflakes flew glittering all around him. He looked big and imposing, very much like an otherworldly being…

Annea followed the druid with apprehension. She had been told to leave her head hooded until the king commanded otherwise, and the only thing she could see was the white, stone floor with golden patterns, and the druid's back featuring that big, embroidered four-headed dragon of the Skyarach. She could hear people whispering, though. 'How many people have come?' she wondered. It sounded like quite an audience... But she had been warned, she had to keep her head down, no matter what happened around her.

Lughan took the rear and walked in the same way behind his little Pandora. He knew this was going to be a tough trial for them. Asttrian had invited every noble man to this scrutiny, which was quite unusual, and he didn't like it in the least.

After what felt like an eternity, the company stopped in front of the king, and the druid was the only one that pulled down his hood.

Meanwhile, very uncustomary, king Asttrian, who had been standing while they approached the throne, moved forward to greet his uncle Thuarnach first.

"Hyo! But look who's here after all this time: my dearest uncle! I thought you had forgotten your nephew..."

"Your Majesty," answered Thuarnach with a scornful look, while he bowed in front of Asttrian.

"But, of course, muin Eonar Drkent Dryd Thuarnach, where are my manners? It seems I got carried away, but you surely understand. See, I'm so excited to finally have a look at what you have brought us today... after all, you have been keeping her all to yourself long enough, dear uncle…" and looking around, Asttrian added, "oh my, I have even forgotten to fix you a place at court to sit. How inexcusable of me!"

Now, moving closer to his uncle, he went on, "but here, you can take my throne to rest for a while. It must be quite exhausting being such an old man."

Thuarnach was as always unmoved by his nephew's remarks.

"Don't bother about me, Asttrian, I'm sure this scrutiny won't take long, and my walking stick is strong and will hold me. Surely you need to attend to other, more important matters."

"Oh, I wouldn't be so sure about that, uncle… This new Gæn Ærin of yours, can she be a worthful Skyarach citizen?" gave back the king out loud, putting up a thoughtful face.

Turning to the nobles, who were now seating and murmuring to each other, Thuarnach went on with his speech.

"As you will all get to understand, this girl called Anneya made incredible progress concerning the use of our language and our traditions. Lughan, here, bears witness to the hard work she has put through, this last month. She is very capable and will be an excellent addition to our guest citizen community–"

"See, sister," interrupted him the king, and turning to Shya, he added, "I told you! She must be a wonderful person indeed if our most honourable Drkent Dryd, praises her like that. I wonder why hasn't our loyal uncle come before to tell us all this? Could it be he wants to keep her for himself?"

The king now climbed the brief flight of steps that was separating him from his uncle, and continued his speech.

"Our faithful nobles here assembled, muin Eonaran, want to be sure before making up their minds. They crave to see her with their own eyes, Thuarnach, and we shall not disappoint them. Surely you understand I have to satisfy my people's curiosity, they want to decide for themselves if she is worth a place in my household. Oh, such a merry crowd!" concluded the king with his arms theatrically wide open, as if embracing his whole court.

Without wasting more time, and seeing that the court remained in utter silence and expectance, Asttrian gave the order Annea had been waiting for.

"Muine Gæn Ærin Anneya, hann ona yissa!"[67] commanded the king solemnly.

She held her breath, and felt her father do the same.

---

[67] Meaning: "pull down your hood".

A moment later, she slowly pulled down her hood, still fixing the floor with her eyes.

The court gave a loud sigh of surprise, and then an unorderly murmur filled the hall.

Even though she had been brought to court in her plain Gænnæriati dress, Annea's face was of such an extraordinary beauty that the Harkan Næl felt bewitched at her sight. They were slowly realising why there was no point in opposing the king tonight. Everyone, including Shya couldn't stop staring at her.

Annea was used to such looks, she had learnt to deal with them. Today, however, it was different. Their eyes were drilling through her, and her cheeks were burning, her heartbeat, rocketing: she was afraid.

'What are they all about? Have they no decency or education?' she thought, with a sigh, 'I'm not a pet of some sort... how long still? I wish this would be over, now...'

The king came closer to her and gently pulled her chin up, forcing her to look at him. He then smiled at her and offered her his hand.

As protocol demanded, she bowed and kissed the ring with the dragon head on his thumb.

Turning to his nobles, Asttrian spoke again, "my loyal and faithful Harkan Næl, here I give you our own Altásva![68] Thank you, uncle, truly!"

And making a sign with his head, he commanded the Drkarach Kechtás, who had escorted the three into the hall, to free Annea from her clothes in front of the whole court.

She did not move, and she did not dare look at anyone. She fixed her eyes on the gigantic golden dragon head perched atop the throne. She pierced those empty eye sockets and kept still, aware of her helplessness and containing her swelling anger, while the two guards started tugging at her garments.

'Thuarnach had warn me about the king's inclinations... I have to keep calm, no matter what,' she said to herself, 'but what have I done to deserve this? why does he need to humiliate me in front of everyone?'

The entire hall was murmuring now, and the buzzing of people's voices was getting so loud, that Annea's head started spinning.

'God, please, please, make him stop. How can I look these people in the eye ever again?!' she thought in despair.

---

[68] Mythological female being from the legends of the ancient Seannarachti Kingdom – see also page 36 for reference.

Lughan, who had been completely ignored by the king, had his head still bowed and covered with his hood. Therefore, he could not see what was happening around him, but he sensed something was going very wrong...

He had to summon all his will power not to look up. It was all it need take for Asttrian to give the order to cut off his head, and he knew it. The new king had been looking for a reason since the day his father had died. And Lughan would be of no help to Annea as a headless corpse. So, unfortunately, Lughan would have to stay hooded and bowed, staring at the floor and in pain for his girl...

It was Thuarnach, however, who first spoke this time.

"This is utterly unacceptable, Asttrian!" cried Thuarnach angry.

"Your Majesty for you now uncle!" countered the king.

The two guards stopped undressing her, and looked at each other unsure what to do next.

"Have you been drinking too much Rheannvid or have you lost your mind?" went on the druid undisturbed, "this is not the Arach way to introduce a new Gæn Ærin to court! This girl, in any case, is not ready to move to Drkent Har, I plea for more time."

"Oh, yes, I know, and I suppose you would offer to continue her training under your exclusive supervision, am I wrong uncle?"

King Asttrian laughed out loud before he went on to address his nobles, "my honourable Harkan Næl, as you can all plainly witness, muin Drkent Dryd Thuarnach, as always, wants to keep the best pieces for himself! I say, he will have to share this time! This woman will stay at Drkent Har with, or without his consent! If he stops arguing against my will, however, I might consider allowing him to visit her once a month to continue her training. As you all know, I care about my people."

Shya, who had so far been silently bearing witness to her brother's stupidity, stood up abruptly.

"Enough! You," she pointed to a royal guest maiden that was standing beside her, "cover that girl up immediately and take her out of this room, we have seen enough for today."

She had to interfere! Not because she would care about the girl, Shya did not know what caring for someone actually meant. No, she had to interfere, and get the woman out of everyone's sight, especially hers, because Annea was even more beautiful than she recalled, and her beauty was a threat to her, who thought of herself as the most beautiful woman in the whole kingdom, and beyond.

Now turning to the nobles, she continued, "Muine honeri Harkan Nælli og tou Skyarachti,[69] I kindly ask you to clear the court and rest assured I will support the king in handling this matter. If the girl is of no use to Drkent Har, she will leave. Thank you for your attendance, today."

And saying no more, Shya left the hall room through the private back door that was accessible for the royal family only, and disappeared out of sight herself, too. She was, as most of the time, fuming over her brother's behaviour.

"Ahhh, my beloved sister, always death's head at a feast!" complained Asttrian, "well, you can all leave the court, now. Summons for the upcoming festival of Dryemoshach[70] in the month of Gloaras will reach you soon."

He then turned to his uncle, who was not showing any sign of leaving the room, anytime soon.

"Muin Eonaran, uncle, what is this dislike on your ancient face? Don't tell me you have grown so attached to a plain guest girl at the eventide of your life. Are you truly willing to oppose me on this matter, your own nephew, your king?"

---

[69] Official formula required by royal protocol to adress the court, meaning: "my honorable host nobles and all the Skyarach people."
[70] Dragon Celebration for the arrival of spring, of the colour green, time of the year when the Dragon lays its eggs in fresh moos, in caves. It symbolizes the promise of riches and abundance for the year.

Thuarnach looked down, tired and disgusted with his nephew's demeanour.

"No, muin Reaghil Drkent Teyn,[71] you are right, so silly of me to think you would deal with this matter in a fair way."

"Careful, uncle, I have sent people to die for much less…"

"Ahhh, I don't doubt that, nephew. More important, however, I still have an offer to make. In exchange for some valuable information that I have been lucky to obtain, I would like to continue teaching the girl at Drkent Har daily."

"And what if I say no?"

"Then, you, my dear nephew, will never know where to find Drkentstar."

"You treacherous, old man! I knew you had taken the sword! You are, of course, aware that this is high treason, Thuarnach. Even if you are my uncle, I will have you arrested straight away. Kechtás!!!"

---

[71] Official formula for adressing the king in the Skyarach language, as used by the druids.

"I wouldn't be so hasty, nephew. I was not the one to hide it from you," he lied, "but I am the only person in this city who knows where the sword is and can retrieve it for you."

All four Kechtás, who were part of Asttrian's personal escort, were marching promptly in their direction, now. The remaining people, who had actually been gathering closer to the entrance to exit the hall, turned to see what was happening behind their backs. But the king raised his right hand and brought his guards to an abrupt halt in the middle of the hall.

"Such a pity," Asttrian said, "it would have agreed with you to stay overnight in my dungeons. I guess, this time I will have to listen to your conditions, muin Eonaran."

'I guess you will…' thought Thuarnach.

Thuarnach knew he could not trust his nephew. He had given orders to place Rayka's copy of Drkenstar, which he had kept within the druid tunnels so far, under druid protection. Should anything happen to him, his fellow druids would devise a way of getting Annea out of the city straight away, which would mean breaking faith with the king once and for all.

This course of events, however, was not the preferred one. Thuarnach needed to buy time, he needed to stay close to his nephew and Drkent Har, as long as possible. Only in this way, would he be of any use to Ara and their cause.

Now, with this move, he was able to get a royal allowance to continue teaching Annea in the castle, while they waited for Ara's arrival. The king had been so eager to believe he was in possession of the sword, he would never see the difference between the copy and the original. Thuarnach, on his part, promised to return him the sword in a month's time, provided he could see Annea daily for another month, until the feast of Dryemoshach.

For today, however, Thuarnach and Lughan had no choice, but to leave Drkent Har empty-handed, and closely escorted by two massive Kechtás.

The king, on his part, could finally rejoice in the idea of both having a grasp on his new toy, and the perspective of his father's powerful sword...

In a dark corner, at far end of the hall, a young, handsome Harkan Næl called Rothar was watching the scene unnoticed by everyone. Like the rest of the nobles, he was used to Asttrian's cruelty and eccentric behaviour. Tonight, however, the king had gone too far. What he had done to that poor Gænnæriati girl in front of the whole court was inexcusable. These were not the morals of a Skyarach king, this was not his king! There and then, Rothar had made up his mind. He was going to contact the druid and offer him his help, he would eagerly be his eyes and ears at court.

<u>Chapter Eighteen:</u> The Anairarachti Princess

Nightfall

10th Day of Wbentas, 300YD,
Daing Mhuir on Inna Skythiarach

It was dark. That last lonely torch at the end of the corridor was the only light, and it was but flickering shyly.

Anuelle was out of breath. She was exhausted and terrified, at the same time.

She had been running restlessly with her heavy satchel through the never-ending corridors of the fortress of Daing Mhuir, trying to avoid the ever-watchful eyes of the royal guard.

Right in front of her, at the end of the last corridor, she could already make out the service gate for the kitchens.

She was almost there.

Early that morning, she had retrieved her leather satchel from its hiding in the wine cellars to make sure she had enough provisions. She had added some Arach crust bread and fruits, nuts and water with elderberry juice to keep her healthy through the cold, just as her brothers had once taught her to do.

Once that had been settled, she had gone straight to the fortress's apothecary cabinets where she had taken some medicinal herbs and potions mandatory for any long journey. She had stuffed everything in her small belt pouch, and then she had returned to her room to stay there until sundown.

It was still very cold for the month of Wbentas. So, she would have to take her warmest riding coat, apart from the fisher's black cape she would be wearing tonight. Luckily for her, she had just received one such warm coat as a present from her father. It had been made especially for her out of the thick wool of the hardy Mhuirarachti sheep and dyed in the colours of her father's house: light blue and a grey fox's fur for the hood. And although it was not as fancy as a Skyarachti cloak,[72] it had been fashioned in the tradition of the isle to resist the strong sea winds, keeping its owner warm and dry through any storm.

Anuelle had her mind set. She was not about to fail them...

---

[72] It had no embroidery or emblem, and the wool was treated differently to resist the rough weather conditions, which made it heavy and rustic.

The four siblings had always been very close despite their age difference, and the fact that the princes had been often away for their training. The boys had been caring and protective to their young, always rather delicate sister, and she had grown to love them dearly, especially her oldest brother, Arachtan.

She was now determined to find them no matter the odds, and no matter what her mother believed.

Queen Scaìthara might still see her as a child, but Anuelle was no such thing anymore, and while the last couple of months had been extremely difficult with her mother, the last few weeks had turned into a nightmare at the castle of Daing Mhuir.

The queen was losing patience and hope with the uncertainty surrounding both her kingdom and her missing sons. She was in a terrible mood, like a caged feline. Thus, Anuelle and her father had been confined to have most of their meals on their own.

Queen Scaìthara was not hiding her frustration anymore.

Her three princes had been missing for over a month, and by now word of the situation under the new Skyarach king was spreading like wildfire over the island of Inna Skythiarach, where the Anairachti nobles were starting to ask many uncomfortable questions, most of which were to stay unanswered...

Anuelle's father, on the other hand, was a completely different story.

Being many years older than his queen, Drearyan was a very wise and sensible man, whose actions were always guided by reason and measure.

He had been the great warrior queen's right hand all throughout the Arach Sea Wars, and he still was. And even if as a couple, they had never been truly in love with each other, their bond was much older and stronger. They respected and cherished their partnership and friendship.

Drearyan felt angry and overwhelmed by the disappearance of their sons – including Arachtan, who he had always considered his own – as much as Scaìthara did. He had, however, recommended to wait and evaluate the situation further, firmly steading his wife's hand for some time. This, in return, was sparking the queen's dragon temper even further.

Anuelle, on her part, knew she was going to hurt her father and betray his trust by escaping like this. Drearyan was a good and kind father, who loved his children above all, and was especially fond of her. It felt dreadful to know that she was going to disappoint him... During the last, difficult months, they had been the only comfort for one another. He was going to be very lonely once she left, but she could not wait any longer...

It was time to leave, now.

Anuelle covered herself gracefully with a hooded, black cape, like the ones the fisher women wore, and passed swiftly through the back of the kitchens into the yard, striding determined to the service gate. The whole place was empty and silent, but one person had been waiting for her in the shadows...

Ryssa.

Early that week, Ryssa had witnessed a quarrel between the princess and her mother, and although she had not been sure, when exactly it would happen, she was certain that the princess would attempt to leave the fortress in search of her brothers... And Ryssa, of course, would be leaving with her.

It had become too dangerous for her at the island fortress. She knew Drkent Har was waiting for her messages, but it was impossible to use the royal jays, without getting in trouble, and all other means took far too long. Both kingdoms had by now mobilized so many spies and knights to oversee their roads and borders, that she was no longer safe here. No, she had to leave, too. Her destiny had been sealed the day Arachtan had left without a word. Ryssa would accompany the Anairarachti princess, even against her will! She had a good plan, and her friend Gællen, the stable boy, had accepted to help her.

For two days now, she had been carefully observing each and every of Anuelle's movements. She had found the backpack with provisions hiding between the casks of wine, and had decided to put her plan into action. Tonight, like a ghost, Ryssa had been patiently waiting for the young princess, under the cover of darkness, close to the service gate.

"Hyo, muine Etayn Anuelle! Late the hour, don't you agree?"

Anuelle froze midway.

She was young and unexperienced, but after a few seconds, she answered pretending composure.

"Hyo, Ryssa! Not late for me, certainly. Perhaps you haven't noticed that I turned 17 two months ago. Now, I can wonder the castle as I please!"

"Oh, silly me. Of course, I remember now, the preparations for the celebration... Drkent Etayn Anuelle na Anairarachti[73] finally received her golden torque! That must have been a scene to remember!" Ryssa laughed sarcastically, "a pity, I was not invited.

---

[73] Dragon Princess Anuelle of the Anairarachti.

No worries, though, muine Etayn,[74] I'm not the vengeful type," she lied.

Silence filled the crispy night surrounding them for a short moment.

"As you will surely understand, however, I am terribly concerned about my dear husband, and I have decided to leave Daing Mhuir tonight and search for him!"

"I'd rather you did not call him that here, mother still does not know…"

"Well, that is because your brother has disappeared without telling her!"

"Shush! They will hear us," said Anuelle, searching the darkness around them.

Ryssa studied Anuelle's reaction carefully. She wanted to convince the princess of the convenience of travelling together, keeping the appearances until the very last moment would help her gather critical information about Ara's possible hiding place. But if the princess resisted, she and Gællen would have to take her with them by force.

---

[74] My princess

Anuelle was taking too long to answer, so Ryssa decided to continue with her argument.

"Muine Etayn, I know you miss your brothers, too. Together, I assure you, we can find them! Together, we could help each other in the wild, and have more chances of surviving the journey! Drkarach only knows, where your brother Ara could be by now!"

The young princess looked back, piercing the darkness she had left behind. No one was coming after her as yet, but still, she had to hurry. Ryssa was an unnecessary complication, but maybe... No, she neither trusted nor liked the woman. It was better to go alone!

"The answer is no, Ryssa. I'm not interested! I'm travelling on my own!" she answered, moving on towards the gate, and passing too close beside the slave girl.

Ryssa followed her closely, and before too long, she grabbed the girl's arm and turned her around to face her.

"Anuelle! Believe me, you will never make it pass Innatyarsach da Aehgamer![75] By the time you reach Eonnal Maelirmer[76] for passage, word of your disappearance will have reached every port city in both kingdoms! Think about it! Be reasonable! I have

---

[75] Great Britain, known as the Island of the Great Water Portal.
[76] Short version of the name Eonnal Skethemarbheal na Maelirmer.

already settled passage for myself in a fisher's boat, which happens to be waiting for me, right down at the Reaghil Sketheamar,[77] now. I could easily arrange passage for one more person for some royal coin. They could smuggle us both straight into Drejkreins!"

'Drejkreins...' thought Anuelle, 'that's our friend Tschiaran's city! With a bit of luck, I could find him, maybe he knows something about my brothers... Oh, Arachtan! What should I do, brother?!'

Ryssa saw a cloud of doubt sweeping through the princess's sweet face, and did not waste time.

"Listen to me," she pressed on, "we don't have much time! The boat is leaving in half an hour with or without us, and we still need to go down the devil's gorge!"

After giving it some thought, and to avoid further discussions, the princess finally gave in, "fine, we can travel together if you please," she said, "but only up to Drejkreins. After that, Ryssa, I'm on my own!"

Together, then, the slave girl and the Anairarachti princess scuttled out of the fortress walls, rushing into the open darkness of the night.

---

[77] Royal Port of Daing Mhuir.

The first part of Ryssa's plan had been successful. Gællen would be waiting for them at the boat, settling the last things. And how could anything go wrong? She had thought through every detail of their escape, paying for fresh horses once they would reach Innatyarsach da Aehgmer. Surely Anuelle would wonder why Gællen was with them, but there was enough time to think about some plausible excuse. Now, they had to hurry, there was no more talking, they had to move as fast as they could to put a safe distance between them and the fortress of Daing Mhuir, where soon mighty queen Scaìthara would find out that also her daughter was now missing.

An Old Friend

14ˢᵗ Day of Wbentas, 300YD,
Drejkreins, Skyarach Kingdom

It had been a four-day journey with almost no rest. The way had been full of dangers and obstacles, and although they had known from the beginning that taking that route was a risk, following the main trading routes connecting the buzzling port cities of Innatyarsach da Aehgmer posed an even greater risk, that of being discovered.

Other than usual, they had sailed with the fishers to the little city of Da b'Œsbajkann,[78] a picturesque fisher port southwest of Inna Skythiarach. They had made sure to keep their identities unrevealed and paid for the fishers silence with precious Anairarachti Tanner.[79]

To continue their uncertain journey west, they had fresh horses waiting for them. So, in silent complicity, the three of them hastily started off, knowing that, by now, the queen must have discovered the disappearance of her daughter, and she would be searching for her everywhere.

---

[78] Meaning the "old, little fisher's bay, which would be close to today's city of Oban, in Scottland.
[79] Royal big gold coin

Nobody, however, would be expecting them to use the old trading route, which stretched from the east coast and followed right through the heart of the impenetrable forest of Tærkerann Tyarcad. This was an extensive forest of mythical legends, of magical beings that supposedly locked intruders forever within its dense vegetation. Some even believed the forest was older than the dragons themselves, and most people would rather be hanged than sent to traverse its expanses.

For Anuelle, Ryssa and Gællen, the forest had surprisingly shown its benevolent side.

They had found fresh water springs to drink from, and they had spent two nights resting within its darkness, with but a small fire to keep them warm. Nothing had troubled them. In truth, nothing had as much as touched them, not even the fallen leaves that from time to time kept dancing up around, whirled by the horses' hooves, while they were riding. It was as if they had been under a protective spell…

And although it had been a strenuous journey, covering the distance on horseback and without many stops had altogether paid off.

They had reached the west coast port of Eonnal Maelimer swiftly, and gained passage without delay. The winds had been kind, and the sea, clear, taking them over to the Skyarach Kingdom in good time.

Now, the three of them were in high spirits for having reached the city of Drejkreins unharmed and undetected. They were, at least officially, out of queen Scaìthara's reach, and somehow, for the time being, it still seemed to be all it mattered.

Ryssa decided to look for lodgings around the city's busy market square, or so she told them. She said the crowds would help them stay unnoticed, while they changed their fisher cloaks to unspectacular Skyarachti Nachtural Brean[80] ones to mingle in.

In reality, however, Ryssa wanted to make contact with Asttrian's spies, so she left Anuelle with Gællen waiting in a shabby inn at the docks.

They had been waiting for about an hour, now, and the princess was starting to get nervous. Gællen, as always, would not make much of a conversation, so she decided to go and ask for another drink.

---

[80] In the Skyarach Kingdom, special attention was given to the colour and material of clothing. It had been established by a royal decree issued by queen Umbriel herself that all, save the royal family, were to wear tartans of different colours. Nachtural Brean, or native farmers, were to use the colours brown, grey and natural wool, and they could wear a deerskin as hood or as collar to their cloaks.

She moved towards the bar self-consciously, wrapping her lean figure with the thick woollen cloak apprehensively, and straightening her hood every time an unruly lock of her hair tried to escape.

She was not going to risk it.

Anuelle's hair was easily recognisable, and was the one thing she had to hide. It was curly and unruly beyond measure, and of a very unusual red-brownish hue, namely the same as her mother's.

The inn was crowded, and the air was thick and salty. It was the last place princess Anuelle would have desired to be, surrounded by tough seasoned sailors of dark demeanour.

After meandering along the large tables, she finally reached the bar. In front of her, a large, square-shouldered man was filling two big glasses with ale.

She came closer.

"Hyo, Bræy Ærin!" he greeted her friendly, "drysti aì?"[81]

---

[81] "Hello, beautiful lady! Thirsty today?"

"Yes, sir, thank you," she answered shyly, "could I have some of that, please?" she pointed at the glasses he had just filled, "or if you have some, I'd much rather have some Úllst...?"[82]

"Certainly, Bræy Ærin, the Sketheamar Inn has everything you want!"

Pulling a bottle from under the counter, the man generously filled a big ceramic mug with the golden liquid.

"Here, the best Úllst you can get!" he said, while giving the mug over to Anuelle.

"Sorry, but... I'm not from here. How much do I owe you?"

"Oh, no worries, we are all from somewhere else here, muine Bræy Ærin. So, let me see... For you only, it would be 4 Dryani[83] if you desire to pay with Skyarachti coin, but we also accept Anairarachti Skræn, in which case, it would only be 1 Skræn," he answered with a broad, toothless smile.

In a dark corner, right to the left of the bar, a man was sitting and listening attentively. He had immediately placed the accent, which

---

[82] Bubbly cidre made of an ancient apple sort.
[83] The two Arach kingdoms had different currencies. The Skyarachti had the little bronze Dryani, the medium-sized silver Thann, and the big gold Dreken, but also bargaining was common place during the time. Anairarachti gold was most precious and mostly preferred around the coastal area facing Innatyarsach da Aehgmer. They used smaller and bigger coins named Skræn and Tanner respectively.

had sparked his curiosity, and now he was sure... If his informants were right, then this "Bræy Ærin" must be the missing Anairarachti princess half the kingdom was searching for!

He hadn't seen her for quite some time, but the way she talked, her tall, lean figure... He decided to approach her.

Anuelle was half way to her table when the stranger intercepted her.

"May I help you young Ærin? Might you be looking for lodging in this strange city, perhaps?"

Anuelle, who had been looking to the ground to keep her hood in place, raised her head slightly, just enough so as to make eye-contact with the stranger, whose particular voice reminded her of someone...

"Thank you, sir. I've already– Tschiaran?! Is it you?!" she whispered excitedly.

"Muine Etayn Anuelle?!" responded Tschiaran in a bewildered whisper, "so happy to have found you! An Drkarach,[84] Anu, you truly have become a beautiful woman... but what were you thinking to come over here?! You are in grave danger, we must leave, this place is full of spies!"

---

[84] Arach exclamation of surprise.

The princess stopped him short, "have you seen Ara, Thuaì or Skeor? They disappeared more than a month ago, and no one has heard of them ever since. I came looking after them… since my mother has taken to merely wonder the castle like a wild animal in a cage."

"Anuelle, listen to me, are you with someone else here?"

"Well, yes, why?"

"We have to collect your things and leave this place, I'll explain later, as I said, the inn is infested with royal spies," he ended in a whisper, while looking around them.

They walked further, but then Anuelle turned around to face him again.

"Why should I go with you? I've managed quite well on my own so far…"

"Because, Anu, I'm your only friend in this city. And besides, your brother Ara would kill me if I let you here with these people."

And without another word, Tschiaran and the princess walked to the table, picked up her leather satchel, and left Gællen complaining with a fresh mug of Úllst. The stable boy was no match for Tschiaran, so acknowledging his defeat, he sat back down and waited patiently for his beloved Ryssa.

The Northwest Wind

16th Day of Wbentas, 300YD,
Drejkreins

Her delicate, pale blue eyes were blurred by a sea of tears, mirroring the troubled waters of the Rheann river outside.

Anu had been in the hiding long enough, she had to move forward or she would never be able to find her brothers.

Tschiaran, on the other hand, was of a totally different opinion. He knew that, despite her bravery, Anu was not prepared for such a journey.

Inclined to music, books, and the arts of healing, she had always been the perfect princess, not a warrior or a ranger. In fact, she mostly kept herself indoors, but for the horse riding, which was also one of her passions. He couldn't possibly let her pursue her goal of finding Ara. He had to bring her back to Daing Mhuir...

Queen Scaìthara had sent a royal order days ago to stop her, wherever she would appear. The queen was furious at what she called her daughter's "childish demeanour". She was offering 20 golden Tanner for the man who brought the princess back, sending the whole city of Drejkreins into madness.

From what Tschiaran knew, Asttrian still did not know of the princess's disappearance, and as long as this was the case, he still had time to smuggle her out of the city, and back to her mother. This didn't mean, however, that local Skyarachti spies hadn't heard the news. The girl had truly no idea of the perils that were awaiting her on this side of the sea...

She stood up and turned her back to the window, through which she had been observing the Rheann vessels leave the harbour in the distance, like tiny colourful fish crisscrossing each other randomly.

She moved closer to Tschiaran and fixed her wet eyes on him.

"I won't stay a day longer hidden in this warehouse, and you will never convince me to turn back, Tschiaran. I set off to find my brothers, and I will!" her voice, trembling with determination.

"Of course, you will. We will all help you, Anu," replied Tschiaran patiently, "but from a far safer distance. The Skyarach Kingdom you knew does not exist anymore, you are no longer safe here. I've arranged passage for you tonight, you will be returning to Inna Skythiarach with your parents. I can't possibly let you continue into the bowels of a monster alone."

He realised too late that he should not have said that.

Now, she came even closer and stared him fixedly in the eyes full of suppressed anger and desperation, her cheeks turning scarlet red.

"And you call yourself a friend?! How can you do this to me? How much money will you be getting from mother? Ah? What am I worth these days? I should have never trusted you…"

She turned around and moved away from him.

"Well, know this, "friend", you will have to drag me home then, for I intend to leave this warehouse tomorrow morning and board a Rheann boat to find my brothers!" she hissed slowly through gritted teeth.

Tschiaran had never seen Anuelle like this.

He was truly taken aback by her sudden stubborn convictions and her refusal to listen to reason. This was not the girl he had met five years ago, playing the Hærlb[85] and singing at court.

He was deeply wounded that she should think he was doing this for the gold, too. He was an old friend of Ara's, he had been at

---

[85] Hærlb was an Arach music instrument very similar to the harp

Daing Mhuir the day Anu had been born, and had witnessed such a bright smile on his friend's beautiful young face... A moment he would never forget. He would do anything to protect the princess of Daing Mhuir.

"You surprise and offend me both, muine Etayn."

He sighed, feeling the burden of decision mercilessly crashing him down.

"I've sworn my friendship and services to your family since I was an orphan boy wondering the cold streets of Eonnal Maelimer. I would do anything to protect you and any member of your family, muine Etayn."

He stopped and listened to her silence.

"I met your brother Ara, ey, about two months ago. We had all received information that the situation at Drkent Har was becoming a threat for all of the Arach kingdoms, if not for the entire known world... Your cousin Asttrian, you see, he has become nothing more than a mad tyrant, and Dryd Thuarnach alone has great difficulty to restrain his actions. The new king listens to no one, Anu, and, what's more, he stops at nothing when he wants something."

"But what is cousin Asttrian after?" interrupted him Anu.

"Absolute power, that is what his heart most desires: to do as he pleases, when he pleases, with whom he pleases. And he will destroy anyone or anything that gets in his way."

He saw her reflecting and quickly added, "Asttrian hates Ara and he sees him as a threat to his ambitions, Anu. He has always hated him. I have information that he hasn't found him yet, so there is hope. On the other hand, if he gets hold of you... Well, he would have a weapon to get to him. Do you understand, Anu?"

She turned around.

"Actually, I do, and I'm sorry, for my words, too. I didn't mean to offend you, Tschiaran. I know how close you have always been to my brother..."

She walked closer to him and took his hands in hers.

"But Tschiaran, if this is so, you have to help me find him before. I cannot go back, now. Daing Mhuir has been cut off, the only information we receive is yours. Thuarnach hasn't sent jays for months, father was never keenly involved in the foreign affairs of our kingdom, and mother... well, she is simply unrecognisable! She's not herself since the old king's death. She is always in a bad mood, always alone... I would not trust her warrior spirit will awaken any time soon. It will be up to us to help Ara, Tschiaran, and the more we are, the more chances we have to succeed. My brother needs us!"

"Hmhh, I was starting to wonder why the queen hadn't been moving her troops to the border, yet. I assumed she had grown more diplomatic over the years, under your father's influence..."

"Ney, Tschiaran, she has retreated within herself, where no one can get close to her. I saw it happening, but have been unable to stop it. My father has taken over daily business at the castle, for more than a year, now. She openly argued that the Skyarach kingdom is nothing she cares for, while she wanders the castle corridors restlessly like a trapped ghost. Now that my brothers are missing, she seems frustrated and overwhelmed, but I'm afraid it's too late, I don't think we'll be seeing Warrior Queen Scaìthara coming back, any time soon, from wherever it is her soul dwells now."

Tschiaran looked troubled. He did not like to entertain the idea of his queen leaving the kingdom open for Asttrian to march in…

"Surely, your father and Thuarnach have stopped her hand, Anu. They would not have war between the two kingdoms, they still remember far too well the last time there was war within the Arach family. It took hundreds of years to heal, and the old Thuatharachti kingdom never truly recovered."

"It's possible that uncle Thuarnach did interfere... Still, she is not the same person since king Urarathan died, so do not expect her to protect the kingdom as she used to."

Tschiaran looked down at her hands and went silent for a moment.

"Anu, there is something I need to know... Who was the person I saw with you at the inn?"

"Why, I thought you had all the informants on your side..." she answered mockingly.

"Ney, Anu, truly. It is important that you tell me. Who travelled with you?"

She let his hands go, and moved to the little table in the corner, where the water jar was. She poured fresh water in a glass and drank before answering.

"No one, just the stable boy of Daing Mhuir. He is a mute."

"And your brother's wife? Was she with you?"

"Don't call her that! My brother never called her so, and so she remains just another slave girl we have rescued. Her name is Ryssa."

"Well, have you seen Ryssa, then?"

"Why would I?" she answered a fraction of a second too quick.

"Anu, stop this. I'm the one making the questions, now… It seems you know something, you're not telling me. The girl went missing at the same time as you did, you know, and the whole kingdom is looking for her, too… I need to know if she was with you."

Princess Anuelle did not like being interrogated. She was not used to lie, and she could not do it well, but she was not sure about the consequences of telling the truth.

She drank more from her glass to have more time to think. Somehow, she suspected Ryssa's involvement in her escape would change things. She was not sure, however, if it would be for the better or for the worse.

She, then, looked up from her glass and risked an answer, "ey, she was with me, as well."

Tschiaran held his head with both hands instinctively, in an expression of concern.

"I should have known…" he muttered to himself.

Then, after a few seconds, he addressed her again, "whose idea was it that you should escape?"

"Mine, of course!" she gave back bluntly, offended that he would not trust her to have enough courage and boldness to put through her own escape.

"But, there is something…" she hesitated, recalling the night of their escape and their peculiar encounter. She had not given it a second thought since then. Now, however, under another light, she thought she was starting to understand the true motivation behind the slave girl's actions.

"But… she was eager to accompany you, wasn't she?" filled in Tschiaran for her.

"Well, yes…"

"I knew it! That is how Asttrian is always a step ahead. That girl is a spy for Drkent Har, Anu!"

He turned around abruptly and started looking for something in a box he had hidden under the improvised lit, where Anu had been sleeping.

"Ryssa? But that's impossible, she is just…"

Suddenly, she remembered about the missing jays and it all made sense.

"Do you truly think so?"

"Yes, it explains many things, Anu."

"But then... well, she knows I'm here... Oh, by the Dragon, what have I done?!" she exclaimed while covering her face with both her hands, while her glass fell to the ground spilling its contents onto the shabby carpet.

"How could I be so naïve?!"

Tschiaran walked over to her and laid both his big, warm hands on her shoulders.

"This changes everything, muine Etayn. We have to move now, we have to leave this city, or Asttrian's men will be on us by dawn. I cannot send you back to your mother, the borders have certainly been reinforced with more Kechtás by now, and your mother's power is miles away from here. Our only path will take us to the very heart of the monster. We'll have to cross Rheann territory, where thousands of royal knights have been positioned, but, as you say, well, I am the man with the contacts. If I can't take you out of this city, nobody can... I promise you this Anu, I won't rest until we find your brothers, and I deliver you safely to them!"

"Oh, muin lævyvljg Meyn Tschiaran, I'm so sorry, I never meant to be causing everyone so much trouble!"

"I know," he smiled at her compassionately.

"But tell me, how are we going to leave the city if every single corner is being watched?"

"Well, we will mingle with the Drejkrenian pottery fleet that trades river inwards, moving from here straight to Kælnamer on the Rheann. There, we will surely have to change trade… Now, as it will take some time to contact the different trading guilds and their fleet, I will have to leave you now to arrange passage. I have friends in many, you see, and I'm sure, they can help us get to the mouth of the Lahir. From there onwards, we'll have to improvise, but, in any case, most Kechtás are positioned on the Rheann and its surrounding valleys. They won't waste too many men patrolling the Lahir. Besides…" he hesitated for a second and then he added, winking an eye to her, "that is the route your brother has taken."

A broad smile cleared her troubled features, while her spirit lightened up.

"Thank you, Tschiaran, you've always been a true friend!"

It was not difficult for Tschiaran to settle things in a blink of an eye. He had so many connections that, by dusk, he and Anuelle were well on their way on a smuggler boat filled with ceramic objects of all sorts, and some very interesting forbidden liquids...

Officially, a vessel belonging to the pottery guild, it was a light ship with enough space for twenty oarsmen, a shabby, old sail and its cargo. The owner of the boat was an Anairarachti sailor that had settled down with a family on this side of the sea, and expanded his trading business by carrying all sorts of illegal substances, or passengers. He hated Asttrian's rule as much as any tradesman, and he was willing to support any man that would stand against it.

Anuelle felt confident that, with Tschiaran at her side, she was finally going to be able to reach her brothers in time. She knew she could be of more help to them there than sitting at her father's side, waiting for her mother to finally wake up from wherever it was that her mind was dwelling since the death of the old king.

Tschiaran, on his part, was not so confident. On the contrary, he was actually very anxious. He knew that this had not been a good move, just the only move possible. They were risking too much. The Rheann valley was tightly in the hands of the enemy.

Thousands and thousands of the best trained men were now searching for Anu all over the kingdom. He did not want to think what could possibly happen if they catch them...

At least, before leaving, he made sure to send out the two last jays in his possession: one to Daing Mhuir and one to Reaghil Bheallemer.

He was not hoping queen Scaìthara would support his decision. On the contrary, she was not going to like it, for sure. But at least, she would know that her daughter was safe for the moment, and maybe, the situation involving her four children would now shake her enough to decide to interfere in the Skyarachti affairs after all... Who could tell?

As for Thuarnach, he knew the Druid would promptly send someone to come their way and keep them safe. That is also why he chose the route of the Kæyns,[86] as the Lahir-Vwylr[87] route was called. In his message, he warned him also about the slave girl Ryssa, who was still at the loose, and told him that until now he had received no news from Ara. He could only say with some certainty that he had not been caught, yet.

---

[86] Temples

[87] The Lahir and the Vwylr rivers, known today as Lahn and Weil respectively, were smaller navigable tributaries to the Rheann that flowed through the Thaunaan mountains from the North East. Following this route, they were certain not to find many important trading cities or villages. It was a route mainly dedicated to the Seann Dryd Kydrachs na Drkarach or the Sacred Ancient Druid Order of the Dragon. And many smaller procession roads connected the Kæyns with each other.

It was dusk, and the waters of the Rheann were now calmer. They had been waiting for less than an hour at port for the winds to rise, and good fortune had been on their side. The mighty Nro, a wind coming from the Northwest, had aroused by the hand of a gentle breeze, and had turned into a constant sailing wind, half an hour later. They had set the big sail, and the light vessel had swiftly disappeared from sight, following the meander of the river.

From the docks, however, a pair of malicious black eyes had followed the trajectory of the boat attentively. In her bloody hand, a dead bird: a jay…

Chapter Nineteen: The Vwylrynn Kæyn

23rd Day of Wbentas, 300YD,
Eno Vwylrynn Kæyn

    It was late, it was the hour of the wolf, and outside only the light of the torches flames subtly hinted at the temple's massive silhouette. It was made completely out of red sandstone, and the walls seemed to be ignited by the dancing tongues of the eight lonely beacons.

Inside, Arachtan was sitting in front of a warm, welcoming hearth, the bright fire, covering all with a friendly tinge of orange light, while behind him, deep scarlet shadows danced frantically on the distant walls.

He was deeply submerged in his thoughts, his right hand, fidgeting with his heavy druid ring, his brow furrowed, and his handsome face heated by the argument he had just had with his cousin Ealator…

Ara and his company of four had finally reached the Eno Vwylrynn Kæyn,[88] after a much strenuous journey. Following Skymnia's untimely accident, they had been forced to wait, hiding in the cave for several days until she was fit enough to continue. Two men carried the barge with Skymnia, while the other two scouted the surroundings, making sure to avoid any exposed areas.

This time, however, they consistently kept clear off the road or the river, both particularly busy with merchants close to the bigger towns of Aarfael and Har na Lahirynn. To oversee this lively buzzing chaos, the vigilant eye of the Dragon Knights was everywhere, here.

They could spot Kechtási patrols several times. Once they saw them questioning the locals. Another time, three Kechtás were on the lurk behind a warehouse. And still another, Thuaì found them hiding beneath the bushes, close to the river shore, just in time, as he was about to go down to the river to get some fresh water.

Fortunately, their decision to keep the high ground no matter the odds had paid off. They turned the untamed forest to their advantage, as they were able to conceal themselves effectively in the uninhabited upper woods. In this way, they actually managed

---

[88] The first of the druid temples along the northeast procession road across the sacred landscape of the Thaunaan.

to remain unseen for the rest of their journey to the first Kæyn, but at a high cost, too.

Progress had been extremely slow and tedious. The area was rocky and irregular, and at times it seemed almost impossible to go on, particularly carrying an injured person. The forest here had been left untouched by human hands, and it was as impenetrable as it was lonely. But they trudged on, until they finally reached the valley in front of the first Kæyn. There, an extremely steep and uneven ascent was waiting for them.

Fortunately, Ara knew the best way to take, and he guided his men safely, as tired and exhausted as they were, all the way up to the Eno Vwylrynn Kæyn. By the time they reached the temple, however, everyone was tired to the bone and famished, too.

As was customary, the temple druids had been warned of their arrival by their guards, and had opened up the huge bronze gates, welcoming them with kindness and warm hospitality. They had promptly taken care of Skymnia, who had still been carried in the old barge and who had vehemently disagreed with being parted from her company, especially from Skeor. But as much as she had protested, the temple druids had made sure to treat her and give her peace of mind, and body, by secluding her in the Ayno or healing rooms of the temple, which were arranged linearly, southwest from the central druidic shrine.

Skymnia herself had never been in such a place before, although she had heard many stories. She was used to lavish castles and generously ornated gardens for sure, but this? This was something altogether different...

A rather peaceful place, the Kæyn was of a natural, simplistic beauty that evocated its surroundings, and of an astonishing brightness, too. Light and fire were at the centre of the structure, and also represented in every corner.

With a landscape gifted by damp, green forests to the north and rich, open valleys to the southeast, and embraced by a streaming belt of water canalized from the Lahir, the Eno Vwylrynn Kæyn had been built on an elevated rocky platform to dominate the area.

Now, due to the icy temperatures, the canal was partly frozen, and the mountains were all covered in white, but still, the views from the Temple were glorious.

The temple itself had been enclosed within a wall system. An outer, circular wall made of a local hard rock called Thaunaan Graichfael,[89] which was light yellow and brownish in colour, enclosed the druids' dwellings, as well as the stables, a smithy, a small market area and the temple itself.

---

[89] Taunus Quartz

The latter was a square-shaped building entirely made out of red sandstone that had been positioned in the centre of the outer courtyard, pointing with its tall, golden corner stone, a sort of hollowed pillar stone, towards the southeast, where the prominent Polarys Kæyn with its druid school and the druid town of Neybhrealle stood many miles away.

From within the golden corner stone, white bright flames, the White Fire of the Dragon, ensued spectacularly, reaching out proudly with long, pale tongues towards the skies.

The centre of the temple, on its part, was marked by an enormous golden dome with a hole in the middle, from which the eternal smoke coming from the inner druid shrine escaped the building.

The inside walls of the Eno Vwylrynn Kæyn were all white, even the vault. Only the floors had been made out of the same red sandstone as the façade. And to reinforce the idea of brightness, all four corners of the square building possessed masterly placed triangular glass panes on the flat roof, which generously allowed light to penetrate into the inner temple.

Hundreds of columns, arranged in circular form, shaped five separated spaces in the centre of the Kæyn. Partly open and partly closed, the druids could use these central circular spaces for their different activities, spiritual, mental, physical, transcendental, and the combination of all four.

All proper rooms, on the other hand, had been laid, following the square shape of the structure, and around the central vault.

To the southeast, there were the kitchens or Teynaman,[90] where the druids not only cooked, but also gained decoctions, herbal infusions, oils and all sorts of medicinal substances from natural products.

To the southwest, six Ayno[91] rooms had been accommodated for the sick and injured. The dividing walls, which could be removed if a bigger room was necessary, had been made out of Zirbe, or pinus cembra wood, from the Alps to promote healing and stimulate proper breathing. Three of the rooms had soft hay beds, while the other three had hard beds with natural fibre mattresses to treat the sick according to their ailment.

To the northwest, the thermal baths were arranged: a spacious room with heated floors, hosting three big pools, one with cold, one with warm and one with hot, salty water, and two massage tables.

Finally, to the northeast, the temple housed the oldest and one of the most complete libraries in the kingdom, only second to the one in the Polarys Kæyn. With ancient scrolls dating back to the

---

[90] The place of fire
[91] Ayno means health and balance.

time of the old red city of Seannanorthai, the Eno Lyvriach, as it was known, displayed a vast collection of books and scrolls from all the places the Arach people had been to, and in many foreign tongues, too.

So, it was not to wonder that when Skymnia was carried inside the Kæyn the first day, she was awestruck and completely speechless. In a way, she began to understand why Arachtan had always been so fond of the druid way of life. She even wondered if it was something, she could imagine for herself…

However, the druid orders strictly separated women from men, which was something she was not really looking forward to. Even if she cherished and respected the peaceful and harmonious atmosphere of the temple, she was already missing her cousins, her mother, her friends at court and, to some extent, also her brother.

As the days passed, Skymnia started recovering her strength steadily, if slowly. The Eno Dryds had assured Arachtan that if she continued responding so well, there was a fair chance she would be able to leave the first Kæyn, in about a week from now, walking, which was unexpected good news.

Only Ealator, as usual, was once more against waiting. Now, his determination seemed to have turned into obsession, he could not think of anything else. He wanted to storm Drkent Har, kill King Asttrian, and rescue his mother Lady Skenya without more delay. From lethargy to madness, as most thought, he appeared to be more concerned about his unfulfilled heroic deeds than his own sister's health, or his mother's life, while putting everyone's patience to the test, at the same time.

True, the healing process had costed them precious time, and since their arrival, only Ara, in his capacity as a druid, had been admitted to see Skymnia, and only once a day for a short time.

She was being held in the southwest wing of the temple, in the Ayno rooms, while the rest had to dwell in the outer courtyard, sharing the druid housing.

Skeorden, who was extremely concerned about Skymnia's health, would make sure some little gifts or short messages would reach her daily. He desperately wanted to keep her spirits up. He knew well that Skymnia was feeling lonely and plagued by doubts despite the druids' efforts to make her rest. She was not someone that would let go that easily, that was also why Arachtan had disagreed to leave her behind.

In truth, Arachtan's youngest brother had always been gentle-hearted and sympathetic, with a particular soft spot for his

Rheann cousin, and he knew how much Skymnia cared for Ara, and how she was troubled by the prospect that he could have married in secret. Altogether, Skeor was by now starting to regret that they had waited so long to interfere with Asttrian. So many things had gone wrong since the old king's death... Skeor could also not help to wonder, if they shouldn't move on and press into the capital with druid support, like Ealator advocated. The druids were peace-loving, but specialised in finest weaponry and the use of magic, nevertheless. They had an armed force of their own, and whereas they might be outnumbered by the king's men, they were skilled enough to face the most dangerous of the Kechtás all the same. On the other hand, he was certainly no one to question his brother's decisions. He trusted Ara more than anyone else, he always seemed to know what was the right thing to do, and Arachtan was against an attack. So, this time, Skeorden kept his thoughts to himself.

Ealator, on his part, had consistently been denied access either to the Ayno or the inner temple. The druids had several times offered to help him with his drinking disorder and his unruly soul, nevertheless. They had tried to comfort and advise him against any rash actions that could cost him his and his mother's life, and perhaps even others'... But to no avail. He had tried to storm into the temple and take his sister with him by force, after which the Eno Dryds had forbidden him to leave his housing, or else he would be sent to the dungeons, the rocky, moisty caves beneath the Kæyn.

Of course, he was extremely vexed about it, and blamed it all on Arachtan. In their latest argument, he had clearly made a point of leaving for Drkent Har with or without his sister, the following day.

In truth, all throughout their journey together, Ealator had been restless and looking for trouble with everyone. It had only been his sister's good nature and Arachtan's patience to stop further escalation.

By the time they had left the Reaghil Dryd Sljk that connected the Rheann fortress with Daing na Lahirynn, he had finally recovered consciousness, and had taken to insult and attack Thuaìden in all ways possible. Arachtan's brother had gathered all his strength to keep his temper, he knew Ealator was frustrated and broken. But he had been unable to steady himself for long, and had punched him in the face so hard, that their Rheann cousin had stopped arguing for a while.

After that, Ara had kept them both as far from each other as he could manage, which was no easy task, since they were travelling together. Every now and then, the two would collide with each other, causing delay and unrest among the company.

Indeed, Ealator was opposing them consistently, and for no reason. Of course, he had been against their escape from the very beginning, and although he hated Asttrian more than anyone else, he was unable to see a way out of their misery without brutal force, hence his intention of a desperate attack.

It seemed that ever since the old king's death, Ealator had become belligerent and restless. He would not participate or offer his help unless it clearly was a matter of life and death. During their journey, it had been almost impossible to keep him away from intoxicating substances, and his moods would swing like a hurricane gale. He had indeed been most difficult to handle, a heavy burden for all, especially for his sister…

And now he was getting even worse. Ara was starting to doubt that it had been a good idea to bring him along, after all.

Chapter Twenty: The Golden Cage

The Reaghil Gæn Tor

6th Day of Gloaras[92], 300YD,
Drkent Har, Reaghil Bheallemer

"Such a beautiful place, it's simply magical!" she said in amazement, while standing alone in front of the south window of her room.

Annea had been assigned a most luxurious room, in the female royal guest tower, Reaghil Gæn Tor, close to the queen's, which had infuriated the king's sister even further. Shya did not like that the king was making so many exceptions for this one.

Despite the excessively extravagant atmosphere of the chambers, which was enhanced by the many flowers and the use of fragrant oils that burned daily, Annea liked the place. It felt like a refuge in the huge fortress. The only place, where she could close the door and leave this strange world behind...

---

[92] Third month of the year

It was shortly after dawn. It was the time the service maid usually came, but today, ironically, she seemed to be late.

She walked closer to the window and laid her hands on its cold, thick glass. She wished she could stay here all day, she was not in the mood to face Asttrian or his jealous sister.

It had been another sleepless night, so many things in her mind, the cherry on top being today's rehearsal for the spring celebration of Dryemoshach, in Arsant Har. The king had even sent her a special dress to wear.

'I still can't believe this is happening to me...' she thought, 'one day I was saying goodbye to Lola, and the next I know, I'm 3000 years back in time, being knocked down and dragged by some glistening men in stiff armour, I meet a gigantic, live dragon, I finally find my father, and his new family, only to be parted shortly after, yet again! Truly, Annea, this did escape the wildest of your dreams!'

Annea rolled her eyes at herself and walked back to her bed, thinking about her friend and her old life, 'will we ever meet again, dearest friend? I wonder... I miss you, Lola, I need you here with me... I wish you could also see it all: the city, the castle, the people, the dragon... I wish it would be just a film we watched together,' she sighed.

After a while, she got distracted by the patterns of spirals and flowers beautifully carved onto the bed poles. Yes, the place was a jewel in many ways. But still, it was not her time, not her place... Now, more than ever, she felt trapped and restless, like a bird in a golden cage.

She did not recognise herself, feeling totally useless and overwhelmed by this new reality. Without Lughan at her side, now more than ever, Annea felt lost among these fickle strangers.

'There must be a way to return home!' she thought, 'if the magic has brought us here, it surely must be able to take us back...'

By now, she had been for a month as Asttrian's Reaghil Gæn Ærin,[93] and she could not complain, he had treated her surprisingly kindly. So much so, that at times, she could not believe this was the same man that had given orders to strip her naked in front of all his nobles. Either he was playing his part well, or he wasn't as bad as everyone had told her. His message, however, was not to be misread: she was his exclusive possession, and totally under his will.

Whatever he was, though, she did not like him. It didn't matter that he was being kind to her. He had terrible mood swings, and he would charge on anyone that happened to be there at the wrong time – that is, anyone, but her. So far, he was contained and

---

[93] Royal guest lady

polite to her, yes, even patient, most of the times. And since he liked drinking, which let his temper get the best of him, he had given specific orders to take Annea out of the room whenever he drank a drop too much.

Still, he behaved mostly like a spoilt child, who would rage if he couldn't get what he wanted, even when he was sober. He was not a strong person, as one would expect from someone exercising so much power. On the contrary, he was insecure and arrogant. Annea did not fear his rage, but was rather surprised that he had been able to take up his father's throne, at all.

Something was very wrong about him, and still she knew she had to continue playing her part, too. Thuarnach had been very explicit, they had to wait, and as long as the king did not force himself or tried to hurt her, she could manage the threat well...

It was as if something would be holding Asttrian back, though. Something she had not been able to figure out, yet. She had the strange impression that Thuarnach was behind it, but for how long would he be able to restrain the king?

His sister Shya, on the other hand, was a completely different story. She was straight out mean to her, whenever or wherever they met. While she was full of bile, and enjoyed threatening her, these threats were not empty ones. She would not hesitate to drop the contents of her glass on Annea's dress, while passing by, or make fun of her in front of other people, or even send her to clean her chambers during meals, even though Annea had been exclusively assigned to Queen Umbriel. To these events there would always follow an argument between the king and his spiteful twin sister. Shya was cunning, however, and she always knew how to get her way, leaving King Asttrian looking pitiful and angry both. After a while, he would resume with whatever it was he was doing, as if nothing had happened.

Once, Shya had made sure to send Annea to work in the kitchens for a full day, without telling her brother. When Annea had finally been able to return to her duties to Queen Umbriel, late that evening, the king had been so enraged that she had been missing, that he had threatened Annea with the dragon. It was only after mentioning Shya's orders, that the king had turned around and left her, mumbling something through gritted teeth.

Not that Annea cared much, though. Thanks to Shya's mean tricks, she had been able to avoid the king from time to time, and she had learned her way around Drkent Har without raising any suspicions.

What a feat of engineering skill it was, with its terraces and balconies, greenhouses and towers, and all interconnected by a myriad of maze-like, serpentine corridors. The person who had designed this fortress had certainly loved to play with light, for the white quartz stone was everywhere, and, contrary to most medieval castles that had yet to be built in this region of the world, Drkent Har had somehow managed to masterly integrate hundreds of windows around the building, which provided the castle with daylight everywhere. What Annea loved the most, however, was the south gardens in front of the main entrance to the castle, which were perched over the landscape like an exuberant hanging terrace. Looking very much like a French garden from a Loire castle, they dominated a fascinating view of the valley below. From there, one could see all the way towards what, thousands of years later, would become the city of Frankfurt am Main, and all its surrounding areas. A vastness difficult to assimilate, it was simply breath-taking!

Annea had been fortunate to be assigned as maiden to the old queen. In this way, she had been able to accompany Queen Umbriel in her walks through the gardens, almost every day. And while the old queen seemed terribly sad and lonely, it was the only time of the day, when Annea felt at ease. Maybe because the queen posed no threat to her – in truth, she wouldn't even talk to her - or maybe due to the surrounding green, she had started to appreciate this daily leisure moments of reflection.

Altogether, the queen did not speak much since her husband's death, she just needed someone to hold her arm when walking, and keep her some company. Annea liked to think of herself as the queen's walking stick. Not that she had not tried to make conversation, but the old queen would just nod or shake her head in response, when she was not completely mentally absent. Very soon, Annea even started pitying her: what sorrow could have caused a woman to become like this? This was certainly something she still wanted to find out about.

Actually, she had so many questions, and no one to talk to, really. She was missing so many parts of the puzzle. If anything, she was sure of that...

'I mean, like, how can a place like this disappear altogether? There were a few ancient remains here, 3000 years later, but how on earth–?' she remembered her father talking about a parallel world, 'could it be true? Could I be living in a parallel reality?' she sighed, 'I have the feeling I won't like the answer, and I suspect father and Thuarnach haven't told me the whole truth about what is going on. I thought finding Dad would change everything. Now, here I am, a royal captive of King Asttrian of the Skyarach!'

In that precise moment, a service girl entered the room, fortunately interrupting her thoughts.

She came every morning to bring breakfast – or something like that – and came back an hour later to help her wash and get dressed for the day. Annea had a very strict routine, and she was not allowed to wander around the castle for leisure, which still felt very much like some mysterious, mythological maze rather than a royal family home. The hallways and rooms were ghostly silent and empty, and she had almost no contact with the outside world, but for some sporadic nobles that conferred with King Asttrian and Thuarnach's visits.

The druid had been visiting her daily, checking nothing bad had happened to her. From the very first moment, however, he had insisted on her accepting her new role and learning to survive at Drkent Har, for hers and Lughan's sake. But during his visits, they hadn't been able to speak freely, as they had always been escorted by the all-knowing Kechtási knights. Besides, they were merely given an hour, before she was to return to the queen. On one occasion, however, Thuarnach had mentioned something about waiting for the right moment to act – whatever it was he meant – and had promised to let her know in due time... She dearly hoped he and Lughan were planning her escape, since it was becoming more difficult by the hour to cope with the eccentric Skyarachti royals.

'Hurry up Dad,' she thought, 'I don't know how much longer the king will behave himself, but if he doesn't, rest assured I will put him back in his right place!' In the end, putting up a fight was better than lingering in this golden cage for ever!

And it was that last thought that finally cheered her spirits up, a little.

Arsant Har

6th Day of Gloaras, 300YD,
Drkent Har, Reaghil Bheallemer

Annea looked at herself in the mirror and couldn't believe what she saw...

She had never seen such a beautiful dress in her life! It was truly precious beyond imagination... Made out of blood red, shiny silk and fine golden seams, and richly decorated on the sides with golden floral patterns depicting apple blossoms, the queen's spring celebration dress for Dryemoshach looked sensual beyond measure on her.

Observing it more closely, she noticed that each apple blossom had a bright red gemstone in its centre, like tiny, red eyes twinkling at her from the mirror.

'Are they rubies?' she wondered... 'it wouldn't surprise me.'

She heard someone approaching and then stop, a few steps behind her.

She did not dare turn around, she knew perfectly well that she was being assessed like some market animal bought to slaughter...

'What is the king up to? Why is he giving me his mother's dress?'

She finally turned around, and curtsied.

Asttrian was wearing one of his radiant smiles on his handsome, delicate face.

Annea thought that he was actually a good-looking man. He was tall and slim, had beautiful curly brown hair, and a sweet face adorned by an elegant nose and bright blue eyes. He wasn't that old, maybe in his early thirties? Of course, he was half Arach, so one could not really tell...

'Another question for my list of questions,' she thought, 'I will need at least two days straight for Thuarnach to answer them all!'

However, the king was neither a charming individual, nor a smart one. She actually considered him to have the IQ of a despotic bat and the appeal of an arrogant ape!

"Muine Bræy Ærin, camra Thay?[94] I am delighted we are finally having our first rehearsal, today, and rest assured, I am very

---

[94] My beautiful lady, how are you?

pleased to see my mother's dress suits you well, muine Lævyvljg,[95]" said the king.

Annea nodded courteously.

"If you like it, it's all yours. My mother won't be missing it, she doesn't participate in official ceremonies anymore. Now, would you mind?" he asked, politely extending his hand to her.

Without a word, Annea put her hand into his, and he smoothly guided her to the centre of the hall, where Mæster Louhin, the dance instructor, was waiting.

"So, today we will practice dah Cæwyldamhsa, our celebration's dance. It will be useful to master this dance, Yahæne Ærin,[96] for you will need it through the year, at least for our four solar feasts called Cæwylgryene. You know the moves already, we've practised that. Today, Anneya, you will be dancing with your king, so be mindful, and please, also pay attention to your movements with this ceremonial dress. You will see, it is a completely different feeling, Lævyvljg, you will have more freedom, and I want you to use it."

'Perfect!' she thought.

---

[95] My darling
[96] Young woman/lady

She had never liked dancing in public. She was not a terrible dancer, but she was very shy, more the type that would rather enjoy an ecstatic dance within the four walls of her own room... Let alone the fact that she was expected to dance with this mad tyrant!

"Ey, Mæster Louhin, I'll try my best," she answered.

The king, on his part, couldn't stop smiling, very much like a four-year-old with a lolly.

And so, the hours passed. They danced time and again, until Mæster Louhin was finally satisfied for the day, and Annea's feet were cramp-bundled. She walked slowly towards the great windows, her feet in pain, and stood there, looking out into the busy courtyard.

The king rejoiced in his achievement, and was in the best of moods. He looked longingly at her silhouette against the bright light, and was just about to follow her, when princess Shya entered, every step thundering through the room, foreboding a menacing storm.

"Muin Læyven Bran,[97] I've looked for you everywhere! Where you hiding from me?" she inquired.

---

[97] "My dear brother"

But then, she saw Annea in her mother's Cæwyldamhsa dress, and forgot Asttrian. This was outrageous! He was simply going too far!

"Are you completely out of your mind, brother? This dress?!"

Knowing his sister, Asttrian hurried to her side, and whispered soothingly, "It's just for fun, Shya, I want to see our nobles' faces when they see her using that dress... you know they aspire to see me married to one of their hideous daughters," he concluded, making a face.

She looked disdainfully at Annea and then turned to her brother again, "never thought to find you here! Don't you have better things to do? Like attend to your kingdom, for example? We have just been reported an important presence travelling towards us on the Rheann..."

"Truly? How delightful! Who can that be? Is it someone we were expecting?"

"Ney, not exactly, but still a more than welcomed guest, brother."

"Stop playing guessing games with me Shya, I'm not in the mood. Who is it?"

"I thought you liked them..." she said in a self-sufficient tone, "it's our young cousin, Princess Anuelle of Daing Mhuir."

"Oh... but how exciting, indeed!"

Asttrian turned to Annea with a mischievous grin, winking an eye in complicity.

"Such good news, muine Lævyvljg! You might be having delightful company soon..." and now speaking to himself, he added, "ey, this is slowly becoming a day to remember!"

Shya was observing her brother and especially Annea with contempt. She knew Asttrian wanted to provoke everyone at court, but this?!

So, without further hesitation, she strode determined towards Annea and strapped off one of the dress's sleeves.

"Oh, I'm so very sorry, Kræyin,[98] just wanted to see if mother's dress was still holding together. But as I see, it is far too delicate for someone like you," she said.

Annea was used to receiving this kind of treatment from her, it was just such a pity for the beautiful dress. Couldn't this woman stop for a day? She felt a surge of unbounded indignation...

---

[98] Girl

"As I see, muine Reaghil Etayn Shya, it is far too delicate for someone like you!" Annea replied out of her guts.

Both the king and his sister turned to her with wide opened eyes in disbelief. She was not supposed to address any of them without being told to, let alone in this tone.

"How dare you?!" started Shya, but, fortunately for Annea, Asttrian acted quicker this time.

"She didn't actually mean you, sister. She was just repeating the words to make sense out of them. Remember? She doesn't speak our language properly, the poor thing," he said, and moved towards Annea to caress her cheek delicately, while winking to her again.

'Wow, that was close!' thought Annea to herself, '… and now, I owe him one…'

"Off you go, come on," continued the king, "go to your room, and change before attending to my mother. You," he indicated a maid standing by the door, "go and fetch the seamstress, I want this dress fixed by tomorrow."

Then, he turned to his sister with a determined look.

"Shya, you know how much I love you, sweet sister. You know you can have anything you want from me. Well, this is the thing, this Kræyin of mine, she is my special toy. Uncle Thuarnach and that Lughan will never get her back, I have decided I want her at my disposition to do as I please, and I don't want you to spoil my fun any longer. It's enough! You will keep away from her from now on."

"Or what, brother? Will you be throwing me to Drkarach?" she laughed whole-heartedly, and then continued, "wow, Asttrian, so you are falling in love with her, now... how pitiful!"

He went on ignoring her, "she has her Kechtási escort, and they will see to it. Do you hear me? I want her to eat from my hand, and trust me more than anyone else. She belongs to me and to no one else, I won't let you interfere. If you do, you'll be accompanying lady Skenya in her confinement. Am I clear, Shya?"

Annea only understood half of what the king was saying to his sister. However, she had the impression that, for the first time, he had said something that had caused a deep impression on the princess. She had silently, if reluctantly, nodded to her brother, and they had both left the hall together towards one of the private towers, where the king unofficially received his counsellors, nobles and spies. It seemed to Annea, that this guest Shya had been talking about before was someone important to them... She would have to tell Thuarnach later on. Maybe in this way she could be of some help.

The Old Queen

6th Day of Gloaras, 300YD,
Royal Gardens of Drkent Har, Reaghil Bheallemer

She found queen Umbriel alone in the gardens, sitting in front of the magnificent central fountain, which was her favourite. It was something like early March, and for some time now, the frosty weather had ceased, and she would spend hours sitting there, staring through water and stone into some ghostly memory. It was still cold, but Annea guessed the sound of trickling water somehow comforted the old queen, and she would sit there in silence until dusk.

The queen was, as always, wearing her hunting wardrobe with a woollen, deep moss-green cape, adorned with wolf's fur around the hood and collar. It was the cape of a host noble, not the one of a queen. But day after day, queen Umbriel would come out to sit in her garden using that cape…

"My most honourable Queen," she said at last, "I have come to be with you until you are taken back to your rooms. If there is anything I can do for you, just let me know."

As always, queen Umbriel did not answer. This time, however, she turned her head slightly to look at the girl sitting beside her. Then, she stood up with some difficulty and lifted her flexed elbow, signalling Annea to accompany her for a walk.

They walked through the medicinal gardens, and the flower gardens. Then, they took to the southern trees garden, and finally reached Drkent Har's Caydúllien Ore, which stood old and proud at the edge of the garden terraces, overlooking the valley beyond.

This was another place the old queen favoured. Under the tree, there was a little wooden bench with exotic, carved flowers and plants and two dragon heads crowning over the back. Annea deduced this was a special place for the queen and her king. At least, it seemed very remote and private to her.

"See that apple there? That is our apple, the one which carries our wedding promise... I should have removed it a long time ago."

Annea was shocked to hear the queen's cracked voice for the first time, and did not dare interrupt her, she seemed fragile and broken, somehow.

The queen went on as if reading her mind, "my husband, the great Urarathan of the Thuatharachti of the North, almost immortal, excellent leader and warrior, loving father and uncle, you have finally gotten rid of your Host Queen, your unacceptable mistake, which cost you so many lives... maybe even yours..."

She laughed as if drunken with forbidden memories.

"Your true love will never know the truth, she will die in agony just like me.
Where did she go, your strong and beautiful warrior cousin? She should have looked after your tender heart, my love... oh, what a delight that feast after your return! That night you thought I was her, and our destinies were sealed."

'She is definitely not talking to me!' Annea guessed uneasy, 'what should I do? Just let her go on? I'm not quite sure I'm supposed to hear all this...'

The queen continued her monologue undisturbed, "that stupid old king had to interfere, he almost ruined everything! But you see, I knew how to get what I wanted: the rightful queen of the Skyarach, great queen Umbriel! No one would have ever doubted me again, why did she have to come back... she had to come to my kingdom, and take away what should have been mine!!!"

The queen broke in tears, but continued to ignore Annea's presence. She sat down on the bench with difficulty, sobbing uncontrollably.

Annea did not know what to do. Shall she speak words of comfort to the old lady? She wasn't sure she was aware of her presence anymore. She decided to lay a hand on the queens shoulder, which the old lady took almost instantly and held fast in her grip for what seemed a lifetime to Annea.

Right then, a service maid appeared in the distance through the maze-like hedges to announce a visitor: Eonar Drkent Dryd Thuarnach.

Chapter Twenty-One: The Magic Stones

6th Day of Gloaras, 300YD,
procession road towards Polarys

"Two days since he left, and we haven't heard a word, Ara! Druids from the Deno Kæyn visited yesterday the temple, and they said they haven't seen Ealator along the way. Where could he go? He couldn't have vanished in thin air... how come he didn't say anything to anyone, Ara?" demanded Skymnia, while urging her horse to keep pace with Arachtan, who had been riding beside her, "it is strange even for him, Ara..."

"Don't worry, muine Kay,[99] we will do everything in our power to find him, I promise," he answered, looking deep into her eyes, "we sent out druid scouts as soon as we realised, he cannot be far," he lied despite of himself.

"I'm afraid it might be not enough, Ara," she gave back troubled, "I know my brother. Right now, with all that is in his mind, he is capable of anything if we do not get to him."

She looked away so that he could not see the twinkling drops rolling down her cheeks, and did not wait for his answer, but

---
[99] My cousin (fem.)

spurred her horse to catch up with Skeor, who was riding at the front.

Ara watched her until she reached Skeor's side.

Skymnia had grown, she was a woman, now. They would not be able to keep her in the dark about the whole truth behind Ealator's disappearance for much longer... But he would wait until they reached Polarys. There, she would be safe, and he could entrust her to his druid masters, while they continued to Drkent Har.

They had left the Eno Kæyn dressed as local Nachtural Brean six hours ago, and were now about to reach the Deno Kæyn,[100] where they would stop to rest and refresh themselves for the night. It was already dark, and the cold was creeping into their bones, but at least they were on their way, and apart from Ealator's disappearance, everyone was content with moving on. Drkent Har was still far, and they could not afford to lose more time.

Eight days ago, Ealator had stolen a Dryd Stællyr,[101] and had vanished from the temple for good. They had searched the area for a day, but had to stop due to a heavy blizzard, and after that,

---

[100] Second temple.
[101] A druid stallion was a special breed that druids kept for their Kæyns. These male horses were bred for resistance, loyality and good temper, all the druids needed from their horses in this mountainous and often woody area.

they had decided to let him go his way. There was nothing else they could do for him at the moment.

At first, they had kept Skymnia in the dark. They had not wanted to upset her, she had been making excellent progress, and the temple Dryds had also agreed it was best that way.

But the day came, when she had asked to see her brother, she wanted to talk to him alone. She had been feeling much better, and having heard that they were leaving the Kæyn in two days, she had planned to beg Eala to stay here, so that the druids would help him with his troubled soul. In truth, she had actually been preparing for a heated discussion with her brother, who had never been easy to convince otherwise…

This so expected conversation, however, had never taken place, and they had been forced to tell her what had happened, wisely omitting some uncomfortable details, such as the precise date of his disappearance and his repeated threats.

Ara knew that Eala was far away and out of reach by now, but he had to choose, and he had chosen to wait for Skymnia to recover. He had used the time to confer with the druids about further possibilities of action against Drkent Har, and to plan his itinerary and strategy meticulously. They had sent secret messages to Polarys and Drkent Har, using the hidden druid tunnels. Ara had to inform Thuarnach of their arrival, but he would not risk being surprised by more Kechtási knights, nor did he want Asttrian or Shya to get information of his whereabouts. Ealator would have to be on his own, they could not risk more exposure. They had done as much as they could for him, for the time being. Now they needed to focus on reaching the capital and Drkent Har unnoticed, and with enough support to overthrow the tyrannical rule of their cousin.

However, on the loose, Ealator posed as much a threat to others as he did to himself, and not least to their cause. So, in case anyone found Eala, they had sent word to the different druid temples along the procession road to seize him immediately. But for all there was to be said against Ealator's attitude, he was a well-trained knight and he knew his ways in the forest, almost as good as his Anairarachti cousins. It was no surprise, then, that no one had even had a glimpse of him since his escape. And this, in turn, was becoming a matter of increasing concern for all.

Skymnia, on her part, could not get rid of the strange feeling that they were not telling her the whole truth. She felt powerless, excluded from the important decisions concerning her and the ones she loved. And then, it was that thing with Ara...

Since she had met Ara in Reaghil Ovsbhealle Rheanna, after so long, she could not really talk to him openly. Not that she did not trust him, it was rather the distance that he kept to everyone. Only Skeor and Thuaì seemed to be able to pierce the veil, and only at times. Most of the times, Ara retreated and was on his own, meditating, thinking, plotting, who knew. Of course, he had always been different from the others, and he was more than kind to her, but he kept on treating her like a little child, which she was most certainly not. He seemed unable to see her for what she really was: a grown-up woman.

Since they were very young, she had known Arachtan wanted to become a druid... But that was different. The distance, the years, and the rumours... Now, she did not know what to believe anymore. Of one thing she was sure, however, there was more to the stories as the Anairarachti princes would let on, and she was intent to find out, one way or the other.

For now, Skymnia was more than grateful that her cousins had taken her to the druid temple to be healed. Her wounds ran much deeper than the eye could see, and she guessed her cousin Ara had suspected from the beginning that there was more than her broken bones to heal...

As things were, the holistic treatment she had received by the Kæyn Dryds had been exceptional, and she still could not believe the wonders she had seen, during their stay at the first temple.

A potent mixture of essential oils and herbal decoctions had always been burning in one corner of her room, cleaning and purifying the air. Over her bed, there had been a special niche in the wall, where the druids placed magical stones. At some point, she had noticed that although they changed them every day, it had always been the same type of crystal. She had asked Dryd Tyrna, and he had explained to her all the healing properties of the stone, and that it needed to be charged again with dragon fire from their altar to make it more powerful. Hænardrkentfael[102] was its name, the celestial dragon stone. With its stored energy, it dispensed with fear and unrest, providing her room with a relaxing, positive atmosphere, which made her feel protected and safe, while connecting her with the powers of the ancestors. This use of magical stones had been widespread in the Arach Kingdoms of old, its wisdom jealously kept through the millennia by the druid orders, but the Hænardrkentfael was known by all to be the strongest of the dragon crystals for protection and healing, if difficult to get.

Skymnia had had to follow a strict routine, too. Starting with a daily hot bath of arnica and cypress oils, followed by a massage with hot stones early in the morning, she would then be given the first of three daily turmeric teas with rich goat milk, ginger, black pepper and honey from the temple bee stock. With the help of a druid, she had been urged to walk, despite the pain, once around the central dome, and to meditate in one of the four shrines of the

---

[102] Angel stone.

inner temple. Sometimes, even Ara came to accompany her during her meditations, but they were not allowed to talk to each other.

She had always been guided to either the fire or the water shrines, she wasn't quite sure why, but it had all felt good, so she had never complained. The druids had simply said that fire would support physical movement, while water was the source of the spiritual fountain, and that was enough for her to know. And although she had never been admitted to the central shrine, every other room of the temple was a masterpiece of druid wisdom and natural beauty. She had been allowed to borrow books about old legends from the Eno Lyvriach, too, making her stay at the Eno Kæyn a joy. She could not recall when was the last time she had felt so happy...

The food had been excellent, as well. She had not been allowed to join in the meals at the kitchens, but she had always been accompanied by a druid of the order, most of the time by Dryd Tyrna, a novice to the order. By the time she had left, however, she had met most of them regularly, and was well acquainted with them. The Eno Kæyn Dryds had been truly friendly and caring. She would not forget. One day, she would pay them back for their kindness.

The druids lived very modestly, but at the same time were holders and protectors of millennia of ancient wisdom, very powerful wisdom. It had not taken long for her to realize that they would be next on Asttrian's quest for absolute power. She knew druids were trained to defend themselves and their temples. They were not alone, certainly. They had their own trained army, their magical powers, and the people, most here would fight until the very last drop of their blood for them. With the reformation of the Arach Law, however, Asttrian's power had grown considerably overnight, and no one knew what his next move would be.

Asttrian's army was the most powerful military machinery in the whole of the remaining Arachti kingdoms. His father, old king Urarathan, had seen to that. 'To keep the peace among the Arach peoples...' he had said, without realising the potential dangers of such a weapon when in the wrong hands.

There was so much her good, old uncle had not realised timely enough... His own son had been recruiting Kechtás and expanding their powers under his very nose. This was a fact no one could deny by now!

Yes, all of the Arachti kingdoms were in terrible danger. And to make things worse, it still was uncertain who the great Drkarach would support. The creature had not been seen flying over the cities of the realm since the death of the old king. It was even said that it was weak and too old, that it would die soon. Skymnia was sure that whether this was true or not, Asttrian would see to it, the moment he was certain the beast would not support him. But what if the dragon did decide to support Asttrian? What then? How long till they targeted the temples, she wondered… They had to stop him!

Skymnia opened a small pouch of smooth silk she had been given by Dryd Tyrna himself before they left. She had it hanging across her breast, just as he had told her to do. Inside a beautiful, round light blue, transparent stone, the Hænardrkentfael.

She took it out and pressed it hard in her right fist.

"Please, give me the strength and the will to help in this cause. Keep mother and brother safe, and help us put an end to my cousin's tyranny for once and for all. Ara is the one, I know it. Whatever he has done, it doesn't matter, I'm no one to judge him. He will be the one to lead us into freedom, I beg you, let me be at his side."

Chapter Twenty-Two : The Warrior Queen And Her Dragon King

6th Day of Gloaras, 300YD,
Drkent Har, Reaghil Bheallemer

"Muine Bræy Anneya, camra Thay aí?[103] They told me you were in the gardens with the queen…"

"Ey, muin Eonar Drkent Dryd Thuarnach. It's been a good day…"

She thought she was not going to go into details about the dance rehearsal with the king, or his sister's poisonous remarks. There were more pressing matters to discuss.

"I have news from afar," she said in a whisper.

The druid raised his eyebrows surprised.

"Ey, muine Yahæn Anneya, Yai draykt,"[104] he answered.

"A princess is travelling from… Daing Murr?" she added, unsure of the right pronunciation.

---

[103] "My beautiful Annea, how are you today?"
[104] "Yes, my young Annea, I see."

"Daing Mhuir?"

"Ey, that is the place."

"What about her?"

"They have somehow found her, she will be coming to visit..." she said in a low voice.

"Hmm, Anuelle?" asked the druid surprised.

"Ey, that was the name of our visitor, muin Eonar."

At that point the two Kechtás, who had been standing close to the entrance, cleared their throats simultaneously as an obvious threat to the two whispering behind their backs.

Thuarnach nodded to her in silence, and they changed the topic rapidly. But this news was extremely preoccupying. He would have to inform Lughan and the noble Rothar, who was their newly acquired spy in the castle, straight away. This was changing everything.

"Tell me, muine Anneya, have you learned something new, today?" he asked out loud to avoid any trouble.

She thought for a moment.

"The queen talked, Thuarnach."

"Really? This is good… I didn't think she would ever talk to anyone again."

"Well, she didn't talk to me, precisely. She was… well, absent, as always, and then she just started talking… I guess she was remembering her life, her king, or something like that."

"Muin Bræye Anneya, I sense there is something you want to ask?" he winked at her.

"Ey, there is…"

She looked down to her hands, which she had folded over her lap, "there is so much…"

"Start with something I might be able to answer, Yahæn Ær."

They did not have much time left and he wanted to give her some comfort, and support her as much as possible during her time alone in Drkent Har.

"The queen, she said terrible things, Thuarnach. She talked about plotting to get the crown and marrying king Urarathan? Could this be true, or was it just part of her state of delusion?"

It was a sensitive state matter they were discussing now, no triviality, so she was not completely sure she deserved an answer at all. Plus, the Kechtás were still listening in… To her surprise, however, Thuarnach looked deep into her eyes with profound sadness, and suddenly, he seemed tired, ancient to her.

So, it was true…

He nodded sadly, "ey, muin Læyve Kræy,[105] it is true. My brother Urarathan, then the crown prince of the North Arach Kingdom of the Thuatharachti, was bound by law to choose. Umbriel had been sentenced to die for what she had done. Only he could have saved her, and only by marrying her."

"It seems kind of unfair for him, right? But, what had she done?"

"Anneya, normally all Arach kingdoms strictly follow the Wbent Teyn Drkent, the Arach Law. I've told you already about the laws that normally regulate our kingdom, you remember? Well, the law of the kingdom clearly states that when a true Arach - princess, prince, king or queen - takes a common person as lover, and

---

[105] "My dear child"

procreates with this person, that person either dies - with the child - or is tied to him or her for life under the bond of marriage."

"Wow, but... so, they slept together and she got pregnant, and then she was sentenced to die for it?"

Thuarnach sighed visibly overwhelmed. He had been keeping his brother's dangerous secrets for too long, and it was weighing on him like the pillars of the heavens themselves. Some years before, he had decided to open up to Lughan, for he knew he could trust him with his life, and it would aid their plans to have someone else understand what they were fighting for.

He had to admit to himself, that he would have to let Annea into Urarathan's secrets, too, if he wanted her to trust him fully. And now that his brother was dead, and the kingdom was under such upheaval, it didn't matter as much anymore. Besides, who knew under which circumstances they would meet again...

"Anneya, we are not what you would understand as normal humans."

He hesitated for a second as he looked into her disbelieving gaze, but then continued, "we were changed by the ancient dragons thousands of years ago. We, so to speak, sealed a blood pact with them. Urarathan, just like me, was a descendant from the Dreà

Arachti, the Peoples of the Dragon. We possess, let's say, other qualities that normal humans don't possess…"

"Right…" she answered, slowly chewing down this new information with considerable apprehension. Weren't it Thuarnach talking, and hadn't she seen Drkarach by herself, she would call for a doctor right away…

"One trait of our people is longevity – some even believe us to be immortal because our lifespan is so much longer than that of common men. It is then our duty, you see, to choose our consorts wisely, to protect our people and guide them by example. We are so powerful, even without the dragon, that no man could challenge our rule if we are united."

"So how old are you, Thuarnach?" she wanted to know.

"Yai er Eonar, muin Kræy,"[106] it was all he answered. He didn't want to scare her with too many details, he knew she was starting to doubt what she was hearing.

They remained silent for a while, but she had to know more, so she pressed on.

"So, did he love her?"

---

[106] "I am ancient my child"

Thuarnach did not hesitate this time, "no, Anneya... Umbriel was beautiful and smart, and she had set eyes on my brother since her family joined court, but..."

After weighing his words, he continued, "my brother's heart had been given away to someone else long before, you see. He had eyes for one woman only, he loved our warrior cousin, mighty queen Scaìthara of the Anairarachti, and he did so until his last breath."

"Thuarnach, that is truly sad..."

"Ey, sad indeed, muine Bræy Ærin.[107] Umbriel gave birth to twins and became Urarathan's wife."

"Asttrian and Shya?"

"Ey. One thing led to another, and our father, King Urukaracht, not accepting my brother's decision, exiled them, and anyone that stood behind my brother, including me, so starting one of the bloodiest wars in Arach history. At this point, the Drkarach flew off to follow my brother, and settled here. The old beast never really liked my father..."

"But why, Thuarnach? Surely, this all seems a little out of proportion to me..."

---

[107] "my beautiful lady"

"Yai kwbent..."[108] he answered with a heavy sigh, "but that is because you are not acquainted with our traditions and values. With great power, Anneya, comes great responsibility, greater than one's own personal desires and wishes. In my father's eyes, Urarathan had betrayed our kingdom by taking host maiden Umbriel as his wife, while in my brother's view, he was saving her from an unfair death sentence. He thought it was his debt to pay: a great price for his great mistake."

"Hmm... the queen talked about a celebration at his return?"

"Ey, that is precisely when everything went wrong. There was a feast in my brother's honour for his successfully completed trial in the South, he had managed to acquire more allies for the Confederation of Arach Kingdoms. He was now ready to replace the old king in the North, our father. Everyone was merry and drank a little too much Reahnnvid, a noble red wine my brother had brought from the new lands he had visited.

In this state of intoxication, Umbriel took the opportunity and seduced him. She was wearing Scaìthara's Dragon Mask, which is the one used in the sun and moon celebrations through the year. She made him believe she was our cousin Scaìthara, and he was so drunk, he believed her. Urarathan never forgave himself for not noticing the difference..."

---

[108] "I know"

"But where was the actual Scaìthara, then? Didn't she love Urarathan back? Surely she had something to say about this."

"Of course, she did, Kræy, she loved my brother more than her own life! But she was too far away, and she had to stay away for long to defend her own title, Anneya. She had also been sent away to a more difficult region for her trial. She was to handle an agreement with the nobles of the isles in the west for fairer sea trading conditions. The task would decide if she was the right queen for my brother, but she was no diplomat. Her trial ended with a cruel war that lasted ten long years, a war she has regretted bitterly ever since… by the time she could return, my brother had left the Thuatharachti Kingdom with a wife and their twin children to found the Skyarachti Kingdom, in the South."

"So… had Scaìthara been promised to him, or not?"

"Well, not quite. That is not a tradition of ours, you see. Our queens and kings are able to marry who their hearts desire, as long as it is someone of Arach descent. This is because the mixture with normal humans brings about malformations and hereditary problems of all sorts. If my brother had accepted to renounce his title as king and had moved far away to live a quiet life with his wife and children, it wouldn't have posed much of a threat to my father's heritage. As it was, however, my brother was determined to rule. He saw it as his innate responsibility, even more so after his self-imposed marriage."

"I don't understand…"

"Scaìthara and Urarathan had chosen each other of their own accord already as children, Anneya. They were inseparable! We all grew up together under my father's vigilant eye. She belongs to the Arach people of the sea, the house of the Mhuirarachti or Anairarachti, named in this way for their seafaring qualities. Her mother, Anneahnem, known also as The Lady of The Woods, came with her parents from the ruins of the red ancient city of Seannanorthai. So, my cousin was a perfect match for my brother: she was beautiful, strong and very cunning. Many men feared her more than my brother!"

There was a rather conspiratorial sparkle in the druid's amused gaze, when he was telling this story. Annea could see, he could still remember every detail of it as if it were today.

After a while he went on, "they fought wars together and they built cities together, and although it had not been written down, they had promised each other eternal love."

"What happened when she found out about his marriage?" she pressed on.

His gaze clouded for a moment, now.

"Well, Scaìthara took a group of her best and most loyal men, and marched south to join Urarathan. When she first met him, she fought him to the ground, in front of all his nobles, and then walked out into the woods without looking back once, where she stayed for some time. He went after her to no avail, she had vanished.

But their love was bigger than life, she could not stay angry at him forever. And so, she appeared back one day, during the festival of Annorashkin.[109] He asked her to stay, and she consented. They worked hand in hand to build up Urarathan's Skyarach Kingdom. She was always at his side, day and night.

Queen Umbriel, who had always despised her, did everything in her power to separate the two, but my brother was very clear from the beginning: he had married her to face the responsibility for his mistake, he had never and would never love her. And, you must know, he never touched her again after that day when she seduced him, back at our father's court. Queen Umbriel started and ended her reign as our Host Queen."

"But Scaìthara did not stay here forever after all, did she? I mean, I haven't even heard her name before..."

---

[109] Dragon Festival in the month of June, when the dragon egg claims its colour and the realm of men are gifted with red fruits.

"Correct, muin Kræy. She had her own duties to her family, you see. She had been entrusted the foundation of a new kingdom in the West, in the same lands she had appeased, during those long years of war. In her absence, however, there had been a void of power, and many revolts among the different peoples and host nobles there, too.
Many even suggest, it was Umbriel's family behind it all. You see, they were rich tradesmen with a vast network in the Thuatharachti Kingdom and beyond. So, after three years of a factual married life, my cousin was forced to leave and take up her new seat at Inna Skythiarach, the Island of the Winged, as it is known..."

Now, Thuarnach's dreamy eyes looked up as if searching for a lost bird.

"I still remember the day that both mounted Drkarach and flew away together, the Warrior Queen and her Dragon King, towards the red, setting sun over the Thaunaan – Believe me, I saw fire rising over us that day!"

He stared in the distance as if he could still see them flying off in front of him.

"He came back some months later, with a broken nose and a broken heart. They never saw each other again. They wrote endless letters to each other, and they trained their children together, as the Arach law demands, but they stayed away from each other until his last day."

"And they never saw each other again, Thuarnach?"

As if not listening to her, he continued with his tale.

"Some years later, Scaìthara married her older cousin Drearyan, descendant of an old Mhuirarachti branch. And she had children of her own, too: Arachtan, Thuaìden, Skeorden and Anuelle, the princes and princess of Daing Mhuir... ey, Drearyan has made a good consort king for her, after all."

"Thuarnach, this is such a sad story. I never met your brother or his love, but I can feel their pain as if it was my own... why do such terrible things have to happen?"

"Muine Læve Ærin, Arach or not, we are all humans, after all. The Arach had been chosen for their strength and discipline. They were selected by the dragon spirit to protect and guide humankind through their journey on Earth. But now, after thousands of years, not even the dragon blood can save us from corruption and decay, and while we might be doomed, we can still save our people, the ones we were here to protect in the first place... This is what I have understood in my very long life."

He looked at Annea compassionately and then added, "so, you see, we have to save as many lives as possible from Asttrian's and Shya's tyranny, Anneya. They are very powerful together, never underestimate their ambitions. And they are especially dangerous for those that stand in the way between them and absolute power."

"Hmm... so, you say, you sort of have some kind of special powers? Do you mean something like magical powers?"

She truly hadn't decided yet what to make out of this whole story of his. Some parts seemed fairly logical, but others... It all just escaped her rational understanding of the world by far!

On his part, Thuarnach had already gathered that this was more than she could handle for a day, and although he was in a hurry to share important things with her, too, he would have to wait for the rest.

"Your people in the future might call it so, muin Kræy," he continued.

"So, what is it that you can do?"

"It is not quite the same for everyone. Each of us, just like all humans, has a special gift, a particular ability, you could say, which is enhanced in the Arach people. Me, for example, I can fairly well read people's minds, among some other things."

"Ohhh…"

"Ey, it can get quite loud at times," he grinned sheepishly at her, "and now, we'll let our dutiful Kechtási knights here finally use the restroom," he chuckled, "I can't come tomorrow, but I'll come the day after at the same time as today, and yes, I will send your love to Lughan… Keep strong, muine Læve Etayn Anneya."[110]

"You too, muin Eonar Drkent Dryd Thuarnach."

He was such an extraordinary person, Annea thought, full of wisdom and kindness…
To cheer her up, he would always say goodbye to her with their secret joke, one her father had started, and the Kechtás better not hear: "muine Læve Etayn Anneya," my lovely princess Annea…

---

[110] My lovely princess Annea.

Chapter Twenty-Three: **Troubled Seas**

7th Day of Gloaras, 300YD,
Daing Mhuir, Inna Skythiarach

"No, there is no word from Thuarnach, muine Drkarach Qvynne, I'm sorry," answered the druid concerned.

"I don't like this, Rœhen, it's been simply too long, now. I might have to intervene, after all…"

"Ey, it is true… I have sent several jays to Dryd Rayka at Polarys, muine Drkarach Qvynne, and I have tried the Eno Kæyn, as well… the temples, they seem to be isolated by the Kechtási force. They must be sending out messages through other means, but the jays aren't flying, and the road takes longer."

Rœhen, like Scaìthara, had already understood that the Skyarach twins were not going to stop until they had destroyed the kingdom their father had built. They were not interested in promoting a prosperous kingdom for their people. They wanted to gain absolute power for themselves, and for such an endeavour, they were going to need to do away with any opposition. First the free cities, then the temples, and then any kingdom that would stand on their way, they would all have to fall to the unleashed power of Asttrian's Kechtás. He would try to destroy them one by one, and Thuarnach and Ara would not be able to stop them without the Dragon or the sword…

"What do we know about Drkenstar? Has it been found, yet?"

"Ney, muine Drkarach Qvynne, da Chlìar Drkent na Teyn er ærgull."[111]

"I don't believe this. My druid cousin would have seen to it…"

"Well, there is one account from our spies at Drkent Har suggesting it has been found and will be returned to the king on the feast of Dryemoshach, but I'm not sure we can trust the source."

"Thuarnach would never risk such a move… what is he up to?"

"My same thought. Apparently, he will be trading the sword in exchange for a favour from the king. It seems he is trying to protect someone, or so my source tells me…"

"But Ara has not reached the capital yet."

"Ney, neya tvæy Noys kænnt."[112]

---

[111] "No, my dragon queen, the dragon sword of the king is lost."
[112] "No, not that we know."

"So, who could be so precious for him to risk the kingdom's destruction? No, this is not a possibility, I know Thuarnach well."

"Maybe, or it is something or someone we don't know about that is also vital to the cause... we simple don't know."

"Hmm, that is not much like my cousin."

"I agree," interrupted them Drearyan, entering the court room dripping water from all corners of his coat.

"What have you been up to?" asked the queen amused.

"Oh, this?" he answered showing his soaked coat in full length, "I was visiting Dabhealle[113] and a storm came up my way," he laughed wholeheartedly, as always.

"What business do you have at Dabhealle, in such a weather?"

"I talked to the fisher."

"And?"

---

[113] The island of Inna Skythiarach, where Daing Mhuir was, marked the periphery of the Anairarach Kingdom to the west, and hence was not heavily populated, having only two small fishing and trading ports and a mediumsized village close to the fortress, where people lived a calm and retrospect life. So "Dabhealle" has to be interpreted as "the village" not "the city" or "the town" in this case, and it refers to Daingbhealle, or the village of Daing Mhuir.

"Well, I was right. They escaped with the fishermen that night. It seems Ryssa and that stable boy were with her... the men swear it was dark and nobody knew it was Anu..."

"You're saying that our daughter escaped right under our very nose with that girl? But she said to me she didn't trust her... I should have expelled Ryssa from our kingdom long ago!"

"Ey, Scaìthara, muine Beag Etayn er raian."[114]

"So, she went on her own accord?!"

"Ey, it seems so, muine Lævyvljg."

"So, what now Drearyan?! Would you still have me wait?"

She walked down the few steps that were separating them, to face her husband.

A tall, proud figure, queen Scaìthara possessed a threatening aura, one that would overwhelm even the toughest warrior.

"For the Dragon, all our children are missing, Drearyan!"

She walked closer, holding his gaze.

---

[114] "Yes, Scaìthara, my little princess ran off"

"You know how much I respect you, you have always been my right hand and a wise one, and although I have not been myself since Urarathan's death, trust me, the mourning is over!" she said, while her strong hands curled up into fists.

Then, she turned and walked past both men, until she reached the centre of the hall.

"We have waited enough! I've made up my mind. We will go back to Urarathan's Kingdom and fight! Fight for his heritage, for his dream of a peaceful, prosperous world, and fight for our children!"

"Muine Drkarach Qvynne," started Drearyan carefully, "we have fought side by side during the Mhuirarachti conquest wars, no one knows you better than I do…
I have never, for a moment, believed that your dragon fire was extinct. I knew you were going to return as brave as ever to defend what we all have built with so much effort, and also with the blood of many innocent and many good men. During the last few months, I've started both reorganizing the protection around our borders inconspicuously, and readying our troops, as I promised I would. Anu's disappearance has proven to me that there is no more time to sit back, muine Lævyvljg…"

He moved towards her slowly, "Scaìthara, a jay reached my spies at the port yesterday… It was from Tschiaran."

"And?"

"Well, he has found Anu…"

"I'm listening."

"He is convinced Ryssa is a spy for Drkent Har, and she has by now certainly informed everyone, including Asttrian and Shya, that Anuelle is out there looking for her brothers… Scaìthara, Tschiaran could not bring Anu back through the border. They had redoubled the Kechtás overnight…"

"I see…"

"He is smuggling Anu through the Lahir-Vwylir-Kæyn route to her brothers."

She slid to the nearest window and watched the angry, foamy waves whipping restlessly the rocky foundations of her fortress.

Scaìthara was no one to know fear… But it was different with her children.

"It is the safest route, muine Lævyvljg. There are Skyarachti spies looking for her everywhere this side of the border, too. My source is reliable…"

"What then? Even if they were able to meet with Ara, Skeor and Thuaì, the whole kingdom is looking for them if Ryssa is a spy…"

"Ey, indeed. They will need our support. We'll march in, but in a different way this time. We don't know where our children are, we don't know what Thuarnach is up to, and we don't know where the sword is… but we do know one thing for sure: where to find Drkarach."

"What are you suggesting, Drearyan?! Drkarach is not our Dragon, he could kill us the moment we set foot in the temple! Without Urarathan, she is as dangerous as Asttrian or Shya for us…"

"But you have a true warrior's heart guided by the loyalty and dedication to your people! Yours is a true Drkent Cœr."[115]

"And yours is full of wisdom, muin Læyv, but on this matter I'm not so sure… I will have to think about it!"

Right there, looking down her window, she started wondering when the storm had started… She had been in the court room most of the day, finally attending to her daily tasks as queen, with

---

[115] Dragon Heart

Dryd Rœhen at her side, while her husband had been fighting the icy, wet gales of their beloved Mermhuir,[116] down at Dabhealle. She had to admit yet again that Drearyan had always been that brave, if more diplomatic, warrior at her side. And despite all troubled seas, he had always helped her master storms wisely... But would it be so this time?

---

[116] Great Ocean

Chapter Twenty-Four: Of Noble Hearts

7th Day of Gloaras, 300YD,
Royal Kechtási vessel on the Rheann, close to the city of Reaghil Ovsbhealle
Rheanna

Anuelle stood motionless, counting the seagulls that flew past them, like dancers in a swirl of white feathers. Birds, ethereal beings suspended in eternal freedom...

She was on deck of the proud Drkent Skythiarach,[117] the largest of the Kechtási vessels, and now, her floating prison. In the distance, the breath-taking silhouette of the Green Terrace of the Dragon, now so devoid of any meaning to her, stood omnipresent over the grey waters of the Rheann.

They had started off three days ago, and an icy rain had accompanied their course most of the time, forcing them to stay inside the cabins.

Today, it was the first time she dared come out.

She felt lost and astray in the huge vessel, and only those cheerful birds flying freely around her lifted her spirits, somewhat...

---

[117] The Winged Dragon, the ship was the most important of the Kechtási vessels, being the biggest and best equipped river warship in the kingdom.

Exactly three days ago, during a promising morning twilight, she and Tschiaran had landed at the prosperous port of Kælnamer an Rheann,[118] one of the busiest cities on the shores of the river. There, they were hoping to change guild and ship, respectively, to erase any trace that could lead to them from Drejkreins. All in all, it had been a rather unspectacular journey so far, and both of them had started believing that their good fortune would last.

After landing, Tschiaran had left Anuelle to wait in a particularly quiet corner of the port, if not smell free, right between the vendor stands, which were being frantically set up, and the fishers' docking area.

He was supposed to arrange the transfer onto the next ship, this time, with the guild of the metal craftsmen. This one had strong connections inwards the Lahir river and all the way to the city of Neybrealle and the Polarys Kæyn, where the art of metallurgy had a strong tradition, and where they would be heading. By now, it would be the safest place to hide and wait news from Ara and the others, if they weren't there themselves already.

Anuelle had been waiting for half an hour, when an old crone wrapped in a rugged and tattered cloak approached her. She had

---

[118] Today's city of Cologne

a basket full with fresh oysters from the northern coast, which was considered a true delicacy.

"Muine Kræyin, camra Thay? Vuoy esmerian dhasi? Frigge na nrothan Sketheamar! Bræt da Thay, muine Kræyin! Bræt da Thay![119]

"Duellich, muine Ærin, Yai er neya Ùydn hor, fallay en'audr Úinne," Anu replied politely.[120]

But the woman was not going to let go easily.

She started tugging softly at Anuelle's coat, begging and arguing she needed the money to feed her sick children.

Anuelle desperately searched with her eyes for Tschiaran, but she could not see him anywhere. The port was starting to wake up, and more and more vendor stands where blocking any further view of the docks.

Now, the woman was pulling harder from her coat and repeating her monotone plea like a chant.

"Doyde, Bræye Kræyin, kæyfe muins Frigge Œstrys, doyde, muine Kræyin..."[121]

---

[119] "My girl, how are you? Would you like to eat these? Fresh from the northern sea port! Cheap for you, my girl! Cheap for you!"
[120] "Sorry, I'm not interested right now, maybe another time."

It was then that, in the fraction of a second, everything went wrong.

The woman's tugging made Anu's hood move slightly backwards, and an unruly auburn curl escaped from its jealously guarded cover, flaming up instantly with the first timid rays of sun that were softly painting the harbour in a myriad of watercolours.

From far away, Tschiaran saw Anu, and started off towards her in a desperate pace.

Suddenly, there was more movement around her, some fisher pulling carts and rolling up their nets. He couldn't see very well what was happening, but he could see several men gathering closer to her rapidly.

"For the Dragon!" he cursed to himself, "they've found us..."

He started running now, but it was too late. A group of four men were dragging Princess Anuelle to a back alley, at the end of the docks.

Tschiaran jumped over some carts and boxes, pushed his way through the chaotic crowd on the narrow docks as hard as he could, hopelessly. Now, he could not see them anymore.

---

[121] "Please, nice girl, buy my fresh oysters, please, my girl..."

He rushed past the last vendor stand, and then hastily took the turn into the alleyway, where he had seen them disappear.

There his heart jumped at the scene he found.

Anu was struggling against two big Kechtás, who were holding her tight from both arms, while two others were striding in front of them with a certain goal: get Anuelle to Asttrian and Shya.

Tschiaran had one sabre-like sword he had won gambling, and he knew well how to use it. Still he was outnumbered by Kechtási knights!

He thought fast, he had to use the surprise factor to his advantage, it was his only chance.

He sneaked silently behind them like a ghost, hiding behind some empty barrels and wooden boxes stacked at both sides of the grey alley.

At one point, one of the Kechtás that was holding Anu, stopped short and turned around. He had definitely heard something.

Luckily for Tschiaran, the other Kechtá was in a hurry, and urged his comrade to continue, without checking on the noise.

Tschiaran took this chance, summoned all his courage, and ran full speed into one the Kechtás, while throwing an empty wooden barrel onto the other, causing great confusion.

"Raian aí, Anu! Raian aí!"[122] he managed to shout.

Anuelle was flung to the ground, but quickly got up and started running back to the port. She wanted to see what was happening behind her. She had heard Tschiaran urging her to run, though, and so she did.

She ran as fast as her legs would take her. She could not hear Tschiaran or the Kechtás anymore.

Once she reached the docks, she stopped running and decided to turn right to look for the ship chartered by the metal guild, the one Tschiaran had arranged for them. He would know where to find her.

Right before she mingled with the crowd, however, she took the chance and turned around to get a glimpse of the men she had left behind.

She could not make out Tschiaran from the rest of the men fighting with drawn swords at the back of the dark alley, so she

---

[122] "Run now, Anu! Run now!"

hastily counted. Still five! Tschiaran was alive! Now, she had to focus...

She strode through the busy crowd always alert, searching for the ship.

There! She had found it!

A sturdy medium-sized vessel with the shield of the guild was resting calmly, lulled by the grey waters of the Rheann, at a wharf some thirty meters away from the last stall.

Anuelle scurried past the vendors not listening to what they were calling. She felt fear crawling up her spine, but she had no time for that, she had to be brave, now.

When she finally reached the wharf, she was out of breath, but still she kept her pace. She had to make it!

Right then, a cloaked woman and a thin, long man appeared out of nowhere to block her way.

At first, she could not see them well, so tightly did she hold her hood around her exuberant curly head. She had also been avoiding eye contact with everyone, but she decided to look up, now. They would have to let her pass!

She recognized them immediately: Ryssa and Gællen, right there, in front of her!

For a moment, she forgot about the suspicions she had had. She was just happy to see a familiar face in this so unfriendly crowd.

"Ryssa, thayng da Drkarach![123] They are after us! We have to hide! Come!"

But Ryssa did not answer, nor did she move.

"Come, we have to go! Ryssa!" Anu urged her again.

But Ryssa stood there in silence.

"What–" she could not finish what she was about to say, when she suddenly saw the two big, cloaked men standing right behind the slave girl.

'Kechtás,' she thought.

Anuelle tried to walk slowly backwards, but after a few steps, she stumbled over something hard. Two big hands steadied her back, while she slowly turned around.

---

[123] "Thank the Dragon" or "thank Drkarach."

Right behind her, two huge Kechtás were towering over her, like statues carved in hard stone guarding the entrance to a temple. One of them was holding Tschiaran's sabre, his hands blood-soaked…

Later, Anuelle would try with all her strength to recall the events of that day, but her effort would remain fruitless.

She could not find out what truly happened to her loyal friend Tschiaran, and she would never know exactly how she got onboard the Drkent Skythiarach either, or how long it took her to find her voice back. Any memory of these events had been erased, forever.

The one thing she would never forget was Ryssa's demeanour, when she finally got onboard the royal Kechtási vessel. She was beaming, she looked triumphant, even defiant… And she was alone. Free from her shade, free from the mute stable boy, no Gællen at her side.

Anuelle remembered wondering, where he would go without her, only to find the answer written on Ryssa's blood-stained hands, while she was trying to hide a small knife in between her clothes.

'It must have happened at the port, right before we got onto the ship, right in front of everyone...' she remembered thinking, 'and no one cared, no one said anything, for who would miss Gællen?'

'Only the horses at home,' said a sad voice in her head, after a while...

It had not been enough for Ryssa to betray them all. She had to do away with any evidence of her wrongdoings, of her dark secrets. It seemed Gællen knew too much, and posed an undesired risk to her. Yes, he was a mute, but maybe not mute enough for that woman.

Anuelle never asked, she didn't need to. Of all that happened on that tragic day, she was certain of this one thing, she would never see her loyal friend Tschiaran or the stable boy of Daing Mhuir again.

Chapter Twenty-Five: The Underground

7th Day of Gloaras, 300YD,
Reaghil Dryd Slijk close to the central market, Reaghil Bheallemer

It had been truly difficult to arrange the meeting without raising suspicions. Thuarnach would have preferred to meet his helpers right after he had talked to Annea, but he was being closely watched, and he had to wait for another turn of the sun.

Today, he had been effectively evading the Kechtási knights for hours, but not without the cunning of years of training. By now, he was out of breath, and he had to move on, or he would never reach their meeting point on time…

As soon as Thuarnach had left Drkent Har the day before, he had sent word to Lughan and to Rothar, their spy at court, that the situation had changed and they had to meet urgently to rethink their plan. Time was most precious, he had written, and he had hinted at the arrival of another important hostage to Drkent Har.

With the arrival of Anu, the situation was getting even more delicate, and Thuarnach couldn't get rid of the bad feeling, that they would have to act without waiting for Arachtan, after all. But he did not think that their resources would be enough to liberate all of Asttrian's hostages, which would mean certain death for those being left behind...

Rothar and Lughan had been there waiting for quite some time, now.

They had been playing the royal game of Ur,[124] sitting concentrated beneath the torchlight, on the cold stone steps leading to the lower levels of the Dryd Slijk, under the main market square.

'It has always been the best place to meet,' Thuarnach thought, with satisfaction, 'the entrances are so well disguised that it is almost impossible to find them without me clueing them in, and the square is busy and chaotic enough to create the perfect distraction...'

"Hyo muin Meyn Lughan! Rothar, En er myrdien thayn Ur gern, muin Meyn?"[125] the druid greeted them, with a grin.

---

[124] Board game played also by the Sumerians.
[125] Hello, my friend Lughan! Rothar, he is killing your Ur (game) again, my friend?" Meaning Lughan is winning the game of Ur again.

The other two raised their heads at the same time to watch Thuarnach walk swiftly down the steep stairs to where they were sitting.

"Hyo muin Eonar Meyn!"[126] replied Lughan, standing up and clapping the druid lightly on the shoulder, "Rothar er Mæd go Ur,[127] he makes it easy to win," he added, with a broad smile.

Rothar's face was red with embarrassment, but fortunately no one could see it down here, in the tunnels.

"Muin Eonar," he replied courteously to Thuarnach with a bow, "Thay vuoy bleyrn da Noys fret?"[128]

"Ey, muin Meyn, there are troubling news from Drkent Har. I'm afraid we will have to change our plan, we can't wait."

"What has Asttrian done now, Thuarnach? Is Annea ok?" wanted to know Lughan, surprised that the druid would favour rush action, instead of waiting for Ara's arrival. After all, they had finally received news that he had reached the first Kæyn, weeks ago.

"Troubling news indeed I have, my friends, troubling news…"

---

[126] "Hello my ancient friend!" This is a friendly greeting Lughan always uses when meeting Thuarnach, instead of the formal greeting used for a royal Dragon Druid or Drkent Dryd.
[127] "Rothar sucks at the game of Ur"
[128] "You wanted to talk to us urgently?"

He then went on to explain the situation to both men, who listened attentively.

Arnya, the royal guest maiden assisting Annea and the queen, had confirmed to Thuarnach that Anuelle of Daing Mhuir was expected to arrive soon. Arnya had been ordered to prepare the next royal guest room to Annea's. She had also said that the tension between Shya and her brother was increasing by the minute, and that Annea was always in the line of fire.

Arnya, Thuarnach knew, was to be trusted, she was a righteous and faithful woman. He had helped her long ago, when she had first set foot in Reaghil Bheallemer, and with time, she had become the wife of a Kechtá, and was forever in Thuarnach's debt.

For months, now, her husband Esthron had been sent off to patrol the Lahir and the Rheann, and ever since, she had waited, in vain, for any news. She loved her husband dearly, but working so close to the royal family, within the castle walls, she had slowly gained the impression that the role of the Kechtás as protectors of the realm had become questionable under this new king.

However, it wasn't just that. She felt empathy for Annea, she pitied the foreign girl sincerely. She had been in a similar situation herself, and although Urarathan had been king of the Skyarachti, then, without Thuarnach's support, she would have never accomplished what she had. She felt that the young king's tyrannical behaviour towards his subjects, and especially his abuse of power towards the Gæn Æri was beyond reason and healthy judgement. Arnya had served the Skyarachti Royals long enough to know that Asttrian was evil, weak and, most of all, insanely ambitious.

She had offered her help before Thuarnach would ask, and she was convinced it was the right thing to do. Even though her husband was a Kechtá, and had been sent to secure the big waterways for the king against any rebellion that might arise, she was not bound by any vows to Asttrian's crown. She would have time to explain to her husband once they met again. Thus, Thuarnach knew, Arnya was certainly their most valuable ally within the royal chambers.

Once Thuarnach completed his tale, Rothar, who had been patiently listening, added some important extra bits of intelligence he had gathered during his visit to the court two days ago…

Rothar's family had been one of the most loyal families to the crown for generations. His grandfather had first served as a notary and advisor to the king. But the family had been gravely affected by a terrible imported disease that had decimated the city some twenty years ago. While in the future there would be a vaccine for this illness, in ancient times, most people got the infection and died. The disease was called Nwyrbesch,[129] and the realm had suffered greatly under its grasp, recovering only slowly.

Thankfully, Lughan had conducted some research and had been able to inform Thuarnach about modern day solutions to such epidemics. The druid had then promptly started working on a sort of vaccine, which would prevent many deaths in the future. But as close as he was to creating one, it had certainly been too late for Rothar's family.

As it happened, Rothar now lived and worked alone with his father, who had been acting as notary to the king for many years himself. Asttrian had threatened to dismiss them, he mistrusted anyone loyal to the old king, but after seeing the convenience of experienced advisors, he had reluctantly let them stay. The relationship between the king and his notary, however, had from early on been put to the test, and it would never recover.

While Rothar had been ever supportive of his father's enterprises, and had assisted him wherever he could, with the years, Næl Royn had become a lonely soul, with no expectations or ambitious for the future of the realm. Rothar and his duty to the crown being the only two things he had left, Næl Royn had made peace with

---

[129] The bite of the serpent, one of the first ancient epidemics of measles.

the despotic rule of their new king, and had kept the promise he had made to the old king despite the differences and constant tensions. He was a loyal subject, and in his heart, he would continue to be one until his last day.

With Rothar, however, things were quite different. He had grown increasingly weary, observing month after month, how the new king treated his father and all other members of court. He had never liked Asttrian much, as most, and he was clever enough to stay clear of the old king's son, as much as he could. He had early on discovered the new king's cruel tendencies towards foreigners, and his heart had made a decision for him, long before he had met Annea. He was not about to sell his soul to the devil. He was determined to be part of a new, different kingdom, a kingdom free from the tyrannic and despotic rule of the Arach twins.

And so, it happened that, being able to gain access to the most confidential information discussed within the closed doors of Asttrian's small council, he shared all he knew with Thuarnach and Lughan, and helped without conditions to build up the resistance literally from the underground of the Golden City.

Chapter Twenty-Six: The Plan

7th Day of Gloaras (well past midnight), 300YD,
Gænnæriati Quarters, Reaghil Bheallemer

Lughan had been sleepless all night. He couldn't stop thinking about his Little Pandora, all alone within the hermetic walls of Drkent Har. She had come all the way to find him, as he knew she would, and now, there was so little he could do for her... She was in great peril, at the mercy of Asttrian's moods. The longer they waited, the more dangerous it would become. Old Thuarnach was right: they could not wait for Ara.

Originally, their plan had included Ara, and would have certainly been much easier to carry out successfully. As things were, they would have to act without him, needing altogether another strategy, avoiding any confrontation, or they would be doomed. The true heir would have to wait, this much was certain.

They would need to cleverly evade all security posts that were in place. They could not afford to be discovered. It was going to be extremely difficult to get Annea, princess Anu of Daing Mhuir, and Lady Skenya into safety. But, at least, they had been lucky to find more help from within the walls of Drkent Har...

Yes, it was best to act now. Especially, since word from Ara had finally reached them, confirming the rumours that Ealator, had disappeared in the vastness of the Thaunaan forests, shortly after arriving at the first Kæyn. The three Anairarachti princes were certain, however, that he was heading towards the Golden City, with the heroic intention of liberating his mother all by himself.

They could not afford another hostage to free, thought Lughan. This was truly getting out of proportion, and would inevitably escalate towards a civil war, what they had been miraculously able to avoid so far.

The festival on Dryemoshach was their last chance! But Lughan still had to talk to his family... He was determined to make them leave the city with Annea.

Lughan had seen many things during all his journeys. He knew how to take care of himself. His young family, on the other hand, was utterly vulnerable. And once Asttrian noticed what had happened, his unbounded rage would turn to those he despised the most and were at hand.

Yes, they would have to go first. He and Thuarnach would follow later on. He dared not think what would happen if things went wrong, but he was sure of one thing: they would not live to tell the story.

So lost in his thoughts, Lughan hadn't noticed that his wife Rasmei had been staring at him in the darkness, across their shared bed.

"Muin Lævyvlig, kvæy har Eonar Thuarnach bredien Thay?"[130] she spoke as if to the ceiling.

"Yai drayk Thay har drym, muine Læyv!"[131] answered Lughan somewhat surprised.

"How can I sleep with you tossing and turning like that," she laughed, "besides, you have been somewhere else in that head of yours since you came back from your meeting today, so I figured there must be something nagging at you. What is it, then? Are you going to tell me?"

"Ey, muine Læyv. Unfortunately, Asttrian has caught Arachtan's little sister, Princess Anuelle of Daing Mhuir. Apparently, she was sailing up the Rheann on her own. She will arrive to the capital in a few days. Now, he counts three hostages..." These last words hung ominously in the darkness surrounding them.

"I wanted to talk to you and the children tomorrow, I wanted to see you rest peacefully beside me, tonight... But if you prefer, we can talk now," he went on.

---

[130] "My darling, what has ancient Thuarnach told you?"
[131] "I thought you were sleeping, my love!"

"Lughan, I will do whatever you need me to do. For us, for the cause, for Annea... I am strong and I will fight at your side, until the end."

He turned to look at her, a black shape in front of him. They laid separated by his dark thoughts, and still he could feel her warmth reaching out and caressing him without words.

"Rasmei, I need you and the children to leave the city with Annea, on the day of Dryemoshach. I need you all to stay out of reach."

"But why? If Arachtan Skyarach is finally here, I can fight for his cause, too..."

"Ey, I know, muine Læyv, that's what we all wanted..."

He paused thoughtful for a moment, and then went on, "he won't make it in time, Rasmei. I'm afraid it will be just us."

"So...?"

"We have enough help from the royal druids, Læyv. Some host noble families are on our side, too. And on top, we are very lucky to have one royal guest maiden working for us, Arnya, who is in charge of service to the royal chambers."

"These are all our resources, Lughan? You know the Kechtás will crush us! How many royal druids are left in the city? Five? Six?"

"Well, they'll have to be enough. Besides, we're not planning to meet any Kechtás on the way."

He smiled to himself, remembering Thuarnach's description of their plan, but Rasmei wouldn't understand their sense of humour, so he kept the details to himself.

"And how loyal are these host families you're talking about? Do you know them well? Without Arachtan Skyarach and Drkenstar, we don't stand a chance. He is the one that was chosen, he has the right to rule this kingdom, and he continues to be completely in the dark about it."

"Rasmei, Thuarnach has his reasons… I'm no one to judge him, nor are you!"

Silence filled every corner of the room.

After some time, Lughan continued, "know this: all these many years, all of what that old man has done, truly everything, has been to protect Arachtan and our kingdom. He knew Urarathan's weaknesses more than anyone else, and he knows how to handle Asttrian and Shya better than all of us together, too. We have to trust him. It is our best chance, now more than ever!"

"So, you're telling me that we are to escape from possibly the most perfectly guarded city in the known world with the loyal help of five druids, a service maid, and some suspicious crown-traitors, who suddenly have found it in their hearts to risk their lofty lives for their kingdom?! Lughan, Læyv, who's going to fight the Kechtás? Me and the children? Anneya? There are dozens and dozens of them, while, it sounds to me, there are in fact very few of us!"

"Rasmei, please, trust me, it is for the best. We have the people we need to make this plan a success. We need no more. Ara will understand that this was the only way."

"So... what about you, muin Læyv? What part do you have to play? Surely, you're not expecting me to leave without you, right?"

He moved closer to her, now.

"Thuarnach and myself will be staying behind for a while. We know where to hide, and we have lots of people we need to help here before we leave, Rasmei. Besides, we still have to inform the druids at Drkarach Aelbstael Cathrie of Arachtan's arrival so they are prepared, and this can only be done in person, momentarily..."

"No! I won't leave you! I made a promise to the Goddess,[132] the day we sealed our promise,[133] Lughan, and I'm not about to break it."

"That is out of the question. You are a reasonable person, Rasmei, and I know you will eventually understand my decision. Please, don't make things even more difficult to me. I love you too much..."

"But–"

"No, Rasmei, it is my last word on this. You will leave on Dryemoshach without me. You will have knowledgeable escort through the wilderness, and, with some luck, you will be within the walls of the Polarys Kæyn within a few days, a week at the most. Harkan Næl Rothar will see to your safety. I trust him."

She felt a cold pearl moisturizing her cheek, and she rapidly turned her back to him. She didn't want him to see her crying. She was a strong person, and she understood, it was not the right time to start being sentimental.

"So... I suppose this is it, then. You have made up your mind?"

---

[132] The "Goddess" was the short form for "Thouar Altærinann" - the ancient goddess of nature, much respected and honoured by mothers and wifes.
[133] In the Arach culture, people didn't need to marry oficially through signing a contract. They could seal their bondage with blood and a promise presided by a druid.

"Ey, muine Læyv."

"Are you at least going to tell me more about your plan? How many of us are leaving the city, for example?"

It was best she started being familiar with the details. She was clever, and they could use her abilities. It was essential she knew her part well.

"There will be twenty-two of you, in all: you and the children; Annea; princess Anuelle; Lady Skenya; Dryd Myrten and Dryd Eykr; host noble Rothar with his father and nine of his most loyal knights; the black smith Ranor the Black; and Arnya the royal service maid."

"Really, so many? It sounds more like a procession to the temples, not a secret escape!"

"Ey, but you will meet outside the city walls at different points. Eventually, you will continue your journey to the Polarys Kæyn together. In a certain way, it is a procession, only a secret one, you will have to hide every step of the way. And always remember, Rasmei, from the moment we steal Asttrian's toys, a death sentence will hang from our necks. It will be extremely dangerous, but it is the only way out, muin Læyv."

He reached out blindly to find her warm body in the cold, damp air of the night. He caressed the back of her neck gently.

She moved closer to him, their two bodies now promising each other reassurance.

It would be fine, they would meet again, in the end, one way or another... She was sure of it.

Chapter Twenty-Seven: The Lady Of The Thriar

10th day of Gloaras, 300YD,
Drkent Har, eastern wing guest rooms

Lady Skenya was observing the rich drops trickling down the rough window glass. One after the other, as if they could not resist the urge to follow the spiralling path that would inevitably take them from the second floor of the castle to the very bowels of the earth.

It was a dark day…

She had not slept well, thinking about her brother Thuarnach's note, it had been raining all morning, and she did not feel like having breakfast with the queen, as commanded by the king.

It had been an absurdity, in the first place, as most of Asttrian's orders. Lady Skenya and Queen Umbriel had never been good friends. One could even say they had barely tolerated each other's presence, and only as long as Skenya's brother, king Urarathan, had lived. But the Lady of the Thriar, as Skenya was widely known, had never had a very high opinion of the Host Queen, and she had never made a secret of it.

Asttrian, being who he was, made this measure part of his punishment and silent threat to Lady Skenya, for not supporting him as king and openly complaining about the dissolution of the Thriar council.

Her whirling thoughts were suddenly interrupted by the service maiden, Arnya, who was bringing breakfast to her room.

"Muine Æriel Skenya,[134] mon er Thay aì?[135]" asked the woman while putting down the tray with the food, and walking towards the window, where Lady Skenya was standing.

"Oh, well, I've seen better days in my life…"

Only then, did she saw Arnya standing right beside her.

"Oh, it's you, Arnya. Thank you, I'm feeling fine. I needed sometime on my own, that is all. That note you brought…"

"Ey, Muine Æriel, I understand."

"He said they had taken my niece Anuelle prisoner?"

---

[134] "My Lady"
[135] "How are you today?"

"So it seems, Muine Æriel."

"But how could Scaìthara and Drearyan let her travel to this place?"

"I don't think they knew she was undertaking such a journey, Muine Æriel. Word has it that she was found in the company of a wanted smuggler called Tschiaran, who apparently died fighting the Kechtás, or so I hear."

She stopped for a while to see if Lady Skenya was still paying attention, and then continued, "she'll be arriving soon."

"What about the other part of the note? Do you know anything about this?"

Skenya turned around and looked at her sincerely. Arnya answered her look, and shook her head decidedly.

"No, Muine Æriel, I'm afraid I know nothing about it."

They remained in silence for a while.

Arnya knew a mother's heart would not be appeased so easily, but still she tried to distract her from her dark thoughts.

"You should go and keep the old queen company, Muine Æriel, they don't like it when you disobey the king's orders. They'll be sending Kechtás to force you... please, Muine Æriel, rest now, but do come to the queen's quarters, later on. They are planning a big dinner tonight, they said it is a family reunion for princess Anuelle's arrival."

Skenya turned again and assented silently. She did not trust her nephew and niece in the least, but she would come.

Without another word, Arnya vowed and left the room again.

In his secret note, Thuarnach had implied Eala was coming. He hadn't written much more, only that her son was coming to rescue her, and this had been enough information for Skenya to understand what he meant.

About six months ago, on the same day as she had been made a prisoner, Asttrian had sent her children away, back to their fortress on the Rheann, as a bait for her nephew Arachtan. Eala had been out of his mind with anger for the treatment they were all receiving, and had fought their escort until he lay knocked down, on the floor. The Rheann Skyarachti had had no chance against the political power of the royal twins, supported by the greatest and most skilful army the world had seen so far.

Years before, it had been Eala who had fought bravely alongside King Urarathan during the revolts, while Asttrian had stayed at court, celebrating their victories. And Arachtan, the king's favourite nephew, conspicuous by his absence during all the chaos that preceded and followed the death of the king, had never returned to Reaghil Bheallemer.

Eala had expected to get, at least, some acknowledgement from the old king, but her brother had died so suddenly and untimely, that no one had been prepared to face what came after. Least of them Eala, who had secretly been hoping to officially become the right hand of the king. To make things worse, he had gathered enough information for the Thriar suggesting that both royal siblings had been behind the revolts, but had unfortunately been prevented from sharing this with king Urarathan. Skenya had to admit that destiny had not been always fair with her children…

On the other hand, she had always been content to know they were growing safe and happy, and would always have their lands at the Rheann. She had never truly wished for more. She had loved and trusted her older brother Urarathan,[136] and she had

---

[136] The royal Thuatharachti children were four in all: Thuarnach, Urarathan, and the girl twins Aenya and Skenya. Two of them had followed Urarathan and had helped him build the Skyarachti Kingdom, or Arach Kingdom of Mists. Aenya had stayed behind with her parents, and after their father, King Urukaracht, had died, she and her mother, Queen Skyra, had taken over the rule of the Thuatharachti in the North, helping apeace the kingdoms. Despite having chosen different sides, both twins remained close to each other, corresponded regularly, and became the main link between both kingdoms.

respected all of his decisions... But Eala was altogether another matter.

Ever since their father, Lord Thuaìrach,[137] had died, both Rheann children had looked up to their royal uncle as a father. With the years, they had developed a loving paternal relationship that most of the time had caused unwanted problems with Urarathan's own offspring. However, the king went on treating all of them, including all of the Anairarachti princes, as his own. He never gave in to Asttrian's or Shya's complaints. In time, even Umbriel had started complaining about it. Sometimes, Lady Skenya wondered if this had not been her brother's biggest mistake...

But now, there was no turning back! Her son was out there trying to get to her, most probably, thinking on how to take revenge on the king and his sister... And while Eala was a brave and intelligent young man, much like her dead husband had been, he had one big flaw: he drank too much! And when he did, his troubled emotions got the better of him.

Furthermore, Drkent Har had become a royal prison for all its inhabitants, after Urarathan's death, and while it was true that Asttrian had sent many men off to secure the Rheann region, someone working alone wouldn't stand a chance against the royal

---

[137] Thuaraìch was Queen Scaìthara's older brother, and Skenya's cousin, and later on, her dear husband. He had died a hero fifteen years ago, in a special quest only the king knew about, in the ancient city of Seannanorthai.

Kechtás. Eala would be facing certain death if he tried anything against Asttrian or Shya.

It would be almost impossible to breach security around the king, or around her… It was a hopeless undertaking. She could only hope that Eala would hear reason in time to avoid being taken prisoner, too. They had to find him first! Otherwise, Asttrian was not going to show him any mercy this time…

Her thoughts now turned to poor young Anuelle, who would be arriving that day.

That girl was nothing like her mother, the poor thing was going to suffer greatly at the royal twins' hands. Yet another toy for those two, she thought, and this time, there was nothing she or the Thriar could do for her… Together with that other poor girl, Anneya, who Asttrian had kept from Thuarnach, they would be now three helpless mice at the mercy of two vicious, crooked vipers.

Chapter Twenty-Eight: A Family Reunion

10th day of Gloaras, 300YD,
west private tower, Drkent Har

She had been summoned for an official family dinner, but Lady Skenya had not been allowed inside the private tower, yet.

She had been secluded most of the day, and the rain had not stopped, until a few minutes ago, so Skenya had decided to use the time for a short walk through the lovely third floor terraces.

She had not been allowed here for quite some time, and she had to admit to herself that this was one of the most enchanting views over the valley she knew, and yet, no match for the astonishing terraces back at her Reaghil Ovsbhealle Rheanna, the pride of all the Skyarach.

Would she ever see them again? she wondered...

At that moment, a nervous service maiden hurried into the west private tower, making the final arrangements before the king arrived.

She would walk back, now, she thought. She did not want to provoke Asttrian any further, today…

When Skenya reached the entrance to the tower, she could see through the wide-open doors, that the King was not there yet. His sister Shya, however, was already talking to a small group of selected guests in a corner, close to the arched windows. She looked radiant. She was wearing a red silk dress, with a light cape made of the same material. Hanging from her neck, she wore the golden dragon torque king Urarathan had given Umbriel for their wedding. Always extravagant to the limit, she was seemingly pleased about something, today. This was easy to read from her broad smile…

With her were Næl Rothar,[138] one of Asttrian's advisors, a young, good-looking Harkan Næl that had already served the crown under king Urarathan and who Shya seemed to like very much, his father, Næl Royn, a plain Gæn Ærin she had never seen before, and Meysters[139] Mayrn and Dryne, Asttrian's scientific and political assessors respectively.

She let her gaze wonder through the room, and discovered Arnya standing with a jar in her hands on the far end of the room. Their eyes met briefly and she raised her head slightly when she saw Lady Skenya entering.

---

[138] Title used to address any Harkan Næl. In this way Rothar would be Næl Rothar, and so on.
[139] Title used to address teachers and assessors of the crown.

While she was walking towards her seat, Shya turned around to greet her.

"Dear aunt, but you look splendid today! Difficult to believe you weren't feeling well this morning... mother missed you, you know. We don't want to upset her more, don't you agree? Make sure you're as crisp as you're right now for breakfast tomorrow, would you?"

Shya strode towards her with a malicious look in her eyes, and a smug grin.

"Now, do relax, auntie. We'll be having some fun tonight!" she added, putting her hand on Skenya's shoulder in a reassuring way, as she passed.

Shya turned, then, to speak to the rest of her guests, while taking a seat at one end of the long table that had been exquisitely decorated with fragrant daffodils from the gardens.

"Dear guests, please, do come closer and take your seats. The king will arrive in a few minutes. He sends his apologies, there was something rather urgent he needed to attend to."

After what felt like an hour, Queen Umbriel made her appearance, lost in her own world as she always was. This time, she was wearing her hunting dress for dinner!

Some of the guests looked at each other confused, but a few seconds later, her son finally entered the room, drawing everyone's attention to him, now.

The king made a pompous entrance, flanked by two most beautiful women, and wearing a most self-sufficient grin on his face. Never had Skenya seen his nephew look so excited and self-satisfied before.

"Welcome, welcome, muin Meyns![140] I'm so happy you could all come, tonight! We have some special guests from far away…"

Skenya almost couldn't recognise the elegant auburn-haired woman at his left side. Only as they came closer, did she saw it was Anuelle, her cousin's daughter! She had grown so much since the last time! She was a beautiful young woman, now. But a curtain of sadness clouded her eyes. What had happened to her?

For all of Asttrian's cheerful remarks, Anuelle did not even bother to insinuate the beginning of a smile. Her look was grim, and she stared in the distance, as if to some distant point in time, when she had lost something, she held dear.

---

[140] My friends

'Poor child,' thought Skenya, 'who knows what she has suffered on her journey...'

Without further ado, the two female escorts were seated at Asttrian's side respectively, and then dinner was served.

The other girl, Bræy Gæn Ærin Anneya, [141] as she was called by all, kept very silent, but observing everything.

She was looking at Anuelle with a worried look, as if she could empathize with her feelings. Maybe she would be of some company for the poor, young princess of Daing Mhuir... Who knew how long they were going to be kept together as royal captives of the King?

On the other side of the table, sat that woman that Skenya had never seen before. Shortly after the king's arrival, she was introduced to them as Ryssa of Daing Mhuir, who had travelled with Princess Anuelle.

At that point, Princess Anuelle looked up from her plate, her eyes bored into the woman's with open disdain. The other, on her part, didn't seem to notice her, she was beaming and too busy, exchanging pleasantries with the king.

---

[141] Beautiful guest maiden Annea.

Skenya deduced that the woman had betrayed the princess somehow... And the king confirmed her suspicions, a few minutes later, with a blunt remark.

"Our friend Ryssa, who appears to also be part of our family, as I hear, has made it possible for our Yahæn Etayn Anuelle to reach Drkent Har safely and timely."

Anuelle didn't bother to look up this time, she was evidently disgusted by the mention of this.

Close to Shya, on the other side of the table, there was one vacant seat that Skenya hadn't noticed before. She wondered if her brother Thuarnach had been invited at all... It wouldn't be a family gathering without him, that was for sure!

As if reading her mind, Shya addressed her brother across the table.

"Oh dear, I almost forgot, our ancient uncle won't be attending the family reunion after all, brother. He sent one of our Kechtás with the message, said he was tired and not feeling well."

The room went silent, every one expectant to what the king's reaction would be...

"How very Thuarnach!" answered Asttrian amused, and both twins laughed at this wholeheartedly.

While the growing tension was luckily only being sensed by some of the other guests, slowly, Skenya was also starting to feel very much like princess Anuelle…

Meanwhile, both Meyster Mayrn and Meyster Dryne continued chattering cheerfully about the coming feast of Dryemoshach, and telling the king how they were organizing the most exotic food and drinks ever served from faraway lands.

Suddenly, two fully armed Kechtás opened the door and interrupted the dinning party.
One of them walked all the way straight to the King, and whispered something in his ears.

Whatever it was he told Asttrian, the king's smile broadened considerably and his eyes started glinting like the metal spikes of steel spears.

"Oh, but what a coincidence, my dear friends! I have to say, this is becoming one of the best days of my reign, so far!"

From across the room, Shya displayed a most irritating smirk.

"Now, we should not let our guests wait, brother," she said.

"No, of course not! Even less so if they are dear family…"

And waving his hands, Asttrian signalled the two Kechtás to bring in a last-minute guest.

Skenya felt a shiver of premonition running down her spine…

A few moments later, staggering between two massive Kechtás, appeared Ealator, her lost son.

"Eala!" she exclaimed, while leaving her place in a hurry to steady her son.

He was in a terrible condition. His clothes were torn and dirty, his skin showed bruises and wounds where the eye could see, one front tooth was missing, and he could barely stand. He smelled strongly of alcohol.

Skenya turned to the king infuriated, "what is this Asttrian?!"

"Muin Reaghil Drkent Teyn, for you aunt!" Shya warned her through gritted teeth.

Asttrian was already sliding gracefully towards Skenya, "Oh, no, no, dear sister, but I do understand our aunt," he said mellifluously, without taking his eyes off Skenya.

When he was close enough, he turned to address all his guests.

"See, my poor aunt here hasn't seen her dear son for quite some time... and now, finally reunited, she has to bear finding him in such a pitiful condition!"

Now, he turned to Eala and clapped his cheeks like an old friend.

"Ahhh, my cousin, you are breaking your mother's heart! Tell us, what has become of you? Our royal drunkard you are!"

He laughed then wholeheartedly, and turning to the others, he offered a toast to his family's health.

He then drank the full content of his cup of Rheannvid, right there, in front of Lady Skenya and what remained of her son.

"What have you done, Asttrian?" Lady Skenya pressed on.

He turned to her with a surprised look.

"Oh, dear aunt," he shook his head sympathetically, "I have done many things in my short life, but this?" he pointed at Eala, "this is your creation alone, not mine."

"You know exactly what I mean, nephew."

"Ahhh, if you mean the bruises and all the dirt... well, they tell me he was so drunk on his way here, he unfortunately stumbled down the big stairs," and looking to the rest of his audience, he added, "a miracle he didn't break his neck!"

And ignoring Skenya's further remarks, he took hold of Eala and dragged him across the room to the empty chair beside Shya, who was already wrinkling her nose in disgust.

"Come cousin, what are my manners, you need to meet the rest of our guests! Please, everyone, welcome Ealator of Reaghil Ovsbhealle Rheanna, the Green Terrace of the Dragon, the pride of our kingdom!"

Asttrian walked back to his seat, and, as if nothing had happened, continued talking cheerfully with his assessors, each sitting on either side of the table, one beside Annea and the other beside Anuelle.

Skenya, acknowledging her precarious situation, went silently back to her seat, inside torn into pieces at the sight of her dear son.

Across the table, Shya was still glowering at her.

In time, the chatter became a throbbing hum that lulled her emotions, Skenya could not touch the food, nor her drink. She felt as if she had eaten rocks for breakfast. But she was not alone...

Annea, Anuelle, Eala, Umbriel, and even Næl Rothar, who had been silently observing every single detail of this family reunion, were all unable to touch their plates. Each for their own reasons, they all had in common that they couldn't wait until this charade was over.

Asttrian, on his part, didn't care to notice a thing. Only Shya did... And she was growing a strong suspicion that these people might all have something more in common than a lost appetite, a thought that made her suddenly feel uncomfortable at her own table.

Chapter Twenty-Nine: Polarys

14th Day of Gloaras, 300YD,

Da Dryan Kæyn Elthanin Polarys, eastern Thaunaan mountains

There it was. Finally, in front of them, rose the colossal shape of the Dryan Kæyn,[142] with its glimmering defence walls of white Graichfael.[143]

Arachtan's heart jumped at the sight of it. Although, on this occasion, he would not have time to stay for long, his soul longed for the company of his fellow druids, most of which he knew very well.

Arachtan had spent many seasons here. He had been a most ambitious apprentice. He had trained hard, meditated, worked, and learned all the skills he needed to become the perfect royal druid. And it had been here, within these walls, that he had received the most holistic preparation of all. He had been personally tutored by the two more skilful druids in the kingdom: his uncle Thuarnach, who would escape the capital's busy life to remain here with him over three full months every year, and his most loyal friend, Dryd Rayka, who lived in the village of

---

[142] Third temple.
[143] Quarz stone.

Neybhrealle nearby, and who would narrate the most fascinating stories from the ancient kingdom of Seannarach.

Yes, he had truly missed the place. It was unfortunate that the present circumstances were quite different…

It had taken them six full days to reach the third of the Vwylrynn Kæyns. They had avoided the procession roads whenever they could, and this had turned the normally short journey through the Vwylrynn into a tediously long one.

Skymnia was thankful she had a horse, otherwise she would have never been able to reach the Kæyn. She still walked with a slight limp, and her legs felt tender and weak. Her strength was coming back, but only slowly.

Her spirits, however, had been high at the sight of the temple. She had never spent so much time among the druids before, and she had discovered that apart from being kind and educated, the druids were caring, hard-working and disciplined beyond anything she had seen before. They had worked miracles with the landscape, true jewels out of pure, raw nature. This Kæyn, in particular, was certainly one of the best examples of their skills with the elements, if not with magic itself.

She had had, of course, Skeor's full attentions. He would help her whenever he could, and stayed at her side most of the way. This, she had to admit, had given her most comfort.

She had not spent so much time talking to her cousin before. One year her senior, Skeorden had played with her as children, but she had always been so obsessed with his older brother Ara, that she had never really noticed him. He had grown since the last time they had met, too. He was much taller and stronger, and his blue eyes had grown in depth and intensity…

Skymnia was starting to long for the quiet moments they would share, when he would tell her stories about Daing Mhuir and the isles, the wild seas, and sea-faring peoples that inhabited their kingdom. She had been to Daing Mhuir only once in her life, and she had been very young, then. Still, she could remember it as if it was today. It had been part of an official visit as envoy from the Skyarach court. Her mother, Lady Skenya, had been sent as a member of the Thriar to discuss important economic matters with the warrior queen, and she had taken Skymnia with her.

A wild place, she remembered. Untamed, green, and carved out of the rock by the winds and slashing waves, but also of a most intriguing mystical character, like some jealously guarded secret kept deep down the ocean's majestic waves. She hadn't enjoyed it much then, though. Or better, she had not understood it fully. It was only now, by listening to her cousin Skeor, that she was able to delve into those mysteries, and, to her surprise, she was liking it, very much.

Thuaì, for his part, had been in high spirits most of the way. He had been counting the hours till reaching Polarys, pleading he was 'soul-thirsty', not having had a good Úllst in ages. Luckily for him, the little town of Neybhrealle, close to the Kæyn, was famous for its apple ciders. So, as soon as they had reached the temple, he had taken a fresh horse and made his way to the village for some drinks with old friends, and new...

The town was noted for being protected from Asttrian's knights and informants. It had always been an autonomous town, politically unbiased, based on traditional craftsmanship and a little trade, with some quite cheerful taverns to share an Úllst or two. Neybhrealle had been founded by a druid hand, which had remained hovering over it, ever since. Ranking the biggest of the druid villages on the procession roads of the kingdom, it was very close to the most prominent training Kæyn, and the druidic guard was ever silently present on its streets, markets and the surrounding forests. Powerful spells protected the whole area, and no Kechtá would dare enter without a formal invitation.

It had been no surprise, then, that Arachtan and his companions had been first greeted by the druidic guard, way before they could even see the temple, and had been kindly escorted, all the way up to the main gates, unspoken suspicion lingering in the air...

Elthanin Polarys, or the Great Dragon, being the main teaching temple of the druidic faith in the Skyarach kingdom, was bigger than the king's fortress, Drkent Har. It was part of a complex system of bigger and smaller temples, mounds and sacred sites that mirrored the heavens on the land, creating a sacred landscape masterly connected through the procession roads.

This druidic mapping of the heavens was of great astronomical importance, for the location of each temple marked the position of a star in a given circumpolar constellation. What we know now as Cassiopeia, Draco, Ursa Minor, Ursa Major and Cepheus, had all been written on the face of the Thaunaan mountains and its surrounding valleys, like an open book for those who were able to read it.[144]

Next in prominence was the Drkarach Aelbstæl Cathrie Kæyn, the Seat of the White Dragon Star. Slightly West from the capital, it marked the position of the former Polar Star, known to us as Alpha Draconis or Thuban. This temple was part of the bigger serpentine constellation of Draco that is wrapped around the smaller Ursa Minor.[145]

---

[144] Within this system, Polarys played a prominent role as it represented the position of the current North Star, around which all circumpolar constellations seem to circle. The star is part of the constellation we now call Ursa Minor, and was widely used for navigation in antiquity.

[145] In Greek mythology the constellation of Draco was said to represent the famous Dragon that guards the golden apples of the gardens of the Hesperides.

But the importance of the Polarys Kæyn was not just astronomical. It was much more than that. It was intimately connected to its central location on that sacred landscape, and its proximity to the capital, which allowed small druidic towns like Neybhrealle to flourish.

After its foundation, the temple had rapidly grown as the most influential druid school, providing housing for at least 500 permanent apprentices and teachers, with equally numbered spaces for men and women. It possessed around 100 spaces for the sick in the Ayno rooms, which were distributed in four wings and arranged towards the four cardinal points and the four seasons of the year, giving Polarys the shape of a diamond. This great temple could also house up to a hundred guests, which made the temple a merging point for the most progressive and visionary ideas.

At the head of the temple was Dryd Erdyn, who had been assigned by Thuarnach himself after the old Keanndryd[146] had passed away. Dryd Erdyn's most significant trait was his stubbornness, and for that he was admired and respected by all. He had come as a Gæn Ær from the lands of Armourean and knew the meaning of hardship, all too well. But he had the resilience of ants and, against all odds, he had finally become a Drkent Dryd, and was leading the most important Kæyn of all.

---

[146] The Head druid or Keanndryd was the leading druid in a temple.

Dryd Erdyn had been expecting Arachtan and his three companions. Still, he was increasingly bothered by Thuarnach's repeated meddling in the affairs of the temple. He had so far been able to keep distance to any political matters that affected the capital, making his temple a safe haven for all, and he wanted it to stay that way. He was not at all interested in attracting Asttrian's or Shya's eyes towards his druidic community. Of course, he revered, and even feared Thuarnach immensely, but he cherished his temple more, and Thuarnach's last message, which he was holding in his hands now, the one he was supposed to share with Arachtan only, meant an open war was brewing over their heads, and their tranquil druid way of life would inevitably come to an end...

As every day, Dryd Erdyn had been meditating on his straw mat in front of the central Caydúllien Ore, when Arachtan passed through the Tærzylen or columns of the Earth.[147]
He had chosen the place on purpose, so that they could talk alone and undisturbed. No one was allowed to enter the heart of the temple without the Keanndryd's invitation. Arachtan, who knew

---

[147] The Columns of the Earth formed a circle in the centre of the temple, dividing the core of the temple into the Blue Expansion or the Heavens, and the inner meditation stone circle. It was considered a transitional space, a threshold or space in-between worlds.

him well, understood to pad slowly, almost cautiously towards the mat the druid was sitting on.

They had not seen each other for some years now, and Arachtan was taken aback by his appearance. The old druid looked exhausted, extremely weary, as if the weight of a hundred years were resting on his bones.

The last time he had been with the druids of Polarys, Arachtan had promised to return the following year to stay, for the last three years of his training, with them. He had not come back, nor had he written to them, since then. So many things were different now…

First, the unfortunate incident with Ryssa, then, the sudden death of his uncle, and after that, Thuarnach's messages, always so cryptic and urging him not to correspond with anyone in the Skyarach Kingdom. The list of things that had prevented him from writing to the druids went on and on, but Arachtan knew he should have somehow communicated with the Keanndryd, who had also seen himself as one of his mentors.

Yes, he owed druid Erdyn an explanation… But was it now the right moment? They had certainly more urgent matters to discuss than his failed druid path.

"Hyo, muin Læyven Læhren![148] Hope you travelled well?" started Dryd Erdyn without opening his eyes, once Arachtan was close enough to him.

"Muin Eonar," answered Ara bowing in front of the sitting druid, and taking the next empty mat to the right of him for himself, before answering his question.

"It has been a long journey, muin Eonar."

"Ey, a long journey, indeed, muin Kræyn."

Silence took over their conversation for some time. It was a peaceful silence, but loaden with unasked questions.

Arachtan saw the druid was holding something tightly in his hands.

"Is that from Thuarnach?" he asked, after a while.

Dryd Erdyn opened his tired eyes, and darted a complimentary glance to Arachtan

"I see you haven't forgotten your teachings, muin Kræyn," he said, "ey, Eonar Drkent Dryd Thuarnach has sent word from Reaghil Bheallemer... for you!"

---

[148] "Hello, my dear apprentice!"

Finally! Arachtan had started to believe this journey had all been part of a trap, and his uncle was either totally unaware of it, or worse, he was already dead.

"This is good news, muin Eonar."

"Ey, indeed it is," answered Dryd Erdyn ironically.

"What does he say?"

Lying in front of them, next to their mats, was a small, green ceramic cup with a dark, hot aromatic liquid inside. It was part of the welcome ritual, within the stone circle, to share a cup of spiced Kyllanan together with fellow druids before any important matters were discussed.

The older druid invited Ara to drink from it before he went on to answer.

"Asttrian has brought princess Anuelle to Drkent Har."

"Kvæy?![149] That is impossible! She was under my mother's vigilant eye when I left. She would have never left Daing Mhuir on her own, and my mother would have never agreed to send her over."

---

[149] "What?!"

"It's true, Arachtan, they have your sister Anuelle."

The druid put back the cup on the floor and continued, "she was caught in Kælnamer an Rheann and brought straight to the fortress… and she is not alone, Arachtan. Asttrian seems to have developed a taste for hostages: he has caught Ealator, has long imprisoned Lady Skenya, and apparently some other, unknown girl, called Anneya, who seems to be of particular interest to your uncle…"

He went silent for some time, weighing his next words carefully.

"She seems to be quite special… " he went on, "Thuarnach is almost more concerned about her well-being than the Kingdom's! Have you ever heard of her, before?"

"Anneya, you say? Ney, muin Eonar, not that I recall. Is she from the capital?"

"Well, she was found astray, close to the Tyarsach Drkent, it appears."

"Hmm… strange, I didn't even know that one could walk close to that place, and live to tell the story. It's the best guarded place in the kingdom!"

"So, I thought…"

"Muin Eonar, uncle Thuarnach urged me to come as quick as possible, nothing more. He used our secret language to encrypt the message. He must have feared that our jays could be intercepted… and so I came. That is all I know."

"Well, I guess your journey will end here for now," gave back the old druid, while extending to Arachtan the small scroll he had been holding in his hand, "here, your new instructions."

Dryd Erdyn stood up and slowly limped his way towards the Hyerst Aegha shrine.[150]

"We'll see quite a lot of each other for a while," he called to Arachtan, "don't you think, muin Kræyn?"

With a surge of anxiety and premonition unfamiliar to him, Arachtan watched the druid disappear into the blue mosaic patio… Dryd Erdyn looked worn out by the years, but his temper was still the same.

Arachtan hesitated for a moment, before unwrapping the scroll. Then, he opened it slowly, even cautiously, as if some poisonous snake could spring out of it, any time.

---

[150] The Autumn Water or Hyerst Aegha Shrine was the western shrine, where the healing spring water fountains were.

The message had also been encrypted, only a well-trained Drkent Dryd would be able to read it. Thuarnach had taught Ara how to decode such messages a long time ago, and he had made sure that his nephew would master the discipline. But as the written lines passed by in front of his unbelieving eyes, his whole world was beginning to crumble down into sharp, tiny shards ready to cut off his bare flesh: his beloved sister Anuelle was in Asttrian's and Shya's hands! How could that be?! Every fibre of his body resisted to imagine what this meant...

His druid uncle continued recounting the events one after the other as he had witnessed them, or as his most loyal sources had informed him. There was no doubt the information was accurate.

His good, old friend Tschiaran was dead, ambushed by the king's Kechtási knights and killed cold-blooded, while he was trying to defend his sister... But what were they doing in Kælnamer an Rheann? How could his sister reach the continent in the first place? So many questions... And his dear friend had been silenced forever, he would never be able to ask Tschiaran, now.

Ara's head was bursting, raging with imminent fear. Fear for his sister, for his uncle, for the Skyarach Kingdom and beyond. He could see everything clearly now, he could see what would happen to all of them if no one stopped Asttrian and Shya...

The message went on. Ryssa was at Drkent Har, she had arrived with Anu, but they seemed to be on bad terms with one another. Ealator, too, had been caught and was being tortured, but he had not told anyone about Arachtan and their escape from Reaghil Ovsbhealle Rheanna. Lady Skenya, his mother, was kept prisoner and was being forced to witness Eala's suffering daily to make sure she didn't forget her place at court.

What would he tell his cousin Skymnia? She would break if she heard what was happening...

Asttrian was now calling back more and more Kechtás from the southern borders, where years ago the first revolts had taken place, to the capital to secure his position... He was in fear of being attacked.

Thuarnach also wrote about this mysterious newcomer, a royal guest maiden named Anneya, he said, and pleaded him to protect her with his life if it was necessary.

Who was she? Why would Thuarnach be so concerned about this stranger? As much as he tried, he could not find a feasible answer for his uncle's behaviour.

But that was not all the druid had written that shook the very foundations of his assessment of the situation.

Thuarnach had finally concluded his message saying there were two things, two secrets he wanted to share with him when they met again, and that for the time being, it would be enough for Arachtan to know that the old king had named him, Arachtan Skyarach, prince of the Anairarachti, as his rightful successor... So Skymnia was right all the while, King Urarathan had wanted him, his bastard nephew, to swing Drkenstar, the king's sword! Thuarnach assured him also that he had hidden it in a very safe place, where he would have to retrieve it from, when the time came.

But for now, his uncle needed him to wait at Polarys. He had a plan to get the hostages unscathed out of Reaghil Bheallemer during the celebration of Dryemoshach. They would take dah Svæg Cryuns Tyarcad's, the Wild Creatures Forest route, over the steep hangs that followed the course of the Vwyl river, and would be reaching the town of Neybhrealle some four days later, the Dragon permitting. He, Arachtan, and his brothers were to escort them safely straight to Polarys, and wait for him, with the rest of them, there... Thuarnach would be leaving the capital a few days later, after he and his friend Lughan had finished some errands.

It seemed a highly risky plan to Arachtan. He knew the kind of Kechtás that were protecting the fortress, and every corner of the city. They would have no chance to come out alive using confrontation, and all main gates would be closed once they had noticed their hostages were gone. They would need to stay undercover and use the secret Reaghil Dryd Sljk, but how were they going to escape the city?

Arachtan stared unbelievingly at the great, old tree in front of him, letting Thuarnach's words sink in slowly. He remembered how many times he had been sitting here with Thuarnach and Rayka, even with Dryd Erdyn. Their long talks, the tales, the discussions about magic, they all seem to be part of an irretrievable past, now...

He would not be able to become a druid after what had happened with Ryssa, he could not go back, and he could not repent from something he could not even remember of.

In any case, he was still convinced that marrying her had been the right decision to protect her and the baby from the consequences of his misbehaviour. He would never love her, he knew, but the Arach Law was very clear on this respect: a non Arach person that conceived a new life with a Drkarach Qvynne, Kynn,[151] or any of their offspring, would be sentenced to death before the child was born if not protected by the bond of marriage. The children would only inherit the title of their Arach ancestors if there was no other Arach sibling from that Teyn or Qvynne, and only if it was so desired by their Arach progenitor.

---

[151] The words Kynn and Teyn were used both with the meaning "king" or "chieftain" indistinctively.

It was a very controversial law that had been upheld for thousands of years to make sure no mixture with other humans took place. The leaders of the Arach kingdoms had to stay loyal to their blood. That had been the one condition of the Dragons.[152] The ancient Dreà Arachti had been warned about the effects of admixture, and they had defended their kingdoms and their people by imposing the Arach Law all over the Arachti Wbent Teyn Kydrachs.[153] While it had been successfully implemented for a long time, it was also true that, in many cases, like with his uncle Urarathan, the breach of this law had split entire families and caused havoc and destruction.

In Arachtan's case, it would not have mattered much because, as a bastard prince of Queen Scaìthara and a dead Arach official, he officially had no title. Now, however, everything had changed...

His beloved uncle Urarathan had decided Arachtan should be the owner of Drkenstar, he should rule over the Skyarach Kingdom! Had he truly thought through on the consequences of this decision? He knew Ara wanted to live a druid's life...

"Uncle, what were you thinking? If you only knew what I've done..." he spoke to the silence, "I'm not worth your trust."

---

[152] Dragons were considered the most ancient creatures on Earth, and the story of how the Dreà Arachti developed their high civilization hand in hand with the Dragons was found in the compilation on mythological scrolls known as "The Altásvas and the Fall of the ancient Seannarachti Kingdom".
[153] Arach Confederation of Knowledge (fire).

Considering the character and behaviour of his royal cousins, Arachtan had to admit that the old king might have not had another option, but to bestow Drkenstar, and therefore, the rule of the Skyarach Kingdom onto him. Bastard-born or not, Arachtan was a true Arach, his dead father allegedly being a distant cousin of the Thuatharachti. This also made evident why Asttrian, deposed by his own father and being who he was, was doing everything in his power to find him before he reached the capital.

'Your choice of heir will have long lasting consequences for all, dear uncle,' he thought.

Chapter Thirty: **Dryemoshach**

Da Denne Etaynne[154]

21st Day of Gloaras, 300YD,
Royal Guest Tower, Drkent Har

It was a beautiful, clear morning. The weather was showing some mercy, and seemed to have attuned to the celebrations with cloudless skies that were opening up to a bright, spring sun.

'Finally,' thought Annea, 'I was missing the light!'

Someone had pulled the heavy fabric covering the thick windows apart, so that quite a few rays of sun were whimsically tickling her nose.

When she was young, in days like this, she would run out of bed, and into the garden to see if any of granny's flower buds had finally open up… How she missed her, still! She would be so happy to know Annea had found her dad, after all those years… If only they could return…

---

[154] The two Princesses

A sweet humming melody coming from the opposite side of the room brought her slowly back to the present.

She turned around and searched her bed.

"Anu?"

Annea was surprised not to find the princess sleeping beside her.

Anuelle had been assigned the room next to Annea, but almost every night since the beginning of her forced stay, she had paid nightly visits to Annea, and asked her if she could sleep beside her, in the same bed. The poor thing was having terrible nightmares.

"Ey, Yai er hjer...[155] Sorry, I didn't want to wake you."

"It's alright, I also love getting up early when the sun is out. It seems we will have the chance to go to the garden without wearing our cloaks today!"

The weather and their imminent escape suddenly filled Annea's heart with warmth and hope, feelings she had almost forgotten.

---

[155] "Yes, I'm here."

"When does the celebration start, Anu? Maybe, if we are fast enough, we can get out into the garden for a walk, just you and me… and our escorts, of course!" she said, looking at the closed door.

"Well, it won't start until two hours past midday, so we should have time to get ready once we're back, not that it matters too much…"

In utter silence, Anuelle padded listlessly to the thick windows, a sadness within her was fighting the bright rays than danced joyfully on the wooden floors.

"But it does, Anu. I know you and I have seen terrible things we would never have dreamt of. And surely, there was nothing we could do to change them, then. But today, we will have our one opportunity to show the world what we are made of, we have to be brave! We have to laugh, circulate, talk, dance, all of it, even if we are breaking inside. We don't want to make them any more suspicious than they already are."

Only silence met her words.

"Anu, look, I know you're sad about your family and your friend who died, but now, for this one day, you have to let go of those feelings. You are not responsible for what happened! It was not your fault!"

"Oh, but it was…"

Anuelle turned around, now.

"Nothing would have happened if I hadn't defied my mother's will," she said, "I wanted to find them, my brothers… I wanted to be of help, to show them that I'm not a child anymore! It was so selfish of me–"

"No," interrupted Annea, "I know, it might have not been sensible of you to escape, but these are difficult times for everyone!" and difficult places, she thought.

Annea remained thoughtful for some time, and then went on, "you are of immense help to me, Anu. Truly, I don't know how I would have survived the last few days without your company! See, there, God takes you through paths you could have never imagined…"

"God? Who is that?" asked Anuelle somewhat confused.

"Oh, sorry, it's an expression where I come from… never mind, what I mean is that even if you set off with a goal that doesn't turn out the way you expected, life has many ways to fix things in different ways. You just have to be open and grateful when the time comes…"

Annea was thinking about her own journey and how she also, just like Anu, had tried to be helpful, to find her lost father and bring him home, to show the world what she was capable of... And in the end, she had also ended up stuck, here. But their stories were certainly not over, yet. They could still bend things to their advantage, and for now, they needed to focus on their imminent escape.

"You know, I never intended to be here, either. In fact, my path has been very similar to yours. I still don't quite understand why all this is happening, but talking with Thuarnach has healed many wounds, he has opened my eyes: we have to take life as it is, as it comes, and like with a stream of water, just let things flow, Anu, just let things flow..."

Anu was hanging on Annea's words, and coming back towards the bed, she took both of Annea's hands and pulled her playfully out of the sheets.

"Thayng Thay, Anneya, muine Bræy Meyne!"[156]

---

[156] Thank you, Annea, my beautiful friend!" The meaning of the word "Bræy" here is synonym with "good or "best."

A Promise of Riches and Abundance

21st Day of Gloaras, 300YD,
Almost two hours past midday,
Drkent Har

Annea was striding, as fast as queen Umbriel's magnificent Cæwyldamhsa dress would let her, through the Teyn Sljk to reach the main stairs to Arsant Har, where the spring festival was about to begin.

She was late...

She had helped Anu get into her borrowed dress – one of Shya's exotic robes – and got delayed. Thankfully, Arnya had come to help timely, and together they had just managed to finished on time. But that was certainly not all the service maiden Arnya had helped with. She had been the one in charge of preparing their escape from within the walls of Drkent Har.

Tonight, it would all be about the right timing. Security within Drkent Har was as tight as ever. They had to be precise like a clockwork, or they would be discovered. The change of guards would occur somewhere around midnight, and they needed to be well under way by then.

They would have to disguise themselves as male Harkan Næl, to evade the Kechtás. And they needed comfortable and warm clothes and boots for the journey on foot, not fine, silky robes or slippers…

Rothar had provided the clothes and cloaks, and Arnya had hidden the bundles under her own bed. They would change there, and together, all three of them would take the East wing service corridor, on the ground floor, and would leave the castle through the kitchen service door, at the side of the building. From there onwards, they would need to be very careful to reach the inner Caydúllien Ore, at the heart of the gardens, where a secret stair would take them to the last gate to freedom: the Tyarsach Drkent…

This time, they would not be able to use the druid tunnel on the East wing due to the overload on food stocks, lying right on top of its entrance. It would take ages to take all the wooden boxes and potato bags off it. But the kitchens were just the perfect place to disappear in the chaos and confusion of cheerful, feasting service men and women, and the busy cooks and kitchen maids, who were still trying to get on with their work. Besides, there was only one Kechtá positioned at that entrance, and he was a good friend of Arnya's husband. It would be easy for her to provide him with enough sleeping potion in his cup, to knock down an army.

By the time they would risk their escape, everyone would be drunk, and nobody would notice their absence. Arnya would have provided all key guards in the building with enough Rheannvid and sleeping potion, for them to have the time to escape safely. Thuarnach himself had given her the strong herbal decoction to mix a little into their cups so they would sleep as soundly as babies through the evening and night. At least, that was the plan…

Lady Skenya, on her part, would have to free her son alone, and they would then take the Dryd Sljk underneath the dungeons. It was the safest way for them, but she would also need to be very careful not to disappear too early from the feast, or else people would start to suspect something.

She also would dress in male Harkan Næl clothes to avoid being recognised in the corridors, and would be in possession of a copy of the original keys to the dungeons, including the one for the entrance to the Dryd Sljk, which Thuarnach had especially made for the occasion.

Five people then, in all, would try to escape the castle alive that evening. Each of them, however, would have to get rid of a full time, personal escort of two Kechtás, plus the guard at the kitchen entrance, and all the others that kept patrolling the castle at all times. They were going to need a lot of that sleeping potion, indeed…

'Thank God,' thought Annea, 'I've made it before the king!'

She went down the stairs in a hurry. In a few more minutes, the king would be appearing, and she wanted to mingle with others before he or Shya searched for her.

She saw Anu waving in her direction, and hurried the few steps to stand next to her.

"Do you have something like Dryemoshach where you come from?" Anu asked her as soon as she got there.

It was just then, that looking around, she opened up to the beauty of the place. She had been in such a hustle the whole day, that she had completely overseen the magic of her surroundings.

She took a deep breath, and now mindfully let her gaze linger on the thousands of little things that surrounded her… What she saw, exceeded her wildest expectations.

"How extraordinary, Anu! No… No, actually, I don't think I've ever seen something like this before… you know, in a way, I do feel lucky to be witnessing this… as an archaeologist, I mean, I would have never imagined a place like this could have ever existed…

life does have its strange ways!" she answered absentmindedly to a somewhat confused Anu.

Within hours, Arsant Har had been transformed into a fairy forest! Colourful and fragrant floral bouquets of early spring blossoms were hanging from every corner of the hall. The floors had been completely covered with fresh moos that had been masterly laid out like a soft, green carpet, while also being used to decorate tables, chairs, mirrors!

Some of the flowers she could even recognise, mostly bulbous plants, for it was quite early in the spring, while certain flowers had been brought all the way from the lands south of the Ælben.[157]

Fragrant pink and blue hyacinths, yellow and white daffodils, bright tulips, sweet-scented lilies… Iris, crocuses, tiny snow drops, all playing a melody together like different instruments in an orchestra to turn the room into a world filled with magic.

'There are no other words to describe this,' she thought, 'this is pure magic!'

She thought of the time when she was learning about past civilizations at college, and how the ancient world had been seen as primitive and uncivilized… Well, to these people, to this

---

[157] The Alps

civilization, nature meant everything. The changing of the seasons, when was the right time to harvest, when to seed, when to dry the hey, when the calves were born, all these marked the changing of the seasons. They seemed to remember to be grateful for this eternal cycle of life, and this was truly something that would slowly get lost in modern day societies. Dryemoshach was a hymn to Mother Nature's blessings!

Suddenly, a cheer went through the crowd, and Annea felt Anu's elbow on her ribs.

She turned to look, and saw him strutting down the great stairs: Asttrian, King of the Skyarach, with that self-sufficient look on his face.

He surveyed the hall with satisfaction, but as if searching for something or someone. And there, his eyes met Annea's and he gave her his most charming smile.

'How false,' she thought, 'handsome or not, this man is very much like a poisonous snake.'

Once he arrived at the bottom of the stairs, Thuarnach, in his office as Reaghil Drkent Dryd, presented him with the most magnificent sword Annea had ever seen in her life. How it glittered with the lights, it seemed to have an inner light. Was this even possible?

The druid said a few words, and then walked together with the king towards the centre of the room, where a richly decorated moos nest was holding an oversized, golden egg.

"What is that?" Annea asked.

"Oh, you have never seen a dragon egg before? They bring it out from the Drkarach Aelbstael Cathrie every Dryemoshach. It has been painted with gold so it lasts for ever. I was very impressed the first time I saw it, too. It is said to be quite ancient, and that the druids were the ones who first brought it to the Kingdom. I have seen two myself, but we don't possess one in Daing Mhuir, unfortunately. I think they are very beautiful..."

"I didn't know..." managed to say Annea.

"Ey, and for the celebration of Annorashkin, later in the year, it changes colour! Well, not completely, it does remain gold but it gives off a different light from within. And then, every year the colour of that light changes, too."

"So, is it alive?"

"Oh, well, I don't think so. Dragons are not coming back, Anneya, if anything, they are disappearing from Earth. Besides, the egg is too old to hatch!"

"So, where have you seen the second egg, then?"

"Well, I'm not supposed to tell, but since we are together in this… It was at my grandfather's Daing, back in the North Kingdom of the Thuatharachti. I used to visit every summer when I was younger, of course, only after the Great War ended, and uncle Urarathan made peace with his mother. He was the one that had given the egg to my grandfather in the first place."

"So, what is it with dragons and the Arach?" Annea pressed on.

"Thuarnach is the one who knows every detail of the story. You should really ask him… This much I know, however. We have scrolls and books telling of the first encounter with dragons and how our family became entrusted with the responsibility of bringing the Dragon Knowledge to humankind. Sooner or later, they would leave us to our own destiny, that was part of the deal we sealed with them. It is also said that dragons are the oldest creatures on Earth, it would be a pity if also Drkarach fades away, don't you think?"

"Ey… but, what do you mean fade away?"

"The White Dragon is the last of them, and druids say it is just waiting for its final task. Once dragons have completed their tasks, they vanish from our world, forever."

"So, they just disappear?"

"Ey, I guess you can call it that, but no one really knows where they go..."

Annea went thoughtful for some time. She had seen the Dragon herself at her arrival to the Skyarach Kingdom. It had been truly impressive, and somehow beautiful and fascinating, at the same time.

"Have you seen Drkarach, Anu? I mean, have you talked to it?"

Anu was surprised by this question, "ney, why would I? Dragons are dangerous, no one goes close to the Dragon. It is the Dragon that summons a person, not otherwise. And they don't talk, why would they? They are said to be pure thought!"

"But–"

"Believe me, Anneya, you don't want to meet face to face with a dragon. Drkarach was my late uncle's dragon, he spent hours with the beast, he even flew it wherever his heart desired. But he is dead now, and the White Dragon is sleeping in her cave underneath this very mountain, now. It hasn't been seen flying for at least three years, they say."

"So, you think it is never coming out again?"

"Oh, no, that is not what I said. It's just, no one can force it out, it will come out on its own accord, when the time is right."

"Right…"

Annea didn't know what to make of all this Dragon Lore of the Arach. She would have to ask Thuarnach more questions about these mystical creatures. She had never read anything about dragons in her life because she had believed them to be mythical inventions, products of human fantasy, nothing more.

At that precise moment, the crowd around her put on their dragon masks and started to make space for the king, who was striding decisively towards Annea.

"Drkarach's blessing on you, muine Meyne!" she heard Anu say.

And then, the music started, the king took her hand and the world went spinning for hours.

On the Run

21st Day of Gloaras, 300YD,
two hours to midnight, Drkent Har

Her heart was pounding as if it would burst out of her breast. It was now, or never!

She looked across the room to Anu and nodded slightly.

The King was asleep beside her. Still partly on his chair, half his body hung onto Annea's seat, their escorts, who had been positioned at the entrances, nodding off at this precise moment. Shya was nowhere to be seen.

She searched the crowd with concern, but did not find her.

People were merry and careless, some were sleeping with their heads flat on the tables, others dancing or singing wildly.

No Kechtá had been positioned within the Hall of the Arts, it had been Asttrian's explicit wish, maybe to make believe his nobles that he trusted them. Who could tell? But he had insisted, in spite of Shya's repeated tantrums.

Quite a few Kechtás had been, however, located at every single access to the hall, that is, every single one, but the east wing service entrance . It was the closest and most direct way to the kitchens, and, luckily for the two of them, both the stairs and the corridors were too narrow to have a person permanently positioned there.

Annea and Anuelle stood up, and started moving slowly, trying not to attract any curious looks.

Arnya would be waiting for them in her room, so cautiously, they made their way through the crowd, and reached the east wing entrance without being noticed, or so they thought…

Then, they rapidly took the stairs to the service corridor, and started going faster. It was darker and colder down here, and it took them sometime to get used to the lack of light. Annea stumbled a couple of times in her silky Cæwyldamhsa dress.

"Vyen aí, Anneya, fret,[158] they could be coming after us this moment!"

"I know! I'm trying to…"

At that moment, right from behind, a dark shadow jumped onto Annea and thrashed her back to the ground with unleashed rage.

---

[158] "Come on, Annea, hurry…."

"Thay!" Shya screamed, while pulling from Annea's dress, "Yai kænnar en!"[159]

Annea struggled hard to get rid of her, but it was useless. The dress was all entangled around her, and with Shya's weight on top, she could not move.

Anuelle came to help, and started yanking at Shya's arms.

For a moment, it looked as if the two would manage to get away, but then Shya, screaming furiously, started tearing off parts of Annea's dress, and scratching her fiercely.

Luckily for the them, Arnya, who had heard the screams from down the corridor, came to their help.

When she saw Shya, she rapidly took one of the small busts decorating the niches of the corridors and, without hesitating, hit her hard on the head.

Shya fell to the ground like a ton of bricks, and did not annoy them again for the rest of the evening.

"What do we do now?" said Anu.

---

[159] "you!"... "I knew it!"

"No worries, we will hide her in my room," said Arnya, "by the time they find her, we'll be long gone!"

They dragged her together, tied her to Arnya's bed, and filled her mouth with a piece of cloth, so she wouldn't scream when she woke up. Then, they hastily changed their clothes, and picking up their supplies for the journey, they left the room silently towards the kitchens.

The corridor to the east wing kitchens was bustling with servants, and it took them a few more minutes to reach the kitchens, so far undisturbed. They rapidly mingled in the chaotic cheerfulness and warmth within. Careful not to awake suspicion, they made their way across the busy room, where men, as much as women, were sharing a good time, oblivious to the three women in disguise.

They were making good time, despite their unfortunate encounter with Shya. A few metres only, and they would reach the side exit.

Right then, two women, believing them to be some handsome Harkan Næl, who had lost their way in the kitchens, wrapped themselves seductively around Annea's and Anu's shoulders.

"Oh, my dear, you are indeed very attractive, but we must leave! You see, our pigs have a very bad indigestion, unfortunately..."

managed to say Anu, faking a man's voice as well as she could, while trying to untangle herself from the iron grip of the brawny kitchen maid.

"Ey, another time perhaps..." added Annea quickly, supressing a burst of laughter and gently unwrapping the other woman's arm from around her neck.

Both women looked somewhat confused, but let them continue without complaining.

"Our pigs? Really?" said Annea.

"It was the first thing that came to my mind, and it worked!" answered Anu, both amused and relieved.

"Thayng da Drkarach!" said Arnya in a low voice, "come, over here," she pointed to an open door, right next to a row of massive kitchen cabinets.

'We made it!' thought Annea, 'we're out of the building!'

As predicted, the Kechtá who had been positioned there, was snoring louder than a bear. And so, the three of them could exit the kitchens without further obstacles.

Once out, they had to cross the expanse of the inner patio very cautiously, for there were patrolling Kechtás not only in the gardens and on top of the defence walls, but also on the towers and all across the paved patio. Luckily for them, tents of various colours and shapes had been set up there to welcome some guests, who were coming from afar to witness the Dryemoshach celebrations. These helped them to hide along their crossing, until they were able to reach the tall, defence wall.

From there onwards, they had to stay in the shadows and follow the whimsical path of the wall as silently as cats, since only the darkness was their shield.

They made their way with difficulty, crouching and extremely slowly. They could not afford a second encounter, for this time, they were surrounded by Kechtás.

After what felt like hours, they reached the east entrance to the orchard gardens. Silently, they opened the gate and now moved faster across the maze-like gardens, little paths dividing the different cultivated patches of green. They had to avoid the main walkway, or else they would risk being seen. Thankfully, it was much easier now to cross from the orchard straight into the herbal gardens, and from there, it was only a few more metres to reach the south end of the gardens, where the Caydúllien Ore stood strong, watching over them all.

Finally, they could see the tree!

From there, they quickly moved towards the secret stairs that Thuarnach had shown Annea a few days ago. The only way to open the entrance was through pushing hard on a brick of the last perimeter wall, which had a minuscule golden apple on it. To find the brick, one needed to count from the point where the bushes started growing, the fifth brick to the left, and from the floor, the fifth upwards.

The three of them were so concentrated on their quest, that they had not heard the loud sobs from behind. All of a sudden, an audible, tired sigh came through, and they stopped short.

They did not dare turn, but they were close enough to some bushes, and hid swiftly behind them.

"Who's there?" asked queen Umbriel anxiously, "show yourself this moment, or I call my escort!"

'Damn!' thought Annea, 'what now?'

After a few seconds, just as Annea was about to come out of their hiding to talk to the queen, Arnya stopped her and shook her head.

"Where are the Kechtás? We haven't come across any in the gardens..." whispered Anu.

All was silent again.

The queen, as always, had already forgotten all about the noise, and had started lulling herself back to the trance she had been in before they interrupted her.

After what felt like ages, Annea carefully came out of the bushes again, and swiftly pushed the brick with the golden apple further into the wall.

There, in front of them, a steep, coiled stairway carved out of stone opened up into unbounded darkness. As promised, lying at their feet was a torch Thuarnach had left for them to illuminate the cavernous entrails of the Drkarach Krayns.

They put the brick back into the wall, and closing the entrance, they started their descent, not really knowing what to expect on the other side. Only Annea, who had been to a similar place before, knew that these stairs were leading them straight into the Dragon's monumental den. Thuarnach had thought she would be capable of convincing the dragon to let them pass, but how? During their last talk about dragons, Anuelle had reminded her how dangerous these creatures were: "nobody goes and talks to them just like that Annea," she had said... Well, they were going to find out! One way or the other, only the Dragon was now standing in their way to freedom!

Chapter Thirty-One: Drkarach's Secrets

21st Day of Gloaras, 300YD, close to Midnight,
Drkarach Krayns, underneath Drkent Har

The stone stairs to the cavernous tunnels were extremely steep, worn out and slippery. The three women descended step by step, with great difficulty. It took them almost an hour to reach the bottom of the cave, and by that time, they were both exhausted and anxious, the events of the evening starting to weigh on them.

Thuarnach had told them to walk straight ahead for about half an hour, when they would find an illuminated chamber. Annea, he had insisted, should be the one to enter first.

But before they continued, Annea suggested they paused to drink something. She felt she was going to collapse any minute, and the other two were happy to join her, too.

There, in silence, they drank from the elderberry juice Arnya had brought from the cellars. It was delicious, especially sweet and strong, almost like wine, but much more invigorating. It would help them get on their feet again, for they still had a long journey ahead.

As soon as they felt better, they started to walk again, in that dark and forsaken underworld.

'Who would like to spend time in here?' Annea thought.

But right then, they saw it: an absurdly brightly illuminated chamber ahead. There was nowhere, where the light could come in from, except…

"What–?" started Anu, but Annea interrupted her.

"Wait here," she said.

"But Anneya…"

Annea turned around and looked at Anu with a determination she had not yet seen on her friend's face.

"No, this time, I'm going alone, Anu. You two will wait here."

And without looking back, she cautiously walked into the chamber, alone.

She recognised it very well, it was the dragon's awe-inspiring den. She found its unique brightness, despite the hundreds of metres under the earth, still bewildering. She was entering through another passage this time, which is why it took her some time to recognize it. This must have been the king's, as it was conveniently placed in front of the castle's Caydúllien Ore, the private heart of the royal gardens. Anu said the king always talked to his dragon…

Thuarnach, on his part, had warned her she might meet Drkarach again. The tunnelling of the mountain range was vast, and the dragon moved freely in his realm, but such a clever creature always knows where to find intruders. However, the druid had been confident that the dragon would let them pass.

With its permission, the three would be able to reach the entrance to the Reaghil Dryd Sljk, and from there, take the passage straight northeast that led them to the Wild Creatures Forest.[160] Once there, they would need to follow a green trail for some time, which ended at a stone circle. There, the rest of the company would be waiting for them.

---

[160] The Arach name for it was "dah Svæg Cryuns Tyarcad", and it had been given that name due to the untamed animals that lived there, and their wild habitat. The area was protected and respected to the point that no Skyarach would dream to hunt there, it was simply too dangerous. But it had been meant, above all, as a refuge, and no one was going to look for them there, since it was as wild as it was almost impenetrable. It would take druids to guide them out of it, and it would be a difficult and long path.

Lost in her own thoughts, she had not noticed the swirls of air that presently bounced on every rock, in the cave.

"So... Etayn Anneya, here we are again," surprised her the dragon's voice in her head.

She looked around and saw no one.

"Are you talking to me?"

"I never talk to anyone... you should know that by now: I am thought, I am dream, I am knowledge... I am."

"But somehow, I seem to hear what you're saying, right?"

Drkarach did not answer to this, instead it went on, "you have stayed with the Skyarach, you did not go back to where you came from... hmm, it is because of that man, Lughan, you are attached to him... attachment is never a noble feeling, you would be wise to let him go, Etayn Anneya."

"I'm not a princess–" Annea started to protest, but then interrupted herself, "what do you mean, I would be wise to let him go?"

"If you go back through the passage you came from, certain death would you find, and the last quest of the Arach would be lost forever. But know this, Etayn Anneya, Lughan is not to return with you, he does not belong with you."

She did not want to make sense out of this statement. Instead, she shook her head, trying to clear her thoughts, what could the dragon know about her and her father...

"Everyone says you are dangerous, but you haven't hurt me although you had the chance."

"Great power entails great danger. We dragons are powerful creatures."

"What does that mean?"

"Humans would be wise to fear us more. Greed, however, nests in their hearts, and most of them would do anything to gain such great power, to control its source and bend it to their will."

"I see…"

"It has never been the purpose of the Dragon to kill or destroy humans. We, as the most ancient protectors of Gæya,[161] came to help you lead mankind into a brighter world for all living beings,

---

[161] Mother Earth in the Arach language.

when the rule of wisdom and light triumphs over darkness and folly. And so we did, with our power, we helped the Arach spread wisdom and justice across many regions, and the Arach kept their part of the covenant over thousands of years, and prosperity touched every region of the planet that came into contact with the Arach civilization... But the greed of men has great power, too. And year, after year its seed persistently eroded the very foundations of the Arach kingdoms. One after the other, the ancient kingdoms fell, and all the dragons, but one, have disappeared forever with them."

"But now there is hope, is there not? You are still here, and Thuarnach said–"

"Ey," interrupted her the great beast, "the old fool has a brave soul, for that you can let him know, I have spared his Dryd friend, although he had taken from us some very precious things..."

"Do you mean you wanted to kill one of Thuarnach's friends?"

"Rayka, tell him, is wandering the woods close to the White Seat.[162] He was almost dead when I found him, a sadness and regret I've never sensed in a human heart before, I could not take his life for that. But what he stole from us has finally broken him."

---

[162] Short form for Drkarach Ælbstæl Cathrie.

Annea was struck by a thought, "Was he the one who brought the dragon eggs to the new Arach kingdoms?"

"Perhaps..." said the dragon, "and perhaps he also took away something even more precious to us..."

"But what could that be?"

"A Dreà Arachti baby, Etayn Anneya, the last sacred child that had been born without a dragon. Untamed or left in the wrong hands is such a child a danger for mankind and even Gæya herself. It has been part of the covenant since the early times, as precious as such a child is, it is extremely dangerous and cannot be left to live without its dragon."

"So, an innocent baby was condemned to die?"

"Ey, it was, from the very moment that the ambitions of power had already killed its dragon and destroyed its kingdom. All Arach know this..."

"Which kingdom was that?"

"The Seannarach Kingdom, home to the ancient Red City of Seannanorthai and the first druid order of Seann Dryd Kydrachs na Drkarach."

Right then, like awakening from a long trance, Annea heard all of a sudden Anu's voice calling for her.

"Oh, I am sorry, I had almost forgotten, I need to ask a favour of you."

"I know."

"And? Would you let us pass?"

At that point Drkarach made itself visible in front of her, and came closer, lowering its huge head to look Annea straight into the eyes.

"You are clever, but not always wise, your greatest gift is the power of your heart. Keep following it, and hope will never die. Run now and take your friends, there is still a chance that we will save them all and meet again. This is my last trial, Etayn Anneya, once we are finished with the Skyarach, me the white Drkarach will fade from the memory of men, to never return again... And so, will you."

"What? Are you saying I will be able to go back to my time?" Annea wanted to inquire further, but the dragon had already disappeared in a swirl of wind and light, leaving no trace of its presence.

She did not wait, however, and rapidly called the other two women, and without further hesitating the three of them continued their journey through the extensive, maze-like tunnels, moved between anxiety and wonder.

"Where are we?" wondered Anu out loud.

But Annea did not tell her, not then, at least. She was still too confused about Drkarach's words, which in retrospective sounded both like a promise and a threat at the same time.

'How unnerving!' Annea thought, 'most of the times, the dragon speaks in riddles, how am I supposed to understand what its talking about?'

At that point, she remembered the words of the dragon: 'I don't talk…. I am thought, I am dream…'

What if this all was a whimsical, chaotic dream? What if they all were the product of someone's creative imagination gone wild? Somehow, deep inside, she still hoped she would at some point wake up, and nothing of this would be true… It would be so much easier!

Chapter Thirty-Two: To No Fair End

21st Day of Gloaras, 300YD, close to Midnight,
Drkent Har

Finding Ealator had been much easier than Lady Skenya had dared hope. Thanks to Arnya's beverage, her personal Kechtási guards had been sleeping soundly in front of her bed chambers, while she had made her way through unknown passageways that connected the courtroom to the dungeons. Using Thuarnach's original floor plans that included several hidden doors, she had skilfully found her way through endless stone stairs and windowless corridors. Finally, she had reached the dungeons unnoticed.

It was moist and cold down there, a contrasting picture to Arsant Har and the Dryemoshach celebration's that were still going on, above her head.

She had taken the keys Arnya had provided her two days ago, and methodically tried each one on every cell she walked past.

It had taken her some time, but then, all of a sudden, the iron gate to the last cell opened: it was her son's!

Eala was, as expected, in a terrible condition. He looked even worse than the last time she had been allowed to visit him, ten days ago. It seemed they were not giving him proper food any more, just strong beer to keep him alive. The smell in the cell was unbearable, and Eala was beaten, weak, and drunk.

"We have to get away from this hell," she thought out loud.

She put his arm around her shoulder and straightened him, as best as she could. He was conscious, but not helping much. He was murmuring something absentmindedly.

"Eala, it's me. We have to leave, now!"

He looked up to her, his gaze confused.

"Mother?"

"Ey, Yai er. Vyen aì, Noys raian!"[163]

She dragged him with all her strength out of his cell and into the dark, damp corridors.

Very slowly, Eala and his mother trudged and stumbled their way through the underground maze of Drkent Har, which would take them from the dungeons to the nearest entrance to the Reaghil

---

[163] "Yes, it's me. Come on, we have to go!"

Dryd Sljk. Every time her son fell to the ground, the Lady of the Thriar would kneel beside him and urge him to go on, not to give up. She would help him up, and they would continue advancing like this, bit by bit, with little hope of ever seeing open skies above their heads again.

At some point, Eala seemed not to manage to get up any longer. His mother was on the brink of desperation, what could she do, all alone? She would never be able to carry him all the way…

Suddenly, out of the next turn, Lughan came into sight.

"How–?" Lady Skenya started to mutter.

"There is no time for explanations muine Æriel, we have to go on," he said politely, while ungently pulling Ealator back onto his feet.

Fortunately for them, Lughan had managed to evade the Kechtás, as well, and suspecting the difficulties Skenya would be facing, he had made his way to the dungeons to help her with their escape.

"Thayng da Drkarach!"[164] she managed to say, while they started moving faster now, "you are a true soul, indeed, dear Lughan!"

It appeared that good fortune had finally come their way, and they were going to make it without further disturbances. After the

---

[164] "Thank the Dragon!"

next left turn, just a few meters more, and they would reach the hidden entrance to the druid tunnels.

Skenya went at the rear, she had thoughtfully started searching for the bundle of keys to open the Tyarsa[165] that would separate life from death, freedom from confinement. It was a heavy bundle, with many keys, and she had to pull hard to take it out of under her cloak...

So concentrated was she in her search, that she hadn't noticed that someone had appeared from behind, and was now following them.

They took the turn left, and then all of a sudden, a thunderous male voice called them to a halt:

"Thay! Rem oan Thay er!"[166]

They stopped short, and turned around very carefully to find an extremely young Kechtá with a stretched bow, ready to shoot.

"I was asked to take the prisoner and his mother to the Guest Chambers," Lughan managed to say.

---

[165] Door or gate.
[166] "You! Stay where you are!"

"Silence! I know who you are! You will come with me, now! I have already sent for reinforcement, and they will be here any minute."

Lughan could not remember to have seen him before… He was no older than fourteen, maybe fifteen… So now Asttrian was recruiting children as part of his royal guard!

"We won't do anything," said Lughan, "but I need to put the King's cousin down, or my back will break in two."

He moved cautiously, he did not want the Kechtá to panic and shoot. But right then, without any previous warning, Lady Skenya jumped towards the young Kechtá screaming madly.

The Kechtá, taken by surprise and not knowing what else to do, let his arrow fly instinctively.

For the first time since he had met him, Lughan saw a fleeting emotion cross Ealator's pale, scarred face.

Then, all they heard was the arrow hitting its target, and Lady Skenya fell instantly to the ground.

"Ney!!!" cried Ealator, and stumbling along and crawling, he tried to reach the spot, where his mother had fallen.

Lughan used the confusion of the moment to take out his hidden knife, and threw it like a bolt straight into the Kechtá's breast.

The young knight, looked at him surprised, and plummeted to the ground just like Lady Skenya had done, seconds before.

Lughan quickly went to where both Ealator and his mother were lying.

Now, both bent over her to assess the damage. The arrow had cleanly pierced her heart, so she was bleeding to death. She sighed in pain, she could barely breath.

"Eala, pro.. promise me…" she managed to utter.

"Ey, mother," said Eala, "Yai er hjer!"[167]

"You… You will go! Leave this place… Find Arachtan and your sister!"

She grabbed Ealator's arm firmly, "fight for our kingdom, son! Fight until the end!"

Ealator's face was carved in stone, but his eyes showed infinite pain.

---

[167] "I am here."

"Ey, Yai er..."[168]

But the brave Lady of the Thriar could not hear him anymore, she had passed away not knowing the kind of resolution that was taking shape in her son's heart...

Not wanting to lose more precious time, Lughan shook Ealator gently, and looked him with determination.

"Rai, Ealator, aì!"[169] and taking the keys from Skenya's white, cold hands, he added, "this one here will open the entrance to the Dryd Sljk. Go now! I will take your mother to Thuarnach for a proper burial, I promise. But since I won't be able to make my way to the Drkarach Aelbstæl Cathrie, as was the original plan, you will have to take the message to the Drkent Druids. Tell them about the fugitives, about what happened tonight, tell them Asttrian is ready to unleash his rage on all the kingdom, and tell them also that Ara has arrived at Polarys but will have to stay there to receive the fugitives and make sure they are safe. He will come to collect the king's sword after, and they should be prepared... And Ealator, I'm counting on you! May the white fire of the Dragon guide you in the darkness!"

---

[168] "Yes, I will..."
[169] "Go, Ealator, now!"

"Ey, may the Dragon guide you in the darkness, too!" repeated Ealator, and kissing his mother for the last time, he plunged into the darkness of Thuarnach's secret druid tunnels.

Lughan summoned all his strength and, picking up Skenya's lifeless body, he made his way towards the little secret entrance he had come from before. He would take Skenya into the first service room he found, and search the fortress for Thuarnach.

His journey, however, would take an unexpected turn altogether…

A double patrol of eight Kechtás came his way, and the moment they saw him with his burden, they all unsheathed their swords almost simultaneously.

There was no talking this time…

Right there, the royal knights charged onto Lughan mercilessly, and did not stop until he went on his knees, still holding the Lady of the Thiar in his arms.

Bit by bit, as if not wanting his precious burden to ever reach the ground, he collapsed, his blood and hers merging into a wild red river that meandered at will through the cold stone floor, and never seemed to stop.

Then, Lughan saw no more, and heard no more…

He thought of his Little Pandora, all alone in this wild world, and of his young family, who were risking their escape this very moment… What a pity it was he would not see his children grow up, he would not share Rasmei's hearth any more. She had been sure they would see each other again, but had never said where…

End of Book One

Epilogue

October 22nd, 2022 (our count),

International Airport Ing. Aero. Ambrosio L.V. Taravella,

Cordoba, Argentina

Six months since the last time she had seen her friend! It seemed impossible to Lola that this could be true.

Looking out the large, dirty airport windows, she wondered if she was perhaps standing right where her friend had been, before taking the flight that had changed their lives for ever...

Lola had had a terrible time, ever since. She loved her friend dearly, and she could not get into her mind that Annea would disappear just like that. It was as if she had evaporated into thin air.

For months now, Lola had been in close contact with Annea's host family in Germany. The Beckmann's had been more than willing to pass on all the information they had, as, somehow, they felt guilty for what had happened.

As soon as the Beckmann boys had returned home alone that fateful snowy day, the family had contacted the local authorities who had searched first the area, then the province, and then the whole country for her friend. By now, they had extended the search with the involvement of the European Interpol, and even Scotland Yard… A few weeks more, and they would stop the active search. From her friend, however, still no trace!

Lola had finally made up her mind, she would fly to Germany. She had to see the place, where Annea had been sighted for the last time. She would find no peace of mind if she stayed in Argentina, and let the others do the work. In the end, Annea was more than her best friend, she was like a sister to her!

For this, she had quarrelled loudly, and several times with Lara Menard, Annea's unnerving mother, who was sure her daughter would turn up sooner or later to ask her for money, and had openly communicated she was not planning on spending her time or energy with a search. After all, she had said to Lola, Annea might just as well have joined her father in hell.

How could such contempt and negative feelings prevail in that woman for so long? How could she feel like that about her own daughter?!

After all, Lola thought, if she was not coming with her to Germany, it was her own fault. Lola would go anyways, and was determined to find out what was keeping her friend away, one way or the other.

Within a week, she had settled everything for the trip. She had dutifully left Annea's cat, Ludwig, back home with her parents, and she had arranged to stay with the Beckmann's, too, as it was very close to the place, where her friend had last been seen. As for her master's degree, that would have to wait now!

However, even if all was running according to plan, something still bothered her...

Why was she feeling so anxious?

A voice in her heart, which was becoming louder and louder by the day, kept telling her that she might not like the truth behind her friend's vanishing, after all...

Lola looked out for the last time to the scorching bright sun of her homeland, and then turned to search for the check in counter.

Whatever had happened in Germany, Lola had made up her mind, she would be there for Annea, always!

Vocabulary of the Arach Peoples:

Aarglas	January/sleep and rest
Aehg	Water
Ælben	of white colour/white/pure// the Alps
Ællinas	May
Ær	Person/people (always written in capitals)
ærgull	Lost
Ærin	Woman/ maiden
Æriel (Muine Æriel)	(my) Lady = noble title
Ærn	Man
Aesg	Fish
Aesgir	Fisher
aí	Today – now
Altásva	High Mare (originally, the title of beautiful witch Queens of old, modern for the king's horse)
Althayan Priestess	Priestess of the Great Mysteries
an	From/by
Anairarachti	Peoples of the West Arach Kingdom (of Anairarach) founded by Scaìthara
Ann	Ancestors/ancient/of old
Annoras	June

Arachti Wbent Teyn Kydrachs	Arach Confederation of Knowledge
Armourean	Territories of southern Spain and France
Arsant Har	The Hall of Arts in Drkent Har
Ásv	horse
Ásva	Mare
Ayno	Health and balance
Ayno rooms	Healing rooms
Bajk /j/	Bay
Beag	Little/small
Bhealle	City/village
Blaàthas	April
bleyrn	To talk
Bran	Brother
Bræt	Cheap (barato)
Bræy	Beautiful
Bræy(e) Ærin	Beautiful woman (way of addressing an unknown lady)
Brean	Farmer
Cathrie	Seat
Cayd	Tree
Caydúllien Ore	Golden apple tree
(dah) Cæwyldamhsa	The celebration's dance (offcial dance)
Cæwylgryene	Sun celebrations

Chlíar /jleer/	Sword
Chlìar Drkent	Dragon blade (sword)
Cœr (Drkent Cœr)	Heart (corazón) Dragon heart
da	To
Da b'Œsbajkann /j/	An t'Òban, little fisher bay
dah	The
Daing	Fortress
Daing Mhuir	The fortress of the Ocean, name of the fortress of queen Scàithara on the isle of Skye
Daing na Lahirynn	Lahir Valley Fortress = today's city of Bad Ems
Den(ne-pl fem)(e-s)(s-pl masc.)	Two
Deno	Second
Dhasi	These
Doyde	Please
drayken	To see: yai draykt (I see)/ think
Dreà Arachti	Adj and noun, of the True Dragon People
Drejkreins	Trading city of Utrecht (Latin: Traiectum), Netherlands
Drejkrenian	of Drejkrein
Dreken	Skyarachti big gold coin (1)
Drkarach	Dragon
Drkarach Ælbstæl Cathrie	The Seat of the White Dragon Star, Alpha Draconis (Thuban), the former

484

	polar star/main entrance to the undertunneling for one remaning Drkarach. Name of the druid kæyn on top of today's Feldberg, only visited by Drkent Druids. It had special temple guards for protection, as well as very powerful spells to stop the unwelcomed.
Drkarach Kechtás	Dragon Knights of the Syarachti (royal guard)
Drkarach Kynn	Dragon King of the Skyarachti
Drkarach ney!	Salutation of the Drkarach Kechtás
Drkarach Qvynne	Dragon Queen (traditional title)
Drkenstar	King Urarathan's sword, symbol of power
Drkent	of the dragon, adj.
Drkent Dryd	Royal Arach Druid/ Dragon Druid
Drkent Har	The Court of the Dragon
Drkent Skythiarach	Winged Dragon was the name of the main Kechtási vessel on the Rhine
Dryan	Third
Dryani	Skyarachti little bronze coin (100)
Dryd	Druid
Dryd Stællyr	Druid Stallion
Dryemoshach (21/3)	Celebration of the arriving of spring, of green, the Dragon lays its eggs in fresh moos, in caves, promise of riches and abundance for the year
drysti	thirsty
duellich	sorry

Echt /j/	Emphasizing affirmative exclamation, like "doch" in German
en	It/he
cn'audr	another
Eno	First
Eno Lyvriach	First library (in Eno Vwylrynn Kæyn)
Eon	Age
Eonan ælbenvid an Rheann	Ancient/aged white wine of the Rheann
Eonnal Maelirmer	Abbrev. For the city of Edingburgh
Eonnal Skethemarbheal na Maelirmer	First Port City of Great Trading, area around the city of Edingburgh, offering passage from the North to the Netherlands
er	am/ is/ are
Erian	To be (verb)
Etayn (ne – pl)	Princess (es)
ey	Yes
fallay	maybe
Fael	Rock/ stone
fret	Urgently/fast
frigge	Fresh
Gæn Ær (i. =pl)	Guest Person/ People = foreigners coming to live to the Arach Kingdom, they had not many rights, but they were free to move and take up work. They were abliged to learn military skills so as to help protect the

	kingdom in the hour of need
Gænnæriati	Adj and noun, of the Gæn Ær people
Gæya	Mother Earth
Gloaras	March
go (prep.)	In
Graichfael	Quartz stone
Grhain	France
Gryen	Sun
Har	House/hall/court
Hænardrkentfael	The celestial Dragon stone
Hænar	The sky
Harkan Næl	Host Noble/Person = native nobles of the territoties ruled by the Dragon people.
Hærlb	Music instrument similar to the harp
hjer	Here
Honer(i)	Honorable (pl)
hor	Today – now
Hyo	Hi there!
Inna	Island
Inna Skythiarach	Island of the Winged = isle of Skye
Innatyarsach da Aehgamer	The Island of the Portal to the Great Water = today's Great Britain
Kay	Cousin (both fem and masc)

Kælnamer an Rheann (on the Rheann)	Urban settlement almost equivanlent to the place where now the city of Cologne stands
Kæyn	Temple
Kæyn an Drkent Dryd	Temple of the Dragon Druid
Kechtá(s)	Knight(s) (from the word "keicht" for riding, and "Ásvas" for horses)
Kechtási	Adj. As in kechtási knights or salutation
Keann	Head
Keanndryd	Head of a druid temple
Krayns	Cave
Krayn na Drkarach	Dragon Cave (the area around the Tyarsach Drkent or Portal of the Dragon)
Kræy (ne)	Child/ kid (dren/s)
Kræyin	Girl
Kræyn	Boy
kvæy	What
Kydrachs	Alliance/confederation/order
Kyllanan	Elderberry juice
Lahir	Lahn river
Lahirynn	Lahir Valley
Læyv	Love, amor
Læyve (-n for male)	Lovely, dear
lævyvljg	Darling

Lyvriach	Library
Mar	Sea
mæd	bad (also to suck at sthg)
Meadh a'Oighe (21/12)	Mid winter celebration, marking the darkest day in the sun cycle of the human Year
mer	Big/ great
Meyn(e – female) (s)	Friend(s)
Meyster (title)	Master (counsellor, adviser to the crown)
Mheyn	Main river
Mhuir	Ocean
Mhuirarachti or Anairarachti	Adj and noun, of the Anairarach Kingdom
Mohir	Mosel river
mon	How
Muin(e/s)	My (fem/ pl)
Muinærnd	Husband
Myrd	Death
myrdien	To die/ to murder/to kill, can be used figuratively as "to lose" (e.g. losing a game of Ur)
Myzær Kæyn	Oldest temple and fortress of the Skyarach on today's Altkönig peak, Germany
na	of

Nachtural Brean	Native farmers living within the Arach Kingdom
ney	No
neya	Not /never
Neybhrealle	Small beautiful city with skilled craftsmen to the northeast of the Golden City
Neyen	No one
Noys	We/ us
Nro	Northwest wind – good for sailors on the Rheann, tavelling upstream.
Nrothan	North, northern
Nuar	Ring
Nwyr	December/the dark Lord/winter/Serpent/Snake
Nwyrbesch	Measels or Snake Bite
Nwyr Krayns	Caves of the Serpent (Lord of Winter and darkness)
Nyamás	Death
Nymmædnwyr	Evil-poison snake (a snake species coming from central Eurasia)
Oer	Ear
og	And
onn	Or
Ore	Gold
Oreash	Patience

Pennian	Punishment
Polarys Kæyn	Second biggest druid temple, forming the constellation of Ursa Minor, close to the city of Neybhrealle, northeast of the Golden City
Quaranien	Peoples natural to Switzerland, Austria and Northern Italy
Qven	Who
Raeth	Wheel
Reaghil Bheallemer na Caydúllien Ore	Great Royal City of the Golden Apple Tree = today's Heidetrank Oppidum
Reaghil Drkent Teyn	Royal Dragon Chief (Great King)
Reaghil Gæn Tor	Royal guest Tower (where guests to the crown reside in Drkent Har)
Reaghil Dryd Sljk	The royal druid tunnel/ way
Reaghil Ovsbhealle Rheanna	The Royal Western City of the Rhine, also known as the Green Terrace of the Dragon = today's area of Koblenz
rem	Stay
Rhea	River
Rheann	Rhine
Rheannar	Citizens of the Rheann city
Rheannynn	Rheann Valley
Rheanvid	Precious red wine of the Rheann region
Rœnneral	Nebra astronomic disc
Seann	Adj. used for old, ancient things,

	disused arcaic use for old red/ocre/colour of gold(en)
Seann Dryd Kydrachs na Drkarach	Sacred Ancient Druid Order of the Dragon
Seannanorthai	The Red Ancient City of the Seannarachti (first great city)
Seannarachti	Adj and noun, of the Ancient Arach Kingdom of Seannarach with the oldest capital in Seannanorthai/ the Peoples of the Ancient Arach Kingdom
Sgyth (Pl. -i)	Ski
Sketheamar	Port
Skræn	Anairarachti gold (small coin) in 100 units
Skyarachti	Adj and noun, of the Skyarach Kingdom
Skylliad	Craftsmen or Tradesmen
Slijk	Tunnel/way
Sryath	Stream (of water)/ smaller river/rivulet or brook
Sryath	A stream or brook called Ursel Bach, in Oberursel, Germany
Stæl	Star
Stællyr	Stallion
Star	Power
(dah) Svæg Cryuns Tyarcad	The Wild Creatures Forest
Tær	Earth
Tærzylen	Columns of the Earth/World

Tærkerann Tyarcad (forest)	Mythical forest covering southern Scotland
Tanner	Anairarachti gold (big coin) in 100 units
Teyn	King/ fire/ chief
Teynaman	Kitchen/ the place of fire
Thann	Skyarachti medium-sized silver coin (100)
Thaunaan	Taunus (mountain range in Germany)
Thay	You
Thayng	Thank
Thouar Altærinann	Goddess of nature, Mother Nature
Thriar	The Council of the Wise, made up of a Druid and two royal women. For the Skyarachti it was Thuarnach, queen Umbriel, and the old king's sister Lady Skenya of Reaghil Ovsbhealle Rheanna
Thuatharachti	The Peoples North Arach Kingdom (of Thuatharach)
Tou	All
Tvæy	That/ thing
Tyarsa	Door
Tyarsa Raeth an Fæl	The wheeled chamber with the carts under the Rheann fortress
Tyarsach	Portal
Tyarsach Drkent	Portal/Threshold of the Dragon (doorway to the Dragon's lair)

Tyrcad (a)	Forest (s)
Úinne	Time
Úllien	Apple
Úllst	Ancient cidre
Ur	Board game played by the Sumerian
Ùyd /Ùydn	Interest/ interested
vuoyen (Thay vuoy)	To want/will (you want)
Vwyl	Weil river
Vwylr (ynn or valley)	Valley of the river Weil
Wbent Teyn Kydrachs	Knowledge/ wisdom/ Arach Confederation of Knowledge
Wbent Teyn Drkent	Bright/white Fire of the Dragon, wisdom and knowledge
Wbentas	February
Yai	I
Yahæn	young
Yhiria Færianásva	The Wide Green Plain of Horses (heaven)
Ynar Drkent (YD)	Year of the Dragon
Ynaria	Years of the Dragon, also 100 mortal years
Ynn	Valley
Yrwpa	Europe
Zirbe	Pinus cembra